KISSING WITH FANGS

ASHLYN CHASE

Cover illustration by Chad Michael Ward
Cover design by Brittany Vibbert/Sourcebooks
Photography by Jon Zychowski
Model: Kenny Braasch

Published by Sourcebooks Casablanca, an imprint of Sourcebooks, Inc.
P.O. Box 4410, Naperville, Illinois 60567-4410
(630) 961-3900
Fax: (630) 961-2168
www.sourcebooks.com

Printed and bound in the United States of America.
WOZ 10 9 8 7 6 5 4 3 2 1

To Gaye T. I'd include her last name, but it's one of those seven-hundred-letter-long jobbies with no vowels. She'll understand. She doesn't even use it, and not because she's a lazy slug like me.

Chapter 1

Anthony closed his eyes and pinched the bridge of his nose in front of the burnt-out wreck that used to be his bar, Boston Uncommon. Even in the darkness he could see the destruction too well. His dear "aunt" Sadie rested her hand on his shoulder. Neither spoke for a few reverent moments.

At last, Sadie said, "I know it's bad, but at least no one died…per se."

Anthony slowly opened his eyes and stared at her. "Per se?"

His only living relative pursed her lips. "I don't know if I should tell you this…"

Anthony sighed. "You have my attention now. Tell me whatever it is, whether you think I ought to know or not."

"It's Claudia. She's in trouble."

Now his psychic aunt *really* had Anthony's attention.

Claudia had been on his mind too, but not because he thought anything was wrong with his beautiful, stylish bar manager. He assumed a smart woman like Claudia would find another job in a snap—and he would miss her terribly.

He'd trusted her completely with his business, and not just because she had an MBA. She was always there during the daylight hours when he couldn't be. He missed her cheery smile and their private conversations in his office, and if he were honest, he'd admit to missing *her* more than his lost income.

She'd never know that, though. He had to hide every emotion he had toward Claudia from his psycho ex-girlfriend, Ruxandra, for Claudia's safety.

"Come to think of it, she hasn't called to ask for a reference. What's wrong?" he asked.

"I'm not sure. I get the sense she's in emotional turmoil. It's more than an unhappy feeling I'm picking up. Possibly, she's very depressed—or worse. Call her."

Anthony dug his cell phone out of his suit jacket pocket. As he pushed the number 1 on his speed dial, he realized again how important she had been to him. If she was depressed, he needed to give her more than a phone call.

It rang a few times before she picked up. Her garbled hello alarmed him.

"Claudia?"

"Who wans to know?"

"It's Anthony. Are you all right?"

After a long pause, he repeated the question.

"I'm jus' fine an' dandy."

"You sound drunk."

She snorted. "So? I'm over twenty-one. I'm in my own 'partment. Don't I have the right to drown my sorrows?"

He gentled his voice. "What sorrows, Claudia? What's happening?"

She laughed. "I los' my job. I thought you knew that. You were my boss."

It had to be more than that. "Claudia, I'm coming over."

"No! I mean, please don't. I'll be fine."

"I'm on my way." He hung up and dropped his phone back into his jacket pocket.

He touched Sadie's arm. "Thank you for telling me."

"Call me later and let me know how fucked up she is."

Anthony raised his eyebrows.

She raised hers right back at him. "You can't be shocked at my language. You've heard it before. Listen, I wouldn't have had a vision if all was well. Oh, and be sure to tell her I'm thinking of her."

He nodded and jogged around the corner to a deserted side street before he took off at top speed. After all, he couldn't let the constant crowds on Charles Street see him virtually disappear. They weren't supposed to know vampires existed—along with dragons, werewolves, and any other number of supernaturals. Boston Uncommon had been a safe haven for all of them. Anthony couldn't help wondering where they'd all go now.

He had Claudia's address memorized. Even though he had never been to her high-rise apartment overlooking the river, the big sign bragged, "If you lived here, you'd be home by now." It took him about two seconds to reach it.

A doorman. Shit. If the gentleman opened the door without asking him to come in, it didn't count as an invitation into someone else's home. Without it, he couldn't get in. So, Anthony tried for a little small talk.

"Nice evening."

"Yes, sir." As predicted, the man opened the door but didn't invite him in.

Anthony spotted the concierge behind the desk inside. "Uh, I don't live here, but I'd like to see someone who does. What should I do?"

"Speak to the concierge inside."

That sounded like it *might be* an invitation. Better to be sure. "So, I should go in?"

The gentleman's brow wrinkled. "Yes, sir."

"Thank you." *That was a trifle awkward, but it did the trick.*

The concierge offered him a welcoming smile but when asked to notify Claudia Fletcher that she had a visitor, he gave Anthony the unexpected news that she had moved out.

"Where is she now?"

The concierge looked uncomfortable and said, "I'm not at liberty to give anyone that information."

Anthony leaned in until he held the other man's gaze. "If you have the information I just asked for, you will give it to me, and you won't remember divulging it."

"Yes, sir." In slow motion, the gentleman reached under the desk and drew out an old-fashioned index-card box. He thumbed through the alphabetical tabs until he located Fletcher, Claudia, and offered the card to Anthony.

A Cambridge address in Claudia's handwriting occupied the space for forwarding mail. At the bottom she'd scrawled, "If I continued to live here, I'd be homeless by now."

Anthony took off at a brisk jog to her Cambridge apartment. He could no longer fly since he didn't know exactly where he was going. On the way, he reflected back to when he'd first met the klutzy waitress who became his bar manager…and how Ruxandra had instantly spotted the attraction.

He had been gazing with appreciation at one of his waitresses, Claudia, a blond with a pixie cut. She caught him staring at her, and the tray she carried crashed to the floor. She gasped and quickly stooped down to gather the large pieces of glass.

Anthony had to force himself to ignore her perfectly rounded bottom and help her. "Hang, on, Claudia," he called. "I'll be right there." He found the broom and long-handled dustpan while Joel brought her a damp towel.

"I'm so sorry, Anthony. Ouch!" She'd pricked her finger on a piece of glass, and a tiny red bead seeped out.

His mouth watered. The smell of her blood was intoxicating, but he wrestled himself under control. It would have been so easy to lick that wound and stop the bleeding instantly…if he could resist more than a taste. *No snacking on the staff, no matter how wonderful she smells*, he ordered himself.

"This sort of thing happens, Claudia. Step back and let me sweep up the shards of glass."

"I should do that. I made the mess. I—I feel like such a spaz."

Little did she know he found her flustered reaction to his gaze adorable. He'd better keep that to himself, however. Otherwise he might have to "clean up aisle one" a lot more.

"It's all right. I've got it. Just replace the drinks you were bringing to your customers."

Claudia sagged as if defeated and returned to the bar where Joel was already re-pouring the order.

"What happened?" Joel whispered to her.

Anthony wouldn't have heard the exchange if not for his superior vampiric senses.

"I just didn't have the tray balanced properly. I've never waitressed before. I'll get used to it eventually, I'm sure."

"Don't take too long," Joel said as he set two new cocktails on a dry tray.

Claudia let out a little groan and carefully walked the drinks over to the waiting customers.

In only a few minutes, the spill was cleaned up and everything seemed to be returning to normal. Anthony had just laid a hand on Claudia's shoulder, ready to reassure her that she wasn't in any trouble, when suddenly the door burst open and Ruxandra strutted in.

"I knew it!"

Anthony growled. "Ruxandra." He straightened his six-foot frame and strode over to his ex-girlfriend, now nemesis. "You're not welcome here."

"I can see that. I might spoil your plans with your new *whore*."

"Ruxandra!" He didn't know what else to say in front of a full bar of staff and patrons, so he grabbed her arm and dragged her outside.

"What are you doing here?" he demanded.

She flipped her long blond hair over her shoulder. "I came to bring you back where you belong, lover. With me."

"I'm not your lover anymore, and I belong where I say I belong."

Unconcerned, she finger-walked her way up his chest. "Then I must belong here too, because we belong together."

"No. We do not."

She ripped her arm out of his grasp and pouted. "But I always took care of you, Anthony. You need me. Why do you keep running away from me?"

"Because you won't let me go." His posture sagged.

"Look. You took good care of me when we were together, it's true. But your jealousy ruined our relationship. I can't have you ruining my business too.

"But I'm no good without you." Her lower lip jutted out as it did whenever she was trying to manipulate him. Her pretty pout used to work but not anymore.

"I'm sorry you feel that way. I'm infinitely better off without you controlling my every move."

"You're my maker. You're responsible for me." She folded her arms and tipped her head back as if daring him to defy her logic.

"You can't talk like that in public." He grasped her arm again and led her back inside to his office. As soon as they were behind the closed and locked door, he took a deep, steadying breath. "I've taught you all I know—including not to use words like 'maker' in front of humans. We are not lovers anymore and haven't been for decades. You're not even my friend. My duty has been met, and you have no claim on me."

She stomped her foot and the hardwood floor cracked. "But I need your protection. It's a big, scary world out there."

He couldn't help it. He leaned back and roared, laughing. When he had composed himself, she was glaring at him.

"If anything, the world needs protection from you, Ruxandra. My bar is off-limits. I cannot prevent you from staying in the city, but I can ban you from my business."

"It's a public place. I don't need an invitation."

"It's my bar, and I can ban anyone who doesn't behave themselves in it."

"I haven't done anything—yet."

"I'm afraid you have. You called one of my waitstaff a whore."

She snorted. "Is that all anyone has to do to get banned? Use a bad word? Ha! You won't be open very long if that's the case."

"I won't be open long if you cause a scene every time you get jealous."

She tipped her nose in the air and sniffed.

He'd had all he could stand of her. "Ruxandra, I need to get back to work." He unlocked his office, marched her to the front door, and gave her a shove. "Now, go away."

A couple passed them on the sidewalk and stared.

"I'll go for now, but I'll be back. Mark my words. You'll regret throwing me away like trash."

Anthony had to bite his cheek to avoid the retort he so badly wanted to mutter. Instead, he just hoped he'd have a bar to run the next evening.

Stepping out of his flashback, he found the street he'd been looking for near Central Square and stopped to catch his breath—what there was of it.

At the brick apartment building's entrance, a few buzzers showed names of tenants. He located the one for C. Fletcher and pressed it. No answer. *She wouldn't have left because I said I was coming over, would she?* He leaned on the buzzer and didn't take his finger off until Claudia's voice shouted, "Cut that out!"

"Claudia! It's Anthony. Let me in."

"I tol' you not to come," she slurred.

"Well, I'm here, and I'm not leaving until I see you."

After a few tense seconds, a third-story window slid open. When Anthony looked up, Claudia leaned out. "There. You've seen me. Now go away." She swayed and he was afraid she might fall out.

"Let me in, Claudia." He was tempted to jump up to that high window, but she didn't know what he was.

It might scare her straight, but I couldn't enter without her permission, so I'd just wind up hanging off the side of the building and that *wouldn't attract attention* at all.

A young man stared as he walked by. Anthony couldn't help feeling a little stalker-ish, standing on her doorstep and begging to come in.

At last, Claudia let out a loud sigh and said, "Oh, all right." She slammed the window shut, and a few seconds later she buzzed him in.

Now what? Is a buzzer enough of an invitation when someone doesn't want you to enter? He opened the door and cautiously extended his foot past the threshold. *Whew. I guess it is.* Either that, or Claudia really *did* want to see him. He went with that assumption and genuinely hoped he was right.

Jogging up to the third floor, he wondered what he should say to her. *I miss you? I can't believe I won't see you every day?*

She opened the door just a crack, but it was enough for him to see her face. Her eyes were red, puffy, and ringed with smudged black mascara. He never dreamed he'd see her like this. She always seemed so smartly put together, but clearly she was falling apart.

"Claudia," he said softly. "May I come in?"

She hesitated but eventually let out a deep breath and opened the door. "Why not?"

It wasn't much of an invitation but would have to suffice. She didn't look like she was going to welcome him with open arms.

"Thank you," he said as he stepped into her living room. She had always kept his office immaculate, so he was shocked to see her apartment looking like a Tasmanian devil had torn it apart.

A pizza container, empty glasses, and paper plates littered the coffee table and floor around it. Empty beer cans and liquor bottles were strewn across the open kitchen counters. Pillows lay on the floor and sported black stains.

"Have you been crying?"

She swiped at the smudges under her eyes. "No."

"Don't lie to me, Claudia. Have you been depressed ever since the fire?"

She wandered over to her sofa and plopped down on it, dropping her head into her hands. Anthony followed and sat beside her. When she didn't answer his question, he softened his approach.

Rubbing her back, he said, "Tell me what's wrong, Claudia. This can't all be because the bar is gone. Even *I* don't feel that bad about it, and I owned the place."

She chuckled.

It was a welcome sound. Maybe she still had her sense of humor. If Anthony could get her to see things in a lighter way, he might be able to save her. He picked up a beer bottle from the floor and set it on the coffee table. "I see you decided to open your own bar."

She raised her face and frowned at him. "I drink when I'm upset. What of it?"

"I'm sure you know this, but alcohol won't help. If anything, it will make you even more depressed."

She sighed and sagged against the colorful pillows. "I missed the smell of Boston Uncommon. I know that's nuts, but it's the truth. So, that's why..." She made a sweeping gesture toward the well-stocked kitchen-counter bar. Only then did he notice that all the bottles were open and most were empty.

He doubted that was the only reason why, but now was not the time to discuss a possible drinking problem. The thing was, he'd never smelled alcohol on her at work. They shared an occasional brandy when they discussed business before she left for the evening, but he'd never seen her have more than one.

Claudia's eyes shimmered with new tears, and she turned her head away from him.

Anthony couldn't refrain from touching her any more than he could fly to the moon. He reached over and pulled her into his arms.

She leaned against him and sighed. Then she turned her face into his shirt and inhaled deeply. *If she knew I ran all the way here, she might not want to do that.* As it was, she seemed to melt into him.

"Claudia, Claudia, Claudia...what am I going to do with you?"

She leaned away from him and looked up into his eyes, searching, yearning—but for what?

Could she have harbored feelings for me and hidden them so well that I never recognized them? Well, why the hell not? He had done the same thing around her for the last five years.

From the day she walked into his office to apply

for a waitressing job, he had felt the instant pull of attraction. If not for his jealous ex-girlfriend, Ruxandra, showing up, he might have considered acting on it. For Claudia's safety, he had kept her at arm's length. Now here she was safe in his arms, feeling like she'd always belonged there.

Claudia's blond highlights might not be natural, but they made her hair shine like spun gold whenever she stepped under the lights of the bar. He cherished the memory—especially now when it looked as if she hadn't brushed her shoulder-length bob in days.

She seemed to be fading fast. Her eyes fluttered closed, and eventually her breathing took on the long, slow rhythm of sleep. She might have passed out, but Anthony chose to believe she felt so safe in his arms that she could finally relax and let go.

He vowed to hold her until just before dawn, if she didn't wake up before then. At that point, he'd have to leave. Otherwise, he would appear to be the one who'd passed out cold…more like dead. He didn't think she could handle that in her fragile condition.

Hours later, Claudia's intercom buzzed. Anthony considered waking her to answer it, but Claudia looked so angelic sleeping in his arms. He edged out of her delicate grasp and laid her down gently.

Who would come to see her at five in the morning?

He touched the intercom speaker button and whispered. "Who is it?"

After a brief delay, a woman's voice said, "Is this Claudia's apartment?"

"May I ask who you are first?"

An impatient male voice called out, "It's her parents. Who the hell are you?"

Oops. Caught in a girl's apartment at 5:00 a.m. by her parents. That hadn't happened in a while. Anthony glanced over at Claudia, who was softly snoring. The apartment was still as disheveled as it had been when he first saw it. If he was concerned for her after seeing that, her parents certainly would be.

"Give me a few seconds to wake her," he said.

An oath from her father was cut off halfway as Anthony let go of the buzzer. He used his vampiric speed to clean up the apartment. Finding the trash can under the sink, he grabbed the bucket and loaded it with empties until it wouldn't hold any more. Then he simply hid the rest of them. He zoomed around the room once more, putting pillows back on chairs, mascara side down, and placing the empty pizza boxes on the kitchen counter.

He stopped to appraise the job he'd done, and everything seemed neat. Then he shook Claudia. "Wake up. Your parents are here."

She protested with an *agh*.

He shook her harder and called out, "Claudia, wake up!"

At last, she opened her eyes and blinked. "Anthony? What are you..." Then she groaned. "Oh, yeah. I remember now." She looked shaky as she pushed herself up to a sitting position.

The intercom buzzed again.

"Your parents are here."

"What?" She shot to her feet and swayed.

Anthony grabbed her arm and clasped her around her waist to steady her. "You need to buzz them in."

"No. They're in Florida."

"They're here. If you don't let them in, I'll have to."

"No! They can't know you're here. Quick. Hide in the bedroom." She pushed at him, but he didn't move.

"It's too late. I answered the intercom the first time it buzzed."

She hit him. "Why did you do that?"

He turned her toward the door and marched her over to it. "Let them in. They're probably as worried about you as I was."

She sighed. "Okay, but first I need to make sure it's really them." She leaned on the intercom button and said, "Mom? Dad?"

A soft click was followed by her mother pleading, "Open the door, honey," and her father bellowing, "What kind of daughter lets her parents stand on the sidewalk while she—"

Claudia let go of the intercom and buzzed them in. "That's them all right."

"I'd better go," Anthony said.

Claudia glanced around her apartment and her eyebrows rose. "You cleaned up after me?"

"Just a quick tidying up."

She rested a hand on his arm. "Thank you."

Anthony held her gaze for a moment. Something unspoken but deeply meaningful passed between them. He was fairly sure it was more than gratitude on her part. It certainly was on his.

A hard knock on her door broke the spell.

"Time to face the music—or the cacophony," Claudia muttered.

Anthony buttoned his suit jacket a moment before she opened the door to reveal a bedraggled-looking couple.

"We drove thirty-six hours straight to get here, young lady," her father blasted. "You'd better have a damn good excuse for not answering your phone or emails."

"I—uh…"

Her father turned his anger on Anthony. "Are you the reason she was unreachable for a week?"

"No, Dad," Claudia quickly said.

Someone upstairs opened their door and yelled down, "It's five o'clock in the friggin' morning. Shut the hell up and let people sleep!"

Claudia opened her door wider. "Come in and try to calm down."

When her parents were inside the apartment, Anthony extended his hand. "I'm Anthony Cross. I was concerned about her as well."

Her father stared at Anthony's hand. At last he grasped it and shook twice. "Your hand is cold. You must have arrived just before we did."

Her mother added, "Even if he's been here all night, she's a grown woman and allowed to have a boyfriend, dear."

Anthony didn't quite know how to respond to that. Should he let Claudia's father think they were a couple? Fortunately, he didn't have to confirm or deny. Claudia jumped in.

"He's not my boyfriend. He's my old boss."

"Old boss?" her father said. "Did he fire you? Is that why you look like hell?"

She sighed. "No. He didn't fire me. The fire fired me." Claudia faced Anthony straight on and shot him a poignant look. "The building that housed the import-export business burned down."

Import-export? Was that code for "my parents don't know I worked in a bar"?

"Oh! Were you hurt? Is that why we couldn't reach you?" her mother asked, wringing her hands.

Anthony glanced at his watch. He had to get going in order to make it to his lair in Chinatown before the sun came up. It would happen about 5:44 a.m. at this time of year.

"Excuse me for interrupting, but I have to go," Anthony said.

Claudia smiled gratefully. "Yes, I suppose you must be tired. Thank you for listening to me, uh, talk your ear off."

Anthony was glad his suit wasn't rumpled and it looked as if talking was all he'd been doing, but how would Claudia explain her appearance?

"I'm glad we talked. I'm sorry I got you out of bed by arriving so late. I'll call you soon so we can continue putting together a plan to get the business back up and running."

She waved away his fake apology. "Oh, don't worry about getting me up. I'm just glad you're including me in your plans to rebuild."

"I couldn't do it without you."

Her parents smiled and seemed to buy into their explanation. Whew. Not bad for a cockamamy story on the fly. He shook hands with both of them, waved to Claudia, and left.

He'd have to zoom back to his place. Public transportation wasn't fast enough. Standing on the sidewalk, he checked for witnesses, and dammit, the garbage truck was rumbling down the street and people were scrambling to get their trash out in time.

Panic gripped him as he noticed the dawn approaching and pictured his bad self bursting into flames in the sun.

Chapter 2

As soon as the door closed, Claudia's parents both began talking at once.

"Where were you?"

"Is he really your boss or your boyfriend?"

"What happened?"

Claudia held up both hands. "Whoa. Let me make some coffee first."

"Oh, yes. Coffee would be nice," her mother said. "I'm glad you haven't forgotten your manners."

Manners are all that's keeping me from throwing you out the door.

While Claudia headed to the kitchen, her father said, "So, tell us why you moved from your other apartment. It was so much nicer."

He dropped into her chair and a crunching noise surprised him. "What the…?" He popped back up and lifted the cushion.

Oh no. Now she knew where Anthony had stashed the empty beer bottles.

He pointed to the cracked brown glass. "What's this? Some dangerous version of a whoopee cushion?"

Claudia felt her face heat. "Um, no. Of course not. I had a few friends over before Anthony surprised me with a visit. I just stashed the bottles there because I didn't have time to clean up." *That sounds reasonable.* She hoped they believed her, because it was the best story she had.

Meanwhile, her mother had made it to her kitchen and opened one of the pizza boxes. "It looks like you weren't worried about impressing your friends. Really, Claudia. Pizza and beer? I thought we raised you to be more refined."

She smiled. "Sorry, Mom."

"And look at all these glasses in the sink…" Her mother was about to open the dishwasher, and only God knew where Anthony had stored the hard liquor.

"Mom, please! Get out of my kitchen."

Her mother gasped. "Excuse me? I'm sure you can rephrase that to sound a little less churlish."

"Sorry. I just—Please, sit on the couch with Dad and let me make you something to eat. You must be hungry after your long drive."

"That's more like it." Her mother sniffed and turned on her heel, marching back to the living room.

Claudia usually liked apartments with an open floor plan so she could talk to guests while preparing food, but in this case, she'd rather stick them in another room—or another city—and gather her wits.

She opened the refrigerator, knowing there was precious little to offer anyone in there. *Butter. Peanut butter. Jam. Cheese.* She'd better find a way to make something edible. If not, she was toast. She bolted upright. *Toast!*

It wouldn't impress, but it would fill their stomachs. *If only I had time to run to the coffee shop. Ah!* A brainstorm in her otherwise fuzzy mind formed a solution.

"Why don't we all go to the coffee shop down the street? They have some lovely pastries…"

Her mother studied her with raised eyebrows. "You aren't considering going out like *that*, are you?"

Claudia sighed. As usual, she couldn't do anything right. "Well, we have a choice. I can get cleaned up and we can go out, or I can make PB and J, and grilled cheese sandwiches."

Her father smiled. "With the crusts cut off?"

Her mother wrinkled her nose. "That's hardly a decent breakfast." She started to return to the kitchen. "Is that all you have?"

Claudia grasped her mother's shoulders before she could reenter and spun her around. "I've been away…on a camping trip. That's why I have no food and why you couldn't get in touch with me. There's no cell reception up in the Maine woods."

Whew! Two explanations with one lie. She felt brilliant. Now if she could just down a gallon of coffee, she might make it through this inquisition—er, visit.

Anthony woke up in unfamiliar surroundings. *Where the hell am I, and what is that stench?* Then he remembered. He hadn't made it back to his lair in time and had to resort to prying open a manhole and hiding in the sewer to accommodate his death sleep.

Now that it was evening again, he considered going back to Claudia's, but he reeked. Besides, her parents might still be there. A long, steamy shower in his apartment sounded like a much better idea.

He climbed the ladder until he reached the manhole cover. Now to play "guess if anyone is up there or not?" He couldn't use his sense of smell. That was compromised. *Bloody hell, I might not get the disgusting smell out of my nose for days.*

He lifted the lid slightly and listened. Noise of the city met his ears. Mostly traffic rumbling along the busy main drive a block away. He didn't hear any clicking of shoes along the sidewalk, so he pushed the manhole aside and climbed out.

A couple of men who had apparently been leaning against a nearby building spotted him but said nothing. They simply stared as he straightened his lapels, stood tall, then strode off in the direction of his home with his head held high.

He was halfway home when he heard his name being called.

Maybe it's another Anthony. He hoped so. He was close enough to the Italian North End for the name to refer to dozens of men.

"Hey, Anthony! Wait up."

There was no mistaking the voice now. Tory Montana had caught sight of him. Even though Tory was quite a way off, he'd know that Anthony, with his vampiric senses, could hear him. *I can't very well pretend I don't know one of my former best patrons.*

Anthony swiveled around. Despite the darkness, he spotted the African American ex-linebacker jogging toward him. As soon as he'd spotted Anthony waiting for him, Tory slowed to a walk.

Almost five years ago, Anthony had been chatting with Claudia in his office when a loud crash came from the bar. Voices shouted and another crash followed.

They charged out of the office, tripping over each other. A bar brawl was in progress, with one gentleman clearly getting the worst end of it. The bouncer, Kurt, jumped between them and pushed. The guys stumbled back a few feet but came at each other with renewed vigor.

Anthony was removing his jacket when Kurt called out, "Stay where you are. I've got this."

He took down the guy who reached him first and sat on him. Just as the other one was about to take advantage of the situation, another customer tackled the guy, rose, and tucked him under his arm like a football.

"Where do you want this one?" he asked Kurt.

Kurt got up and yanked his guy off the floor by his belt. "You toss that one out the back, and I'll send this one headfirst out the front door onto the sidewalk."

The helpful customer simply nodded, carried the stunned fighter to the back exit, opened the door, and tossed him into the alley.

Meanwhile, Kurt opened the front door, and despite the guy's loud protest, did what he said he'd do…sent the other fighter sprawling onto the sidewalk.

As the helpful, yet unfamiliar, customer returned, Anthony stuck out his hand.

"Thanks for your help."

"Anytime." He grasped Anthony's hand and shook it. "Are you the owner?"

"Yes. Anthony Cross. And you are?"

"Tory Montana."

Someone at the bar whirled around on his stool and said, "Tory Montana. I thought you looked familiar. You played for the Steelers, right? What are you doing in Boston?"

Tory tucked his hands in his pockets. "House-sitting for friends. I'm flattered you remember me. I retired in 2006."

"Seriously?" As the two customers began a conversation, Anthony strolled over to Kurt, who was setting a chair upright.

"What happened?"

Kurt shrugged. "To be honest, nothing. They just walked in here and started throwing punches like they'd already been having an argument.

Anthony lowered his voice. "Montana's *freakishly* strong, if you know what I mean. Maybe we should invite him to the back booth for a free beer—and careful discussion."

"I read you loud and clear, boss."

And that's how the coyote shapeshifter became Anthony's second bouncer.

Returning from his memory, Anthony waited for Tory to shake his hand, but the shifter came to an abrupt halt and wrinkled his nose. "What's that smell?"

Anthony sagged against a tree. "I was visiting Claudia in Cambridge this morning and couldn't get home in time. I spent the day under the street."

Tory's eyes widened. "In the sewer?"

"It was the best option I had."

Tory laughed. "So it would smell." He held his nose but continued talking, with a nasal tone. "How's Claudia?"

"She'll be okay." *I hope.*

"So, Cambridge, huh? Did you hear about the lab over there?"

"What lab?"

"Jesus. I thought you knew. Some of the werecops think there's a secret lab over there doing testing on paranormals. They suspect that some kind of screwup exposed the existence of paranormals and caught the attention of a brainiac group. Now scientists are trying to capture as many as they can and study us like lab rats."

"Shit. Where's this lab located?"

"That's just it. We don't know. Nick Wolfensen heard about it from his cop buddies. He and Kurt Morgan have been looking for it but aren't having much luck. As a wizard, Kurt can avoid capture pretty easily simply by becoming invisible or using that neat time-stopping trick he has, but with no leads..."

"I see. How can I help?"

Tory clapped a big hand over Anthony's shoulder. "Just help yourself. Try to be as inconspicuous as possible." He sniffed the air. "You might want to start by washing off that stink soon."

"You're not saying they could overpower a vampire..."

"I don't know. They've found a way to disable weres long enough to get them to the facility."

"How do you know this?"

"A paranormal they'd held for a while escaped. She told a couple of police officers who happened to be werewolves. Unfortunately, she didn't know the area and couldn't retrace her steps or give them much information. The cops didn't take it too seriously at first because the scientists thought she was some kind of new animal. Then a few weres began disappearing."

"Crap. Maybe they were seen shifting. That would alert a bunch of overachieving researchers."

"You know how careful we are. I can't imagine a bunch of paranormals suddenly getting sloppy enough to shift and get caught."

Anthony doubted it too. Winding up as an experiment—prodded, probed, and possibly dissected—was every supe's worst fear.

"Is there any pattern?"

"Like, do these disappearances happen only during the full moon or in a particular area?"

"Yes. Anything like that?"

"No. I wish it were that easy."

"Where are you getting your information?"

"Mostly from Kurt and Nick. When he's not helping the police, Nick's been using his paranormal PI skills. Tracking, mostly. His reputation is growing, but I doubt anyone suspects him of the breach. He's always kept our population strictly on the down low."

"What about his wife? Brandee was human. Could she have spilled the beans?"

"Nick insists she absolutely did not. And why would she? If anything happened to Nick, she'd be devastated."

Anthony nodded. "That's true. Besides, she proved herself trustworthy long ago when he revealed our world to her. So what do we do?"

"Nothing. Let Kurt and Nick investigate first. If they need our help, they'll ask."

"If those two are on the case, it's only a matter of time before they find the facility. We can breathe a little easier—not that I breathe much."

Then Anthony remembered how secretive he'd been about his lair's location. Other paranormals were the same way. How could Nick or Kurt find them if they needed help? "I guess the best thing I can do is rebuild our meeting place as quickly as possible. We need to communicate with each other, and there's strength in numbers."

Tory grinned. "I was hoping you'd say that."

~

Maynard peered into his microscope and studied the fish scales from the merman's tail. Said merman was hanging over the side of his giant fish tank, glaring at him.

"That hurt, you know."

Maynard tried to ignore him.

"How would you like it if I scraped a piece off your leg and stuck it on a glass slide?"

When Maynard didn't answer, the specimen continued talking. Indeed, he had to think of these creatures as impersonally as possible to do what was necessary. A Nobel Prize omelet wasn't made without breaking a few eggs. *Hmmm...I wonder if the mermaids lay eggs in the water and the males spread their sperm over them. I'm not going to ask where his dick is.*

"I was minding my own business, just enjoying a swim in the harbor. Who are you to throw a net over me and bring me here?"

"Shut up, fish." Maynard took a break from his microscope long enough to pull his hair back and secure it with an elastic band.

"I have a name. It's Jules. Jules Vernon. Please use it."

Using the specimen's name would make the work a lot harder. Maynard had no problem studying cells from rodents, but this was a man—sort of—and one of the most important discoveries ever made. Maynard had to document scientific data to prove he'd found a whole new species. Ever since the invention of computer graphics, a documentary wouldn't do it.

The merman had proved useful, at first. He tried to buy his way out of captivity by giving up what he knew of other paranormal species. Now Maynard and a few trusted scientists like himself worked night and day to capture as many of these "paranormals" as they could find.

Who knew so many unique creatures were living right under their noses? His work could explain how ancient legends came about. He'd often wondered if these persistent stories had any basis in fact. But he'd be a laughingstock if he made claims of vampires and shapeshifters without solid proof.

"Aren't you going to feed the others?" Jules pointed to the cell at the end of the room.

He felt bad about the woman and her young son who claimed not to be vampires but said they needed blood to live. "Yeah, right. What do you want me to do? Walk in there and expose my neck?"

The merman smirked. "Sure. Why not? All in the name of science, right?"

Maynard snorted. The alleged vampires were beginning to look a bit gaunt and weak, but it seemed like the best way to keep them docile. The researchers had tossed a pig in there a couple days ago and after the mother and son had fed on it, practically draining it dry, they were suddenly much stronger. For a few moments, Maynard wasn't sure the iron bars would hold them.

The naked men in the unbreakable glass cell were just as difficult to manage. They were super strong too, which is why the scientists were using the gorilla room to hold them. They'd refused to transform but had been caught in the act of going from canine to human. Fortunately, none of these creatures seemed able to shake off a Taser on a high setting.

The merman was right. It was time to feed the specimens, but Maynard didn't dare do it without help. As soon as one of his colleagues arrived, they could handle it together.

Sadie was the only one who knew where Anthony's lair was located. She entered the Chinese restaurant, nodded to the woman behind the counter, and ambled into the kitchen at the back. The two cooks preparing food stopped and bowed slightly as she walked past, and she returned the respectful gesture.

Anthony had chosen this part of town to hide his scent from Ruxandra. Among the exotic spices and cooking odors, even the most astute nose could become confused. Moreover, there was a ready supply of animal blood nearby.

He had a sweet setup. During the day, he occupied an unused, completely dark storage room in the basement and locked it from the inside. At night, he had an apartment over the restaurant. The owners lived on the third floor and slept better knowing he spent most of his waking hours right over their precious family business.

When Sadie asked why Anthony didn't just keep a coffin in an apartment bedroom, he blanched. After some embarrassed hems and haws, he'd admitted he couldn't sleep in such a small enclosed space because he was claustrophobic. Not an ideal situation for a vampire.

No one had asked about his pale skin or odd hours, but the Chinese were no fools. Sadie figured they knew what he was and realized if they provided him shelter, he wouldn't bite the hand that fed him…or housed him, as it were.

Sadie crept up the stairs at the back of the kitchen and stopped at Anthony's door. It was midnight, so he should be at home. Then she caught herself. Anthony *used to* be home by midnight after the bar closed. She didn't really know what he was doing with his evenings nowadays. She knocked anyway and waited.

"Who is it?" he called out.

"Sadie."

He opened the door and greeted her with a warm hug. Well, it was emotionally warm anyhow. Physically he was always a bit chilly.

"Come in. I have company, but you're welcome to join us."

"Oh. I thought I was the only one who knew where you were."

"I had to tell one other person."

Sadie glanced over Anthony's shoulder and recognized Kurt the wizard. She hadn't seen him since the bar burned and was delighted when she spotted his charming smile. "Kurt! How lovely to see you."

He rose and surprised her with a big hug.

"Same here. I hope you brought your tarot cards, Sadie."

"I don't go anywhere without them. Why? Do you need a reading?"

"I need a miracle." He glanced at Anthony. "We all do."

"Oh, dear."

"Sit, Aunt Sadie." Anthony gestured to the couch. "Can I get you some Chinese tea?"

She sighed. "If that's all you have."

Kurt chuckled. "You were hoping for a White Russian?"

One corner of Sadie's mouth turned up. "You know me too well, but I was actually worried about the caffeine at this time of night."

"You might need a little to sharpen your psychic senses," Anthony said.

Her gift didn't work like that, but no one needed to know about her trances. As soon as she'd settled onto the couch, she pulled her tarot cards out of her large satchel and began shuffling them.

"I was kind of kidding about the tarot reading," Kurt said. "I was told you don't really need the cards to do your psychic thing."

"That's true. It's mostly for show, but sometimes just one card can lead me in the right direction. What's your question?"

"I'd like to know the location of the lab that's been capturing and holding paranormals."

Sadie's jaw dropped. She'd always worried about humans other than Kurt and herself learning that paranormals were real and living among the residents of Boston. "How… When…"

"What I really need to know is *where*."

"I understand, but I can't pinpoint locations."

"But you said a card can point you in the right direction."

"I meant that metaphorically."

Anthony returned with a small bamboo tray, a cup of tea, a spoon, and a packet of sugar. "Here you go."

Sadie took a sip and wrinkled her nose at the

strange-tasting tea. She added some sugar to kill the unfamiliar taste and tried again. "Ah, that's better." Setting the cup on the tea table, she said, "Tell me what's been going on. It sounds likc I'vc misscd something big."

"A few paras have gone missing. All we have are rumors right now, but if what we suspect is true, we could lose a lot of friends before we put a stop to it," Kurt said.

Anthony sat next to her. "I don't think it's a rumor. I think every paranormal's worst fear is coming true."

"But how? Isn't the number one rule for all paranormals to keep their identity a secret?" she asked.

"It is. But somehow word has leaked out, and just as we feared, we're being hunted."

"By whom and for what?"

Anthony snorted. "Scientists. The government. They could want our supernatural strength and healing power for an immortal military. I don't know." He shook his head.

She laid a hand on his shoulder. "Anthony, did you keep the tea leaves?"

"Uh, no. I tossed them in the garbage. Do you read tea leaves?"

"Yes. I can sometimes figure out timelines by where the leaves land in the cup, but it still won't give me a location."

"I can make more." Anthony turned toward the kitchen, but she reached out and grabbed his arm. "Let me try the cards first."

He nodded and sat nearby. Sadie shuffled them a bit more purposefully. "I'll tell you what I can. I've read you before, Kurt. Do you remember your indicator card?"

"The Hierophant."

Kurt waited on the edge of his seat as Sadie gathered up her cards again. A card jumped out of the deck and fell right side up on the table. It was the Hierophant.

Sadie leaned back and stared at the card. "Now, I'm good, but I'm not *that* good."

Kurt chuckled. "I figured you might need it, so I found it for you."

Sadie shook her head and muttered, "Show-off wizard."

Kurt's grin indicated he didn't take offense.

She placed the card in front of her and set the deck next to it. "Cut the deck and hand me the top card."

Kurt did as she asked, and she placed the King of Swords over the Hierophant, sideways.

"Kings and queens indicate people and places."

"That's good, right?" Kurt asked. "I mean, that's what I wanted to know."

Not necessarily. A king was a formidable foe, and swords meant he had a strategic plan. Sadie worried her lip and closed her eyes. Her deep, steady breaths helped her access the more psychic reaches of her mind. Kurt and Anthony remained silent, giving her the time she needed to get a vision, if one would come.

At last she was standing outside a nondescript three-story building. All seemed quiet. She didn't recognize it or the neighborhood, so that wasn't much help. *Maybe if I astral-project to the roof, I can see a landmark.*

Sadie entered a deep trance and saw out of her mind's eye as she floated up one story, two stories, three stories. At last she found the roof and directed her spirit body to land on it. Glancing around the area, she saw more buildings but none of them familiar. She sensed she was outside Boston proper in a pretty sketchy neighborhood, but she couldn't be sure exactly where. Cambridge? Somerville? Everything was densely packed, and taller buildings obscured her view. Additionally, she couldn't see any street signs.

Deciding to astral-project through the roof into the building, she hoped to view its contents and discover why she had projected there.

The third story held boxes and crates. Some had been pried open, and straw was strewn about the floor. Nothing interesting there, so she continued sinking through the third floor into the ceiling of the second. She found herself in an office. It seemed like this might be an old factory. There was a wall of windows and a metal walkway just outside the office. She imagined the supervisors keeping an eye on things by gazing down at the factory floor.

That seemed like a good idea, so she floated through the wall and stood on the walkway. What she saw shocked her. Cages. Some small enough to hold a rabbit, others large enough to hold a man. Then she spotted a group cell—a very large, glassed-in area with two naked men, a naked woman, and a naked child inside. If that wasn't upsetting enough, a few giant fish tanks stood against the opposite wall. She spotted one with a man inside…and he had a fishtail!

Sadie was about to get closer when a security guard rushed toward her from her right. *Can he see me?*

"You there. Halt!"

Crap! He can! How he was able to see her in astral form wasn't important at the moment. Getting out of there was.

She shot up through the ceiling and then through

the next one, willing herself to return to her body in Anthony's apartment.

Just as she arrived on the roof, her spirit snapped itself back into her body and she fell over.

"Sadie!" Anthony was lifting her upright in a nanosecond. "Are you okay?"

Sadie took a deep breath and allowed her calm to return. "I'm fine. At least I will be. I astral-projected into an old factory and had to snap back into my body abruptly."

"Had to?" Kurt asked.

"I was spotted."

Kurt's shocked expression said it all. "Who or what could have possibly seen you in astral form?"

"That's what I'd like to know," she said. "His speech and uniform seemed old-fashioned, and he carried a nightstick."

"Are you thinking it might have been a spirit?" Anthony asked. "Maybe an old-time cop or security guard?"

"I can't come up with any other plausible explanation."

"Did he seem cognizant? Interested in what you were doing there?"

"Oh, yes. He shouted and began running toward me."

"Great." Kurt tossed his hands in the air. "So, even if we find the place, it's haunted and we can't hide from an invisible guard. Do you think the scientists know he's there?"

"I don't know. I'm sorry I panicked," Sadie said.

Anthony patted her hand. "Don't apologize. You did the right thing."

"This has never happened to me before. Do you think he could do anything to us?"

Kurt paced. "I wish I knew."

Just then the phone rang.

"Anthony?"

A slight hesitation on the other side of the line made Claudia wonder if she should have called. *For God's sake. I was rip-roaring drunk and passed out on him. He probably never wants to hear from me again.*

"Claudia. How are you feeling?" he finally asked.

"I'm…better." She plopped down onto her couch and set the dust rag on the end table beside her. "I just wanted to apologize."

"Apologize? For what?"

She sighed. "Where do I start? My behavior. My parents… Thank you for covering for me, by the way."

"Stop," he said. "You have nothing to apologize for. I should have checked on you much sooner."

"Why? You're not responsible for me."

"I…" There was that hesitation again.

"Anthony, is something wrong?"

He sighed. "No. Well, yes, but it's being handled."

She waited, hoping he'd offer more. When he didn't, she debated what to do. Prod? Leave it alone? What if he needed a friend and she could return the support he'd given her?

"Anthony, tell me. I don't want to see you suffer any more than you wanted me to."

"I can't."

Simple as that? He can't? "Whatever it is, it can't be

worse than what you saw me going through. Please, let me help."

She heard a voice in the background, which was quickly muffled. She pictured Anthony covering the phone.

"Oh. It sounds like I'm interrupting something."

"No. It's fine. We were just finishing up. Kurt said to tell you hello."

Then she heard a female voice.

"Sadie too."

"It sounds like you're having a reunion. Can I come?" Claudia slapped a hand over her mouth. *Why did I invite myself? If he'd wanted me there, he'd have asked me. What a dumbass move.*

"I—I'd like to see you, but not here. Can I meet you for a drink?"

Claudia groaned. "The last thing I need right now is a drink. Besides, I shouldn't have invited myself."

"No. I really want to talk to you."

"You do?"

"Yes. Are your parents still there?"

"They opted for a hotel. I can't say I blame them. They're leaving after breakfast tomorrow."

"So, you're alone for the rest of the night?"

"Yes."

"I can be there in an hour. Will you let me in this time?" He chuckled.

Claudia felt her face heat. *Jesus, I made him beg to come in last time. Way to go, Princess Charming.* "I promise to let you in, if you'll let me make up for my rudeness."

"What did you have in mind?" he said seductively.

A fraction of a second later he said, "I'm sorry. I didn't mean that the way it sounded."

After her own brief hesitation, she said. "Darn it." Then her hand flew up to cover her big mouth.

Chapter 3

On his way to Claudia's apartment, Anthony wondered what she'd meant by her last remark. She had hung up too quickly for him to ask her. On one level he knew. Heck, on all levels he knew. It sounded like she was feeling the same way about him as he'd always felt about her. But had she hidden her feelings for five years?

Taking public transportation was frustrating. At least he was close enough to jog to the Red Line and didn't have to change trains. He was so preoccupied that he might just end up in the suburbs if he wasn't careful.

At last Anthony's car pulled into Central Square, and he was the first one off. He hadn't taken the T to Cambridge before, so he wasn't exactly sure where Claudia's apartment was in relation to the stop, and the streetlights were out. Spinning around, he looked for a landmark. A bicyclist rode toward him, his DayGlo orange stripes gleaming.

"Excuse me, where's Green Street?"

The guy pointed toward a coffee shop. "One block over."

"Thanks." Anthony could barely wait for a break in traffic to sprint across the busy street. When he reached Claudia's steps, he took them two at a time. She buzzed him in, and he dashed up the stairs to the third floor.

She opened the door the minute he knocked, and Anthony walked right into her waiting arms. With no discussion, and none needed, he cupped her head and his lips descended to hers. She tipped her face up to meet his, and they stood for who knows how long in a fervent lip-lock.

When they broke apart, Claudia was brcathing hard.

"I guess we should go inside and close the door," Anthony said.

She giggled. "What? You don't want to put on a show for the neighbors?"

He walked forward while she took a couple steps back. Absently, he kicked the door shut behind them, and as soon as it clicked, he kissed her again. Their hands explored and caressed each other as if of their own volition.

Five years of waiting. Five years of pent-up sexual frustration. Anthony didn't know if he could stop touching and kissing her—ever.

When they finally broke apart, he rested his forehead against hers. Then, they gazed into cach other's eyes for several long moments.

Eventually, he said, "I've wanted to do that for five years."

Claudia smiled. "Me too. What took you so long?"

They both knew the answer to that. *Ruxandra.*

Claudia stepped away and offered him a beverage. Anthony opted for tea since Type O was probably not on the menu.

While she was in the kitchen, he glanced around the room. It was in much better shape than before. Like the woman he knew, it was well put together and immaculate. He remembered her first request as his new bar manager. She'd wanted to wear her fashionable clothes and not the uniform he had her wear as a waitress.

When she returned with his tea, he took a moment to notice her outfit. She wore a little black dress and strappy sandals. He could take her anywhere in that. Of course, all he wanted to do was take her into the next room and remove said little black dress.

But it was too soon for that.

"Have a seat." Claudia didn't specify where, so Anthony sat on the couch, expecting she'd join him there. She set his tea on a coaster next to him and settled herself on his other side.

Kicking off her sandals and pulling her feet up under her thigh, she looked casual and comfortable. He was glad she hadn't suddenly become shy after their first kiss. A lot of women would have.

"It's nice to see you again," she said. "You look well."

Okay. She wasn't acting shy but a little formal.

"You too. I trust you're feeling better."

She groaned and hung her head. "Let's pretend the other night never happened."

"Why?"

She snorted. "You didn't exactly see me in my best light."

Anthony took a sip of his tea while he tried to think of something to say to that. Should he acknowledge her sober assessment? Downplay it? He opted for reaching over and taking her hand in his. Giving it a squeeze he said, "I've seen you in your best light for far too long. It was about time you showed me your flawed human side."

She smiled. "Thanks. Maybe someday you'll show me your human side too."

Doubtful, since I'm no longer human.

She let go of his hand. "Speaking of which, where are

your emotions? You can be upset around me, you know. I won't wilt, and I want to be supportive. I'm kind of surprised you seem so unaffected by everything that's happened. After all, it was your business that burned to the ground."

"I'm just glad no one was hurt. It could have been so much worse."

"That's true." She worried her lip for a moment. "The other night, when you were talking about rebuilding. Did you mean it?"

"Absolutely. I still want a place in the neighborhood for the locals to socialize." *Especially the local paranormals.* "And I'd like to get it under way as quickly as possible."

"Then, as hard as this is to say, I should tell you that you might want to find another manager."

Anthony's brows shot up. He couldn't picture anyone but Claudia running his place during daylight hours. How could he trust anyone else? It not only made no business sense, but he wouldn't have the same enthusiasm. The best part of going to work was knowing she would be there waiting for him at sunset.

"But, why? Do you need money to live on in the meantime? Because if you do, I can—"

She held up a hand to stop him. "No. That's not it." She fidgeted a little, then faced him head-on. "There's something I need to tell you. Something I should have told you long ago."

"Oh?" *This sounds ominous. Could Ruxandra have threatened her?* "Whatever it is, I'm on your side."

She let out a deep breath. "I know, but wait until you hear what I have to say. You might feel differently."

He didn't want to protest; he just wanted her to keep talking. Whatever it was, he was sure they could handle it together—just like they'd handled everything. So he waited and let her gather her courage.

"Anthony, I have a drinking problem. I have no business working in a bar."

Of all the secrets she could have shared, this was one he'd never even considered. "What? Are you sure? I never saw anything to indicate..."

She held up her hand again. "I know. I was...I mean I *am* what they call a functional alcoholic. I could hold it together all day long in order to do my job, but as soon as I got home at night, all bets were off. You're not the only one who didn't know. I was very good at hiding it."

He took a quick glance at the open kitchen where she'd had her booze and didn't see a single bottle.

"It's all gone. I have to quit, Anthony. It's starting to affect my health."

"I see." He really didn't see. How could this have happened? Was the job too stressful? The hours too long? "Claudia, I mean it. I'm here for you. I'll give you any assistance you need. How can I help?"

She gave him a sad smile. "That's just it. You can't. I have to do this myself. I went to my first AA meeting yesterday, and it sounds like I have a long road ahead of me."

Anthony blew out a rare breath and shook his head at the floor. "I wish I had known sooner. It must have been difficult for you."

"You could say that. As soon as I explained it all to my parents, they wanted me to move back to Florida where they could keep an eye on me. I had to promise them I'd go to AA and call them regularly before they'd agree to drop it and go home."

"So they're on their way?"

"Yes. It's a long drive and my dad doesn't trust anyone to run his business correctly while he's away. At least he's given up the idea that I should take over for him someday."

"I can't imagine anyone else I'd want running my business—whatever it is. Claudia, I don't have to reopen as a bar. I could make it a coffee shop."

"With a bakery and coffee bar right next door? I'm sure they'd love that."

Anthony was desperate to think of something. Not only did he want to help Claudia, but he also wanted to be sure Sadie was taken care of. Both women were too proud to take his charity. He'd have to find a way to employ them both. Sadie just needed a booth to read tarot cards. But now that Claudia was a teetotaler…

As if a lightbulb hovering over his head suddenly went on, Anthony grabbed his cup and blurted out, "Tea! A tea room! Sadie can read tea leaves. She told me so. You can make the place over however you want. I can picture you serving high tea and offering special blends from all over the world. It even fits better with the upper-class flavor of Beacon Hill than a bar."

"You mean like the places with tablecloths and bone china?"

"Exactly." Suddenly Anthony pictured a big werewolf like Nick holding a delicate teacup with his pinkie sticking out. He almost laughed, but the hopeful excitement on Claudia's face stopped him.

"We could have light lunches—like soups and salads.

Of course the requisite finger sandwiches, scones, tea, and other beverages too, but no alcohol," she said. Jumping up, she added, "Maybe we could even strike a deal with the bakery next door and have them make the scones and cakes for us."

If Anthony had second thoughts, he'd just have to squelch them. A tea parlor would be perfect for the two ladies in his life. And who knew, maybe paranormals would be willing to meet there, even without the alcohol.

He could see the female paranormal population more comfortable in a place like that. And he remembered how Kurt and Tory always complained about the lack of available women. *Well, guys, problem solved.*

Almost. First he had to rebuild. Getting permits, hiring contractors, all that would take time, but he'd done it before. Telling his old regulars about the new venue without becoming a laughingstock would be trickier.

The following evening, Claudia answered her buzzer and was delighted to hear Anthony's voice.

"I bring glad tidings."

"Oh? And what are those?"

"Books about our new business, so we won't come off as neophytes to avid tea aficionados."

"Oh, thank goodness. Come on up!"

When he arrived at her door, she was ready and waiting to greet him. She'd combed her hair and put on makeup. It had felt good to make the effort.

He smiled at her. "You look like you're feeling better."

"I am."

"Good, because I want to take you out to other tea

rooms in the city. My research has turned up only a few, and most are in pricey hotels, so…"

Her face fell.

"What did I say?"

"Oh, nothing."

"Claudia?"

Over the past five years, she'd learned to read his various facial expressions, and the one he was wearing now meant, "Don't try to spare my feelings. Just tell me the truth."

"I—uh…I'm embarrassed about how badly I let myself go. It's a wonder you want…well, anything to do with me."

He placed gentle hands on her shoulders. "How can you think that? I care about you. More than you may believe right now."

She nodded. She cared about him too—definitely more than he suspected. She was in love with him and had been for years.

Anthony sat on the couch and patted the spot next to him. "Let's begin before we get distracted."

She sat a short distance away. If she were going to minimize distractions, she'd have to avoid touching him.

He read aloud. "With more varietals in China than there are wine grape varietals in all of France, tea dazzles us with its diversity. But there is only one plant. Even with the endless complexities and variations in all the teas of the world, every tea springs from the singular plant species *Camellia sinensis*."

"Well, there's something," Claudia said. "Only one complicated scientific name to memorize."

"I don't think we need to memorize species, genus, and phylum, darling."

"Good, because my brain isn't cooperating yet."

"What do you mean?"

She hung her head. "I mean, I'm still just clearing up. I knew the bar business backward and forward and could run the place in my sleep—or a stupor, as it were. This is new learning, and I'm a little afraid."

"Afraid of what?"

"That my previous stupors turned me stupid."

"You're not stupid. If anything..." Anthony sat closer and put an arm around her shoulder. "We have plenty of time and we'll learn it together."

"I don't know. I've already forgotten the name of the species."

Anthony chuckled. "So have I. Let's not worry about that now." He returned his attention to the book. "Black tea is the most common tea in North America. It is produced when withered tea leaves are rolled and allowed to oxidize. This darkens the leaves and develops flavor, color, and body in the leaf."

He rubbed her shoulder as he continued to read. "The tea is dried to halt the oxidation process and lock in these characteristics. The result is a robust cup with bright or lively notes that are perfect for breakfast teas, with about half as much caffeine as a similarly sized cup of coffee."

"Anthony, stop."

"I'm sorry. Was it the word 'oxidation' that threw you?"

She shook her head. "Not the words this time. It's you."

He leaned back and studied her face. "Me?"

"Yes. Rubbing my shoulder, your thigh against mine. All I want to do is throw that book across the room and kiss you."

He laughed. "I'd like nothing better." He started to close the book.

"No. We *have to* learn this. I—I just think I should sit in the armchair." She rose quickly and moved to the chair. Now there was a table between them. "Okay. Keep reading."

He paused and she could sense his inner struggle. Maybe he was getting distracted too.

At last, he refocused on the book. "Green tea is gaining popularity in America. It is produced when tea leaves are heated or steamed right after being harvested. This halts the oxidation process, preserving the leaf's emerald hue and naturally occurring antioxidants and amino acids… Uh-oh. Here comes another one of those words. Theanine."

He placed the book upside down on the table. "Why don't I just go through this with a highlighter and pick out the stuff we really need to know?"

"But I really want to—" Her protest was cut short when he picked her up and laid her on the sofa, then covered her body with his and kissed her.

She snaked her arms around his neck and back. As their tongues dueled, she grabbed a fistful of hair at the nape of his neck, intending to pull him away. She couldn't do it. Instead, she released her grip and combed her fingers through the hair covering his collar. Her other hand caressed his back. His cock grew and teased her in just the right spot. The flare of desire caused her to buck against him.

A sane thought finally broke through her lust-filled haze. *We can't do this. Not yet.*

Fortunately, Anthony's restraint seemed to kick in at the same time. Pushing himself to his feet, he said, "I'm sorry."

She struggled to sit up. "Don't be. It's just Mother Nature's way of ensuring the human species continues."

His brows shot up.

"Oh, no," she quickly added. "I didn't mean that we should… You know…"

"Procreate?"

She giggled. "Sorry. This whole thing is a discussion for another time."

"Maybe not." He sat beside her. "I can't have children. You should know that in case you want one."

"No! I mean, no. I have enough to deal with."

"Yes. Right now you do. But you should know that for the future. If you were hoping for a family someday, it wouldn't be right for me to keep you from that goal."

"Anthony, I'm not harboring secret dreams of white picket fences. The work staff and regulars were my family. I'm fine with keeping it that way."

"Are you sure?"

"Absolutely."

He sagged against the back of the sofa and stared at the ceiling. "I can't tell you how relieved I am."

She was relieved too. The thought of caring for infants, then chasing toddlers around, and finally coping with teenagers scared her to pieces. As far as Claudia was concerned, this was just another indication that they belonged together.

Over the next two months, Anthony and Claudia studied the tea business in public places.

He used the excuse that they needed clear heads to discuss products, equipment, and staffing, and if they were alone in her apartment, he might not be able to keep his hands off her. That much was certainly true.

What he also needed was a way to keep Claudia safe from Ruxandra.

He thought he'd spotted his jealous ex-girlfriend following him one night. Fortunately, he was able to lose her—that time.

For now, he had to make his romantic relationship with Claudia appear as if it were strictly business. That was the opposite of what he wanted, but he needed time to deal with a certain dangerous vampiress. How to do that—short of killing Ruxandra—utterly mystified him.

Claudia seemed to understand his explanation of needing to put the business first and reluctantly agreed. She had her own work to do. The AA program had specific steps and she was taking them seriously. She admitted she wasn't looking forward to taking a moral inventory of herself, but Anthony couldn't imagine any of her actions being remotely immoral. If she only knew his history…her worst sin would pale in comparison to some of his *normal* behavior.

For now, she was attending meetings during the day and leaving her evenings free for him. If she kept to that schedule, he wouldn't have to worry about Ruxandra getting her alone in a dark alley.

His plan was working, at least temporarily. Each time they saw each other, they'd find a secluded table in the back and go over business decisions while waiting for their meals. Well, Claudia's meal. Anthony explained that he was on a special diet. Not untrue.

They tried really hard to keep their hands to themselves, but by the time dessert came, they were playing footsie, or if they had one of those padded-bench seats where they could sit side by side, they groped, kissed, and tried to stop short of getting thrown out for lewd behavior. Anthony didn't know how much longer he could postpone the inevitable.

He was going to sleep with Claudia. It wasn't a matter of if, but when.

"Have you considered my proposal?"

Her eyes rounded. "Your what?"

Whoa. Maybe I should have been more specific. "My offer to give you the apartment over the shop? It's brand new, very chic—like you, and the commute can't be beat."

"Oh." She chuckled. "That. Yes, I've thought about it, but I won't take it rent free. I know you could get upward of three thousand a month for that place."

"True, but I like to know who's living in my building." He reached across the table and took her hand in his. "I'd like to know *you're* living in my building. I want you safe."

"But I already owe you so much."

"You earned every penny I paid you. Who else would work seven days a week without complaint?"

She smiled but kept her eyes down. "It's very generous of you, but it could be awkward if things don't work out between us."

He let go of her hand and leaned back in his chair. "Why would you think that'll happen?"

"I don't. I mean…nobody does when the relationship is new. But things could change."

"Would you quit your job?"

"Of course not."

"Good. Then I don't foresee a problem."

"I'd still feel better paying rent."

Anthony sighed. "I'll work it into your new salary."

"Oh, yeah. That's something we haven't discussed yet. I assume the tea shop won't make as much money as the bar, at least when it's brand new. I guess I'll have to take a pay cut."

"No, you won't."

"Huh? Anthony, we can adjust it as we go along, but I know how much it costs to run a place like that, and you probably won't break even for a while."

"Don't worry about my money, Claudia. I can afford to pay you a good salary, and I will."

She lifted her chin. "And what if I say it's too much?"

Anthony burst out laughing.

"Hey. That isn't funny."

He dabbed at the corners of his eyes as he tried to wrestle the humor out of her refusal. "You're cute when you shoot yourself in the foot—or try to."

Claudia folded her arms over her perfect chest. "I'm trying to keep you in business."

He looked at her sternly. "Claudia, I'm a multimillionaire. I could run this business in the red for a hundred years, and I'd still have more money than I need."

She rolled her eyes. "Well, since neither one of us will be around that long, I can't very well call you a liar, can I?"

Whew. She obviously has no idea what I am. That was small comfort, considering he'd have to tell her eventually if things worked out—and he found himself desperately hoping they would.

"Not to change the subject, but how's the sobriety going?"

"Good. I'm enjoying the AA meetings. It's as if I've

discovered a whole new set of close friends I didn't know I had." She grinned.

An unexpected pang of jealousy hit him. He was genuinely happy for her, but part of him wondered if those friends would come between them at some point.

"I just got a sponsor," she said.

"Oh? That's great. Tell me about him." He tried to sound nonchalant. If he didn't tamp down the twinge of jealousy that had just stabbed his heart, he could threaten her sobriety. As much as he wanted to be her whole world, he wanted her health and happiness more.

"It's not a him. It's a her. Women sponsor women, and men sponsor men. It can get complicated otherwise."

"I see." He relaxed, trying not to let out the breath he'd been holding—for about ten minutes—in a big whoosh.

"I'm afraid I can't tell you anything about her. It's an anonymous program."

"Sort of like Las Vegas? What happens in AA stays in AA?"

Claudia rolled her eyes. "Vegas got a lot of people into AA."

He chuckled. "Well, you look happy. I'm glad to see you smiling again."

After a brief hesitation she said, "You have a lot to do with that. Unfortunately, that brings up a new wrinkle."

He lifted his eyebrows. "Wrinkle?" *That doesn't sound good.*

She fidgeted. "Newly sober singles are supposed to stay out of relationships for a year."

Anthony's jaw dropped. *Oh, hell no.* "A year? But we've already waited five!"

"I know. I explained that to my sponsor. She said it was up to me, and that I should take into consideration your… influence. She was concerned because you owned a bar."

Now he wanted to find this woman and throttle her. How dare she question his "influence"? Hadn't he decided to tailor his whole business to Claudia's needs?

She rubbed his leg. "I told her you were turning the bar into a tea room because I'm a teetotaler now."

"Oh? And what did she say about that?"

"She wants to know if you have a brother."

Mother Nature hummed as she worked in her indoor garden. The glass bubble over the top floor of the Boston office building provided plenty of light, especially since she could control the weather to her liking.

"Excuse me, Gaia."

She whirled around. "Oh, it's you, Apollo. What do you want?"

"Balog is here to see you."

She automatically balled her fists and tried not to curse. *So much for relaxing.*

She removed her dirty gloves and flung them onto the raised flower bed, narrowly missing a petunia. "What the frig does he want?"

Apollo shrugged.

Muttering about how useless and lazy gods were, Mother Nature strode to the bank of elevators where Mr. Balog was waiting.

She folded her arms and glared at him. "What?"

"I—uh, I thought you might want to know that the paranormal meeting place on Charles Street is reopening."

Gaia's eyes grew wide. "You mean that vampire hasn't learned his lesson? The fire didn't show him how dangerous a place like that was?"

"Yes, ma'am—I mean Mother—I mean *Goddess*."

Trying to remain calm, she took in a deep breath and let it out slowly. She counted to ten. Eventually, she slapped a hand over her eyes, gave up, and screamed. "*Gaaaaah!*"

Balog took a giant step back.

After her outburst, she felt better. An upholstered chair materialized under her butt and she plopped onto it. "Tell me everything you know."

Balog smiled and said, "*Everything* I know? That might take a long time."

Gaia rolled her eyes and mumbled, "I doubt it."

Balog cleared his throat. "I'm sorry, Goddess. I was just trying to lighten the mood. Of course you meant everything I know about the tea room."

"Tea room?"

"Yes. Anthony Cross rebuilt the first floor of his building as a tea parlor. It's quite fancy."

Gaia's jaw dropped. Then it occurred to her that if Anthony was trying to reopen a front for a supernatural gathering place, a tea room was an odd choice. "So, is he no longer trying to gather paranormals for some kind of deranged peace talks?"

"Oh, no. He's up to his old tricks," Balog continued with a smile. "I can't wait to see the werewolves trying to hold those tiny watercress sandwiches in their big, meaty fingers." He laughed, but she wasn't amused.

"Are you sure your information is correct?"

"My intelligence-gathering has shown that the same

customers who frequented the bar are interested in the grand opening of the tea parlor."

Gaia was tempted to make a crack involving the word "intelligence," but not even sarcasm would alleviate the worry invading her gut.

"So the paranormals are still planning to gather in a public place, increasing their risk of a slipup around humans. But it hasn't opened yet?"

"Correct. The grand opening is the day after tomorrow at 11:00 a.m. I could take my wife, but I'd stick out by myself."

It sounded as if the human crowd would likely be female. *Observant, meddling, gossiping females.* Gaia bent over and covered her face with her hands. "This is such a bad idea."

"I'll keep an eye on the place as always, Goddess. Reporting any problems to you immediately."

"Well, do it from a distance. You can't help me if your cover is blown."

"I managed to rent the third-floor apartment from Mr. Cross again. Because my family lived there before the building burned, he gave us a chance to rent it first." Balog puffed up his chest. "Apparently he still doesn't know we're spying on him."

She rose and the chair disappeared. "Good, but I want to see this place for myself. You're excused, Balog."

She spun on her heel and marched over to her forest in the corner. "Now to create a hat that's fit for a tea party."

Claudia sat next to her sponsor, Gaye. When it came time to introduce herself, she said what she knew she was supposed to say, but it still felt strange and difficult. "My name is Claudia, and I'm an alcoholic."

Everyone said, "Hi, Claudia," like she hadn't just confessed her worst secret…as if she'd just said, "I like ice cream."

Her sponsor followed suit. "Hi, I'm Gaye, and I'm an alcoholic."

Someone behind them chuckled and said, "So am I."

Another deep voice echoed, "Me too."

Gaye turned around. "Ha. Ha. Very funny."

The room erupted in giggles, but Gaye smiled, taking the good-natured ribbing well. Claudia couldn't help but be impressed with the woman's unshakable serenity. She hoped someday she'd be that comfortable in her own skin.

Her mind was racing. The members were taking turns reading a paragraph at a time from the book outlining the twelve steps. When her turn came, she wasn't even aware of what she was reading. All she could concentrate on was not stumbling over her words. She stumbled once anyway.

"Sheesh. I don't think I comprehended a thing I just read," she whispered to Gaye.

Gaye leaned toward her and whispered back, "Bring the body. The mind will follow."

"But—"

"Shhh. 'Learn to listen and listen to learn.' We'll talk later."

The woman could be a hard-ass, but thank goodness she had someone with experience helping her through this. Claudia couldn't imagine trying to navigate all the changes she was going through alone.

For the first month, Claudia couldn't help crying easily when someone brought up a situation that had contributed to their problems—and hers. Poor self-esteem, isolation, fear...the emotional gamut. But her sponsor said it was normal to feel a little raw in the beginning, especially since she was feeling emotions she'd shut away or tried to dilute with alcohol. *If only it had worked.* The more she drank, the worse it got.

She'd gone from feeling pleasantly buzzed to crying uncontrollably when she'd drunk too much and self-pity kicked in. Someone described her struggle in a way Claudia could totally understand. She said she was a high-bottom drunk with low-bottom emotions. Another guy said he felt like he was in a slingshot when he drank. He never knew where he'd wind up.

For Claudia, the emotions were the worst part. She'd never woken up on a stranger's front lawn or passed out in a friend's closet while looking for the bathroom, but she identified with the feelings of shame expressed at meetings when even the toughest guys cracked.

No one she'd heard speak in AA had the exact circumstances she did—a dear departed sister and survivor's guilt—but everyone seemed to understand her tears and fears nonetheless.

Her sister, Marion, was two years older and the "better" daughter. Claudia should have been driving that night, but Marion came to get her because Claudia had celebrated her high-school graduation a little too much. You'd think that would have made Claudia want to stop drinking—and it did, for a while. But nothing dulled the pain like oblivion.

After the meeting, she and Gaye went out for ice cream. Gaye had encouraged her to complete the twelve steps of the AA program. The first time Claudia read them, she wasn't sure she wanted to. Make amends? How the hell was she supposed to do that with her parents? Her tendency had been to make up for feelings of inferiority by overachieving. It didn't exactly work, but at least she felt less like a schmuck.

"I've been trying, but I can't take all these steps at once," she confessed to Gaye. "For once, I want to be less than perfect."

"It's not a contest, and rushing through the steps won't do you any good. In fact, it could mess you up even more. But you're not alone. Lots of people have thought it was impossible. You'll take the steps as you're ready for them," Gaye said. "And I'll help you."

"I'm having a hard time just letting memories wash over me and facing reality without a drink."

"That's normal."

"But how do I cope when that happens?"

"You call me."

"And if you're not available?"

"Leave me a message and then call someone else. Or if for some reason, you can't reach anyone, repeat the Serenity Prayer or something like 'This too shall pass' until I call you back."

The program relied heavily on clichés, but those tidbits of wisdom were helping Claudia nonetheless. She felt like she was hearing some of them for the first time. *Live and Let Live. Easy Does It. One Day at a Time.* And, oh, yeah…*Keep it Simple, Stupid* was a kick in the pants, but one she needed when she was tempted to overdo it. Life was complicated enough, yet apparently alcoholics were adept at mucking it up even more.

Soon she'd be moving and her schedule would change. Her job at the tea shop would keep her busy during the day, and meetings would occupy her evenings. That seemed simple enough.

Gaye reached into her purse and extracted a pen and paper. "Here. I want you to write a gratitude list. Right here. Right now."

"A what?"

"A list of all the things in your life that you're grateful for. Nothing is too small or silly to write down. It's not for anyone's eyes but yours. Write down at least fifteen things."

"Fifteen? But what if I can't—"

"You can. Think about it. I'll give you as long as it takes for me to finish my ice cream. Now, start writing."

"Sheesh." Claudia thought a moment and began.

I'm grateful for…

Steady job.
Cute apartment.
I'm reasonably healthy.
I have an MBA.
Mostly natural blond hair.
Stylish clothes.
A few true friends.
I'm compassionate—especially to underdogs.
I'm making new friends.
Parents who love me in their own annoying way.

Then she scratched out the word "annoying."

> *Growing and learning in AA.*
> *Sobriety is making me feel healthy again.*
> *A good sponsor.*
> *Caring boss/boyfriend.*
> *Can actually write a gratitude list and mean it.*
> *I can see I didn't cause my sister's death.*
> *I look forward to learning to forgive myself.*
> *Hope.*

She stopped writing when she felt tears burning behind her eyes. "I don't know what I'd do without you and Anthony, Gaye."

"Well, I know why you need me," Gaye joked. "But what is Anthony good for?"

Claudia bit her lower lip. "Call it unconditional love. We all need someone to accept us for who we are. Good and bad. Warts and all. Anthony is that man."

Gaye smiled. "It sounds like you have some stuff to be grateful for."

"A lot, actually. I was feeling so alone, even before the fire. Then afterward my best friend got married, and I didn't want to take her away from her first few months of wedded bliss." Claudia chuckled. "Her name is even Bliss."

"Like my name is Gaye. Is hers any less ironic than mine?"

Claudia smirked. "She was never this blissful before hooking up with her hottie fireman. Maybe you need a handsome firefighter too."

Gaye lifted one eyebrow. "I don't think so. I'm

not ready for that kind of emotional turmoil, and I might never be. Speaking of which, how are things with your boyfriend?"

"Anthony is wonderful. His ex is giving him a hard time, though. I don't know why she won't leave him alone." Claudia studied her bowl of melting rocky road.

Gaye sighed. "Are you sure you're ready to handle a relationship? There's a saying, you know. KISS. 'Keep it simple, sweetheart.'"

"Yeah, yeah. I know that one. Only they usually say 'stupid' instead of 'sweetheart.'"

"In my opinion, we need to be a little gentler with ourselves. We called ourselves stupid hundreds of times when we were drinking. Staying in recovery is one of the smartest things you'll ever do. So, sweetheart…the boyfriend?"

"Why should I give up one of the best things that ever happened to me just because some bimbo he doesn't care about anymore doesn't like it? I think she needs a program of recovery too, but I don't know what it would be. Is there a Pains-in-the-Ass Anonymous?"

Gaye laughed. "I wish. I can think of a few people I'd like to send there—but remember the Serenity Prayer. The only ones we can change are ourselves. That's what they mean by live and let live."

Claudia sighed. "I'm used to being in charge as a manager and working with people who do what I ask them to."

"Welcome to the real world, kiddo."

Chapter 4

Ruxandra had to keep her distance while following Anthony. She had always wished they could communicate telepathically, but now she was glad they could not. One stray thought could tip him off. As her maker, he could easily recognize her scent, so tracking his haunts and habits had proved tricky.

She knew he spent a lot of evenings in Chinatown and suspected his lair was someplace in that area. Maybe he was getting animal blood from the local restaurants, but he was almost always there before dawn when she had to run back to her own dark hiding place for her death sleep.

Luckily she had found an unoccupied building in the Beacon Flats area with a basement entrance. Prying open the door was easy. Sealing it against light and curious passersby had proven a bit more challenging, but she was a clever girl and had remembered a great new invention called duct tape. It worked like a charm.

She worried about Anthony protecting himself without her help. He had taught her to take no chances, but lately he seemed to be taking more and more risks with his own safety. Like now. Why was he in Cambridge?

She'd had to occupy the subway a few cars behind his and was surprised when he got off in Central Square. Why here? Everyone knew there was nothing worth seeing between MIT and Harvard Square.

She quickly checked the wind direction and was

glad to find it blowing his scent toward her and not the other way around. She hung back and wrapped her scarf around her hair, which was so blond it shown like a beacon under the streetlights.

Suddenly he was crossing the street and rounding the nearest corner. She had to jog between cars after the lights changed, but she caught sight of him again as soon as she rounded the same corner. *Whew.* Tracking him all this way just to lose him in—

Ruxandra halted when he stopped a few feet from a moving van.

What the... Another blond was facing away from him, but he came up behind her and slipped his arms around her waist. He must have whispered something funny in her ear, because she giggled. Then the slut turned around.

Claudia!

Ruxandra began to seethe. All those years ago, she'd accused the klutzy waitress of being his whore and they'd both had the nerve to deny it—but it was true! They'd probably been making a fool of her all this time.

Anthony had claimed he needed to spend a few minutes each evening in his office with Claudia so she could fill him in on the business of the day.

Ruxandra needed all of her self-control to keep from rushing at the bitch and tearing her head off. Anthony had frequently accused her of jumping to conclusions and so, as painful as it was to watch, she had to wait until there was absolutely no doubt about his betrayal.

He's kissing her. And she's kissing him back!

Ruxandra couldn't take any more. She flew at the unsuspecting couple. Anthony must have sensed her a millisecond before she reached them, because she fell on her ass as he blocked her with his arm and pushed Claudia toward the nearby stairs.

"Get inside, Claudia!" he yelled.

"Yeah, run. He doesn't need you. He needs *me!*" Ruxandra sprang to her feet, ready to grab her slower rival, but before she could get to Claudia, she was on her ass again and one hundred eighty pounds of vampire was sitting on her chest.

"Ow! Anthony, you're hurting me."

He paid no attention to her. Instead he called to Claudia, "I'll hold her until you get inside. Don't open the door for *anyone*."

Ruxandra heard footsteps scuffle up the concrete stairs. Then a heavy door opened and shut. When it was just the two of them on the sidewalk, he focused his angry gaze on her. "What the hell is the matter with you?" The intensity she saw in his eyes was almost too much to bear and she turned away.

He grasped her jaw and roughly turned her to face him, but he didn't say anything. Instead he glanced up, and a moment later, she heard an unfamiliar voice yelling, "Hey. Get off of her."

Thank goodness for the stupidity of humans.

"It's not what it looks like," Anthony called out.

"Yeah, right."

When she craned her neck, she caught sight of the guy pulling a cell phone from his pocket.

Ruxandra saw her chance to make Anthony admit their relationship as *she* saw it. "He's my husband. Don't call the police. We'll work it out."

Anthony growled.

The guy hit some buttons on his phone, ignoring them. A moment later he was saying, "Yeah, there's some kind of domestic dispute on Essex Street. Looks like the woman is getting the worst of it."

Shit. Now both she and Anthony had to disappear fast, and he wouldn't let her follow him again.

Well, that backfired.

She'd just have to wait until the woman was alone. He couldn't protect her every minute, and now Ruxandra knew where her rival lived. Or not. The moving van… Was it for Claudia? Was she moving in with him?

Ruxandra saw red.

Claudia wondered why Anthony was taking so long to get rid of Ruxandra and come back with the news that the coast was clear. Either the coast wasn't clear, or… *No. I refuse to believe that. He'd never go back to her.*

Pacing, she pondered her situation. She had the moving van for twenty-four hours. After picking it up at noon and loading the lighter boxes into it herself, she'd waited for Anthony to help with the furniture. He didn't get there until eight and it was about nine thirty now.

Well, if I have to spend the night here, at least I still have a mattress to sleep on. Damn. I was looking forward to getting out of this hellhole and moving into the beautiful, brand-new apartment over the tea shop.

Claudia had never come right out and directly asked Anthony why he insisted on never being disturbed during the day. She respected his privacy, and so far it hadn't been a problem. But what if he never came back tonight? Would some kind stranger help her load her furniture in the morning?

She almost snorted out loud. Even friends were scarce when it came to moving.

She was just about to give up and unpack a book when a knock sounded on the door.

Thank goodness.

She sprinted to the door and looked through the peephole. "Kurt?" *What the hell is he doing here?* She left the chain fastened and opened the door only the few inches the chain would allow.

"Where's Anthony?"

"He's been delayed. He asked me to help you move. Tory is here with me."

Tory Montana peeked around the doorjamb. "Heard you could use an ex-linebacker to move some heavy furniture."

Claudia sagged with a mixture of relief and concern. "I don't suppose it matters that he told me not to open my door to anyone."

Tory grinned. "We're not just anyone, sweetheart. We're the cavalry."

That's for sure. These two were her favorite regulars from the bar. She'd never pictured missing their daily presence in her life until the building went up in flames.

She slid open the lock, opened the door wide, and walked into two bear hugs.

"So, is Anthony coming back?"

"He said it was safer for you if he didn't."

She glanced from one to the other. "Do you know about Ruxandra's hissy fit? How she reacts whenever she thinks we…I mean, that Anthony and I…but we never have!"

Kurt chuckled and laid a hand on her shoulder. "I was there the day the bar opened, the first time she threatened you. She'd act the same way toward any beautiful woman Anthony looked at for two seconds."

"She called me a whore!"

"She's just projecting the worst of herself onto you."

"You mean, she..."

"I shouldn't have said anything. Just ignore me." Kurt sported his silly grin. "You know how full of shit I can be."

"Don't worry," Tory said. "We won't let anything happen to you. And Anthony can take care of himself."

"Where is he now?"

The guys looked at each other.

"Tell me."

Kurt cleared his throat. "I think he's trying to convince Ruxandra to leave town."

That sounded like an exercise in futility. How many times had he asked her to leave now? Twenty? Thirty?

Claudia's shoulders slumped.

Tory rubbed her back. "I know. She's been a pain in the ass for years, but I think he's come up with some inventive new threats that might work."

Claudia didn't know how she felt about that. She certainly wanted Ruxandra out of the way, but did she want Anthony threatening anyone? And would he be able to follow through?

As if Kurt could read her mind, he said, "Don't think about it. Please. Anthony knows how stressful this has been for you, and he'll take care of it. He wants you to be able to relax and live your life."

"It doesn't seem like too much to ask," she muttered.

Tory put an arm around her shoulder. "Grab your keys. This furniture isn't going to move itself."

Anthony hated the idea of spending any more time than absolutely necessary with Ruxandra, but he had to protect Claudia. He lured his irksome ex to the Harvard Square area, in the opposite direction from where Claudia, Kurt, and Tory needed to go.

They shared a patch of grass on someone's front lawn. The fragrant foliage wasn't enough to overcome the irritation of being forced to give Ruxandra his undivided attention. Or it would have been undivided, if he could get Claudia out of his mind.

Why he'd begun a relationship with the beautiful human he'd lusted after for five years was anyone's guess. But he refused to call it a mistake. He and Claudia had put their happiness on hold for far too long.

The few months they'd spent together since their first kisses were the happiest he'd had in a long time. Under the guise of planning the new business, he'd given Ruxandra the slip and met Claudia in various places around the city. It hadn't been easy, but he'd become fairly good at it. Unfortunately, he'd gotten cocky too. Now Claudia was in danger, and it was all his fault.

"I've told you over and over again…you don't love me. You're obsessed. It's as if you want me just because you can't have me."

"That's ridiculous. I want you because I love you. And you *need* me."

"You don't know what love is. If you loved me, you'd want me to be happy."

"I can make you happy. I can hunt for you. I can defend you. I can keep up with you sexually. Do you think a mere mortal can do all that? If only you'd give me a chance…"

"I did give you a chance—many chances—and we drove each other crazy. Face it. We're just not good together."

"That was before. I've grown since then."

"Yeah, right. You've grown into a bigger pain in my ass than ever."

Over the last century, he had tried reasoning with the volatile vampiress, threatening her, and putting thousands of miles between the two of them.

Inevitably, he got sick of failing to banish her from his life and would work around her. As it turned out, that was his mistake. She knew she could wear him down and wouldn't stop until he let her hang around.

Eventually, the attention she demanded would drive him to distraction again. If he didn't come up with some kind of permanent solution to Ruxandra's interference, it would go on for eternity.

"Ruxandra, you're driving me into the sunshine."

"Is that the vampire's equivalent of 'You're driving me to drink'?"

"Essentially, yes."

"But that makes no sense. If you want to drink, we should be together. We can drink from each other or share our thralls."

Logic was wasted on her. She had her own, and as much as he hated to admit it, in some ways she made sense. It would be more convenient to be with another vampire. No need to hide what he was. Hunting with a lookout was infinitely easier. Or they'd have twice the chances of finding a willing thrall.

Unfortunately, logic was also wasted on his heart. Claudia was the only woman he felt right with. He totally trusted her, relaxed with her, enjoyed her company. And it didn't stop with companionship. The sexual attraction was overpowering. Claudia was the only woman in decades that his traitorous body had demanded he take to bed. It was all he could do to keep his pants on until he could figure out what to do about Ruxandra.

His own resources weren't enough, but how could he take out a restraining order on a vampire without putting innocent law-enforcement officers in mortal danger? Perhaps Sadie could use her psychic insight to help him think of a solution.

"Are you listening to me?" Ruxandra shouted.

"Huh? No. I can't hear you when you yell. Besides, I've heard it all before, Ruxandra. We have nothing else to say to each other. I think it's time to call it a night."

She lunged at him and pinned him to the ground. "We'll 'call it a night' when I say it's a night."

Anthony simply sighed. If he wanted to, he could toss her into the bushes easily. But he'd done that before—and she'd clung to his retreating back before. They'd done it all before.

And he was thoroughly sick of it. He was almost ready to lie there and fry when the sun came up, but she'd fry too. He didn't think she was willing to kill them both, but who knew?

"What are you going to do? Anchor the two of us here until dawn?"

"If that's what it takes for you to see the light."

Seeing the light. Anthony snapped out of his despair.

Didn't Sadie or Kurt or somebody mention a vampire who could walk in daylight?

He'd heard the story months ago. The humans at his bar had discovered the existence of paranormals, and before all hell could break loose, Kurt had frozen the room. Because this happened early in the afternoon, Anthony was in his death sleep. Nick knew of another vampire he could call. A vampire able to arrive before the sun went down and compel everyone at the bar to forget what they'd heard.

If only he could discover that vampire's secret. He could be with Claudia during the day, and Ruxandra would be powerless to stop them.

Then he remembered he'd have to protect both of them during the night, and his pleasant fantasy went poof. *Damn. There has to be a way to end this without bloodshed.*

Four hours later, the guys had moved all of Claudia's furniture into her new apartment over the tea shop and were getting ready to leave.

"Oh. I almost forgot something," Kurt said. He pulled what looked like a chess piece out of his pocket.

"What's that?"

"It's called *the little warrior*. It's a charm for protection. Call it a housewarming gift."

Claudia accepted the piece and turned it over in her hand. It was a little larger and more elaborate than a chess piece. The warrior looked like a Viking wearing armor, a helmet with horns, and a fierce expression. He was even holding a sword.

"Uh...thanks."

"What are you going to name him?" Kurt asked.

Claudia was about to smirk when she noticed that Kurt looked perfectly serious. He was rarely serious, so she stopped and considered the question. Maybe he was superstitious, but that was no reason to make fun of his gift. "How about Alexander, for Alexander the Great? He looks like he needs an impressive name."

Kurt nodded his approval. He spoke directly to the statue. "Alexander, this is Claudia. She is a good friend and a woman of great integrity. She deserves a safe haven in which to live. You are now honor bound to protect her and her home."

Claudia didn't know what to make of this. Should she laugh? Something told her not to. Maybe changing the subject would be best. "Uh... Can you both stop in tomorrow for a free lunch? I want to thank you for your help tonight, and it'll give me a chance to prep for the grand opening the next day."

Tory grinned. "I'd never turn down a free lunch."

"Neither would I," Kurt said. "But are you sure you want to do that with only one day to unpack and settle in before the madness starts?"

"Absolutely." She hugged them both and said good night. As soon as her door was locked, she leaned against it and sighed. Glancing across the living room, she spotted Kurt's extra key to the building on the side table.

Oh, shoot. She could wait to give it to him the next day, but he was right here. She grabbed it and opened her door ready to trot downstairs. Then she looked at the warrior in her hand. When she heard their voices, something made her stop and listen.

"I know. I'm worried about her too."

"At least we got her out of Cambridge. I'm almost sure that's where the facility is. With so many of us over there trying to find it, she'd be bound to wonder sooner or later."

Facility? What facility? Were they talking about me? Ruxandra? Could this night get any stranger?

Just then the outer door opened and shut, cutting off their conversation.

What was going on? Did it have something to do with Ruxandra finding her? She figured Anthony's jealous ex had simply followed him there.

And what kind of facility could they be looking for? Had Ruxandra opened a secret gym or something? She was always in great shape and was certainly strong as hell, which she demonstrated anytime she heaved a chair at somebody's head.

I should ask. I wasn't really eavesdropping. It was more like accidentally hearing, and it sounded like they were protecting me from something they didn't want me to know about. But perhaps she needed to.

Claudia set the warrior on the half wall beside the door, then charged down the stairs and flew out onto the sidewalk. "Kurt! You forgot your keys."

The two guys turned around. Kurt strolled back to her and held out his hand. "Sorry about that."

Claudia pulled the keys away and held them firmly in her fist. "What were you two talking about just then?"

Kurt glanced over his shoulder at Tory and asked absently, "Uh, just when?"

"When you were leaving. I heard you say something about a facility in Cambridge."

Tory's eyes widened and he quickly joined them. "It was nothing. Nothing to do with you, anyway."

Claudia narrowed her eyes and tried her stare-down technique. It usually worked with employees. "Are you sure about that?"

The next thing she knew, she was in her apartment wondering, "What was I just about to do? There was something..." She searched her brain, but nothing came to mind. Scratching her head, she shuffled off to her new bedroom to unpack.

"I'm sorry I'm late. I had to be sure Ruxandra didn't follow me—again."

Claudia stepped aside and let Anthony into her new apartment. "Mmm-hmm. So, did you come up with any more threats? Maybe something effective this time?"

She wasn't yelling, but that wasn't Claudia's way. Her hand on her hip and lack of a smile showed her annoyance. She only broke out the sarcasm when she was really ticked off.

"I don't blame you for being upset. This should have been a monumental evening for the two of us. Instead, I left and had to send a couple of friends to pick up the pieces."

She stalked away and threw her hands in the air. "When is this going to end? Do I have to keep looking over my shoulder for the rest of my life?"

He wished he could say an unequivocal "no," but he could not. "I'm sorry, Claudia. I know this can't be easy for you—"

"Do you? Do you have any idea how *not* easy this is? Sometimes the urge to drink comes out of nowhere and seems unrelated to anything going on. Then I think about the stress I'm under and wonder why I haven't relapsed before this." She sat down hard on her couch.

"Did you pick up a drink tonight?"

"No. But I could have."

"I imagine you could at any time."

She stared at him. At first her expression was hard. Then she let out a deep breath and sagged against the cushions. "You're right. I called my sponsor and she calmed me down."

"Good." He sat next to her and rested his hand on her knee. "I don't know much about it, but I think that's what a sponsor is for. Right?"

"Not just that, but yes. Talking to her helped."

He tried to joke. "Maybe I should talk to her."

"You?"

She obviously didn't get it.

"I'm kidding. But I do wish I had someone like that at times."

"You should have me." Her voice was barely above a whisper, but he'd heard her clearly.

He squeezed her knee and then wrapped his arm around her shoulder. "Don't worry about me. I just want you to be safe. I have plenty of friends who will give me an objective opinion—even if I don't ask for it."

She smiled. "I imagine Kurt and Tory are good for that."

"They certainly are. In fact, I plan to talk with them just as soon as I tuck you into bed."

She glanced up at him coquettishly. "You're going to tuck me in?"

He realized his mistake too late. If he went into her bedroom, there was a good chance he'd forget about coming out, and he'd asked his friends to meet him in half an hour. "I, uh… Maybe I should wait on that."

She snorted. "Good. Because I was going to say, 'Not tonight, honey. I have a backache.'"

Whew.

"Thanks for getting Claudia settled in, guys," Anthony said. "I'm afraid I have another favor to ask of you. Maybe just some advice or ideas."

Kurt settled against Anthony's couch. "Shoot."

"I'm sorry to take any time away from your searching for the lab, but I need to keep Ruxandra from finding Claudia. Her life is in danger. Ruxandra obviously knows she was moving, but I'd rather she didn't know Claudia lives right over the tea shop."

"Why don't you just mesmerize her?" Tory asked. "Make her think Claudia moved to Timbuktu."

Anthony dropped his head in his hands. "If I could trick her into letting me mesmerize her, I'd just erase all suspicion of me and Claudia as a couple. I had her convinced it was all business between us until…"

"Until you were swapping spit on the sidewalk," Tory said.

Anthony rolled his eyes.

Kurt scratched his chin. "I'm thinking…"

Anthony had hoped his wizard friend would come up with a magical solution, but he didn't want to come right out and ask. The man had powers Anthony didn't understand. Only Kurt knew what could be done and what the consequences might be.

"I can do a spell to make Claudia invisible, but that

might become a problem if a customer wants to *see* the manager." Kurt smirked.

Anthony and Tory groaned.

"Sorry. I shouldn't joke."

No. You shouldn't. I'm desperate here.

"Maybe I could..."

Anthony leaned forward.

"Nah. That wouldn't work," Kurt muttered. "I'd need her cooperation for that."

"Ruxandra's cooperation? That's unlikely."

"I know." Kurt held up one finger. "On the other hand, I've never *bound* a vampire before, and I'm not entirely sure I can since she's dead and all, which is kind of the ultimate binding." He shook his head, as if another idea was out the window.

Kurt's thinking out loud was driving Anthony crazy, but if that's how Kurt's thought process worked, he'd have to let him do it.

"I've got the solution. I just have to spell it out. Get it? Spell?"

"You're killing me, Kurt."

"Relax. I *think* I can do something. I might be able to make Claudia invisible to Ruxandra only. I just hope Ruxandra's not too bright and won't question a teapot floating in midair."

"Unfortunately, Ruxandra's very bright and questions everything."

"Shoot. Just the way I like 'em," Kurt mumbled.

Anthony raised his eyebrows. "Hold on. Are you saying you might be interested in her?"

Kurt squirmed. "Don't take this the wrong way, but I can't figure out why you two drifted apart. I wish I had a gorgeous woman as devoted to me as she is to you. Women can be so damn fickle."

"Is this about the Dear John letter you received during your deployment?"

"Two deployments. Two Dear John letters."

"Ouch. That's rough. You can have Ruxandra if you can transfer her affections from me to you. Is there some magic spell that can do that?"

Kurt laughed. "I'd really be messing with the universe if I magically made her love me instead of you. That's major manipulation."

"But she *doesn't* love me. Not really. She's obsessed with me and mistakes it for love."

"All the more reason not to shift her feelings from you to me. I don't want a stalker any more than you do."

Tory elbowed his friend. "What if you do it the old-fashioned way? Steal her affections? Bring her flowers and shit."

Kurt and Anthony stared at each other. Eventually they both burst out laughing.

"What the hell. It's worth a try."

Anthony's jaw dropped. Apparently, they were laughing for different reasons. "Seriously? You'd do that for me?"

"Hell, I'm doing it for me. I'd love to have a fling with a feisty blond bombshell."

"And you're not afraid she'll devour you?"

"Don't worry about me. I can take care of myself. There's nothing the universe likes more than a good protection spell."

"Then you can do a protection spell for Claudia. Right?"

"I gave her a talisman."

"But a talisman can be lost or stolen. Is there a way to surround her with magical protection wherever she goes?"

Kurt nodded.

"Why didn't you suggest that right away?"

"She has to agree. And at first I didn't think it would be enough. Ruxandra would still get between you two. But maybe that coupled with me as a distraction..."

"Try it. Please. If it'll keep Claudia safe, I'll find a way to make her agree to it without telling her too much. And if you're willing to take on Ruxandra..." Anthony put all the hope he could find into his voice.

Kurt grinned. "Challenge accepted."

Chapter 5

"I must be out of my mind," Claudia said.

"Trust me. If you'll let me do this one itty-bitty spell, it will protect you from Ruxandra. I promise."

Claudia poured more tea into Kurt's cup. "You really believe in magic?"

"Yup."

Tory hadn't said a word. She wondered what the down-to-earth ex-football player thought of this. On the other hand, Kurt, an ex-marine, believing in magic was a big enough surprise.

As if he'd heard her, Tory spoke up. "I've seen it work. I don't pretend to understand it, but Kurt does. He really has a gift."

"Can Anthony be here while you're doing…your thing?"

"Why? Don't you trust me?"

"Not as much as I trust Anthony."

"Didn't he call you last night and ask you to accept my help today?"

"He left a voice mail, but I thought he meant moving furniture or something."

"He meant magical help. Ruxandra's got it in for you, and believe me, you do *not* want to go up against her. I also have ways to protect the shop itself. And after last time…I know it wasn't Ruxandra who burned the bar to the ground, but it *was* a jealous woman."

"That's right. Drake had one date with her, and she

turned into a psycho stalker when he dumped her for my friend, Bliss. Oh, boy." Claudia sighed. "I guess it can't hurt."

"Exactly." Kurt rubbed his hands together. "So, you'll let me give you a little magical protection?"

She rolled her eyes. "Why not?"

"That isn't a yes."

"You want me to say, 'Yes'?"

"Yes."

"Okay, then. Yes. I guess."

"Good enough. I have a few supplies with me." He plunked the gym bag he'd brought with him on a chair.

"What the heck? Are you going to hang stinky socks around the place to ward off evil spirits or something?"

Kurt laughed. "Not exactly." As he pulled nine candles out of the bag, she noticed a hollowed-out portion at the bottom of each. Then he withdrew some kind of botanical mixture and began stuffing it inside the holes.

"Anthony said you had some glass candleholders—enough for nine tables."

"We have more than that, in case one breaks."

Kurt grinned. "After I'm through protecting the place, *nothing* will break."

"Seriously?"

"Trust me. Now, where are the candleholders?"

"On the shelves under the cash register."

"I'll get 'em," Tory said. He jumped up and rounded a display case with special teas in tins or bagged and ready for sale. Returning with as many candleholders as he could carry, he had to go back for the rest.

Claudia watched, fascinated, as Kurt held the stuffed candles upside down and placed the hurricane glass over each, then flipped them over one by one. None of the ingredients spilled out. If she hadn't watched him fill the hollow, she'd never have been the wiser.

Kurt held his left hand over each candle in turn and murmured some words in another language.

It was all Claudia could do not to laugh. *Does he really think these candles are some kind of magical talisman or something?*

Kurt opened his eyes and began setting one in the center of each table. "You'll never need to replace these."

"What do you mean?"

"I mean, they'll appear to burn down an inch or so, but won't go any further. You can light them first thing in the morning if you want and let them burn until closing every night. Don't give them another thought."

The next thing Kurt extracted from his mystery bag was a set of bells.

"You're not going to hang those over the door, are you?"

He stopped in mid-stride. "Yeah, I am. Why?"

"If they tinkle every time someone opens the door, they'll drive me crazy."

"They'll keep evil from entering."

"Okaaay." Claudia tried not to smirk.

Kurt took a deep breath and let it out in a frustrated whoosh. "You've heard of exorcisms, right?"

"Yeah..." *What's he getting at? Is Linda Blair a big tea drinker?*

"There are always bells. And churches...always bells. Just go with it, okay?"

If I was coming in hungover, they'd drive me nuts, but I'm sober now. "Okay. I'll try to get used to them."

"Good." He hung the bells and murmured some more

strange words. "Now that I've finished out here, can we use the office for a protection spell specifically for you?"

"Sure."

Out of his bag, Kurt withdrew a long, wooden branch studded with brightly colored stones. A pointed crystal was attached to one end.

"You aren't going to make me lie down while you walk around me with a magic wand, are you?"

Kurt tipped his head. "Do you have a problem with that?"

Holy crap. "Seriously?"

"I wasn't going to have you lie down. You can sit or stand, but I *am* going to cast a circle of protection around you."

Claudia shook her head. "I don't know why I'm letting you talk me into this."

"Because Anthony wants you to be safe."

She rose. "Fine. Let's go."

Kurt grabbed his gym bag off the chair beside him and followed her.

After he'd rolled up the carpet, he scrubbed the hardwood floor with some clear mixture he'd brought in a mason jar. After that, he poured a circle of salt around both of them. Then he placed various rocks and plants just inside the circle and poured another circle of salt, trapping the various items between the two lines of salt.

"Seems like overkill," she muttered.

"It's an extra-powerful barrier between you and anyone who wants to harm you."

"So I have to stand in here anytime the boogeywoman comes after me?"

Kurt laughed. "No. Once the spell is cast, you'll be protected wherever you go. Well…you'll see."

Claudia was through protesting and questioning. She'd do this for Anthony's peace of mind and no other reason. Wait a minute…she had one more question.

"I just thought of something. What if Ruxandra has one of her fits and knocks the candles over? The place could go up in flames—again."

"Won't happen. Trust me."

She took a deep breath and tried to believe he knew what he was doing.

Kurt grabbed his wand and pointed it at the place where the wall met the ceiling. Then he walked around her, speaking more gibberish. She felt ridiculous until she saw a blue light glowing inside the crystal at the tip of the wand.

Hmm…must be some kind of trick of the light. Like a prism or something.

On his last pass, a stream of blue light shot out of the tip, tracing the entire circle, and she gasped.

Anthony lifted his fist to knock and wondered why he was so nervous. It wasn't as if he hadn't visited Claudia at her apartment before. But this time she was in *his* apartment building and it was the night before *their* grand opening. Perhaps because their lives had become so completely intertwined—at his insistence—he now felt a greater sense of responsibility for her.

No. Responsibility came naturally to him. That wasn't it.

Without analyzing himself further, he knocked twice.

A few moments later, Claudia opened the door and beamed when she saw him. She wore a dress he hadn't seen before. It was purple and set off her blond hair beautifully. He realized he was grinning too.

"Are you ready for the grand opening tomorrow?" he asked.

She lowered her head and looked up at him through hooded eyes. "There's another kind of grand opening I'd like to get to tonight."

Anthony raised his eyebrows and swept her into his embrace. After a long, impassioned kiss, he was dying to take her into her bedroom.

Hell, why waste any more time?

He hoisted her over his shoulder and carried her there while she giggled. Fortunately, her door was open and most of her things had been put away, so he had a clear path to his destination. He dropped her onto her bed and she bounced, laughing.

Anthony dove over her, trapping her body beneath his.

She was beautiful. Not that she wasn't always pretty, polished, and put together, but tonight she glowed. Her eyes were clear and searching, as if she were looking at him for the first time. Perhaps she was. She had described her newfound sobriety as a catalyst to the serenity she had always sought.

"You're breathtaking, Claudia."

She laughed. "You don't need to butter me up, you know. At this point, I'm pretty much a sure thing."

"I'm not buttering you up. I'm telling the truth." He brushed a lock of hair away from her chin. Then he lowered his lips to hers and kissed her more reverently.

The words "I love you" flowed through his mind, but

it wasn't a good time to say them. Could she say them back? She had enough to deal with tonight. He was just happy she hadn't let her sponsor talk her out of their budding relationship.

"You surprised me. I had hoped to have candles lit and a negligee on when we finally got to this point."

"No need for atmosphere as far as I'm concerned. But if you need to feel romantic…"

"Oh, hell no." She cupped the back of his head and dragged his lips to hers. He kissed her again thoroughly.

"I—uh…I wonder if you'd mind if I hung up my dress. I was just trying it on to be sure it fit, so I could wear it tomorrow."

"Of course." He backed off of her and helped her up.

She turned her back to him and said, "Would you mind unzipping me?

He smiled. *Mind?*

Anthony lowered the zipper slowly, revealing her skin a little at a time. When he came to the bottom and peeled back the shoulders so she could step out of the dress, he groaned. Her fair skin was shining. The curves of her lower back and bottom were as perfect as he'd imagined.

As if she'd known he was coming, she wore only a matching black bra and panties. No hose to contend with, thank goodness.

She hung her dress in her well-stocked closet and turned around.

His breath hitched.

She smiled shyly. She must have seen the lust in his eyes as he boldly admired her.

"Your turn," she reminded him.

He whipped off his suit jacket, tie, shirt, pants, and underwear in record time. This time she was the one to stare, apparently fixated on the part of his anatomy that was more than ready to please her.

"Come here," he commanded and was surprised to hear the hoarseness in his voice. She strolled to him, deliberately seductive, and let him envelop her in his arms. He caressed her back and kissed a trail down her neck, pausing over her pulsing jugular vein.

Someday, perhaps. He knew he could heighten the pleasure of sex for both of them with a loving suck there, but she wasn't prepared. She would have to know what he was and trust him completely.

With the delightful fantasy in his head, he unhooked her bra and helped it slip off her shoulders. When she pulled back enough to remove it, she revealed the creamiest set of full breasts his hands could hold.

"God," he whispered.

She smiled and shimmied out of her panties. With them standing as naked as Adam and Eve, he had to force himself not to tackle her to the floor and take her right there.

Damn it all. I've held back long enough.

He grasped her and while they kissed desperately, he lowered them both to their knees. They tumbled to the brand-new carpet and continued to kiss and grope. When she grabbed hold of his cock, pleasurable sensations shot through him and he groaned unconsciously.

He rolled her onto her back and bent over her breasts. Cupping one, he suckled as she arched and moaned. Then he switched to the other, and while he sucked, he rubbed her sweet spot until she writhed and begged him to fill her.

"Not yet," he said. He leaned back enough to see her face as she came apart in his arms. Her cries of climax filled him with satisfaction. She went limp in his arms and whispered, "Oh, my God."

As soon as she caught her breath, she asked, "Are you ready?"

He laughed. "Honey, I've been ready for five years."

She grinned and parted her legs. He kneeled between them and held her gaze as he gently entered her. She bent her knees and raised her hips to meet him. When he was fully seated, she closed her eyes and cooed.

"Are you all right?"

She gazed at him with hooded eyes. "Never better."

He feathered kisses down her neck and found his rhythm. She rocked with him, meeting every thrust. Her soft moans encouraged him. The indescribable sensations sparked a fire he had long forgotten. A white heat burned within. Eventually, he felt the inevitable tingle at the base of his spine.

He sped up and bore down on her pelvis, hoping to bring her over the edge with him. When she threw back her head and let out a strangled cry, he tumbled over the brink. The most incredible sensations shook him to his core. He rode her to the last aftershock and finally stilled when her cries faded. Her hands slipped off his back and flopped out to her sides. She grinned even as she was inhaling lungfuls of air.

He smoothed the hair off her dewy forehead and smiled back at her. "Was it all right?"

She giggled loudly. "If by 'all right,' you mean incredible."

He buried his nose in her hair and kissed her temple,

her cheek, her chin, and made his way to her lips where they shared a long, meaningful kiss. It was as if they were sealing their hope for a future together.

"God, I love this man."

Was that telepathy? Anthony almost broke the kiss to ask her what she'd just been thinking. But how crazy would that sound? He didn't want to scare her. Besides, she might not be ready to commit to those words out loud.

When the time was right, he'd explain that some immortals could establish telepathy with their soul mates. As pleased and hopeful as he was, there'd be plenty of time to explore the details later.

Claudia felt more relaxed than she would have expected to on the morning of their grand opening. She credited last night's gymnastics with Anthony for that. Just thinking about him made her smile.

The cook had arrived early and was unwrapping the bakery items when Claudia poked her head into the kitchen. He was fresh out of culinary school and she hoped he'd be satisfied enough with the limited menu to stay.

"All ready for our first day, Chris?"

"*Oui*," he said with a charming fake French accent. "*C'est bon.*" Then he smiled and winked.

Claudia surveyed the spotless kitchen and realized Chris had everything well in hand.

She lit the candles and inspected the tablecloths, making sure they were clean, and wished Anthony could be there when she welcomed the shop's first customers. But, as usual, he'd said he'd arrive in the early evening.

Where the heck does he spend his days?

In the five years they'd known each other, she'd never asked. She could sense the information was of a personal nature. Maybe he visited a sick relative. Or perhaps he held another job—something volunteer but close to his heart.

The desire to find out was gnawing at her. Part of her said she had a right to ask, and the other part said she might not want to know. She didn't really want to discuss it with her sponsor, because any normal woman would caution her or tell her to confront him.

Claudia knew Anthony was a good man and had dismissed the suspicions that rolled unbidden through her brain. Anyone who didn't know him might think the worst—like maybe he had a family in the suburbs.

A knock at the door disrupted Claudia's musings. The shop wasn't due to open for another fifteen minutes, but she was grateful for the distraction.

Peeking through the window, she could see the top of Sadie's gray head. Her braids were wrapped Gretel-style across her crown. Claudia had almost forgotten that Anthony's aunt would be arriving a few minutes early to set up her table where she'd read tea leaves.

Claudia welcomed Sadie inside. The elderly woman hugged Claudia and smiled.

"How are you? I've missed your calming presence."

Claudia chuckled. "I've missed yours too." It was good to see Sadie's familiar face. Claudia hadn't realized until that moment how important a role the old woman had in the bar before, and she'd bet Sadie would become a fixture in the new business as well.

She watched Sadie wend her way through the tables

to the one in the farthest corner. Sadie put her satchel down on the floor beside it. "Is it all right if I pull this one slightly farther away from the others to give my customers a bit of privacy?"

"Of course. Can I help?" Claudia quickly made her way over to the corner table, pulled out the chairs, and grasped one side of the table.

"Just a foot or so toward the back should be fine."

When they'd rearranged the back corner, Sadie set her hands on her hips and surveyed the whole room. "It looks lovely. Are you sure you don't mind my throwing off the arrangement like this?"

Claudia laughed. "The day I become so anal that I can't tolerate a table being moved a few feet is the day I should hang up my apron."

Sadie looked her up and down. "But you're not wearing an apron. Come to think of it, aren't you afraid you'll spill something on that gorgeous purple dress?"

"That's what dry cleaners are for. Really, Sadie," she teased. "Priorities."

Sadie settled into her chair. "And what *are* your priorities, dear?"

That took her by surprise. Was she being serious? "What do you mean? I was just joking about fashion taking precedence over practicality—although I'm not going to wear an apron. I want the atmosphere to be like a home where I'm the hostess and the customers are my guests."

"Can you handle all that by yourself?"

"I prefer being busy to being idle."

Sadie nodded. "Is that what your sponsor told you?"

Claudia's jaw dropped. Anthony wouldn't have told

anyone she was in AA, would he? Didn't everyone know what those letters stood for? Particularly the second A for "anonymous"?

"I can see I surprised you," Sadie said. "And before you ask…no, Anthony didn't tell me."

Claudia slowly lowered herself into the chair opposite. "You knew that because you're psychic?"

Sadie chuckled. "No. I knew that because I saw you going into the Sacred Heart Church's basement entrance one Sunday evening. *Then* I got my psychic flash."

"Oh." Claudia felt her cheeks heat and she hung her head.

"Don't be embarrassed. I'm proud of you. You're doing what you need to do to take care of yourself."

"I'm not exactly embarrassed. More like ashamed. I had no business working in a bar for so long."

"Did you drink the profits?"

"Of course not!"

"Then you have nothing to be ashamed of. Anthony wouldn't have trusted you with his business if you weren't doing your job. And now he's trusting you again."

"That's just it. Somehow I managed to work sober, but when I got home I'd drink the rest of the night away."

"And now you have something better to do with your evenings."

Claudia gave Sadie a grateful smile. "Yes, I do."

"I still worry about you."

Claudia's jaw dropped. She didn't know whether to be insulted or just accept that people would be concerned for a while. Maybe Sadie was just honest enough to say it out loud.

"But not for the reason you think," Sadie added. "I

knew you and Anthony were fighting a growing attraction to each other. I figured it would only be a matter of time before Ruxandra discovered it."

Claudia groaned and rolled her eyes. "I don't know what to do about her."

Sadie reached across the table and took Claudia's hand. "Let Anthony handle her. It's the only way."

The little bells over the front door tinkled, letting the women know they had a customer.

Before Sadie let go of Claudia's hand, she whispered, "Good luck, dear. I'm here if you need me for anything."

Trepidation that Claudia hadn't felt earlier suddenly enveloped her…until she looked over to see who had come through the door.

"Brandee! Angie!" She rushed over to her first customers. They had been her employees at the old bar, and now she thought of them as dear friends.

Things might work out okay after all.

Chapter 6

Claudia hugged Angie and Brandee in turn, then invited them to sit anywhere. She took two square menus over to them and grinned like an idiot. Realizing they needed a minute to look at the offerings, she flitted off to the cash register.

The little bells tinkled over the door again and a woman she didn't recognize entered. She was dressed like a Victorian lady in a long dress full of lace and ruffles. A huge, foppish hat covered in flowers and vines partially hid her face.

"Um… Welcome to the Boston Uncommon Tea Room. Sit anywhere you like," Claudia said brightly.

The hat nodded.

As the woman found a table, Claudia grabbed a menu and followed her.

Brandee looked up and caught sight of the woman, and her eyes rounded, as if she were ducking school and about to get caught. She tried to hide her face behind the nine-by-nine-inch card.

Hmmm…I wonder what that's about.

Just as Claudia was about to hand the woman her menu, the bells over the door tinkled again. In came more familiar faces. She grinned and waved to Kurt and Tory.

"I'll be right back to take your order," she said to the stranger.

The woman held up one finger. "No need to rush off and come back. I know what I want."

"Oh. Of course. What'll it be?" Claudia said as if still in the bar, but then gave herself a little mental slap upside the head. *Reach back to your refined upbringing, dumbass.* Her casual manner must have come from seeing the old bar's regulars walk in.

"I'd like the raspberry and chocolate scone with Devonshire cream and a small pot of Darjeeling tea."

"Wonderful choice," Claudia said. As she jotted down the order and strode toward the kitchen, she wondered how the woman had managed to order something on the menu without even reading it. *That's weird. Maybe every tea house offers those items.* She made a mental note to ask Chris to come up with some signature offerings.

"Sit anywhere you like, guys," she tossed over her shoulder. Kurt and Tory headed right over to Angie and Brandee, taking the table beside them.

It seemed like old home week when Claudia returned. The guys were chatting with the girls, and Sadie stood between the tables with her hands on Tory's and Angie's shoulders. Claudia hated to break up the animated conversation, but she didn't want to ignore customers, either.

"Have any of you decided what you want?"

"I want a job," Angie said.

Claudia was taken aback. "Seriously? I thought you were bartending at one of the local hotels. One of the *nicer* hotels."

"I was...I mean, I am. But my boss there is so hoity-toity. I miss everyone here. Maybe you could use someone part time?"

This was the answer to a prayer. The only other

employees Claudia had hired were a couple of students who could only work evenings.

"Think about it," Tory said. "As I recall, you became the bar's manager because you were a klutzy cocktail waitress. It was bad enough when you bathed someone in beer, but imagine spilling hot tea in a customer's lap."

Claudia's cheeks heated. It was true, but she'd hoped her sobriety would result in a steadier hand.

The bells jingled again. *More customers.*

Angie nodded to the front door. "It looks like you could use some help. I've already handed the guys our menus."

"Hey. I was just about to…" *Whoa. Take your pride and shove it,* she told herself.

Sadie caught her eye and gave her a slight nod.

If I don't take Angie up on her offer, I should fire myself. "Can you start right now?"

Angie laughed and jumped up. "You betcha."

Claudia ripped the order pad and handed half of it to her. "Grab a pen from behind the counter and have at it. Give the orders to Chris in the kitchen."

Brandee ordered a cup of Irish breakfast tea and plain salad, reminding Claudia she was lactose intolerant. The guys asked for coffee and cucumber-watercress sandwiches. Kurt joked that he just ordered them to find out what the heck a watercress was.

The day progressed smoothly and Claudia's prediction about a slow start couldn't have been more wrong. Every regular from the old bar and a bunch of new faces showed up. Had Sadie known this was going to happen?

The one thing that really baffled Claudia was why the woman wearing the giant hat was staying all day. She sipped her tea slowly and nibbled at her scone. Claudia checked on her regularly and was always dismissed with a wave of the woman's gloved hand.

Eventually, Claudia talked her into a fresh pot of tea, figuring the other one *must have* grown cold by then.

When she picked up the pot with both hands, heat seared her. *"Yikes!"* She quickly set it down and blew on her fingers. Chelsea, one of the evening waitresses, rushed over. "Are you all right?"

Claudia inspected her fingers. They stung and were dark pink, but not red or blistered. "I—I think so."

Chelsea mumbled under her breath, "You'd better get a good tip after that."

The strange woman rose and faced them. "You want a good tip? Here it is… Try picking up teapots by the handles, numbnuts."

Stunned, Claudia watched the woman glide to the cash register, drop a twenty-dollar bill next to it, and saunter out the door as if nothing had happened.

Anthony straightened his tie, using the shop window as a mirror. He was anxious for some inexplicable reason. He trusted Claudia completely, and Ruxandra had promised to stay away, so what could possibly go wrong?

Breezing into the small office sandwiched between the checkout counter and the entrance to the kitchen, Anthony spotted Claudia rubbing something onto the palm of her hand. As soon as he caught sight of the tube of ointment with the Red Cross symbol on it, he rushed to her side.

"What happened? Are you all right?"

Claudia sighed. "Yes. I was just stupid. I picked up a hot teapot by the base instead of using the handle."

Anthony took her hand in his and inspected the burn. "I'm no doctor, but I'd say it's a minor burn. No blisters. Does it hurt?"

She shrugged. "Not as much as it did a few minutes ago. It's just a dull throb now."

"I'll take you to the emergency room, just to be sure."

Claudia held up her glossy hand. "No! They might try to give me pain medication. I won't take anything addictive."

"Won't Kurt's protection spell take care of that?"

"I don't know, and I don't want to take any chances with my sobriety."

"You're amazing." Anthony lifted her palm to his lips and placed a gentle kiss on her fingertips and another on her wrist. Then he kissed his way up her arm until he met the column of her neck and nibbled his way up to her jaw. She giggled and scrunched her shoulder and jaw together as if it tickled.

He captured her lips in a passionate kiss and she twined her arms around his neck, kissing him back just as fervently.

When they broke the kiss, she grinned. "You kissed me like Gomez Addams kissing Morticia."

"Who?"

"Morticia. You know. From *The Addams Family*?"

Anthony shrugged. "I've never heard of them. Do they live around here?"

Claudia laughed. "No. It's a TV show. You probably missed the reruns, but it was hilarious. Someday I'll pull up an old episode on my computer and we can watch it together."

"That would be nice." Doing *anything* with Claudia sounded good—especially if it inspired more hot kisses.

"So I imagine you want to know how our first day went, other than this slight mishap."

"Absolutely." Anthony took the chair beside the desk and let Claudia sit in the larger one behind it.

"It was surprisingly busy. We saw many of the old regulars from the bar, as well as new faces. There was a whole group of ladies all wearing red hats. We had to push some tables together, but it worked out just fine."

"Red hats?"

"Yeah. They weren't all the same type of hat...like they weren't all wearing red berets or anything. Just fashionable hats for the—um, older female set."

"Ah, yes. I had heard we might be visited by the Red Hat Society."

"It's a society?"

"Yes. As I understand it, they just get together to have fun. A member spoke to me about the upcoming grand opening when she saw an ad."

"Ah. So the online ad worked."

Anthony looked at her sideways. "I thought we weren't going to circulate flyers or put ads in the newspaper."

Claudia grinned and shrugged. "I didn't do those things. I used the Internet. We had a little money left over because Kurt provided the candles." She touched his hand. "I just want you to succeed."

"And I wanted to start slowly so you wouldn't be overwhelmed."

She sighed. "Maybe you were right. But Angie came to my rescue."

"Angie? Our Angie?"

"Yup. Apparently she doesn't like her job at the

fancy-schmancy hotel, so I hired her on the spot. She's happy. I'm happy. And I hope you're happy."

Anthony remembered having to mesmerize the bartender who almost cried wolf—or "werewolf," as it were. It was the bar's closest call to being outed as a paranormal meeting place, and what a disaster that would have been.

"I think she'll work out great," Claudia continued. "Whether it's tea or beer, she has a steady hand. I've never seen her spill a drop of anything. Me, on the other hand..."

True. Time to change the subject again. "So, it looks like the crew is getting back together."

She chuckled. "Seems that way."

"And how did Sadie do?"

"I think she had a good day too. Some of the Red Hat Society ladies had their tea leaves read and said they'd tell their friends."

Just then a shriek came from the tea room. Both Anthony and Claudia dashed out of the office to see what had happened.

The door was wide open and a furious Ruxandra stood on the stoop. She was trying to step inside, but her foot kept bouncing off an invisible barrier. She had just raised her fist, as if she was about to smash through it.

Bloody hell. Anthony strode out the door, grabbed Ruxandra's arm, and dragged her a few feet down the sidewalk.

"What the hell do you think you're doing?"

"I'm trying to enter a public restaurant," she spat.

Anthony crossed his arms. "And why do you think you can't?"

"I don't know, but I imagine you and your *whore* have something to do with it." She pointed through the window at a shocked-looking Claudia. "What is she? A witch?"

Anthony dragged Ruxandra to the nearest side street and rounded the corner with her.

When they were out of sight of the evening crowd, he growled. "Why did you come? You *promised* you'd stay away."

Ruxandra folded her arms and turned up her nose. "I found a loophole."

"A what?"

"A loophole. You made me promise to stay away from *your* tea room. But as I see it, any restaurant that invites the public in is a *public* place. And I didn't promise *the public* I'd stay away."

"Unless the public signed the deed, it's not the public's tea room. It's *my* tea room…and as I recall, you promised to stay away from my tea room."

"Are you sure it doesn't belong to you and your little whore?"

Anthony had to use every fiber of his inner strength to keep from grabbing her around the neck and ripping her head off. Through gritted teeth he said, "Do. Not. Call. Her. That."

She whipped her hair over her shoulder. "Why not? You pay her, don't you?"

"I pay her to manage my business."

"And you set her up in a nice apartment in a building where, you admitted, your name is on the deed. What do you call her now?"

"A renter." *Shit. How did she know about that?*

Suddenly he was glad Claudia had insisted on paying rent, but *dammit, Ruxandra knows where she lives.*

Rounding the corner, Kurt stopped and opened his eyes in surprise. "Ruxandra. I didn't expect to see you here." He took a step back and eyed her appreciatively. "Wow. You look…stunning!"

She smiled and touched her hair a couple times. "Why, thank you, Kurt." Then she turned her angry gaze on Anthony again. "See? Other men appreciate my beauty."

Kurt laid a hand on her arm. "Oh, Ruxandra. You're so much more than mere beauty."

Careful, Kurt. Don't lay it on too thick, or she'll see right through our ploy.

But Ruxandra seemed to be eating up the compliments. "Really? What else do you like about me?"

"Well, for one thing, you're loyal. To a Marine, that means everything." He lifted his sleeve and exposed his tattoo. "See? Semper Fi."

"Semper what?"

"Fi. Short for *fidelis*. It means always faithful."

She narrowed her gaze on Anthony. "I wish everyone felt that 'fi' was important."

"And I wish everyone kept their promises." Anthony and Ruxandra stared each other down. At last, Anthony cleared his throat. "Well, I should be getting back to the shop."

Ruxandra's hand shot out and grabbed his arm. "Not so fast. You haven't told me how you performed that little trick with the door."

He yanked his sleeve out of her grasp. "And I don't intend to. Consider it a warning. Stay away." As he stormed off to make sure Claudia got home okay, he heard Kurt ask Ruxandra to a movie.

"Oh, go to hell," she said.

Crap. So much for that plan.

Claudia paced across the office floor, wondering what, if anything, she could do about a jealous ex-girlfriend interfering with her new relationship. She stopped in the middle of the floor, sighed, and whispered the Serenity Prayer.

"God, grant me the serenity to accept the things I cannot change—Ruxandra; courage to change the things I can—um..." She hated to admit it, but about the only thing she had control over was dating or breaking up with Anthony. "And the wisdom to know the difference." She slumped into the small chair beside the desk.

Giving him up was the last thing she wanted to do. They had already pushed their feelings aside and sacrificed five years of their lives. To surrender would hand Ruxandra the victory she wanted.

Claudia leaned over and dropped her head into her hands. After allowing herself a moment of self-pity, she straightened and said aloud, "I think it's time to call my sponsor."

She dialed Gaye's number and waited through two rings. She was just about to chicken out when her sponsor answered.

"Claudia?"

"Hi, Gaye. How did you know it was me?"

"Caller ID showed your number."

"You know my phone number?"

"I have a good memory for numbers."

Claudia snorted. "I don't have a good memory for anything these days. I feel like my mind has turned to mush."

Gaye laughed. "That's normal too. Hang in there. It'll get better, I promise."

"I hope so. I have a situation, and I can't figure out how to handle it. Do you have a minute to talk?"

"I have as many minutes as you need."

"Good." Claudia already felt a little better. Less alone with her problem, at any rate. "I told you about my boyfriend, Anthony, right?"

"Uh-oh."

Claudia's spine stiffened. "Uh-oh? I haven't even told you what's bothering me yet."

"You're right. I'm sorry. Tell me what's going on."

"It's his jealous ex-girlfriend."

Gaye groaned.

At that moment, Anthony entered the office, looking sad and defeated.

"Uh…I should go. Anthony's here, and I should be talking about this with him, anyway."

Anthony's brows lifted.

"Fine. Just remember, your sobriety comes first. If anything threatens that, it's gotta go."

Claudia smiled. "Yes, ma'am."

"I'm glad you called. Try me again later when you can talk."

"I will." Claudia hung up and faced Anthony. "Well?"

Anthony crossed his arms. "I don't know what to tell you. Ruxandra promised to stay away, but obviously I can't trust her to keep her word."

As hard as it was for Claudia to bring up the only logical solution, she had to. "Maybe we should stop seeing each other."

"*No!*" he roared.

Claudia took a step back. She had never seen Anthony lose his cool. Not once.

"I will not let a spoiled brat run my life. She'll get over it. Meanwhile, I'll need to keep you close at all times so I can protect you."

Claudia set a hand on her hip. "At all times? What am I? Your prisoner? I have a life too. I need to go to meetings and—"

Anthony held up a hand. "I'm sorry. I didn't mean during the day. Just the evenings. She won't bother you during the day."

Claudia scrutinized him. "Anthony, I've never asked you what you do all day. I figured it was none of my business…until now."

Anthony shifted from foot to foot and avoided eye contact.

"What is it? Are you reading to the blind? Shopping for new suits? Or does it have something to do with Ruxandra?"

His gaze snapped to hers. "It has nothing to do with Ruxandra."

"Then you should be able to tell me about it."

He scrubbed a hand over his face and paused so long that she began to doubt he planned to answer her at all.

"Look. I'll take care of Ruxandra's interference. I promise I don't see her during the day, and I won't see her in the evenings as soon as I can figure out how to get rid of her."

"Get rid of her? What are you going to do?"

The alarm must have shown on her face. He said, "Don't worry. I wasn't planning to kill her."

Claudia smirked. "Darn it."

Anthony pulled her into a tight embrace and kissed her hard.

"What was that for?"

He stepped back and turned pale—or paler, if possible. "Did I hurt you?"

"No. I'm fine. But I still want to know what you do during the day."

He turned toward the door and grasped the handle. "I'm going to check outside. Stay in the office until I'm sure it's safe, and then I'll escort you to your apartment. Promise you'll stay inside tonight."

"I'll do no such thing. I need to go to an AA meeting—especially when things get nutty—and the way you're acting is pretty nutty right now."

"Look. I can't help it. At some point, I'll tell you about my days, but not now. There's a right time and place for everything."

"Maybe this isn't the right time for us."

She didn't get a chance to say anything else. In a flash he was holding her and grasping her chin, staring into her eyes. "Don't say that. I need you…to trust me, I mean."

Chapter 7

ANTHONY HAD CAPTURED CLAUDIA'S GAZE AND mesmerized her. *Or so he'd thought*. Instead of the slack-jawed, unblinking response he'd expected, she frowned, blinked, and said, "What the hell? Your eyes are turning colors."

He quickly looked away and sucked in a deep breath. *She wasn't under? Am I losing my touch?*

"Seriously. One minute your eyes were the color of milk chocolate, like I'm used to, and then they shimmered gold and then a little purple and finally blue."

Anthony laughed. "It must have been a trick of the light."

She hesitated. "Either that or I'm losing my mind—again."

"What do you mean by 'again'?"

"Uh, you know. Sometimes when I was coming off a bender I thought I saw things that weren't really there."

He snapped to attention. "You hallucinated?"

She shrugged and grinned sheepishly. "Only a little."

"Has it happened since you've been sober?"

"No. I shouldn't have said anything. I'm sure it was just a trick of the light or something. I'm getting better every day. I didn't mean to worry you."

"Let's not dwell on it. You're probably just tired. I need to get you home."

"And I need to get to an AA meeting. Maybe the

people who've been through this before can tell me if seeing weird stuff is normal."

Shit. "Fine. I'll take you."

"You can't do that."

"I'm afraid I have to. I don't trust Ruxandra."

Claudia tossed her hands in the air. "So I'm supposed to hide from her until she gets the hint and leaves us alone? Do you really think she's around every corner, gunning for me?"

The word "gunning" shocked him. But he couldn't let her see his momentary panic. Anthony caressed her arms and kissed her forehead. "I can't take that chance. You're too important to me."

"Someone needs to be here in case Autumn or Chelsea runs into a problem. The tea room is brand-new, and there are bound to be a few bumps to smooth out."

Anthony sighed. He had to know more about the protective spell Kurt cast around Claudia to keep her safe. Would it work if Ruxandra was literally gunning for her? Massachusetts had strict gun laws, but there was nothing to prevent her from mesmerizing a gun-shop owner in New Hampshire.

That seemed far-fetched, even for Ruxandra. Maybe he *was* being overprotective. "Fine. What if Kurt goes with you?"

Claudia's cheeks grew dark pink. "Kurt knows? Did you tell him?"

"No, but I'm sure he'd understand."

She rolled her eyes. "Oh, sure. He was at the bar every day and hardly drank at all. Angie told me he could nurse a beer for five hours. I'm sure he'd know exactly how I feel."

Should he tell her Kurt was his undercover bouncer? He paid him out of his own pocket and Claudia knew nothing about it. Kurt was needed there in case the paranormals got out of hand. Then Anthony remembered that Kurt was helping Nick on a paranormal PI case right now. *I shouldn't keep taking him away from that.*

"Claudia, isn't there something else you can do? Aren't there meetings online?"

"Oh, for the love of..." She sighed. "I'll call my sponsor. Maybe she can come over and we'll have our own meeting."

Uh-oh. That was the woman who'd cautioned Claudia to wait a year before getting into a relationship. He mulled over the possible consequences and figured that anything was better than losing Claudia permanently.

"Give her a call. Meanwhile, I'll go check on the girls and see if there are any problems."

Claudia smiled, but only slightly.

As soon as he left the office, he strode to the men's room to call Kurt. He had to know how safe Claudia really was—before she kicked him to the curb for being overbearing and paranoid.

"I'm not giving up on dating Ruxandra. She's just playing hard to get," Kurt said.

"I don't know, buddy. I heard her tell you to 'go to hell,' and I'd say she meant it. If you intend to keep trying, you'll have your work cut out for you."

"Maybe you can give me some tips. You know her better than anyone. What does she like?"

Anthony leaned against the stall in the men's room and groaned. "Me."

On the other end of the phone, he heard Kurt laugh. "Well, that's not going to help. Can't you give me any other ideas? Does she have a favorite flower? Favorite color?"

"You know her. She has very expensive tastes. Are you prepared to buy her diamonds and furs?"

"Hmmm… How about tickets to the ballet or opera? Does she enjoy those things?"

"No."

"Museums?"

"Only if she can knock one over and steal its priceless artifacts."

Kurt chuckled. "That might make an interesting first date."

Anthony pinched the bridge of his nose. "Maybe this was a bad idea. I don't want you spending your life savings or getting arrested, and Ruxandra is trouble with a capital *T*."

"There must be something she enjoys that's not illegal. Long walks on the beach?"

"No. She likes long bouts of hot, sweaty sex."

"Now we're talking!"

"But, as far as I know, only with me."

"Wasn't she a prostitute in the seventeen hundreds?"

"Yes. And she occasionally worked in a brothel in the eighteen and nineteen hundreds. What of it?"

"She can't be that opposed to new partners."

"It was a means to an end. Money is the only thing she understands…well, that and making my life a living hell."

"Why? What makes her so attached to you?"

"I'm the one who found her near death in a ditch outside the Marquis de Sade's castle. One look at her innocent beauty, and I would have moved heaven and earth for her. I knew looks could be deceiving, but I chose not to believe it that day."

After a short pause, Kurt said, "Don't worry. I know how it goes. Hot girl. Cold dick."

"Tell me about it."

"How and when did you two break up?"

"I masked my scent with some hooker's overpowering perfume and fled New Orleans like it was on fire."

"So, it sounds as if you two spent some time together if you found her in France during the reign of the Marquis de Sade and were still an item recently in New Orleans."

Anthony flopped against the back of the couch. "We were together for over a century, and after that, off and on. I was obligated at first. I taught her what she needed to know to survive—something I never learned from my own maker, but that's another story. Ruxandra and I even had a few happy decades. Unfortunately, that makes it worse. She remembers the good times but conveniently forgets that things haven't been good between us since the turn of the century."

"2000 wasn't that long ago."

"I was talking about 1900, the century before."

"Oh. So, where does she sleep?"

Anthony paced the nine-by-nine room in two strides. "I don't know, and I don't care."

"Whoa. Aren't you supposed to look after the vampires you turn? Isn't that some kind of vampire law or something?"

"I fulfilled my obligation to her years ago. She knows as much about survival as I do. Maybe more. There's nothing more I can teach her, other than how to let go of me and move on. She seems unwilling to learn those lessons."

"So, what you're saying is, you're kind of fucked."

"Unless you can find some way to entice her far, far away from here."

"I, um…I'll have to think about it."

Something in Kurt's voice told Anthony he had an idea but wasn't willing to share it yet.

"Meanwhile, my friend, I need to know that Claudia is safe—no matter what."

"She is. Trust me. She can go anywhere and do anything she likes. The protection spell won't wear off or fade with distance. She could leave the state and still be fine."

The idea of Claudia being miles away bothered Anthony, but he didn't have time to examine that now.

"You're sure?"

"Positive."

"Okay. Thanks, buddy. I owe you."

"You sure do."

Kurt laughed, but Anthony meant every word. Claudia's safety was worth whatever promises he had to keep.

"So, how's the investigation going?"

"Not well. Every time Nick thinks he's found a lead, the trail goes cold."

"Are more paranormals disappearing?"

"A few. At first it was just wolves. Now, it seems a couple of vampires are missing."

"Vampires?" This development hit home for

Anthony. "Who? Where? Are you sure they're missing and not just moving on?"

"According to Nick, a family reported their mother and young son missing. They seemed genuinely distraught. Said there was no way they'd ever leave the rest of the family willingly. Considering they went to a werewolf for help, they must have been desperate."

"Shit." *How did humans sneak up on a vampire—never mind two of them—and then manage to capture them?*

"Exactly. A werewolf capture is hard enough to understand, but they can't move quite as fast as vamps can when threatened. They must have been shot with some kind of fast-acting sedative."

"That's the only thing I can think of. Is there anything that works so fast it could take down vampires before they disappeared?"

"Not that I know of."

Anthony scratched his head.

Kurt elbowed him. "If I find out what it is, maybe I can use it on Ruxandra. Then lock her up until Stockholm syndrome kicks in and she falls madly in love with me. That would take care of your problem."

Anthony laughed bitterly. "How did you know what I was thinking?"

Claudia had made sure everything was okay and said good-bye to her waitresses. She figured she'd better beat it before Anthony handcuffed her to his side. She took two strides toward her apartment entrance, but before she reached her door, Ruxandra stepped in front of her. Dressed in red as usual, she was hard to miss, but she also wore gobs of sparkly jewelry and a fur stole. The only things missing were a tiara and long, white gloves.

"Yikes. You startled me." Claudia glanced all around. "Where did you come from anyway?"

Ruxandra's frown edged up into a slow, creepy smile. "Never mind that. We need to talk. How about if you invite me up…for a drink." Her teeth seemed to gleam and looked sharper than Claudia had remembered.

Doing her best to mask her alarm with annoyance, Claudia blew out a deep breath and dug in her purse for her keys. "What about?"

"I think you know."

"Sorry. I don't, and I'm…I have to be somewhere in…" She glanced at her watch. "Ten minutes. I barely have time to change."

"Into what?"

Huh? She's just trying to get to me. Claudia didn't actually have to leave her apartment for another hour, but letting the pushy blond know that would be a mistake.

Ruxandra reached out as if she were about to grab Claudia's arm, then recoiled and said, "Ouch. I broke a fuckin' nail. What are you made of? Iron?"

Claudia tried to step around Ruxandra, but the woman maneuvered herself directly in front of Claudia again.

"I won't take much of your time."

Claudia closed her eyes and blew out a deep breath.

"May I *please* come up to your apartment so we can talk in private?" Ruxandra asked in a syrupy sweet voice.

Claudia was about to tell her to take a flying leap

when Anthony flew out of the tea shop and wedged himself between the two women.

"Do *not* invite her in, Claudia."

How did he hear what was said from inside the shop? She was tempted to defy him and invite Ruxandra upstairs just to show him she could do whatever she liked, but technically, it was his apartment. And considering how much Ruxandra wanted her out of the way, defying him on this—or anything else where the blond bombshell was concerned—would be just plain stupid.

"Honestly, Anthony. Are you going to tell me what to do every minute of every day? I mean, evening."

Come to think of it, I've never seen Ruxandra during the day, either. Did they really spend their days apart? Is that why his former girlfriend feels she still has some kind of right to him? Claudia told herself she was being ridiculous. Anthony wanted nothing to do with the buxom blond.

He put a hand on the small of Claudia's back. "Why don't you go inside? I need to have a little talk with Ruxandra."

"And she says she needs to have a talk with me. Maybe the three of us should just sit down and talk until we all have nothing more to say." Claudia glared at Ruxandra. "I'm getting sick of being ambushed." Then she faced Anthony. "...and ordered around."

"That's not a good idea," Anthony said. "I'll handle this."

"Handle what?" She folded her arms. "Did you two break up or not?"

Ruxandra tipped her nose in the air. "What we have is something that can't be broken."

"And yet," Anthony said through gritted teeth, "it's been broken for a long time."

What the hell cryptic nonsense are these two saying to each other? "You know what? This is between you two. I'll be upstairs getting ready to go out. If you're still here when I leave, pretend you don't see me."

"Claudia, wait." Anthony started to follow her.

She yanked open the door to her stairwell and said. "No. I've waited long enough."

Anthony hoped Claudia wouldn't refuse to let him in. He needed to talk to her. She must be wondering what Ruxandra was babbling about when she said their relationship couldn't be broken, and he had to do damage control.

He knocked and heard Claudia mutter, "Frig," from the other side.

He waited impatiently until he saw her hazel eye peer into the peephole. He was relieved…sort of. On one hand, he wanted to give her an explanation of why his ex-girlfriend wouldn't go away, and on the other hand, he had to walk a fine line between the literal truth and something that wouldn't expose what he was.

She opened the door slowly and peeked around it.

"She's not with me," he said.

When Claudia opened the door wider, he added, "In any sense of the word," and then he strode inside and closed the door behind him. When he reached for her, she took a step back.

In disappointed surprise, he let his arms drop. "What's wrong?"

"I think I'm entitled to an explanation, and I don't

want to get distracted by your talented mouth and hands before I hear it."

He smiled sadly and nodded, acknowledging the backhanded compliment.

Claudia plodded over to the armchair and gestured for him to sit on the couch. He wanted to sit closer so he could soothe her. Stroking her cheek or caressing her back might have helped, but apparently she knew his moves.

"I want to know about a number of things. First, why is she being such a pain in the ass? It can't be just because she thinks she can break us up. What did she mean by 'what you have can't be broken'?"

Anthony let out a long sigh. The truth was about to get twisted. "In a way, we're related."

Claudia's jaw dropped. "You're what? Wait a minute… Are you married?"

"God, no."

"Divorced, but she won't accept it for religious reasons?"

Tempting, but he didn't even want entertain the thought. "No."

"Cousins? Isn't that illegal?"

"It's more distant than that." *Hey, I turned her in the distant past. That counts as distant.*

"So, distant cousins. Can't she just see you once a year at a family reunion?"

"You'd think, but for whatever reason, she wants it to be more."

"Okay…that brings up another question. I never see you two during the day. Are you spending your days together?"

"Absolutely not!" He had already formulated an explanation using a rare genetic illness if she ever asked about the daylight thing. Now, perhaps he could use the "relatedness" to back it up. "My, er—'family' has a rare condition, and photosensitivity is a major problem for us."

"Really? What's the condition called?"

"Xeroderma pigmentosum." He was proud of the fact that it rolled right off his tongue.

"Sounds made up."

"It's very real, I assure you. Cancer is about three hundred times more likely in those who have this condition. The best defense is no sunlight at all."

Claudia's hands flew to her cheeks. "Oh, no. How awful. I'm so sorry. Is there anything I can do to help? Should I know what symptoms to look for?"

"No. I'll be fine and you're already helping. Because of you, I was able to flip my sleep schedule to daylight hours."

She shook her head slowly. "Oh, my God. I had no idea. I'm so sorry, Anthony. No wonder you didn't want to be bothered during the day—even with emergencies at work." She rose and moved to sit beside him.

This is working better than I had hoped.

"Does Ruxandra have it too?"

"I'm afraid so."

"Oh, dear. Now I'm sorry I was mean to her."

"Please, don't be."

"But she's your relative and she has this terrible illness. I should invite her to have dinner with us sometime. Maybe just letting her know someone cares will help. She must think you're the only one who understands…and she's probably right."

Oh, crap. That backfired. "No. I don't want you anywhere near her. Sometimes, um, people with this condition become very volatile and violent."

Claudia's eyes rounded. "Does that mean that you…"

"No. Not at all. I have a mild form of the condition, and as long as I avoid all sun, it won't get worse."

"So Ruxandra's condition is severe?"

"Yes. I'm afraid so."

Claudia placed a hand over her heart and flopped back against the sofa cushions. "I feel so awful for her. Isn't there anything we can do?"

He put on his saddest expression. "No. There's nothing. I mean, I could institutionalize her, and at some point, I might have to…"

Claudia gasped. "Oh, my God. I hope it doesn't come to that."

"Me too. Really, the best thing you can do is stay away from her."

"So, you're saying she won't fly into rages if she's not jealous?"

Uh-oh. Anthony had a feeling he didn't like where this was going.

Claudia folded her hands in her lap and stared at them. "Maybe we should break up. It's the only way to make sure she stays calm."

"No! Please don't do that. I've put my life on hold too long as it is." He pleaded with his eyes. "I want to live before I die." *Good Christ. Could I have laid it on any thicker?* With every lie, he dug a deeper hole. He'd need to fix it so it wouldn't collapse and bury him. "We don't like to talk about it. I hope you can be discreet and tell no one. Don't even mention it to Ruxandra if you see her. Having this disease makes her angry. Let's not remind her of it."

"I understand the anger. Having alcoholism made me angry at first, but talking about it at meetings really helps. You should consider letting her express her feelings."

Shit. I should have known Claudia's compassionate side would complicate things. This bullshit has gone too far. Fortunately he could mesmerize her and take it all out of her head. Then he'd just have to come up with some other explanation for Ruxandra's behavior…if he could figure it out himself. So far all he could gather was that she was sociopathically obsessed with him. That in itself was concerning, but he'd just have to find another way to deal with it. He was sick of the blond bombshell ruining his life.

He turned to Claudia and held her gaze. *Trying to mesmerize her before didn't work, so I'll have to really concentrate.*

"There! It happened again," she said.

He quickly glanced behind him while his eyes returned to normal. "What? I don't see anything."

"Your eyes. They changed color."

He chuckled. "It must have been the light reflecting off my clothes or something."

"Your shirt is white. Your pants are black."

"Well, they could have been reflecting something else."

She glanced all around. "The place is beige, but your eyes were brown, then shimmered gold, then turned purple, then blue. I've never seen anything like it."

Damn. Why did I paint the place with neutral colors?

Chapter 8

Anthony had talked Claudia into believing she was just very tired and ought to nap until she had to leave for her meeting. He said he'd wake her. He hoped she'd fall sound asleep and stay in for the evening. He could come up with an excuse for not waking her later.

Meanwhile, he had to research why his mesmerism wasn't working. Maybe Kurt would know. He stepped into the hall and dialed Kurt's number.

"Anthony. What's up?"

"Are you busy?"

"Kind of. I'm in Cambridge. Nick and I might be getting close to locating the lab."

"That's great! What makes you think so?"

"We keep losing the trail over the Memorial Bridge, but at least we have a consistent direction. I believe it's a matter of following a fresher scent. We might need your help when we finally find it."

"If it has to do with my powers of mesmerization, I might not be as helpful as you think."

"Why not?"

"I can't mesmerize Claudia. Was it something you did in the protection spell? Maybe by protecting her from Ruxandra, you made her immune to my powers too?"

"I don't think so…at least not on purpose. I used a piece of Ruxandra's hair to represent any and all malevolent forces, but maybe one of yours wound up in the circle too. We did it in your office, after all."

Anthony nodded absently. "Maybe. Or maybe it means I'm evil too."

Kurt laughed. "You? Evil? You won't even kill to live. How's that chicken-blood diet, by the way?"

"Meh. But getting back to Claudia, is there any way you can fix what's happening—or rather, *not* happening?"

"Other than removing the spell and doing it all over again?"

"Yes."

"Then, no."

"Shit. I don't think your wizardry includes the power to erase memories, or does it? Otherwise you wouldn't have needed a vampire when all hell broke loose at the bar last year, and you wouldn't need me now."

"Correct," Kurt said. "I could freeze everyone in their tracks…at least all the humans. Then I need a vampire to wipe their minds."

"Who did you use last year? Some day-walker?"

"Yeah. Nick knew him. Do you think he might be able to help?"

"Possibly. If I'm losing my touch, maybe he knows why."

Suddenly a female voice he didn't recognize came from around the corner near the upstairs landing. "Yes. Get in touch with him. You should have a *competent* vampire handy who can erase minds, seeing as how you've become useless."

Anthony's jaw dropped as a strange woman gracefully descended the stairs. She had long white hair and wore a full-length, filmy ivory robe belted in front with vines.

"I—I'll call you back." He dropped his cell phone into his jacket pocket without taking his eyes off the mysterious woman.

She paused one step above him. "Do you know who I am?"

He cleared his throat. "Mother Nature, I presume."

"Good. You've heard of me. It gets so tedious having to explain that, yes, I really do exist. I am to be called Gaia or Goddess. I watch what's happening on the earthly plain—when I feel like it," she muttered. "Yada, yada, yada..."

"What are you doing here? I mean, why are you interested in me?"

She smirked. "I've been watching you for some time. Ever since you opened your little watering hole for paranormals."

Anthony sucked in a breath. *She's been watching me for five years?*

"Yes. I've been aware of your experiment," she said as if she could read his mind. Now he was really unnerved.

Anthony stood his ground. "It's helped diffuse the tensions between many shifters and vampires. I'd like to continue—"

"Hush. I'm not here to talk about your tea shop. It seems harmless enough. At least tea isn't a fire accelerant." She crossed her arms. "Is there somewhere more private where we can talk?"

"Hmmm..." He didn't want to take her to his lair. It was bad enough that she knew where he worked.

At that moment, Claudia's door opened and she stood there holding her coat and purse.

"Hey. You were supposed to wake me up."

"Sorry. I got sidetracked." He cast a quick glance toward Mother Nature. Suddenly she was wearing a sky-blue dress. *Weird.*

The goddess folded her arms. "Aren't you going to introduce us?"

"Uh… This is Claudia. My…uh…" *How can I protect Claudia from a deity's interest and keep her off Gaia's radar? Call her my tenant? My friend?*

Claudia sighed deeply. "His girlfriend. Who's this, Anthony? Another ex?"

"No. Nothing like that. This is…uh…"

Mother Nature rolled her eyes. "His business partner. I saw you at the tea room, but I didn't know you were Anthony's girlfriend."

Anthony slipped his arm around Claudia's waist. "We've been keeping things on the down-low. You know, since she's dating the boss and everything."

A light of recognition entered Claudia's eyes. "Oh, I remember now. You were one of our first customers at our grand opening. Beautiful hat, by the way."

"Thank you."

An awkward moment ticked by. Anthony hoped that Mother Nature didn't spill the beans about his being a vampire or that she was a goddess or that paranormals were frequenting the tea room. He'd have to tell Claudia at some point, but he'd hoped to wait until she had more sobriety under her belt. If anything could trigger the craving for a drink…

At last, Claudia shrugged. "Well, I've got to get going, or I'll be late." She shook Mother Nature's hand, then kissed Anthony's cheek and said, "G'night."

"Wait. I want to go with you," Anthony said.

Gaia jammed her hands on her hips. "You're busy. You'll see her later."

Bloody hell. There wasn't much he could do. Defying a goddess was probably a bad move. He'd just have to trust Kurt's word that Claudia was protected by his spell.

Claudia turned, gave them both a confused look, then shook her head and left.

"Nice girl. So, where can we have that heart-to-heart?" Gaia asked.

Crap. If I'm in trouble with the powers that be, I might as well get it over with. "How about the office downstairs? I can get you a nice cup of tea."

"Darjeeling," she said. "No sugar. Light on the milk." Then she passed him and descended the remaining stairs.

I must be nuts. I know Ruxandra is hot as hell, but do I really want that psycho babe transferring her obsession from Anthony to me?

Kurt looked at his watch, which wasn't a watch at all. He had changed the analog dial to act as a homing device. Soon he'd be zeroing in on Ruxandra—and dusk would be descending on Boston.

Anthony had said that if anyone could "handle" Ruxandra, it would be Kurt. Now he wondered why the challenge had seemed so irresistible. What was he trying to prove?

Suddenly his watch hands pulled together and pointed in the same direction. He was close. The second hand was slightly off, pointing toward the eleven, so he adjusted his direction accordingly. At last, all three hands lined up. He gazed directly in front of him and faced a brick building in the Beacon Flats. *Here?*

How could a vampire afford to live in this part of Boston? Real estate in the Flats cost less than on the Hill, but it was still pricey for a woman who had no job. *Or did she?*

Kurt decided to hang back and observe. The streetlamp wove shadows with a few trees and nearby bushes, affording a spot where he couldn't be seen, but that didn't mean he was safe. Ruxandra could smell him. He tested the wind and found the best place to stand where her scent would travel toward him, not the other way around. Fortunately, she wore the same perfume all the time, and he'd know it anywhere. Not that he knew the name, but the fragrance was heavy with oriental spices.

A door leading to the building's basement creaked and opened slightly. Kurt flattened himself next to the tree trunk and peered over his shoulder. A male voice said, "Thank you, mistress. Will there be anything else?"

The man came stumbling into view with Ruxandra right behind him, arm extended. It looked as if she had just pushed him toward the brick sidewalk.

"One more thing, whatever-your-name-is..."

"It's Louis."

She rolled her eyes. "I wasn't asking for your name. I don't care who you are. Just come back tomorrow night at eight, and bring more money."

"Yes, mistress."

She held his gaze and said, "You will not remember anything about me or where you've been. You won't even remember my asking you to come back. You'll simply find yourself here for no explainable reason, and you will wait outside until I let you in."

"Yes, mistress."

"All right. You can go now."

With that, Ruxandra swiveled him toward Charles Street and gave him a shove. He caught himself before he fell and glanced at the ground, as if wondering which cobblestone he had tripped over. Meanwhile, Ruxandra strode off in the opposite direction.

Kurt groaned inwardly. She had a thrall. That explained a few things. Where she got blood, for one thing. And it sounded like she'd found someone of means to support her too.

Now where is she off to?

Kurt followed at a distance until she rounded a corner and he lost sight of her. Jogging to keep up, he was about twenty feet behind her when she stopped. Without turning around, she asked, "Why are you following me, Kurt?"

He slowed his pace and she pivoted, waiting until he came face to face with her.

She folded her arms. "So? Why are you following me?"

Kurt tried to charm her with his smile. "Ruxandra! I thought that might be you. Lucky for me I was able to catch up."

"Oh? Why is that lucky?"

"I had hoped you'd consider a proposition."

She raised one eyebrow. "Why, Kurt Morgan. You know I don't do that anymore."

He chuckled. "I didn't mean it that way..." Then he raised a brow right back at her. "Unless you wanted me to."

She spat out a sound of disgust and strode off in the direction she had been heading.

"I was kidding," he called after her. She didn't stop, so he trotted until he caught up with her and they were striding side by side. "I need your help with something."

She didn't look at him or even slow down. "You need help, all right, but I'm not qualified to give it to you. Look in the phone book under psychologists."

"Oh, you kidder," he said, trying to maintain his sense of humor. *This is harder than I thought.*

When she arrived at the corner of Beacon Street, she stopped momentarily before crossing the busy road.

"So, where are you going?" he asked.

"What's it to you?"

He shrugged. "Just curious how a beautiful woman spends her time."

She stuck her hands on her hips and gazed at the oncoming cars, waiting for a break in traffic that didn't come. At last she let out a frustrated breath. She whirled on him and stared right into his eyes. "You will step out into the street and raise your hand to stop traffic. You will stay there until I cross, and then you will go back where you came from."

He took a step back. "Why would I do that? I might get mowed down."

Her jaw dropped.

"Were you trying to mesmerize me?"

At that moment, the light changed and traffic came to a stop. Without answering him, Ruxandra scampered across the street toward the Public Garden.

He caught up to her again. "Wait.

She broke into a run and crossed Arlington Street.

"Ruxandra. Wait up," he called. She was fast and easily outran him.

She kept running until she turned the corner onto Newbury Street. *Ah, she's probably planning to spend that guy's money at the designer boutiques.* By the time he reached the corner, she was gone. He'd lost her to some store, café, or salon.

Kurt stuffed his hands in his pockets and slowed to a leisurely stroll. He kept his eyes open for her, but doubted he'd find her again. If she applied her vampiric speed, she could have already reached the Prudential Center.

The fact that she'd tried to mesmerize him and it hadn't worked really sparked his curiosity. Anthony had had the same trouble with Claudia. *What's going on? Are vamps losing their powers one by one?*

He decided to ask Anthony about it and turned around. At least he knew where to find him. He was at Claudia's a few minutes ago, and by now he'd probably returned to the tea room. A nice, hot cup of tea and company that wouldn't run away from him sounded good. Maybe they could puzzle it out over a pot of Bombay chai and a plate of cookies.

Anthony sat at his desk across from Mother Nature. He steepled his fingers and waited for her to speak.

She took a sip of her tea and set it down on his desk. "Mmm. Not bad."

Anthony didn't acknowledge the compliment, hoping she'd just get to the point and leave. "So, what's your proposition?"

"I have no business proposition for you. Not really. I just came to deliver a warning."

He sat back and hoped he wasn't in some kind of serious trouble.

"Or maybe it *is* a business deal. Do what I say and I'll let you stay in business. How's that for a proposition?"

"I don't understand."

"The human girlfriend. Get rid of her."

"Excuse me?"

"You heard me."

"What does my love life have to do with you?"

She laughed. "What does *love* have to do with *nature*? I'm not going to honor that idiotic question with an answer."

He leaned forward. "All right. Let me put it a different way. What's your objection to my relationship with Claudia?"

"You're a vampire. She's a human. Even a simpleton should be able to see the problems inherent in that."

Anthony hung his head. "I know. It isn't ideal."

Gaia laughed. "Not ideal? Now *there's* an understatement." She rose and paced. "How and when were you planning to tell her?"

He sighed. "I don't know."

She rolled her eyes. "Let's pretend for a minute that you get up the nerve to tell her everything. What's to prevent her from laughing in your face and telling all her girlfriends about it?"

"Claudia's not like that."

"Oh, yeah? Is she going to believe you and accept you *just the way you are*? Is she as delusional as you are?"

"She'll ask questions, but she'll listen open-mindedly. She's very intelligent. Not to mention loyal, caring, resourceful—"

Mother Nature raised her hand. "Fine. You think she's the greatest. For now. What about later when you see the faults I've given her?"

"I already know them, and I don't care."

Gaia threw her hands in the air. "You have an answer for everything, don't you? Oh, wait. You have an answer for everything *except* how to tell her you're a vampire."

Anthony slumped. "When the time comes, I imagine we'll have an honest, adult conversation."

"Dream on. She won't believe you. Were you planning to give her a demonstration?"

"No."

Gaia stopped and whirled on him. "You've really thought this out, haven't you? I have a suggestion. Break up with her *before* you have to explain yourself."

"Apparently, even vampires can't choose who they fall in love with. If you're worried about her, just know that I would never harm or drink from Claudia." *Unless she wants me to.*

"So, you're telling me you'd go against your own nature to be with this human?"

"Yes."

She folded her arms. "I don't believe you."

Anthony rose. "Why not? I'm telling you the truth."

She smashed her fist on his desk. "Because I know the power of nature. Here. Let me give *you* a demonstration."

Anthony didn't have time to blink, much less speak, before he found himself shivering on a snowy mountaintop. A goat walked up to him and stared him in the eyes.

"What did you do to piss her off?" he asked.

The goat bleated.

A moment later, he was back in his office. Mother

Nature shook her head. "He can't answer your question. He's a goat, stupid."

Anthony folded his arms. "What do you want from me? Besides walking away from Claudia, because I won't do that."

She raised one eyebrow. "Isn't it obvious? I want you to dump your human girlfriend right fucking now. But, I'll let you think about the consequences if you disobey me. Someone is about to barge in on us, and I don't want to be here when he does."

A knock at the door drew Anthony's attention for a millisecond. When he turned back to Mother Nature, she was gone.

Kurt poked his head around the door and saw Anthony standing in the middle of his office, clenching his fists.

"Is everything all right, buddy?"

"Uh, yeah. Come in." He rounded the desk and sat behind it. Unusual for Anthony. Back when he owned the bar, he was much less stiff and formal. Maybe he was trying to seem more professional for some reason.

Kurt took a seat on the opposite side of the desk, but stretched his legs out and leaned back with his fingers interlaced behind his head. If Anthony didn't want to be comfortable, that was his problem.

"You came to see me about something?"

"Yeah." Kurt sat up and leaned forward. "Ruxandra tried to mesmerize me."

Anthony's spine straightened even more than it had been with the broomstick up his ass. "What do you mean, 'tried to'? It sounds like she didn't succeed."

"Correct. She looked directly into my eyes and told me to step into traffic."

"Jesus!"

"Yeah. Her eyes turned some kind of funky gold and purplish color, and she seemed genuinely shocked that I didn't do as I was told."

"I'm sorry, Kurt. I didn't think she'd try anything like that. Stay away from her. I'll figure something else out."

"No. It's okay. I'm glad to know she can't make me do her bidding. In that way, I'm probably the best man for the job, Operation Distraction. Even more than that, though, I think she can be useful if and when we find the lab."

"Have you gotten any closer to locating it?"

"Maybe. Maybe not. Sadie described her surroundings and tried to get back to the place, but she's being blocked for some reason."

"How is that possible? Who could prevent her from astral projection? That specter of a security guard?" Then, for some reason, Anthony pinched the bridge of his nose and groaned. "Never mind. I think I just realized the answer to my own question."

"Really? Because the only explanation she can come up with has to do with her spirit guides protecting her. Have you got some other possibility in mind?"

Anthony took a deep breath. Something Kurt had never seen him do. He seemed to be mulling something over. Finally he said, "Never mind. Let's get back to Ruxandra. I need to know that your spell to protect Claudia is rock solid. There's no way she can be mesmerized by me...I know that. I tried. But do you think Ruxandra could make her do something like step into traffic?"

"I doubt it."

Anthony shot to his feet. "You *doubt* it? That's the best reassurance you can give me?"

Kurt held up both hands and pushed Anthony into his chair without touching him. By the look on Anthony's face, he seemed surprised and a little impressed.

"How did you do that?"

Kurt grinned. "I don't give away my trade secrets."

"Hmmm...maybe I should hire you to be Claudia's undercover bodyguard."

Kurt rolled his eyes. "Yeah, she wouldn't catch on to that at all."

Anthony slumped over his desk, his hands covering his face. "What the hell am I supposed to do? I need to protect her, but I can't."

"I don't know. I've done what I can. I'm not ready to give up on Ruxandra, as long as I know she can't mesmerize me. By the way, why do you think that is? Are vampires losing their ability to mesmerize humans?"

Anthony rose and came around his desk. "Let's find out. You *are* human, right?"

Kurt leaned away from him. "You're going to mesmerize me?"

"Why not? I'm a vampire. I *think* you're human."

Kurt smirked. "Watch the insults. I'm one hundred percent human—just a well-trained wizard."

"I won't make you do anything dangerous. I hope you know that."

"Of course. I trust you. You need me." He smirked.

Anthony let out the long breath he'd inhaled a few minutes ago. He leaned down and caught Kurt's eye. All Kurt had time to do was blink—at least it felt like he'd just blinked. He was sitting in Anthony's chair, looking at a piece of paper on the desk with the word "black" written in his handwriting.

"Impressive," he said. "Why did I write the word 'black'?"

"I asked you to write down your favorite color. Black seemed like an odd choice, but you're an odd guy." Anthony shrugged.

"Hey. I thought I told you to watch the insults. I said 'black' because I love all colors and black is what you get if you mix all the colors together. Besides, I look awesome in it." He tugged the shoulders of his black T-shirt.

"Okay. So, vampires aren't losing their touch. Maybe your spell to protect Claudia from Ruxandra protected her from me and you from Ruxandra?"

"Not very likely, but I don't have a better explanation."

Chapter 9

Anthony exited his office to check on the tea room. Angie was sitting with Tory and Nick. He was surprised to see her still there. He waved to Sadie, who was doing a reading, and approached the table of three.

"Didn't you finish your shift a couple hours ago, Angie?"

"Ah, yeah." She fidgeted. "Is it all right if I become a customer in the evening?"

"Of course. I just didn't think you'd want to hang around where you worked. I guess you don't hate it here."

She laughed. "Not at all. I like it. The job is easy, even if I can't get any White Russians here and the clientele is the same old, demanding bunch." She pointed at Tory and Nick with her thumb.

"You love us," Tory said. One side of his mouth quirked up.

"And you're best friends with my wife," Nick added. "Insult me, and she'll have to stop hanging around with you."

Angie laughed. "Yeah, right."

"Actually, Nick, I've been meaning to talk to you about something. Can you come into my office for a few minutes?"

"And leave these two unchaperoned?"

Tory shoved his thick arm. "Please. I think we can manage without you."

"Fine. I know when I'm not wanted." Nick rose and

followed Anthony, but before he reached the office, he called over his shoulder, "If you need my protection, just yell."

"I think I'll be okay, Nick," Angie called back.

"I was talking to Tory," he said. He closed Anthony's door on her indignant sputtered retort.

"You like to give Angie a hard time, don't you?" Anthony asked.

"Been doing it ever since I've known her. She'd miss it if I didn't. So, what did you want to see me about?"

"Have a seat." Anthony waited for Nick to get comfortable, then asked, "How's the investigation going?"

"Which one?"

"You have more than one case?"

"Yeah, but they seem to be related. Apparently there are more paranormals missing, and if they're being taken to a secret lab in Cambridge, we can't find it."

"You know it's in Cambridge?"

"I think so. I've followed scents over the Memorial Bridge several times. That's where I lose them. I think the wind off the river interferes with tracking beyond there."

"Then it *does* sound like you're getting close. Has Sadie confirmed any of what you've seen with what she saw during her astral projection?"

"She said it was too dark and she can't get back there for some reason."

"That's weird. I wonder why not."

"She said maybe her subconscious is protecting her, refusing to let her go somewhere dangerous or mentally disruptive."

"I don't know... She seems mentally sound, and how much danger can she be in when she's in astral form?"

Nick shrugged. "I don't know how her gift works. I just wish it did—now more than ever—and unfortunately her subconscious, or whatever, isn't cooperating."

"What if you took her around the area during the day? Would she recognize anything?"

Nick shook his head. "She says no. She didn't pay attention to the outer surroundings. Just the roof she landed on."

"Maybe Kurt could take her up in a helicopter. He's a pilot—or at least he was in the military."

Nick rose. "That's brilliant. I'm just sorry I didn't think of it sooner."

"Glad I could help."

"Don't tell anyone I discussed the case with you. If it works, I'm taking credit for it." He laughed.

Anthony cuddled Claudia on her couch, but she seemed distracted. He stroked her cheek and tucked her hair behind her delicate ear, careful not to disturb her pearl earring.

"What's wrong, honey?"

"Nothing."

"In my experience, when a woman says 'nothing,' there's always something. Come on. Out with it."

She sighed. "I wish you'd spend the whole night with me sometime. I don't understand why you can't. I'm perfectly willing to black out all the windows. Is it that you don't want to see my morning face with no makeup and bed-head?"

Shit. Maybe it was time to let her in on his secret. He still didn't know if she could handle it sober, and he'd feel horrible if he caused her to start drinking again.

No. Not yet. Trying to sound natural, he said, "Don't be ridiculous. You're beautiful when you wake up."

"How would you know?"

"I woke you one morning. As I recall, you had cried off your makeup, and bed-head didn't begin to describe your hair." He grinned, hoping to lighten the mood and let her know he was teasing at the same time.

She groaned. "True. I guess if you saw me like that and didn't run for the hills, you really aren't bothered by appearances."

"You won't get rid of me that easily." How could he get her off the subject of staying overnight? He shifted so he could hide his erection. "Speaking of getting rid of people, Kurt is trying to romance Ruxandra."

Claudia sat up and faced him. "You're kidding."

"Nope. He's not having much luck at the moment, but he seems determined to win her over."

Claudia covered her mouth with open fingers. "I don't know whether to be grateful or horrified."

"Be grateful. He's a grown man, knows what he's getting into, and seems willing if not eager to tame the shrew."

Claudia laughed. "Unbelievable." Then she quieted. "I know she's beautiful...I mean, absolutely *gorgeous*, but what else does Kurt see in her?"

Anthony shrugged. He couldn't very well say his friend was doing him the favor of a lifetime.

Her eyes widened. "You don't suppose he's after her money, do you?"

Anthony almost asked, "What money?" but stopped himself. Letting Claudia come up with her own plausible answer might be wiser.

"I don't know," he said.

Claudia spoke softly as if thinking out loud. "I never thought of him as opportunistic, but I only know the convivial, flirty Kurt. Come to think of it, he does seem kind of superficial, and she's always dripping in diamonds and furs. She must be loaded. And as far as I know, he doesn't currently have a job."

"I never ask about people's finances. You could be right."

"And I never asked about yours, but you volunteered the fact that I shouldn't worry about the tea shop."

"True. I don't tell people unless they need to know. You're the manager and needed to know we could afford to take a risk."

He stroked her cheek with the back of his fingers and jokingly whispered in her ear, "Now that you know I'm loaded, do you think you could love me for my money?"

She laughed. "I never expected you, of all people, to be so blatant about gold diggers. And, for your information, I'm not one of them."

He grinned. "I know. And I'm glad." *If only she knew about my time in Alaska during the Gold Rush. I knew plenty of them.*

He turned her chin to face him. "You're perfect." He was about to kiss her, but Claudia dropped her gaze, bit her lip, and closed her eyes.

Uh-oh. "What's the matter?"

She shook her head.

"Whatever it is, you can tell me. You know that, right?"

She hung her head. "I'm so far from perfect it isn't funny. There's something I've done..."

There was something momentous in the atmosphere. As if she were about to reveal a horrible secret.

"It's not the kind of thing I like to talk about, but you should probably know. I killed my sister."

Anthony couldn't imagine his sweet, gentle Claudia being capable of killing anyone. It had to have been some kind of accident. Something she'd been blaming herself for.

He took both of her hands in his. "Tell me about it."

She looked away.

"Claudia, honey. I'm not here to judge you. Is this something that contributed to your drinking?"

"Yes," she whispered. "Most definitely."

Hell, it was a wonder he didn't end up with a drinking problem, too, with all the lives he'd taken. "I understand confession can be good for the soul. I'm far from priestly, but I'm willing to listen if it'll help."

She sighed. "I had a sister two years older. She was the brainy one. Really, really smart. My parents couldn't afford to send us both to private colleges, but she got a partial scholarship to Dartmouth. She wanted to be a doctor. A pediatrician. Meanwhile, I was lucky enough to get into BU. My parents took out a second mortgage on their house so I could go. I should have gone to a state school..." A tear shimmered in her eye.

"Marion had just come home for the summer after her sophomore year. I was celebrating my high school graduation at a party on the other side of town. Of course I'd had too much to drink. Since Marion was the smart one, I distinguished myself by being the social one. I had lots of friends, went out every weekend, and drank a lot.

"Anyway, that night I knew I was in no shape to drive

and our designated driver left us all in the lurch after a fight with her boyfriend, so I called good ol' reliable Marion. She took the highway, probably to get there faster. Another car crossed the center line and hit her head-on in a high-speed crash. The driver of the other car was drunk and apparently bounced. He survived. My sister did not." Claudia broke down and sobbed.

Anthony grabbed her and held her tight. How could she blame herself for an accident like that? He wanted to shake her, but that was the last thing she needed. Instead, he stroked her hair and murmured, "Shhh…" until she stopped.

"Claudia, honey. You can't blame yourself for an accident."

"Yeah, but if I hadn't—"

"Listen. You couldn't have known any of that would happen. It sounds like you didn't expect her to take the highway. You couldn't have known there'd be a drunk driver on it. If anyone should be blamed, it's the driver of the other car, but regardless…guilt and shame doesn't help anyone. We live our lives. We make decisions. We make mistakes. It's part of finding our way through the unknown."

"My father hated me after that."

"I'm sure he didn't. Some men don't know how to deal with or express strong emotions. They lash out in frustration. Did he ever say it was your fault?"

"Not in so many words."

"He doesn't hate you. I saw his concern for you myself." He took her face in his hands." I wish I could take away all the pain, but I can't." *Because apparently my power of mesmerism is on the fritz.* "Look, we don't know why some things happen. They just do. It's how we handle them that tells us who we really are."

Claudia clenched her fists. "Then I'm really a horrible person."

"You are not!" He rose and raked his hand through his hair. "I wish you'd stop beating yourself up. Isn't there something in the twelve steps about asking people to forgivc you for things you've done under the influence?"

"Yes. It's the ninth step. I'm not quite there yet."

"Well, when you get there, talk to yourself first. You need to forgive yourself. In the meanwhile, know that I forgive you. Maybe that will help."

She sighed. "I don't deserve you."

"You're right."

She looked up with questioning eyes.

"You deserve better."

Anthony wished he could help by sharing some ghastly stories of his own. So she was indirectly responsible for one measly death. He had fed on hundreds of humans, many of whom didn't survive until he learned how much he could take without killing someone. In a way they'd both had drinking problems.

She'd be appalled. Most humans would, but Claudia with her gentle heart couldn't handle it. Not now, and maybe not ever. *What was I thinking?*

A knock at the door disturbed their intimate conversation. When Claudia didn't answer right away, the pounding increased and a frantic female voice shouted, "Anthony! Are you in there?"

It didn't sound like Ruxandra.

Anthony rose. "It's Angie." He buttoned his suit jacket as Claudia strode to the door.

"Angie, what's wrong?"

"It's Tory. Someone Tasered him, hauled him into a white van, and drove off."

Anthony flew down the stairs faster than he should have, but he needed to catch whoever had done this. The MO seemed to fit the facts Nick and Kurt had shared with him.

Once on the sidewalk, he scanned the area as far as his vampiric night vision could see.

Nothing. Damn it.

He dug his cell phone out of his pocket and called Nick.

"Hey, Anthony. What's up?"

"Our kidnappers just took Tory."

"Shit! What happened? Tell me everything."

"I should put you on the phone with Angie. She witnessed it." He jogged upstairs, still talking. "By the time I got down to the sidewalk, I didn't see anything out of the ordinary."

He knocked and waited for the click that meant Claudia had locked the door. Thank goodness she kept her promise to keep it locked at all times.

As soon as she let him in, he put the phone on speaker and said to Angie. "It's Nick. Tell him what you saw."

"Hi, Nick. Tory and I were just standing on the sidewalk outside the tea shop, talking. A white van pulled up next to us, and two guys wearing black ski masks got out. One of them shot him with a Taser. Then they hauled him into the van through the sliding side door and took off. I screamed for help, but no one would get involved."

"That doesn't surprise me. Did you get a license number?"

"By the time I got over the shock and remembered to look, I only saw a couple numbers and one letter."

"Even a partial might help. What were they?"

"13O."

"Are you sure the *O* was a letter and not a number? Could it have been one thirty?"

Angie hesitated. "Damn. I'm not sure anymore." Her voice shook. "I was so scared. I'm still scared…for him."

Nick's voice gentled. "Angie, it'll be okay. You know I'll do everything I can to help."

"And so will I," Anthony said. "I'm a pretty skilled hypnotist. If I hypnotized you, would you see more of the license number?"

"Maybe," she said softly.

"Nick, can you hold a few minutes while I do that?"

"I'd rather make a couple calls right away and have you get back to me."

"Of course. I'll talk to you soon."

"Will do," Nick said and clicked off.

By that time, Angie was crying. Claudia had an arm around her and guided her to the sofa. Then she said, "I'll get you some tissues," and hurried toward her bedroom.

Angie sniffed, wiped at the tears, and looked up at Anthony. "I had just told my family that it was too damn bad if they didn't like it. I'm going out with him anyway."

"Are they prejudiced?"

"Yeah, but not because he's black. They can't stand the fact that he's from New York. My father, grandfather, and brother all hate the Yankees and the Giants."

Anthony rolled his eyes. "I've heard of crazy Boston sports fans, but that's ridiculous."

Claudia returned with tissues and handed the box to Angie.

"Tell me about it."

"Do you think you can handle hypnosis right now? Maybe we should wait until you're feeling a little—"

"No. Do it right now. I want to help Nick find him, and the sooner the better."

Claudia had gone down to the tea room to make Angie a pot of chamomile tea, per Anthony's request. He seemed to want to be alone with Angie while he hypnotized her. Claudia wasn't about to fight with him about it. Maybe he was afraid of hypnotizing her at the same time. Or maybe he thought Angie would relax more if she didn't have an audience. Yeah, that was probably it.

She made the tea and stepped out onto the sidewalk. As she was locking up again, someone called her name with an incredulous expression in his voice.

"Claudia?"

She glanced over her shoulder and recognized her old boyfriend Maynard. "Hey, Maynard. Nice to see you. How are you doing?"

"I'm great," he said and puffed up his chest under his brown leather jacket. "I'm working in Cambridge now."

"Oh? Where in Cambridge? I used to live there."

"Central Square."

"Really? That's where I used to live. It's funny that I bumped into you over here instead of in Cambridge."

"Yeah. Well, I was just in the neighborhood. What are you doing here?"

Claudia tipped her head toward the tea shop. "This is where I work. I'm the manager."

"Just the manager? I thought you'd own your own business by now."

Claudia didn't know how to take that. Was it a compliment about her intelligence? Or a slam for her lack of success. "Uh, well, the business is brand new. We've only been open a few days. I designed it, hired and trained the staff, created the menu, found suppliers…the whole nine yards. I get to call the shots since the owner is rarely around." *Why am I bragging? Oh, yeah. When I did AA's fourth step, I discovered one of my worst character defects is pride.*

"Cool. Sounds like my kind of boss."

"Yeah, he's great. Are you still into science?"

"More than ever. I'm head of a research lab."

"Cool. I know that's what you wanted. What are you researching?"

"Oh, you know…a lot of stuff."

Was he being evasive or did he remember how bored she'd gotten with his long, drawn-out scientific explanations?

"So, I guess you graduated from MIT."

"Nah. I went three years, then a friend of mine offered me this opportunity and I never looked back."

"Well, good. I'm glad you're doing well." *Especially since I dumped your ass. Now I can stop feeling guilty.* "Uh, I need to get this tea upstairs before it gets cold."

"Oh? Do you deliver?"

She laughed. "Not usually. I have a friend up there who's a little upset. There's nothing like a good cup of tea with honey to comfort someone."

"That or a good cup of rum." He winked.

Ugh. He remembers how I used to cope with…everything.

"Yeah, well, I gotta go."

"Hey, maybe I'll stop by when you're open."

"Sure. And tell your friends about us." She hoped he was just being polite. Bumping into Maynard on the sidewalk was one thing, but being buddies wasn't something she wanted to do. She edged away and hoped he took the hint.

"Well, bye. It was good to see you." *But not really.*

"Yeah, same here."

By the time Claudia returned to her apartment, Anthony had uncovered the rest of the license plate number and was on the phone with Nick. She passed by without looking at him but felt his eyes on her.

"What do you take in your tea, Angie?"

"Honey and lemon, if you have them."

Claudia poured Angie a generous cup and stirred.

"Is everything all right, honey?" Anthony asked Claudia.

Angie's brows lifted.

"Uh, yeah. Fine." Claudia handed Angie the tea and felt her cheeks heat.

Angie looked from Anthony to Claudia. "So, are you two…"

Claudia looked over at Anthony, wondering what had possessed him to call her "honey" in front of their employee. He slipped his arm around her waist and warmed her with a side squeeze.

"Yes," he said. "We are."

A glow of pride fought with her better judgment, but eventually her sentimental side won. She wrapped her arm around him too. "We've been keeping it quiet."

"I hope you will too," Anthony said.

"Hell, yes," Angie said. "Does Ruxandra know?"

Anthony closed his eyes. "Unfortunately, yes."

"Jesus! Aren't you afraid she'll try to harpoon Claudia like she did Brandee when she thought you were into her? What's to prevent raging Ruxandra from becoming a bull in a bone china shop?"

Claudia tried not to smile. It was a serious concern, but Angie's spin on it…well…

"She's been warned. You're both safe. If you weren't, I'd hire another bodyguard."

Angie and Claudia glanced at each other. "Another?"

Anthony sighed. "You might as well know. Remember how Kurt and Tory hung out at the bar all the time? I had asked them to keep an eye on the place."

Angie set her tea down and folded her arms. "I thought Tory was there to see me. Are you telling me he was working there?"

"I'm sure seeing you was a major bonus, Angie."

She muttered something under her breath, but Claudia decided to leave it alone. The girl had been through enough for one night.

Chapter 10

THE FOLLOWING EVENING AT THE TEA ROOM, ANGIE seemed a little better. Apparently Nick had found out who owned the van and was hunting him down. Claudia had just been thinking about her accidental meeting with Maynard yesterday when the bell over the door tinkled. She looked up.

Speak of the devil.

"Maynard. I didn't expect to see you so soon." She kept her feet firmly planted on the other side of the counter in front of the cash register.

"I couldn't resist your invitation. I even invited some friends as you suggested."

Angie peeked up from her order pad as she wrote.

"Sit anywhere you like," Claudia continued. "How many friends are you expecting? We can push together a couple of tables if you're a party of seven or more."

"Oh, no. Nothing like that. Just two others."

"Okay. Can I get you something while you wait for them?" She handed him a menu.

"Just a glass of water…unless *you're* on the menu, of course," he said, and winked.

Oh, gross. A smooth operator Maynard was not. Claudia chuckled anyway, much like she'd seen her waitresses do when the place was a bar. *Must be nice to the customers.* "Sorry." *Not in this lifetime.*

He shrugged. "Oh, well. I had to try."

Angie seemed to be glaring at them. *Oh, no. She doesn't think for a minute I'd cheat on Anthony...*

Maynard surveyed the room and headed toward the table Sadie used. She had taken a dinner break but would be back to read tea leaves within the hour for her six o'clock appointment.

Angie blocked his path. "Not that table. It's reserved," she said a little too abruptly.

"Oh? I think *your manager* said I could sit anywhere I liked."

Typical Maynard. He took things literally and seemed to do it on purpose. That was one of the things Claudia remembered she didn't like about him.

Angie looked to Claudia. "It's okay, Ange. If he wants that table, we can move one for the party that requested privacy." She sent a pointed expression Maynard's way and hoped he'd get the hint. Either he didn't or didn't want to. He sat at Sadie's table and made himself comfortable by stretching out his legs and leaning back in his chair, hands clasped behind his head.

Stubborn ass. Claudia made a mental note to put a "reserved" sign on that table when she knew Sadie would be reading.

The bell tinkled and a young couple entered. They spotted Maynard and joined him at the table. "A tea room, eh?" one of them said. "Since when do you drink tea?"

He smiled at Claudia. "Since I found out the manager is an old friend of mine...and maybe a future friend if all goes well."

Gack.

The couple turned and looked at Claudia for the first time.

"Oh," said the male. He lowered his voice and said something to Maynard that made him smile. It made Angie's eyes widen and she almost stomped off to the kitchen.

Whoa. Claudia didn't want Angie getting the wrong idea, so she followed her.

"Angie."

When she turned around, Angie's lips were so thin that she looked like she was trying to hold back a barrage of words.

"Maynard's an old boyfriend who makes me uncomfortable. Would you mind waiting on him and his friends? I really don't want to give him the wrong idea."

Angie let out a deep breath. "Only if I can dump hot tea in his lap."

Claudia laughed. "If that was allowed, I'd do it myself."

Angie smiled for the first time since Maynard walked in. She must have finally realized Anthony's heart was safe.

As if there were any comparison.

"Okay. I'll try not to spill it directly on him." Angie's evil grin would have given Claudia pause if she didn't know her so well. Angie would be professional…to their faces.

"I'll be in my office for a few minutes. Knock if it gets busy, okay?"

"Will do," Angie said.

Claudia knew she was hiding. So what? Maynard *did* make her uncomfortable. Her sponsor's voice was in her head. Gaye would tell her to remove herself from unnecessary stress, and that's exactly what she was doing.

While she was in there, she pulled out the menu to

see if anything they ordered regularly could be adapted for children's fussy taste buds. Her latest brainchild was having tea parties for kids.

Chris, the cook, was working out well. Not just on time, but often early. She'd felt badly about his waiting on the sidewalk for her to come down and open the door, so she'd given him his own key.

Let's see…starting with the brunch menu. Kids would probably like quiche, but not the ones with asparagus or broccoli. She tapped her lower lip with the eraser end of her pencil and thought about what would please both kids and their parents. She ruled out hot dogs the minute that idea popped into her head. A. Choking hazard, and B. She wanted to keep the high-end integrity of the… *Wait. Mac and cheese?* She scribbled it down and planned to talk to Chris later about the feasibility of adding it to the menu.

The office door opened and in walked Maynard, like he belonged there.

"Is something wrong, Maynard?"

"Not at all. I just thought we should visit while I'm waiting for dinner."

"I'm kind of busy, and I thought you had friends to visit with."

Maynard plunked himself onto one of the chairs opposite her desk. "I won't take much of your time. I just wanted to ask if you were busy Saturday night."

"Yes. I'm afraid I'm quite busy every night now."

"Oh, come on. I'm sure you can find a hole in your schedule."

She was about to protest that "no," she really couldn't, when a knock sounded on the door and someone peeked his head around the corner. It was Maynard's male friend.

"The indicators just went off like crazy out here," he said.

Maynard jumped up and strode to his friend who showed him some kind of handheld equipment.

Claudia rose and was about to ask what the device was when the pair returned abruptly to the tea room. Curious what sort of "indicators" they had been looking for, she followed.

As soon as she exited the office, Anthony and Nick spotted her and waved her over.

"Hey, guys. How are things going?" Just for good measure, she stood on tiptoe and gave Anthony a peck on the lips.

He smiled…and so did Nick. The PI didn't look surprised, so either Anthony had told him they were a couple or he'd figured it out for himself.

Claudia glanced over at the trio of geeks and all of them were frowning. Surely they couldn't *all* be upset that she had a man in her life. Something wasn't adding up.

Angie exited the kitchen, carrying a tray with a large teapot and three plates of salad. She grinned in their direction and called out, "Hey, Nick. Hey, Anthony."

"Hey, yourself," Nick called back.

Claudia lowered her voice and asked Nick if he'd located the van.

"Not yet. But they've got an APB out for it. I expect someone will spot it soon."

She focused on Anthony. "Can I talk to you in the office?"

"Of course. Is anything wrong?"

She worried her lip as she glanced over at the party of three, all of whom were still staring in her direction. "I don't know. Maybe."

"Do you need my help?" Nick asked.

"No. It would be better if you could hang out here and talk to Angie. I'm sure she'd appreciate knowing what you just told me."

"Sure," he said and took a table near the front door.

"Angie, I'll be in the office if you need me. Get Nick whatever he wants…on the house."

Anthony smiled but didn't say anything as he followed Claudia into the office.

As soon as she closed the door, he swept her into a strong embrace and angled his lips over hers. After a long, breathless kiss—even though most of his kisses were nearly breathless—he tucked her head under his chin and stroked her hair.

"Is everything all right?"

"I don't know." She took a step back and looked him in the eyes. "One of those guys at Sadie's table is an old boyfriend of mine. Not that I'm still interested or anything," she was quick to add.

Anthony's eyebrows lifted before he could stop his surprised expression. *Of course she has old boyfriends. She's a beautiful girl and could have several.* Still, a twinge of jealousy stabbed his heart, and for a split second he wanted to rip the guy's throat out.

"I'm just telling you this because he asked me out, and I want you to know that will never happen. Even if he was the last man on earth, I'd want nothing to do with him."

Anthony chuckled. *I'm far more apt to be the last man on earth.*

"What's so funny? You don't think I'm attractive to other men?"

"No! Not for a minute." He cupped her face. "I know how beautiful you are, believe me. The thing is…I trust you."

She smiled and her posture relaxed. After a brief hesitation she said, "I trust you too."

Was it time to say, *I love you?* It seemed like a golden opportunity. But would she say it back?

As he was pondering, she moved on to another subject. He didn't hear her at first and had to drag his attention back to what she was saying.

"His friend handed him some kind of metal instrument and they've been frowning over it ever since. What do you think it could be? Some kind of air-quality thingy? Maybe they're measuring our dust mites? I try to keep the place clean…"

"Whoa. What did you say?"

"Dust mites?"

"No, before that. The first thing you said."

"I said his friend was upset that his 'indicators were going crazy.' At least that's what I think I heard. Now they're all acting pissed off."

"Is he a health inspector?"

"No. He's a research biologist."

Anthony scratched his chin. "Hmmm… Let me go talk to them."

Claudia nodded. "Thanks. I'll wait here, if you don't mind."

"I think that's a good idea. They might not want to say anything if you're right there." He grinned. "Especially if he's trying to charm his way into your pants."

Claudia rolled her eyes. "So not possible."

"Good." He winked and left the office, closing the door behind him.

The three people sitting at Sadie's table were crowded around some kind of instrument. It must have been the item Claudia had mentioned. It was about the size and shape of a brick, but made of metal. He saw a light and a dial, and the device did seem to be reacting to something. One of the guys muttered, "Off the charts," under his breath.

"Is everything all right here?" he asked the trio.

One of the men smirked, while the other guy and the woman looked uncomfortable. "Depends on what you call 'all right.' The food is edible, if that's what you mean."

"Just edible?"

"I assume it's great. I haven't eaten yet. I've been… distracted."

"Oh? Does your distraction have to do with that little box you're studying?"

He grinned. "You could say that."

"May I ask what it is?"

The other guy gave him a head shake, but the cocky one kept on talking.

"It measures paranormal activity, and this place is a hotbed of it."

Anthony straightened. "I don't know what you mean. Are you saying our building is haunted?" He leaned over the object, and it made a *ping* sound.

"Oh really? You really don't know what I mean?" He moved toward him and lowered his voice. "Does Claudia know?"

"Know what?"

The guy folded his arms. “You can drop the innocent act.”

But Anthony couldn’t. His only defense was denial, or blaming his abilities on something else. “I’m not acting. I really don’t know what—”

“Let me spell it out for you. You and your friend over there”—he nodded toward Nick—“set off our EMF device the minute you walked in.”

“Hmmm.” Anthony tipped his head and tried to look confused. “I’m sorry. I think your machine that goes ‘ping’ must be broken.”

The guy snorted.

Anthony rejoined Claudia in the office, and as soon as he’d shut the door, he leaned against it.

“What’s wrong? You look like…well, like you’re nervous. I’ve never seen you nervous before. *Ever.* What did he say?”

Anthony held up one finger. *How the hell am I going to explain this? I need to talk to Nick, but not while Claudia’s in here. On the other hand, how can I let her go out there, knowing the “researchers” might tell her something that will scare the daylights out of her? Shit. I knew I’d have to tell her someday, but they’ve just forced my hand.*

“Claudia, honey. There’s something I need to tell you, but this isn’t the place. Maybe we can close early tonight.”

“Close early? But Sadie has a client scheduled. Not to mention it’s bad for business—”

“I don’t give a shit about the business!” Anthony paced

and raked his fingers through his hair. At last he took a deep breath and dropped into one of the chairs. *If only we hadn't given up the extra office space for the kitchen. I'd still have the couch and maybe I could get her naked on it. At least it would keep her from leaving the office.*

Claudia didn't look ready to leave the office, though. She sat in the chair next to him and laid a hand on his arm. "What's wrong, babe? Whatever it is, I'm here for you."

Yeah, but would you stay here if I told you I was a vampire? He wished he could revel in the fact that she'd just used an endearment for the first time. Instead he was so pissed off and worried that he had to put his mental energy toward damage control.

She angled her body toward him, reached out, and took both of his hands in hers. The gesture nearly did him in. She wasn't the least bit afraid of him. Not yet, but he couldn't kid himself anymore. The beautiful little bubble he'd been living in was about to burst.

"Claudia. I—"

The door opened and the weasel poked his head in. "Uh, Claudia. We should speak."

"Get out, Maynard," she said.

Wow. That's not how Claudia would have acted toward a customer in the past. Even a troublesome ex. *Brava, darling.*

Maynard's jaw dropped. When she glared at him, he retreated but left the door ajar. "I'll be right here if you need me."

"I don't need you—for anything. Please, leave."

Anthony rose and shut the door. For good measure, he turned the lock. When it clicked into place, Claudia looked even more concerned, if that were possible.

"What's going on, Anthony? I want to hear it from you." She rose and strolled over to him. Her arms slipped around his waist, and she held him while searching his face for answers.

If only I could mesmerize her…

He wrapped his arms around her and buried his face in her hair. Inhaling her minty shampoo, hoping it wouldn't be the last time.

A loud knock sounded on the door again.

"Oh, for the love of…" Claudia marched over to it. "This crap is not good for my serenity." She closed her eyes for a moment and took a few deep breaths before unlocking and opening the door.

"If you don't leave me al—Oh! Hi, Nick."

Nick tipped his head in confusion. "Bad timing?"

"Sorry. I was being pestered, but not by you. What's up?"

"Three of your customers just walked out without paying. Angie wanted to run after them, but I stopped her."

"Good," Anthony said.

Angie's voice from behind the door said, "Can you put me down now?"

Claudia swung the door open wide, revealing the six-foot-three ex-cop holding the diminutive waitress under his arm like a football.

Claudia covered her mouth as she tried not to chuckle.

"Yeah, yeah," Nick said and set Angie on her feet.

Angie set a hand on her hip and addressed both of her bosses. "Are you just going to let customers leave without paying? Because word will get around that we're serving free food."

"I doubt it," Claudia said. She faced Nick and

continued, "Maynard is an old boyfriend of mine, and when he kept bothering me, I practically tossed him out on his ass."

"Oh." Nick's eyes narrowed. "Did you say, 'Maynard'?"

"Yes. May-nerd. Emphasis on the 'nerd.' Why?"

"What's his last name?"

"Wisenheimer. Oh, wait. That's just what we called him. It's really Oppenheimer."

"Shit. That's the guy I'm looking for!" Nick took off and almost mowed Sadie down as she was coming in. He mumbled, "Sorry, Sadie," and charged out the door.

Angie's eyes were wide. "*That's* the guy who kidnapped Tory?"

"Anthony, why on earth would a Cambridge researcher kidnap an ex-NFL player?"

Anthony shrugged. *Should I make up something stupid like he might be studying the effects of steroids on head injuries?* In the end, he opted for silence.

"Maybe the nerd wanted a muscle transplant." Angie shook her head. "I can't believe I waited on him…and was nice to him despite what an ass—Oh sorry, Claudia. I didn't mean to call your old boyfriend an ass."

"Don't worry. He deserves it."

"I hope Nick tracks down the ass, then. If he's got Tory…" Angie's lips thinned and her eyes shimmered.

Claudia grabbed and hugged her. "Nick will find him. Don't worry."

Anthony wanted to get Claudia out of there before there was any more speculation. He also didn't know how much Claudia had heard regarding their scientific equipment. If Maynard called her later… *Shit. I* have *to tell her.*

"Claudia, you've had a rough day. Why don't you go upstairs and I'll take over here. Don't go anywhere, though. I need to talk to you."

"But I was going to…" She glanced at Angie who was still standing there, listening intently. "Never mind. I can cancel. Come up as soon as you can."

~

Ordinarily Claudia would have refused to leave in the middle of a situation, but she was emotionally spent. AA taught her not to get too hungry, angry, upset, or tired. They called it HALT. Wait a minute…what she'd spelled was HAUT. Okay…so it was hungry, angry, *lonely*, and tired. Either way, it seemed appropriate to go to her apartment and take a load off.

She was supposed to meet her sponsor later and go to a meeting with her, but Anthony said he needed to talk. Considering his earlier reaction, she felt she needed to be there for him.

She could say she wasn't feeling well but she was a terrible liar, so she decided to sell it by holding her nose as she spoke to her sponsor on the phone.

"Gaye. I'b sick. I can' go out todight."

"Oh, no. I'm sorry to hear that. You seemed fine yesterday."

"Yeah, it cabe on sudd'nly."

"Would you like a visit? We could have our own meeting in your living room."

"Uh'd no. I'b contagious an jus' wanna go to bed."

"Okay…"

Somehow Gaye didn't sound convinced, and Claudia

got the impression that her sponsor suspected there was more to it.

The program asked members to be rigorously honest with themselves and implied that they should be honest with other human beings too, and yet there was that little loophole…"except when to do so would injure them or others."

She'd fess up later.

She signed off with a polite "Good 'ight" and told herself that when she found out what was bothering Anthony, she could tell Gaye.

She had just decided to make two cups of hot cocoa when a knock sounded at the door. She thought it was too early for Anthony, so she looked through the peephole. Anthony stood there, gazing at the floor with a pensive expression on his face.

She opened it and stood aside. "Why didn't you use your key?"

"I figured I'd give you the option of letting me in or not. It's your place, after all."

She chuckled. "Why wouldn't I let you in?"

He shifted uncomfortably from foot to foot. "You might not after you hear what I have to say."

A ripple of uneasiness made her nerves tingle. "Why don't you have a seat? I was going to make some cocoa. Do you want some?"

"No. My stomach is too upset." He sat on the sofa. "Go ahead and make some for yourself, though."

She decided to skip the beverage and sat next to him. "Babe, what is it? You're making me nervous."

He stared straight ahead and his spine stiffened as if facing a firing squad. "I lied to you."

She leaned away and studied his face. He seemed perfectly serious. What on earth could he have lied about? His feelings for her? Did he want her to go back to Maynard? Did he want to go back to Ruxandra? She told herself that was ridiculous, but the longer she waited, the crazier her ideas became.

"Well, don't stop there. What did you lie about?"

"I don't have Xeroderma pigmentosum." He dropped his gaze to the floor and his posture slumped.

"Oh. Isn't that good news? Why do you still look so sad?"

Uh-oh. Maybe he really was spending his days with Ruxandra. Any minute now he's going to tell me he's in love with her, and adios, Claudia.

"You may not believe me, but I swear what I'm about to tell you is the gods' honest truth."

She waited for what seemed like days. The anticipation was killing her. Suddenly she wanted a chocolate martini, not a hot cocoa. *Stop that right now*, she told herself. *Whatever it is can't be that bad.*

"You and I have been through a lot together," he began.

She nodded.

"You've always been the bright spot in my…life."

She cocked her head, still not sure where he was going.

"But even though…" He stopped and raked his hands through his hair. "I'm afraid there's no way to sugarcoat it."

"Anthony, honey, whatever it is, I want you to tell me."

He took a deep breath, turned, and looked directly into her eyes. "I'm a vampire." His eyes searched hers as if waiting for some kind of condemnation.

Of all the things he could have said, that was *not* what she was expecting. "Um… You're a what?"

"A vampire. Creature of the night. One of the undead."

She bit her lip. *Any minute now he's going to crack a smile, and the joke will be on me.* But why would he do that? Then she remembered a documentary she'd seen once. Apparently there *are* people who think they're vampires. They sleep in coffins during the day, cut themselves or each other, and drink blood…*ewww.* But on some level, they know they're not *really* undead.

"Are you saying you belong to some cult where people act like vampires?"

He sighed. "No."

"Okay, maybe 'cult' is the wrong word. I know there are people who sleep in coffins and drink blood. Usually they wear goth makeup to make their skin white." She swiped his cheek and checked her finger. *No makeup.* Not that she thought he wore any. His skin was naturally pale and she blamed that on his "condition," which she now knew he didn't have. Apparently he just reversed his sleep patterns.

She shrugged. "I'm okay with it, Anthony. I mean, you gotta be who you gotta be. Right?"

His posture straightened. "Are you serious?"

She cupped his cheek in a loving gesture. He turned into it and kissed her palm.

"I can't believe how well you're taking this. I mean, I expected the very worst. I thought you'd scream. Run from me. Never want to see me again."

She chuckled. "Of course not, silly. I…" She stopped herself half a second before she said, *I love you.* For one thing, she wanted him to say it first, and for another…

He swept her into a tight embrace, and as his lips crushed hers, she forgot what she was thinking. All she could do was feel.

Chapter 11

Gods, I love this woman, and it's time to tell her so.

As soon as he broke the kiss, he cupped her face and said, "I love you. Truly. So much."

She smiled and her expression grew into a grin. "I love you too. I have for years."

"Really?" He scrutinized her and saw nothing but complete sincerity. "Is that why you didn't date anyone seriously?" He caught himself. That was assuming a lot. "Well, not that it was any of my business. I wasn't keeping track of what you did every minute of every day."

Her gaze dropped. "I tried to. I told myself it was useless waiting for you to notice me. You had Ruxandra."

He snorted. "Since the day I met you, I've wanted no one but you. I held off as long as I did because of her. I didn't know if I could keep you safe, and I couldn't bear it if anything happened to you because of my *former* relationship with her."

"Are you saying you and she haven't been together since we met?"

"Yes. That's what I'm saying. Furthermore, I moved to Boston to get away from her, but somehow she tracked me here."

"Tracked you?"

"Yes. Vampires have superior senses of smell, vision, and hearing. I thought taking a train from New Orleans would mask my scent. Perhaps it did. Maybe Boston was just a lucky guess on her part. After all, she knew I lived here in the seventeenth century."

Claudia leaned away, and confusion wrinkled her pretty brow. "You mean it was so long ago that it *felt* like the seventeenth century. Right?"

After a long pause, her eyes widened. "Right?" she repeated a little louder.

"Uh, no. I actually lived in the seventeenth century. I was born in Avon, England. I sailed to America as an indentured servant in sixteen-seventy-two. You should have seen the seventies, back then. Waaaay different." He attempted a smile, but she didn't move a muscle. Her jaw hung slack, and he had to snap his fingers to be sure he hadn't accidentally mesmerized her. She blinked.

"I, um…" She never finished her sentence. She just turned away and appeared to be pondering deeply.

"I suppose I should have mentioned that vampires are immortal. Did you not know that?"

She bit her lip and stared at him.

"Claudia, say something."

"What do you want me to say?"

"Say that you believe me. I'm telling you the gods' honest truth. Say you don't hate me just because I revealed what I am. Say *you know* I'd never hurt you."

"I…"

Apparently she couldn't say any of those things. Or anything else. Anthony took a deep breath and scrubbed a hand over his face. "I shouldn't have told you so much and expected you to accept everything all at once."

"No. It's not that…"

"Then what is it?"

"I—I don't know what to do. I've never had to tell someone they needed professional help before."

He straightened his spine. "Professional help? Oh, my gods. You think I'm delusional?"

"Well…" She gave a little shrug and blushed. "Lil' bit."

He let out that deep breath he'd taken in a whoosh. "I knew you were accepting this too easily. Did you believe any of it?"

"Some. You said you're a creature of the night, and since I've never seen you during the day, I figured that was true. I've never seen you drink blood, but I was willing to give you that one. I figured it was probably tomato juice that you pretend is blood. Or wine. Superior senses? Okay. But immortality? Really?"

"Really."

"I, um…"

"What?"

"I need to talk to my sponsor about this."

"No!" He regretted shouting immediately.

She jumped backward about a foot. "I'm sorry, but I have to. Don't I? I'm supposed to tell her everything that might affect my sobriety."

His jaw dropped. "You're going to drink? Because of me?"

"No. Of course not."

"Then why should you tell your sponsor? Would you tell her if you got a letter in the mail?"

"If that letter said something life-altering, yes. If it was another sale flyer or credit card offer, or a charity begging for money I don't have, then no. I'd toss those letters in the trash and never give them a second thought."

He rose and paced. "Claudia, you *cannot* tell Gaye. It's not your secret to tell."

"Oh," she said quietly.

When she didn't say anything more, he reseated himself beside her. He took both her hands in his and was relieved when she didn't recoil. "My touch is cool, isn't it?"

"Yes. It usually is. I just thought you had poor circulation."

"You could say that. I haven't fed recently. I'd warm up if I fed from a live source. However, I rarely do that… And when I do, it's from a pig or chicken. *Not* humans."

After a long pause she relaxed slightly. "Well, I guess that's something."

"Yes. I do what I can."

She bit her lip and searched his eyes.

"What is it?"

"Ruxandra. Is she…"

"A vampire? Yes. I'm afraid so."

"Does she have the same—um—ethics about drinking blood from humans?"

Holy shit. What can I say, honestly? "I don't know what she does anymore. And I don't care to."

"Do you know where she lives…or un-lives? Is that a word?" She shook her head. "I'm so confused."

Anthony pulled Claudia into a gentle embrace. "You are my only concern. You and Sadie. She's my niece, not my aunt. My seventh great-niece."

Claudia slapped a hand over her eyes, as if to say she'd had enough of this. But there was more he had to tell her.

He tipped up Claudia's chin so she could see the sincerity on his face. "I know I'll outlive you, and that's another reason I tried to stay away. Some vampires lose so many friends and lovers over the centuries that they decide not to get involved with humans at all. It's grim going through heartbreak after heartbreak." He swept a lock of hair behind her ear. "Please don't break my heart before we've had a chance to enjoy what makes the risk worthwhile."

The expression on her face could only be viewed as sympathetic. "So, have you? Gone through heartbreak after heartbreak, I mean?"

"No. I've had plenty of casual affairs with humans, but nothing serious. Especially not if Ruxandra was around. She's sabotaged every relationship I ever had a chance at."

"How?"

Anthony rolled his eyes. "She's very creative, and I think she considers it a game. She wrote a letter to one woman saying she'd won thousands of dollars and had to go to Denver to claim her prize. She made others think we were married. She told a whole group of women I had syphilis. Basically, she'll stop at nothing to get in my way."

Claudia worried her lip again and looked at the floor.

"What is it, honey?"

"Has she ever killed anyone?"

Fuck. That was the one question he didn't want to answer.

As if she'd read the answer in his eyes, she continued, "Do you think she'd kill me if she could?"

He stroked her cheek. "Kurt assured me you're safe."

"That's not what I asked."

He hung his head. "I know."

She straightened. "I know what you're thinking."

"You do?"

"Yeah. You're thinking we should never have taken our relationship beyond friendship. That you put me in danger. Right?"

He nodded.

"I want you to know I don't regret a minute of it. I wouldn't do anything differently. Well, except maybe not wait five years to tell you how I feel. You're the best thing that's ever happened to me. She can try to ruin it if she wants to. I won't let her."

Claudia cupped his cheek in a loving gesture that he didn't deserve. How could she be so understanding?

He remembered their conversation about her sister. Perhaps that's what made her...*her*. Someone able to empathize. Someone able to love. Someone he could love forever—if only.

He dove for her mouth and she reclined out of necessity. His kiss made her weak in the knees and her head spun. Hands were everywhere. One of his arms held her tight against him while his other hand traveled down her back, over her bottom, down her thigh, and back up. He dragged her skirt up almost to her waist.

Meanwhile, she was fondling his muscled chest with one hand and using the other to shove at his jacket, trying to push it off his shoulder.

She felt a sharp prink on her tongue and retracted it. But just the pressure of their lips and the vacuum produced by the suction felt delectable in and of itself.

He broke the kiss just long enough to whip off the restricting garment and fling it. She didn't know or care where it landed. She simply wanted the rest of his clothes to join it.

He was more adept at removing her clothing. He had unbuttoned her blouse and was massaging her breast without her even feeling a tug. Her bra popped open in the back and her skirt's zipper rasped.

I'd better concentrate on getting his clothes off, or I'll look like I lost the world's fastest game of strip poker.

She had to use both hands to unbutton his shirt and lost the tenuous balance that was keeping her on the couch. Anthony reached beneath her and caught her before she hit the floor. Instead of hauling her back up, he lowered her gently and joined her on the thick area rug.

He swept her hair back off her forehead and stared into her eyes as she finished fumbling with his shirt buttons.

"I love you, Claudia. I never thought I'd say those words to any woman."

She'd just started grappling with his belt and stopped. "What? You've never said 'I love you' before?"

"Never."

Claudia was speechless. Just as well. He used the opportunity to finish what would have taken her another few minutes. In seconds, they were both naked on the floor.

He leaned over her and kissed her at length. His hand fondled her breast and created electric sensations within her. After caressing the other breast, his hand slid lower. When he touched her sweet spot, she arched and moaned into his mouth. He leaned back and smiled.

She seized his cock and began stroking it. His eyes closed and he let out a low groan.

I've never imagined a cock could get so big.

"I'm glad you're impressed."

Had he just spoken? Had she? Claudia stopped what

she was doing. He opened his eyes and stared at her, even though his lids were only half open.

"Did...did you just read my mind?"

"I think so. Yes."

"And you replied in your mind?"

"Yes. I didn't speak."

"Holy..."

Claudia was about to sit up, but he grabbed her arm.

"Where are you going?"

"Nowhere. I just..." What *was* she about to do? Sit up and talk? *Yeah, right. Talking could wait.* Lovemaking was what needed to happen now, and knowing how much pleasure his body could bring, she didn't want to wait.

He smiled and said, "I agree."

"Shoot! Are you reading my mind again?"

"Don't worry about it. There's only one thing on both our minds."

He crushed his lips to hers in a deep, drugging kiss, and she forgot everything except how he was making her feel. *Good. So good.*

He broke the kiss and his tongue swept over her nipple. She shivered. When he latched onto her breast and sucked, his fingers found her opening. He inserted first one and then two fingers while she writhed in pleasure.

He added his thumb to the frenzy and rubbed her clit. She arched right off the floor and let out a surprised gasp. He moved to the other breast and suckled as he continued what he was doing with his hand. The onslaught to her senses had her moaning uncontrollably.

She was close. There's no way she could hold off until he was inside her. He seemed to understand and rubbed harder, faster, until she came apart in his arms. Her cries of ecstasy continued, and her thighs vibrated as she rode the wave of sensation. When she didn't think she could take any more, she whimpered, "Stop…please."

He withdrew his fingers and held her close while she came back to earth.

"Oh, my God," she said.

He grinned and kissed her again. When he let her up for air, she murmured, "I love you." With a glow in his eyes she hadn't seen before, he said, "I love you too."

There was nothing like it. She'd never made love while she was *in* love before. Suddenly she understood a quote she'd heard: "For men, sex is ninety percent below the neck, but for women it's the ninety percent above that counts," or something like that. Anyway, it made sense to her now.

Thinking about Anthony's ninety percent, she opened her legs, as wobbly as they were. "I'm ready," she whispered.

He kissed her forehead and asked, "Are you sure?"

"Try me."

They both grinned as he positioned himself at her opening and entered her slowly until he was fully seated.

She cooed—that was the only word she could think of to describe the sound that came out. He felt so right filling her.

"It feels good for me too," he said, and she was reminded about that mind-reading thing. At the moment, she didn't care. She just wanted him to make love to her.

He began a slow rhythm of thrusts and parries until they acclimated to each other and moved together. She wanted to satisfy him as completely as he had her. The desire in his eyes was so authentic that she could feel it.

Or maybe it was just her own yearning for him. Either way, having sex with him was more beautiful than she could have imagined, and she'd imagined it plenty over the years.

He surprised her by raising himself in a one-arm push-up.

"There are certain advantages that come with a vampire lover," he said.

His free hand found her sweet spot and rubbed, bringing back the intense sensations she'd experienced only moments ago.

"Oh, my," she whispered. "This is for you, Anthony. You've satisfied me already."

"I want us to climax together."

It took only seconds before her inner muscles clenched and exploded, sending her up and over some invisible cliff. She felt like she was flying…or like her spirit had left her body. The whole time, she was screaming in a voice she didn't recognize.

Anthony's body stilled and then jerked a few times.

When Claudia finally quieted and stopped vibrating, she opened her eyes and realized he had been watching her. He smiled like the cat who got the cream, so to speak.

Claudia grasped him around his neck and hugged him hard. He lowered his body to gently rest on top of her.

"Am I too heavy for you?"

"Never."

A few hours later, Claudia was sitting on the edge of her bed, pulling on a pair of socks. "Are you sure you have to go?"

"Yes. You aren't ready to witness my death sleep."

"Who says?"

Anthony sighed. "Claudia, it's disturbing. My blood drains away from my face, and my body goes rigid. Seriously. I appear clinically dead—with rigor mortis. You couldn't rouse me if you wanted any afternoon delight anyway, so what's the point?"

Claudia gingerly pulled up her jeans. "I'm too sore for much more nookie. I just wanted to—you know—prove I can handle it. If you need to crash here some night, I want you to feel that you can."

Already dressed, Anthony strolled over to her and gently cupped her cheek. "I have no doubt you'd take care of me in an emergency, but this isn't one."

"We still need to talk about that mind-reading thing. What *was* that anyway?"

One side of his mouth quirked up, like he was thinking about smiling but suddenly changed his mind.

"There's someone I'd like to talk to first. I've heard certain things, but I'd like to make sure it's true before I spread rumors."

"Would you like to invite him over? I'd be interested in hearing what he has to say too."

"It's almost dawn. He's a day-walker, but I'm not. I'll try to speak to him some night this week."

Claudia's eyes rounded. "You mean there are vampires who can walk around in daylight?"

"I only know of two. They're a married couple who live here in Boston."

"But how?"

He shrugged. "That's another thing I'll ask them."

Hope for a normal life started to emerge, but Claudia

tamped it down quickly. She didn't want to set herself up for disappointment. *Still, it would be nice to go on a picnic or something if we wanted to.*

"Look. I have to go, but you have a great day." He rested his forehead against hers. "I'm sorry I didn't let you sleep much."

"I'm not. I feel more relaxed and rejuvenated than I would have with ten hours of sleep."

"Well, don't be afraid to tell me you need to leave early if you're tired tonight." He walked her to the living room with an arm around her waist.

"I'll be fine." She tipped up her chin, puckered, and closed her eyes. He answered with a passionate kiss that made her toes curl. *Wow.*

"Wow, indeed. I love you, darling."

"Love you too," she said aloud, letting him know she heard him.

"See you tonight. Remember, I'm trusting you not to tell *anyone* what I told you," he said.

"I won't. I promise."

"Good girl." He smiled, then strode to the door and let himself out.

A little patronizing, but I can work with that. Instead of following behind him and locking the door, Claudia made a detour to her kitchen. Suddenly she was starving. She pulled a loaf of bread out of the cabinet, planning to make toast. Something easy.

A few seconds later, someone knocked on her door.

She set down the bread and strode to the door, pausing to look through the keyhole. Anthony was still there.

"Lock it!" he called out. Then he disappeared and she heard him trotting down the stairs.

She smiled. *He* does *love me—in a kind of controlling way.* She turned the dead bolt and slid the chain across for good measure. *So, he's a little domineering. I guess everyone has their faults.*

Chapter 12

Claudia's fatigue had made the next day seem extra long. She smiled as she remembered the reason for it. She'd known making love with Anthony would be incredible, but she'd never expected him to have the stamina to last all night long. *Is that a vampire thing too?* She had so many questions and still wondered if he might just be delusional.

AA taught acceptance and advised members to live and let live. *Isn't that what I'm doing?* She had no idea if that advice applied to learning about the existence of vampires or not. Her sponsor had said to use the Serenity Prayer in all instances, so it was worth a try.

"God, grant me the serenity to accept the things I cannot change..." *If Anthony is a vampire, I don't think I can change that.*

"Courage to change the things I can..." *I'm totally ignorant when it comes to his "condition" or whatever it is, but I can ask questions and learn.*

"And the wisdom to know the difference." *I have no wisdom right now. Maybe I'll get some later.*

Autumn worked the earlier shift so Angie could have a much-needed day off. Nick hadn't managed to capture the researchers and hadn't found the van. They must have taken off in it before he reached them, and the APB hadn't produced results, either. Nick said it must be parked in a private garage.

If only Maynard had given her an address or phone number, Claudia thought. If he showed up in the tea room again, she would throttle him and make him hand over his contact info. Correction. She'd get the information first, *then* throttle him. What he wanted with Tory was still a mystery. So far, no one had contacted Tory's family in New Rochelle for ransom. Now his family was worried sick, too.

Claudia's heart leaped when the little bells over the door announced Anthony's arrival. She grinned automatically and he mirrored her expression.

"Anthony and I will be in the office, Autumn," she called. "Knock if you need us."

"Okay," the quiet college student said.

As soon as they were behind closed doors, Anthony swept Claudia into a tight embrace and captured her lips in a fervent kiss. She slipped her arms around his neck and kissed him back with equal enthusiasm. Their tongues met and swirled. He applied a bit of suction, and she felt that slight prick of pain again.

This time she pulled away and touched her tongue. A tiny spot of blood showed on her finger when she checked it. *What the hell?*

"I'm sorry, darling. My fangs descended without me realizing it."

"Fangs?" she asked aloud.

"Well, yes." He opened his mouth and lifted one side of his upper lip.

Sure enough, what she'd call a fang occupied the incisor space and hung lower than the rest of his teeth. *Why didn't I notice that before?*

"Because sometimes strong emotions trigger the bloodlust."

He opened his mouth, and she watched as the incisors shrunk to normal size.

"Holy shit. You mean, you can really bite someone and drink blood through your fangs?"

Suddenly she became light-headed.

He nodded. A moment later, he said, "Slow your breathing, honey." Anthony must have noticed she was hyperventilating before she did. He braced her around her back and under her forearm, and escorted her to a chair.

Either that was an amazing trick, or he really is *a vampire!*

His face fell. "I thought you believed me."

"I—I did. It's just that, in the light of day, and with a clearer mind, I wondered…"

"You thought you were wrong to believe it, and that I was delusional."

"Yes," she said, under her breath.

Anthony took the chair next to her. After a long pause he asked, "Are you okay?"

"I—yes. I will be. I just need a meeting and a good night's sleep."

"You won't tell anybody. *Right?*"

"Of course not. I promised. Besides, I doubt anyone would believe me."

He smiled and took her hand. "I'm pretty sure most people would doubt your sanity. I'd advise against putting yourself in that position."

"No shit." She didn't usually swear, but letting a few curse words fly relieved the tension somewhat. She gazed up at him.

Anthony was rubbing his thumb across the palm of her hand. "I know I told you this before, but I'd never hurt you. You believe me, don't you?"

His expression couldn't have been more sincere.

"Yes. I believe you."

He rose. "Why don't I let you go upstairs and take that nap?"

"Yeah." She had no problem taking off a little early. She wished she was upstairs under her covers right now.

She grabbed her blazer from the coatrack. It was getting so cold that even the few steps from the shop to her apartment door chilled her.

"Tell Autumn I'll be out in a minute. I want to make a quick phone call, "Anthony said.

"Okay."

Claudia relayed the message to Autumn over her shoulder as she hurried toward the door. Once she hit the sidewalk, a stranger stepped into her path. She almost walked into him.

"Oh. Excuse me." *Where did he come from?*

"Claudia?" he asked.

"Yes?"

What seemed like only a blink later, she was in a completely different place. The noise of the street had vanished, and other than candlelight, she was standing in the dark. Ruxandra stood in front of her. The guy who'd appeared on the sidewalk stood a few feet to one side.

Claudia took a step backward.

"Whoa. Where do you think you're going?" Ruxandra reached out to grab her arm. Instead she shouted, "*Ouch*," and recoiled. "Damn it! I broke another fingernail on you."

Claudia watched as Ruxandra cradled her hand and her fingernail grew back. *Jesus! Is that another vampire thing?*

Ruxandra faced the guy with her hands on her hips. "See? I can't touch her, and she ruined my manicure. Can you touch her? Try it. Touch anything you want on her."

Claudia recoiled.

The guy laughed. "You didn't pay me for that. You wanted me to bring her to you, and I did. Now give me what you owe me."

"I'll *double it* if you'll sink your fangs into her. No need to drain her dry. Just weaken her so she's less of a problem. You'll get your money, plus the bonus of a good meal."

"You know it's hard to stop once we get started."

Claudia skimmed the room, looking for some means of escape. The only door appeared to be locked, chained, and bolted with a giant board held in place by two iron brackets. She began to whimper.

"Don't cry," the guy said. "I'm not going to kill you. Not for a measly grand."

"I just want to know if you can touch her!"

"Ha!" He sauntered to the door. "Call me when you have more cash."

He lifted the heavy board like it was a stick. Ruxandra crossed her arms and pouted. Claudia figured if she timed it right, she might be able to rush past him when he opened the door to leave. She watched him slip the heavy chain out of its iron ring and got ready. One turn of the dead bolt later, he opened it wide.

She scrambled toward the door, but before she knew

it, she was flying through the air backward. She hit the wall and cried out.

Ruxandra bent over laughing. "How did you do that?"

"Simple physics. Even if there's some kind of force field around her, she can't walk through a closed door. I closed and opened this one so fast that she didn't see it and bounced off—force field and all."

The guy closed the door and Ruxandra stumbled over to it, still laughing, to lock it behind him.

Claudia remembered reading some advice about how to avoid becoming a victim. The article said not to appear vulnerable. "What the fuck just happened?" She rose and crossed her arms. Her backside was sore, but she refused to let Ruxandra know.

"I might not be able to touch you, but it was funny as hell to watch someone else batting you away like a fly. Now, if only I could get him to do that all night, I'd never stop laughing."

Claudia didn't respond. She just stood her ground. Meanwhile, her mind whirred with panicky thoughts. Was there any possibility of escape? Would Anthony look for her? Did he know where to look? Should she talk to the woman or ignore her altogether? Would ignoring her infuriate her more? Claudia guessed that it would.

Still trying not to appear helpless, she initiated the conversation. "So, you want me dead. Do you really think Anthony will love you if you kill me?"

Ruxandra's eyes revealed a flash of indecision…as if she knew he would never forgive her. A moment later, her lips thinned. She straightened her spine and puffed out her chest. Her hourglass figure created the kind of curves in her red clingy dress that any man would find hard to resist. She tipped her nose in the air. "At this point I don't care what he wants. I refuse to be rejected for a mere mortal." A sinister smile spread across her face. "You *do* know what we are, don't you?"

The way she said it sounded as if she hoped Claudia didn't know. Like she couldn't wait to be the first to tell her. As bad as the news was, Claudia was glad she knew the truth and couldn't be blindsided by it. "Oh. You mean that you're vampires?" she asked as casually, as if noting they were both European.

Ruxandra's jaw dropped. "He told you?"

"Mmm-hmm."

The buxom blond appeared unable to speak as she assimilated the information. Finally, she asked incredulously, "And you're not terrified?"

"Not of him. I know Anthony would never hurt me."

Ruxandra snorted. "Ha. I've known him a lot longer than you have. *A lot.* He's killed plenty of people over the centuries. Sometimes, even without meaning to. What makes you think you'll be different?"

Claudia shrugged, still trying to appear nonchalant despite this new information. "I suppose I'll just have to trust him to keep his word."

Ruxandra let out a burst of a laugh. It sounded forced. "You can't trust a vampire. We don't play by the same rules you do. We're far superior to humans. We don't have to stoop to your level. If we feel like taking advantage of you, we will, and there's nothing you can do about it."

"Mmm. I suppose. But if that's true, why aren't vampires running rampant through the streets, making humans their slaves?"

Ruxandra's face turned red and she stomped her foot. "Stop talking. I'm sick of answering your stupid questions."

In other words, you don't know the answers or you don't like them.

Despite the volatile vampire circling her, Claudia remained composed. She was amazed that Kurt's spell was working so well. As she watched Ruxandra's face studying her, she became a little less confident. The woman was trying to figure out a way around the magic. Of that she was sure.

At last, Ruxandra stopped pacing and stood right in front of Claudia, hands on her hips. "So, why can't I touch you? Is it some kind of protection spell?"

Claudia just shrugged. She didn't want to put Kurt in danger by revealing what he'd done to help.

Ruxandra sighed. "I suppose this will be useless, but I might as well try." She leaned toward Claudia. Her eyes turned from blue to gold to purple.

"Hey. Your eyes changed colors. Anthony can do that too."

Ruxandra took a step back. "What? I'm not surprised that I can't mesmerize you, but Anthony can't, either?"

"Is that what you were trying to do? Mesmerize me?"

Ruxandra paced with her hands clasped behind her back. "First Kurt, now you. I can't believe I've lost my power to—Wait. Ah-ha! Kurt. Of course! He's a wizard. He must have done a spell to protect both himself and you from vampires."

Claudia didn't know what to say. She had hoped Ruxandra wouldn't figure it out, for poor Kurt's sake.

Ruxandra's pacing became jaunty. "Well, then. I

guess I'll give Kurt the time of day after all." She tapped her lip. "I'll have to find him while it's still dark. Do you know where he is?" She gave Claudia a smarmy smile.

As if I'd tell Ruxandra anything about my friends. Fortunately, she didn't know where Kurt lived. She just assumed it was near Boston Uncommon since he was there all the time.

"I have no idea."

Ruxandra squinted at her.

"Really. I don't know."

"Fine, but don't think that you can escape, just because I have to leave to look for him."

Claudia hadn't taken a really good look around the dimly lit room. Surreptitiously, she surveyed her surroundings. There appeared to be no windows, only the one door, and a few possessions.

"It used to be a carriage house. Someone restored it, probably hoping to make the place into a studio apartment or something. But with no plumbing and no windows, and a roadblock or two, courtesy of the city building codes..." She smiled as if she knew something—or had made it happen. "It's only used for storage, so I got it cheap." She wandered over to an old trunk in the corner. There wasn't just one trunk. There were two with something between them, acting like a long, low coffee table. Suddenly Claudia recognized it as a coffin and her mouth went dry.

Before she realized it, she had duct tape over her mouth and her wrists were clamped to her sides. She had never seen anyone move so fast. It must be another vampire talent.

"There." Ruxandra tossed the roll of tape back into

one of the trunks and wiped her hands against each other as if to say, "That's that."

"Maa a minim. Ow id ou uh meh?"

"How did I touch you? I didn't. I just spread out the tape and ran around you until it stuck to itself.

Fabulous.

"Now be a good little captive and sit against the back wall while I leave and lock up."

Claudia lifted her chin in defiance.

"I have plenty more duct tape," Ruxandra said, narrowing her eyes.

Claudia knew better than to test the murderous vampire. She plodded to the back wall and slid down until her back was leaning against it. She might need her legs—and her sharp stilettos—later.

Anthony had said good night to Autumn and Chris and locked up after them. He hoped Claudia would be home, but he didn't want to wake her if she was taking a nap. Or maybe he did, he realized with a smile.

He took the stairs to her apartment two at a time and knocked on her door. Not only was there no answer, but he didn't hear anything at all. He pressed his ear against the door, hoping to detect the long, deep breaths of slumber. Still nothing.

Oh well. She must have gone to a meeting.

Wondering how he'd kill a couple hours, he returned to the sidewalk.

"Anthony!"

He knew that shrill voice.

"Ruxandra," he said with a nod when she caught

up to him. That was all the acknowledgment he'd give her.

"Are you all right? You look sad," she said.

He let out a deep sigh. "If I'm sad, it's because of you."

She reared back. "Because of me? What did I do?"

"It's what you won't do. You won't move on. I've been too kind to you in the past, but no more. I refuse to put up with your interference and sabotage. I won't have you ruin another minute of my long life."

Her eyes widened, but she didn't interrupt.

I might as well use this opportunity to get it all out there. "If you loved me as you claim to, you'd respect my rights. The same rights everyone in this country has. The right to life, liberty, and the pursuit of happiness. For the record, you haven't let me pursue happiness for decades—long before I met Claudia. I'm not going to let you ruin this. I've finally found someone I love, who loves me…someone I want to settle down with. I can't keep worrying that you might try to—"

Ruxandra held up one hand. "Stop."

Anthony sensed something was different. Instead of railing at him and pounding on his chest, or crying in some melodramatic pose, she stood quietly, waiting for her turn to speak. He folded his arms and let her proceed.

"I realize I've been a little possessive in the past…"

A little?

"But I've done nothing to deserve your anger lately. I've done exactly what you asked me to. I've left Claudia alone."

Hmmm… Something didn't seem right.

"Besides, I'm with Kurt now."

Anthony's expression must have betrayed his shock.

Her lips twitched up for a second. “What? You didn’t think I’d stay single forever, did you? I can’t wait around for you to come to your senses. If you don’t want my company, there are plenty of others who do.”

“I—I don’t doubt that. You’re an attractive woman, Ruxandra—when you’re not being a pain in the ass.”

“Well, don’t worry. I won’t be.”

He kept wondering when the other fang was going to drop. When she’d start the guilt trip, the begging…

She held out her hand. “I’d like us to be cordial to one another.”

Still no tears. He could barely believe this was happening. Reluctantly, he reached for her hand and shook it.

“There. No hard feelings. Right?”

He wanted so badly to believe her. “Right. No hard feelings…as long as this is genuine. I’ll be twice as angry if I find out you’re duping me.”

“I have no desire to dupe you or anyone else. I’ve always been very honest about my feelings and intentions.”

If she’s talking about her obsessive feelings and intention to control me, she’s not wrong.

“You don’t happen to know where I could find Kurt now, do you?”

“No. Don’t you have his phone number?”

“Silly me. I lost it. Could you give it to me again? Please?”

Anthony didn’t want to throw his buddy in harm’s way, in case this was all an act. “I’ll call him for you.”

She didn’t protest or try to manipulate him into giving her the number.

Maybe this is real.

He dialed Kurt.

Kurt and Nick were scoping out a row of industrial-looking buildings on Lansdowne Street in Cambridge. Kurt had nothing of Tory's to make a tracking device, but Nick had used his powerful sense of smell to follow the latest victim's scent to the edge of Central Square. By combining that with Sadie's description, they hoped to find what they were after.

"Did she say she found the cages in the basement or on the first floor?" Nick asked.

Kurt stopped walking and said, "Let me replay that part in my head." He closed his eyes and used his magic to conjure up a photographic memory of the night Sadie astral-projected into the lab.

Before he had his answer, his cell phone rang. It disturbed his concentration, so he decided to answer it and go back to memory lane later.

"Hey, Anthony. What's up?"

"Ruxandra wants to talk to you."

"Me?" Kurt scratched his head.

"Yeah. Why do you sound surprised? She says you're together now."

"Really? Huh."

Nick's eyes narrowed. With his wolf's auditory senses, he could probably hear the conversation on both ends.

"I didn't think I was making much progress in that area."

"Oh, give me that phone," a female voice growled. A second later, Ruxandra took over for Anthony. "Hello, lover. You knew it was just a matter of time before I succumbed to your charm, didn't you?"

"Well, no. Is that what you're doing?"

"Jesus..." she muttered. Then she switched back to her syrupy sweet voice. "Who could resist you? Don't answer that. It was rhetorical."

"Okaaaaay..."

"I'd like to see you. I want to apologize for being so ungracious and refusing your lovely invitation to the movies."

Nick folded his arms and stared at him. Kurt turned around so he didn't have to look at his friend's doubting face.

"I'm kind of busy at the moment."

Ruxandra huffed. "It figures."

"Don't get me wrong. I'd love to see you. I'm just tied up with something over in Cambridge." Then he got an idea, probably not a good one, but what the hell. "You can come here and help me if you want."

After a brief hesitation she said, "I'd love to. Where should I meet you?"

"There's a Starbucks on Mass Ave. Central Square. You can get here on the Red Line."

She humphed. "Public transportation?"

"Why not? Are you too good to take the T?"

He thought he heard a gasp. Kurt glanced over his shoulder and saw Nick covering his mouth, as if holding in one of his booming laughs.

"Fine," she said. "I'll be there in twenty to forty minutes depending on the whims of the MBTA."

"Great! I'll see you then."

When he hung up, Nick couldn't hold it any longer and burst out laughing.

"What?"

"You and Ruxandra? Have you lost your mind?"

"Probably. Look, it started as a favor to Anthony. We thought we might be able to protect Claudia if Ruxandra didn't feel completely rejected. Then, I considered it a challenge. But the more I thought about it, the more I realized I'd really like a chance with a gorgeous woman who has the ability to be loyal in her nature. Sure, her loyalty has been misguided in the past, but it's there for the reshaping. Do you know how many old girlfriends have cheated on me?"

"No. How many?"

"All of them."

"You're kidding. Are you bad judge of character, or do you just let your pecker do the picking?"

Kurt shrugged. "Hell if I know."

"Look, she's beautiful. There's no doubt about it. But aren't you afraid she'll lose her mind and drain you dry the first time you have a disagreement? Remember, she tried to harpoon my wife."

Kurt lifted his chin. "I wouldn't have asked her out if there was a moment when I doubted I could handle her."

Nick shook his head. "C'mon. She's a paranormal—a supernatural being with powers beyond yours. Vamps are not known for their patience or sense of fairness. Anthony is the exception. Most are loose cannons, and she's the loosest cannon I've ever known."

Kurt reached up and set a hand on his tall friend's shoulder. "Try to hurt me, big fella."

Nick chuckled. "You're kidding, right?"

"Nope. I want you to see for yourself. I'm not stupid."

"I never thought you were, which is why I'm so surprised you'd consider a suicide date like a movie with Ruxandra."

Kurt let his hand drop and stood his ground. "Go ahead. Takc a swing at me."

"I will not. You're my friend."

"And as my friend, I'm asking you to knock some sense into me."

"Oh, well, if you put it that way..." Nick looked like he was going to swat Kurt's face with an open palm.

"Not like a girly girl. Do it like you imagine Ruxandra would."

Nick blew out a deep breath. "You're an idiot, but if this is what you need..." He reared back, formed a fist, and let it fly.

Before Nick made contact with Kurt's face, he did some quick mathematical calculations and jumped out of the way—then snapped back. The motion was so quick that he knew Nick's fist would seem to have passed through him.

"Fuck. I didn't know you could do that."

"There a lot I can do that you don't know about. And neither does Ruxandra. I've gifted myself with every one of her supernatural powers but without the nasty side effects of bloodlust and sun sensitivity. Now do you believe I can handle myself around her?"

Nick scratched his chin. "I'm skeptically hopeful. Let's put it that way."

"You know, I was going to ask Anthony to help us when we locate the lab. We'll need someone to mesmerize the whole staff and make them forget they were ever aware of paranormals."

"Yeah. I remember you saying that. But if you can do everything she can do, can't you mesmerize everyone?"

"Yes and no. I can use regular hypnosis or a spell, but it only works if the other person is willing. If there's someone there who's resistant and can mesmerize me before I do it to them, we're sunk."

"So, you need a backup."

"Exactly."

"What makes you think you can trust her not to mesmerize you into believing anything she wants you to believe?"

"For some reason, Ruxandra can't mesmerize me. She's tried it. But I've seen her use that power with other humans, so it's not like she's doing it wrong or has lost it or anything."

"Hmmm…I don't know."

"Seriously. Let's ask Ruxandra to do it. Anthony's always helping us. It might be a good test to see if she can be altruistic."

Nick let out a bark of a laugh. "I don't know if you're delusional or brilliant when it comes to Ruxandra. For your sake, let's hope it's your big brain doing the thinking, not the little one in your pants."

Chapter 13

Ruxandra had put up with public transportation and the smells of the great unwashed to meet Kurt at the coffee shop. But he wasn't even there. She was about to stomp out in a huff when he finally showed up.

"Nice of you to join me," she said with one hand planted on her hip.

"I can leave, if you prefer." He moved toward the door as if he'd actually walk out on her. The nerve!

Just what I need...another infuriating man. Then she remembered she wanted something from him and stopped herself from making a rude quip. "Wait."

He returned to her and sighed. "Sorry I'm late. I probably should have said that first. Would you like a coffee?"

"No thanks. It dehydrates me."

"Bottled water, then?"

Knowing she needed a certain amount of fluid to keep her blood intake from coagulating—especially those platelet-rich A-positive blood cells, she accepted. Kurt paid for her water and his double espresso and escorted her into the chilly night.

"So, what are you doing over here in Cambridge?" she asked, innocently. "I thought you lived in Boston."

"I do. I live in the North End."

Ruxandra was proud of herself. Now she knew where the wizard lived. Either he wasn't too bright, or he wanted her to know for some reason. She would have congratulated herself on her cleverness, except she knew the man wasn't stupid. He might not be telling the truth. He could be sending her in the opposite direction if she ever wanted to hunt him down.

He slipped an arm around her waist as he continued. "About what I'm doing here…I'm glad you asked. I'm on a mission, one I hope you'll help me with."

"A mission? I thought you were out of the military."

He chuckled. "It's not that kind of mission. This is personal."

His intense stare gave her the opening she needed to try mesmerizing him again. She looked directly into his eyes and began by asking a logical, innocuous question. Something he'd assume was just part of the conversation.

"You must tell me what you mean by this mission being personal."

He blinked. He wasn't under. Not only that, but he looked away and shook his head. "Oh, Ruxandra. You tried to mesmerize me again."

"Why didn't it work? I don't understand."

"Neither do I, darlin', but it's a good thing you can't. Otherwise I wouldn't be here talking to you."

"Why not? Don't you trust me?"

Kurt laughed. "Trust is built. How do you think we're doing so far?"

She halted. "Is this some kind of test?"

"It wasn't meant to be. And speaking of meant to be, Nick thinks I'm nuts for trying to have a relationship with you at all."

"Then why are you?"

"I don't let other people tell me what to do."

She didn't know how to feel about that. Was she included in "other people"? If so, she wasn't happy. She liked having the upper hand in any relationship. On the other hand, she admired him.

She sighed. "Okay. So, back to the mission. What is it, and why do you need my help?"

"Ironically, I need your ability to mesmerize people. But I'm getting ahead of myself. I'll tell you what's going on, and you'll probably *want to* help."

That's one hell of an assumption. "Go on."

"There's a group of researchers capturing paranormals and taking them to a secret lab. We think it's somewhere in this area."

Discomfort rippled over her at the words, "secret lab." Every paranormal's nightmare was to be found out by humans and dissected for his or her powers.

"But surely mere humans couldn't catch a vampire—no offense."

"Not much taken. Apparently no one is immune to a Tazer. Even vampires. No offense."

Her discomfort morphed into shock. "They immobilize us and take us to their lab? Surely the vampires can escape as soon as the effect wears off."

"Apparently not. For whatever reason, only one para has escaped. If not for her, we'd never know the lab existed."

"How did she get out?"

"She said a sympathetic guy on the night shift helped her."

Ruxandra felt a little better. Perhaps the human weakness of compassion meant females didn't have to worry.

"And before you think she's the only female

captured, let me tell you they have at least one female vamp. Maybe more."

Her jaw dropped. When she could speak again, she asked, "What did you mean by this being personal? You're human."

He crossed his arms. "They have Tory."

Ruxandra's mouth went dry. She didn't harbor any love for the ex-NFL player. After all, he and Kurt had thrown her out of Anthony's bar more than once. But Tory was strong. Crazy strong. She didn't know what kind of supernatural he was, but she suspected shifter. He smelled like wet dog in the rain.

"Oh…" was all she managed to say.

"Yeah. They've got my best friend. I need to find this place, break in, free any paranormals still alive, and then make the researchers forget paranormals exist. I have Nick's help, but he can't handle that final step."

"Shit."

"No shit."

He needed her help all right. Suddenly, finding out what he'd done to protect Claudia paled in comparison to the emergency at hand.

"I'll do whatever I can."

Anthony paced in front of Claudia's apartment and raked his hands through his hair. *Where the hell is she?* Meetings didn't last until midnight.

She had mentioned something called an alkathon, meetings around the clock to fortify sobriety over the holidays. People who might be tempted to drink at parties they were obligated to attend knew there was always a meeting they could get to—but the holidays hadn't started yet. It wasn't even Halloween.

He wished he knew her sponsor's phone number. He'd ask for that as soon as this infuriating wait was over.

Had she mentioned going out of town and he forgot about it? Not likely. He would have had to arrange coverage for her at work the next day.

He snapped his fingers. "Sadie." Maybe the psychic could give him some clues about what was going on. After all, she'd known Claudia was in trouble shortly after the fire.

He pulled his cell phone out of his jacket pocket, quickly checked for messages, and upon finding none, called his niece.

She answered sleepily.

"Did I wake you, Sadie?"

"Yes, but don't worry about it. I can tell something's got you upset. What's wrong?"

"Claudia's missing."

After a long pause, Sadie said. "Where are you?"

"At her apartment. Can you tell if she's in trouble?"

"I wish I could say she's out with friends having a good time, but I'm not getting that sense. I'll get dressed and come over."

"Crap. You don't have to do that if you can tell me where to look."

"I'm afraid I don't know, but you might."

"What do you mean?"

"Do you think Ruxandra could have something to do with it?"

Sadie had just voiced Anthony's worst fear.

His voice shook. "I don't know where her lair is. Otherwise I'd be there right now."

"I'm coming over. Maybe we can find it together."

"Thanks, Sadie, but let me come to you. I don't want you walking around alone at this time of night." He dashed down the stairs and onto the sidewalk. Fortunately, she didn't live far.

"Okay. I'll see you in a few minutes."

"It'll take me less than a minute."

"Well, don't fly. I have to get dressed and splash some water on my face."

"Too late. I'm standing outside your building."

Sadie let him in, but she was still wearing her bathrobe. "You know I can't actually locate people unless I have something that belongs to them, right?"

"You have me. I belong to her."

Sadie gave him a sad look. "Oh, Anthony. I'm so sorry." She balled her fists. "If Ruxandra found a way to grab her, I'll…I'll… Well, I don't know what I'd do, but maybe you can wring her neck for both of us."

Anthony ground his teeth. "She'll pay. Believe me. Do you know where her lair is? Or can you tell me for sure that Ruxandra has Claudia?"

"I'm not sure I can tell you much of anything, but I'll try. Let me get my cards."

Sadie left the room, and Anthony dropped onto the sofa. He hadn't been to Sadie's place in a long time. Maybe a year. It was small and neat, despite a lot of *things*. Crystals, candles, vases, books, figurines… He had no idea what most of them were for. Maybe just decoration.

He reflected on the first time he'd had tea with her here, and his whole sordid history had come out. He had just mentioned her dear, departed lover Dmitri, and then he found out she knew more about the vampire world than he'd ever have dreamed.

Surprised then at the depth of her knowledge, he'd asked, "How did you know all that?"

Sadie chuckled. "You have to ask?"

Anthony squinted at his aunt. "What else do you know?"

"What do you mean?"

"Do you know about my history?"

"Only what Dmitri told me."

He nodded and relaxed. Dmitri was his friend and wouldn't tell her anything Anthony wouldn't want her to know.

"Oh! You mean that Salem debacle?" Sadie asked.

Anthony hung his head. "Ah, yeah. That."

She slid her hand across the table carefully, reaching for his. He didn't deserve compassion for what he'd done, but the kindness she offered shouldn't be ignored. He took her hand and she squeezed his.

"That wasn't your fault, Anthony. It was the fault of the one who made you a vampire."

"I—I know. But I made it worse."

"What happened? I don't know the exact details."

Anthony hesitated. It might be good to talk about the incident. He hadn't shared the details with anyone. Not even Dmitri.

"In the late 1600s, I came to Boston from England as an indentured servant. I worked my prescribed number of years and earned my freedom from my employer."

"So this city is familiar to you."

He smiled. "Not at all. None of what existed then looks

like it does today. This was a small settlement on the banks of a river with the sea nearby. A few boats in the harbor, green grass, and some rolling hills were all you'd notice. Although Boston Common was there and used as grazing space for the cows. All the structures have been replaced. When I arrived from New Orleans a couple months ago, I felt as if I'd never been here before."

She nodded. "So, how did you get to Salem?"

"The same way everyone got around back then. By horse. I was lucky and had a good master. My skill was animal husbandry, so I worked in the stables. When it was time for me to go, I asked if I might work for him a little longer and earn enough to buy a horse. He allowed it but let me know he would only sell me an older mare. It was enough. Once I had the horse, I made my way to a settlement I had heard about a little farther north—Salem.

"I lived there, working with the horses the well-to-do townspeople owned. Eventually, I was able to procure a few more and began selling them." He smiled sardonically. "I was the used-car salesman of the time."

Sadie smiled but didn't say anything, probably so he'd continue telling his story.

"Back then in 1692, Salem was divided into two distinct parts: Salem Town and Salem Village. The village was actually part of Salem but was set apart by its economy and class. Residents of Salem Village were mostly poor farmers. Salem Town, on the other hand, was a prosperous port town at the center of trade with London. Most of those living in Salem Town were wealthy merchants. I tried to straddle the divide and get along with both classes, so I saw firsthand what was happening.

"For many years, Salem Village tried to gain independence from Salem Town. The town, which depended on the farmers for food, determined crop prices and collected taxes from the village. The dividing line was Ipswich Road.

"Those who, like myself, lived near Ipswich Road were close to the commerce of Salem Town and became merchants, blacksmiths, carpenters, and innkeepers. We prospered and supported the economic changes taking place. But many of the farmers who lived far from the prosperity believed the worldliness and affluence of Salem Town threatened their Puritan values. Their children weren't even allowed to play with toys. That was considered idleness. All their time had to be spent doing chores or reading the Bible.

"Tensions became worse when Salem Village selected Reverend Samuel Parris as their new minister. Parris was a stern Puritan who denounced the worldly ways and economic prosperity of Salem Town as the influence of the devil. Suddenly, the devil was seen everywhere. If there was a smallpox outbreak that wiped out a family, it was the work of the devil. If the crops died or livestock got sick, somebody must have been practicing witchcraft and calling on the devil to make those things happen.

"A man who had just come off a ship one night asked to see me about buying a horse. A merchant I knew well introduced us, so I had no reason to be suspicious. I took a lantern and showed him my horses. My merchant friend decided to get home to his family and left. When I was alone in the stable with that...vampire, as I now know he was, he grasped me tightly and sank his fangs into my neck.

"I cried out, but the nearest neighbor was too far away and my friend must have been almost home by that time. For whatever reason, the vampire decided to turn me. I thought I was dead, then came back to life with a startling set of new sensations. It was as if someone had cleaned out my ears, sharpened my vision, and intensified the odors around me. Boy, I needed a bath."

Sadie chuckled.

"I didn't take the time to think about or question any of it. All I knew was the devil had somehow taken the form of this man and wanted to enslave me. I grabbed a pitchfork, and before he had a chance to react, I stabbed him through the neck, which anchored him to the stable wall. When all he did was laugh, I was positive he was the devil himself and that I had come upon a once-in-a-lifetime chance to rid the world of evil. I grabbed the ax I used to split wood and cut off his head.

"Then I was well and truly fucked. I had no idea what the sun had in store for me the next morning and found out the hard way. Someone knocked on my door, and when I opened it, my hand and face burned as if I'd been thrown into a raging fire."

He stopped long enough to rub his hand, as if he could feel the burn after all these years.

"The young man at the door ran screaming, Meanwhile, I retreated to the root cellar, which had no windows, and experienced my first death sleep. I don't know if he told anyone what he saw or not, but the next night two men came to my home and asked if everything was all right. They said the stranger who had come to see me had been expected at the inn and never returned. Naturally I was worried that they'd discover him in the stable, so I invited the townsmen into my home. That's when the hunger for blood became overpowering. I couldn't stand it.

"I heard the blood pulsing in their veins, and without even realizing what I was doing, I grabbed one of them by the neck and held him so tightly that I heard his bones crack. Then I sank my fangs into his neck until I drained him dry. His friend was trying to pull me off, and when he decided he couldn't do anything but save himself, he ran. I was so quick that I caught him before his feet touched the grass. I didn't know I could move like that.

"He started to scream, 'Devil,' so I shoved him back into my little house and latched the door. I didn't know what to do with him. My bloodlust had been slaked, so I didn't have to feed on him and was so sickened by what I had done that I thought I'd never do it again. Boy, was I wrong. I wound up tying him to the iron grid in my fireplace and left him there as I escaped on horseback."

At last Anthony stopped and waited for a reaction. Sadie must have some kind of opinion on all of this. He didn't care if it was revulsion. He just wanted to know how his story affected someone else.

She offered him a sad smile. "It wasn't your fault, you know. None of it was. I gather you're blaming yourself for the witch hunts."

"Not for starting the whole thing. It was well under way by that time, but I contributed to the idea that it was real. A lot of innocent people died during the following months."

"Where did you go?"

"Back to Boston, but only long enough to stow away on a ship sailing for England. Half the crew lost their lives on that voyage, but it wasn't due to falling overboard as everyone had thought." *Honestly, how many clumsy sailors did they think there were?*

"And you made it to England?"

"Yes. I stayed in the White Chapel area of London while I sought out a doctor who might know what was wrong with me. It was a poor neighborhood and a few of its solitary citizens went missing, but nobody seemed to notice or care. You know what I mean, don't you?"

Sadie nodded. "You had to feed. By that time you must have learned how to control it somewhat."

"Yes. I still experienced bloodlust, but I knew better than to let it get so bad that I'd grab just anyone and..." A golf-ball-sized lump formed in his throat. He remembered the faces of the orphans and widows he'd lured into a dark corner. How he'd found out he could mesmerize people, although there wasn't a word for it at the time. He just stared into their eyes, and their jaws would go slack. Then they'd stand there completely relaxed while he drank his fill.

Sadie reached over and took his hand again. Her gentle touch and sympathetic expression spoke of undeserved forgiveness.

"Did you ever find a doctor you could trust, who knew the truth and could help you?"

"I spoke to a doctor over a few mugs of ale in a tavern. He had no idea I was talking about myself. I said I had heard about this fellow, and he said he had heard about a prince in Romania with a similar story, and eventually I deduced that I'd find the answer there."

Sadie nodded. "It must have been difficult with no

guidance. No one to explain not only how it worked, but what you were."

"'Difficult' is one way of putting it. 'Fucking impossible' was a little closer to the way it felt."

"I'm sorry you had to go through that."

He nodded, staring at his lap. "Yeah. Me too."

They say confession is good for the soul. Maybe not so much for the soulless.

It took Sadie a minute or two to retrieve her cards from the other room.

She sat next to him and handed him the cards. "Here. Shuffle them while visualizing her. Stop shuffling when it feels right."

Nothing felt right. He had called Kurt and Nick and had to leave messages. Tory was still missing, and now Claudia was, too. He had just finished shuffling and laying the cards on the table when his phone rang.

"Anthony Cross," he answered.

"Anthony, it's Nick. We're at the hospital. What's going on?"

"The hospital?" Anthony's heart beat a little faster. Okay, maybe four or five beats a minute, but faster than his usual one.

"Yeah. Brandee's in labor."

"Oh. I guess this isn't a good time to bother you with my dilemma."

"What dilemma?"

"Claudia's missing."

"Shit. How long has she been gone?"

"Since she left work early this evening."

There was a pause on the other end. "Uh, Anthony... She might have just gone out for the evening."

"I don't think so. Sadie's here and she was about to try her cards to find out what may have happened to Claudia."

"Hang on a moment," Nick said.

Anthony heard him giving encouraging words to Brandee and then breathing funny. Meanwhile he turned to Sadie. "Go ahead with the cards. Nick's busy for a minute."

Sadie spread the cards across the coffee table. "Draw one," she said.

Absently, Anthony reached for the closest one and handed it to her.

"Hmmm...the Magician."

"That reminds me. I can't get ahold of Kurt, either."

Sadie sighed. "Now don't get upset, but the way you pulled it, the card is reversed."

"Shit. That's bad, isn't it?"

Nick interrupted. "Okay, I'm back. Brandee had another labor pain. I'm her coach, so I'll have to disappear every three minutes or so."

"Sadie was about to read the tarot cards for me, but I'm not so sure I want to hear what they say."

After another long pause, Nick said, "Buddy, maybe you should wait a while. Claudia might still come home and wonder what all the fuss is about."

"Hang on, Nick. Sadie, do your thing."

She tapped the card. "This card is about energy. This card describes an energetic, focused, and dedicated person. A person who practices hard at a craft, ambition, or personal goal. In reverse, as you drew it, it indicates the drawer of the card is spinning his wheels. Personal energy is being misdirected or wasted."

"See?" Nick said. "You're probably worried for nothing."

"Are you sure the Magician isn't referring to Claudia? She works twice as hard as most people and is more dedicated than anyone I know."

"I'm sorry. If she were here, it would be about her. This is about you."

"Crap."

"Is there anything else either of you can think of besides waiting it out? I'll go bonkers if I do nothing."

"Sorry, buddy. I've got nuthin'," Nick said.

Sadie snapped her fingers. "Those daytime vampires. Sly and Morgaine. Maybe you can talk to the woman. She's a witch and can do a locator spell."

"Great idea, Sadie. Nick, you know where they live, right?"

"Yeah. In my brother's old apartment building. Sly's the super and his daughter lives upstairs. He babysits his grandson sometimes, so I doubt they'd have moved."

"Where is it?"

"Do you really want to bother them at this time of night?" Sadie asked. "If they're up during the day, they're probably asleep at night. They have to sleep sometime, don't they?"

Anthony pounded his fist on the coffee table and inadvertently broke it in half. Sadie jumped in surprise.

"I'm sorry, Sadie. Are you all right?"

"I'm fine. I'm more worried about you."

"I'll be okay. I'll get the address from Nick and visit them tomorrow night if they're unreachable. Sadie, can you tell Angie and Chris that Claudia's missing and send them home for the day?"

"I have a couple readings booked. Why don't I run the place for one day?"

"I thought you didn't want to do that."

"That was back when it was a bar. I think I can handle the tea crowd."

Anthony leaned toward her but spoke so both she and Nick could hear. "So, you think she won't be back by tomorrow?"

"I didn't say that."

Anthony watched her facial expression carefully as he asked, "Sadie, you get vibes. What is your gut telling you?"

Sadie sighed. "I'm sorry. My gut tells me she won't be back tomorrow."

Ruxandra had been having an unexpectedly pleasant evening. Kurt was funny and flirtatious, making her feel like an attractive woman again. She hadn't realized how much damage to her self-esteem all of Anthony's rejection had caused. Suddenly, she knew that Anthony might not be what she needed—and even more surprising, that she *wasn't* playacting with Kurt. She was genuinely attracted to him. *If only he'd let his hair grow, he'd be every bit as attractive as Anthony.*

Never having much of a filter, she'd probably blurt that out at some point, but now was not the time. She didn't want to spoil the wonderful mood. As they strolled over the bridge, Ruxandra remembered something that hampered her mood anyway. *Claudia.*

She wished she could invite Kurt in, but letting him

see Anthony's girlfriend all duct-taped up and probably asleep on the cold, concrete floor wouldn't make a very good impression.

Why did she want the girl, anyway? And what in the world was she going to do with her now? *Frig. Anthony will probably call Kurt to help him find her.* Pondering her dilemma made her stop in the middle of the bridge.

"Why are you stopping?" Kurt asked.

She took his hand and pointed to the full moon over the Charles River. "Look. Isn't it beautiful? I don't think I've ever seen anything prettier."

Kurt leaned against the railing. "I have."

"Really? What?" She expected he'd say something about flying above the clouds or soaring over a jungle waterfall or something. But instead, he swept a stray lock of her hair behind her ear and said, "You."

She nearly melted on the spot. Grinning at her feet like a schoolgirl, she said, "You don't mean that."

"Yes, I do. I'm a Libra. I appreciate beauty in all its forms. Nature can be breathtaking, but nothing beats a beautiful woman. And you, my lovely, are the most breathtakingly beautiful woman I've ever seen."

Her jaw almost hit the pavement.

"Seriously?"

He nodded and leaned toward her. She tipped her face up, letting him know she was open to the idea of kissing him. He wasted no time and captured her lips in one of the most passionate, toe-curling kisses she'd ever experienced. Even Anthony's sensuous full lips didn't convey the desire radiating from Kurt. And surprise, surprise, she wanted him too.

If only I didn't have a human held captive in my damn lair.

All she could do was prevent whatever damage Anthony might do if he called Kurt and blamed her for Claudia's disappearance.

Which pocket does he keep his phone in? Kurt was wearing an old fatigue jacket with about a million pockets both inside and out. *Crap. Oh, well. I'll just have to feel him up to find it.*

She began caressing his back and chest. He took it as a go-ahead signal to grope her a little too. By the time she located the rectangular shape, he was cupping and squeezing her ass.

"Get a room," someone yelled from a passing car.

They broke apart and giggled like they'd been caught in the act. A little longer, and they might have been. Kurt gazed down at her with heavily lidded eyes. She recognized that look. She hadn't seen it in a while, but she knew it as "bedroom eyes." If only she hadn't blown it by kidnapping Claudia, they'd be making love in about ten minutes.

They recommenced their walk, heading in the direction of her lair. She had to drag her mind back to the task at hand. She needed to pick his pocket and take his cell phone. Then she had to hope he didn't have a landline Anthony could call.

One thing at a time.

When they reached the Flats, she turned to him for a good-night kiss. He surprised her by sweeping her into his arms and dipping her low as he kissed her silly. She had exactly the room she needed to reach into his pocket, grab his phone, and slip it under her waistband.

Fortunately, she'd worn a skirt and sweater instead of a one-piece dress or her catsuit.

When he pulled her back up and she regained her balance, she smiled. "Wow. You're so..." What was she going to say? She never complimented guys. She didn't have to. But she wanted to say something sweet to Kurt.

He smiled in return. "Sexy? Smart? Handsome?"

She chuckled. "I was thinking 'romantic,' but the rest apply, too."

His smile turned into an ear-to-ear grin. His straight white teeth held a certain appeal, but she was a little sad knowing he'd never grow fangs and sink them into her neck in the throes of passion. At least that gave her the moment to cool off.

"Well, it's been a great night, but I should let you get some sleep."

"Why?" he said with a teasing smile.

She laughed. "Look, I like you, and I don't like many people. But let's take it slow. Savor it. Okay?"

He stepped away and held her at arm's length. "I guess I can do that, but I'd better go soon. Otherwise, I might try to change your mind."

Exactly what I wanted to hear. She didn't really want it to end, but at the moment, that's what had to happen.

"Okay. I'll look for you tomorrow night. Unless you have a phone..." He began to reach for his pocket but she stopped him by taking his hand.

"No. Unfortunately, I don't have one. I'll have to meet you somewhere."

"How about here? I'll pick you up and take you somewhere really romantic."

"What about the lab?"

"You don't think looking for a secret lab is a romantic date?"

She chuckled. "Okay. I'll see you here tomorrow night."

"Good." He lifted her hand to his lips and gave her a sweet, old-fashioned kiss on her knuckles.

A few days ago, she'd have skinned those same knuckles on his chin.

Ruxandra watched as Kurt rounded the corner onto Charles Street. When she was sure he couldn't follow her inside, she unlocked her door and entered quickly, locking it behind her. Claudia was still leaning against the back wall, glaring at her.

"Wow. If looks could kill..." Ruxandra muttered.

"Meh ah ta ga ta da ah-rah."

Now, what do I do with her? I can't mesmerize her into forgetting all about this, or I'd just let her go. Ruxandra strode over to Claudia and ripped the duct tape off her face none too gently.

"Ouch."

"Be grateful there was a corner I could grab without touching you. Otherwise you'd be talking garbled gibberish for who knows how long."

"I said, I have to go to the bathroom."

Ruxandra let out a long sigh. "I'm afraid I don't have any indoor plumbing."

"I have a bathroom at my place," Claudia said hopefully.

Ruxandra snorted. "You'd like that, wouldn't you?"

Claudia just dropped her head and stared at her lap.

Ruxandra wracked her brain for a new plan. She wanted to get rid of Claudia, but not by killing her. She really would just let her go if she could count on the glorified waitress to keep her mouth shut.

She began to pace. "You realize I'm not that stupid, right?"

Claudia didn't look up, but she nodded slightly.

"Are you crying?"

Her rival lifted her head and bit out, "No."

"Hmmm… You don't want to give me the satisfaction, I'll bet."

Claudia said nothing, but it was plain to see Ruxandra had hit a nerve. The young woman's jaw was set, as if she was clenching her teeth so hard they might break.

"Look. I'm going to level with you, Claud…"

Claudia's eyes narrowed and her face grew red.

"Oh! You don't like that nickname, do you?"

Claudia didn't answer.

Ruxandra chuckled. "No. I don't suppose you do. If I were going to hang on to you much longer, I'd call you nothing but Claud from now on." She sighed. "But you're in luck. I'm tired of you and I just want you out of my hair."

"Great. Let me go."

Kurt's phone vibrated.

"Hold that thought."

Ruxandra scrutinized the caller ID and hoped it would spell out who was trying to get ahold of Kurt. Unfortunately it was only a number. She waited for the call to be rerouted to voice mail, then inspected the phone.

"Do you know how these things work?" she asked.

Claudia raised her eyebrows. "You don't?"

"I wouldn't be asking you if I did, would I?"

"Yeah. I know how most phones work. If I had my hands available, I could help you with it."

"Ha. Clever girl. Clearly, that's not going to happen." She held the device in front of Claudia's face and said, "How do I get to the messages?"

Claudia shrugged. "How badly do you want them?"

Ruxandra threw the phone on the concrete floor, smashing it. "Not that badly. I was just curious."

"Oh. Well, it would have been nearly impossible since the phone is password protected. I take it that's not your phone."

"Forget the stupid phone." Ruxandra resumed pacing. "What I was going to say before the phone buzzed is that I have to move you."

"Move me? Where?"

"Somewhere that's not here."

Claudia rolled her eyes. "Hopefully somewhere with a bathroom."

Ruxandra halted and stared at her flippant captive. "You really don't get it, do you?"

"Get what?"

"That you should be afraid. That I'm a vampire. That I could rip your head off, bash your skull in, and drink out of it like a goblet."

A flicker of something akin to fear showed in Claudia's eyes. Not fear. Revulsion. Then she reverted back to her annoying defiance. "Then why don't you?"

"If only…"

Chapter 14

THE FOLLOWING EVENING, ANTHONY VISITED THE witch-vampire Morgaine. *Does that make her a wampire? Or a vitch?* He was trying to distract himself from frantic worry by thinking the most ridiculous things. Nothing was helping, though. As he'd feared, Claudia hadn't come home and Sadie couldn't pinpoint her location. He was sure Ruxandra had her.

Morgaine seemed like a smart, sympathetic woman—much like Claudia herself. Sly had made an appearance just to shake Anthony's hand and introduce himself. Then he'd said he had some business to attend to downstairs and left his apartment.

"Can I get you some tea?"

"Not unless reading tea leaves will help find my girlfriend."

Morgaine chewed her lower lip. "I'm sorry, no. Tea leaves are good for estimating time, but not place. I was just hoping a nice cup of tea would help you relax." She tipped her head. "Have you fed recently?"

"Uh, no. Do I look paler than I should?"

Morgaine appeared conflicted for a moment, then strode to her kitchen, saying, "I'll be right back."

Crap. I must look like hell. He glanced at his hands. They were almost white and cold to his own touch.

She returned with a glass of red wine. "Here. Drink this."

Anthony sighed but figured some wine might help steady his nerves. Tipping up the glass, he took a long, deep swallow. The taste was…different. Not quite like any wine he'd had before. There was a bit of a metallic tang, which reminded him of blood.

Something amazing was happening. He looked at his hands again. Color and warmth were filling them. He not only felt calmer, but happier. Never had he experienced a wine that could do this so instantly.

"What kind of wine is this?" he asked.

She smiled. "It's our own vintage. We call it Vampire Vintage, and had we not discovered it, we'd be slaves to bloodlust and at the mercy of the sun again."

"You mean this is how you're able to walk in daylight?"

She nodded.

He noticed another change. He was no longer hungry. It was as if he'd consumed a pint of blood, not a sip of wine. He held the glass at eye level and studied it. It looked like any other red wine. Perhaps a cabernet.

"I don't understand. How is this possible?"

She grinned, leaned forward, and whispered conspiratorially. "It's our little secret." Then she leaned back in her chair with a satisfied smile on her face.

"Where do you get it?"

"We make it."

He almost didn't dare ask for more, but if Ruxandra had Claudia, and Morgaine uncovered Ruxandra's lair, he could walk in there and rescue his lover without a fight. He could even drag Ruxandra's lifeless body into the sunlight and leave her to fry. The thought startled him.

One thing Sadie's psychic senses had been able to tell him was that Claudia was still alive. He hoped his niece wasn't just giving him reassurance out of pity, but he'd never known Sadie to lie.

He leaned forward with his elbows on his knees. "Morgaine, I'd pay you handsomely for a bottle of this. Can you spare any?"

She rose and sashayed to the kitchen. Upon her return she carried two full, unopened bottles. "We don't make Vampire Vintage available to just anyone, but Sly and I discussed it beforehand. Nick vouched for you, so, yes. You can have these two bottles. If you'd like more when they're gone, we can begin selling it to you."

He took the precious wine bottles and set them on the rug beside his feet. "Thank you. I'm extremely grateful. I insist on paying for them, however."

"Insist all you want." She grinned. "We received three free bottles when we first learned about it. We're paying it forward."

Overwhelmed at their generosity, he placed his hand over his heart. "I don't know what to say…thank you."

"You're welcome. Now, you wanted me to do a locator spell?"

"Yes. If you can."

"I can, and I will. I'll even let you pay me *for that*. I studied witchcraft the way doctors study their craft."

Anthony thought "witch doctor" and chuckled for the first time in two nights. *Yeah. I'm losing it.*

Morgaine excused herself for a moment and returned with a few items. She unfolded a map of the city and spread it out across her coffee table. Then she leaned over it, anchoring her elbow on the border. A pointed stone dropped out of her hand and dangled from a chain.

"Okay. We're looking for your girlfriend. Claudia, is it?"

"Yes."

"Do you have anything of hers with you?"

"Yes. I have a key to her apartment and brought a few things with me. I was told it might help." He fished her hairbrush out of his pocket. A few strands of her shiny, light brown, blond-highlighted hair clung to the bristles.

Morgaine took it in her other hand, held it next to her chest, and closed her eyes. After a long pause, she said, "Goddess, please point to Claudia, Mr. Cross's girlfriend. He's very concerned for her safety and needs your help. If it's for the good of most, so mote it be."

The candles flickered, Morgaine fell silent, and at first it seemed as if nothing was happening. Then the pendulum began to swing.

Soon, the stone was swinging in a circular direction, round and round, but it wasn't pointing to anything. The candle flames grew higher, and Morgaine's facial expression became strained.

Shit. What does this mean? Is she… Anthony snapped his mind away from the negative thought so fast he had mental whiplash. *She has to be all right. She just isn't easy to locate. Or the goddess isn't ready to answer. Or something else.*

Morgaine opened her eyes and seemed surprised by the wild swinging of the pendulum.

"This isn't the right map."

Anthony leaned back. "What do you mean? She isn't in Boston?"

"Yeah. This doesn't happen unless the goddess *can't* point her out."

His heart lodged in his throat. "I—uh…hate to ask this, but could it mean she's…nowhere?"

Morgaine's eyes rounded. "You think she's dead?"

"I'm asking you."

"Holy cow. No. She's not dead. She's just outside the greater Boston area." Morgaine shook her head as if Anthony were an errant schoolboy.

He threw his hands in the air. "Hell, I don't know. I'm scared out of my mind and looking for any sign of hope. So far, I've heard nothing except 'She's not dead' to hold on to."

Morgaine gave him a sympathetic, sad smile. "I know. But, hey… That's something, isn't it? She's not dead. We *know* that."

He let out a deep breath. One he'd been holding since he arrived. "I'm sorry. You're right. That in itself is good news."

"I have more maps. Let me go get one for Massachusetts and New England. If those don't work, I can borrow my cousin's atlas. We'll find her."

Claudia's crossed leg wagged as she sat on an ice chest and tried not to get seasick. It was obvious the captain and deck hands had no idea she was onboard. Ruxandra made sure of that when she compelled each one of them. She'd told them to sail east and not to stop until they reached land.

She had to have known a fishing boat didn't have the gas to get to Europe. So here they were—stuck in the middle of the Atlantic Ocean, out of gas, and bobbing on the waves. The captain stayed at the wheel, as if they were still sailing east with no trouble.

And Claudia still had to go to the bathroom.

Kurt stood outside Ruxandra's door, holding a dozen red roses. He knew it was a clichéd gesture but he hoped she'd overlook a lack of creativity since he still didn't know her well. Maybe later on he could bring her something more personal. He smiled, realizing he actually hoped there *would be* a "later on." He was no longer just doing a favor for Anthony. He was seeing Ruxandra for himself.

Her door swung open and she stood there framed in candlelight. Her blond hair tumbled over her shoulders in shiny waves, and her long, red dress skimmed the floor and clung to her curves. *What a knockout.*

"Are those for me?" she asked, delighted.

"They are, m'lady." Kurt couldn't help feeling corny, but she seemed very happy as she took the roses from him and buried her nose in them. Sometimes corny was the way to go.

"I've never seen your place," he said. "May I come in?"

She stepped aside and said, "Of course. Please."

He walked inside the…studio? Bare room? Storage locker? Glancing around, he didn't see anything but four bare walls and a few possessions. At least he could tell Anthony that Claudia definitely wasn't there. He didn't even have to make an excuse to search the other rooms. There weren't any.

Then he spotted the white coffin. *She couldn't be in there, could she?* Strolling over to it, he tried to keep his heart rhythm steady. Ruxandra might be able to hear a sudden change in beats.

"Is this your bed?" he asked innocently.

"Yeah. Not very romantic, but practical if the unthinkable happens and my lair is discovered by someone I don't trust during my death sleep. It locks from the inside." She opened it and pointed to a sophisticated-locking mechanism.

Empty. Claudia's definitely not here. He nodded. "We'll have to go to my place when you're ready," he said with a teasing wink.

She didn't ask what he meant. She simply stared at her feet.

Is she shy? Nothing could surprise him more. Perhaps she was just making sure she was wearing the right pair of shoes.

"I—um…I didn't know how to dress. You're probably not taking me out to dinner…"

He laughed. "I wouldn't know how. But, I'm a practical guy, and I know you've gotta eat. Is that something you need to take care of soon?"

"No." She shook her head, then stopped suddenly as if an important thought had just occurred to her. "Are you offering?"

He took a step back. "Uh, no. I think we should probably get to know each other for a while. From what I understand, that's pretty intimate, isn't it?"

She set a hand on her perfect hip. "And taking me to your bed isn't?"

He grinned. "You got me there. I guess we'll have to figure it out as we go along. Are you up for a stroll?"

"Sure. I need to find a vase and some water for these beautiful roses. Maybe we can make a grocery store our first stop."

"No need." Kurt waved the shape of a vase around

the roses and visualized a pretty aqua glass with water sloshing around the inside. Soon, mass and gravity came together, and Ruxandra grabbed the glass vase before it hit the floor. A few water droplets escaped, but other than that, his execution was perfect. He was tempted to say, *Ta-da!*

"Nice trick," she breathed in awe.

He grinned, thrilled that he could impress a woman without being interrogated or accused of being demonic. Yeah, he no longer dated ministers' daughters.

Ruxandra set the vase on top of the coffin and opened a trunk. She pulled out a red lace handkerchief and used it as a doily on top of the coffin. It complemented the roses beautifully.

"There," she said. "That looks really pretty." She strolled up to him and placed a peck on his lips. "Thank you. It's been a long time since anyone gave me roses without my commanding them to."

He grinned. "I know Anthony's my friend and everything, but if you'll forgive me for saying so, what an idiot."

She laughed. "I'll not only forgive you for saying it, but you can say it again if you like. I'm glad someone thinks I'm worthy…"

Her voice trailed off and she bit her lip. A second before she whirled around, he thought he saw some red liquid shimmering in her eyes.

"Oh, hey…" He said softly as he gently turned her around. She was hanging her head and a red tear trickled down one cheek. "Ruxandra…"

He pulled her into his embrace, but she pushed away. "No. I—I'm sorry. I have to pull myself together. I don't do self-pity, and besides, I'll get blood on your clothes." She grabbed the red handkerchief from under the roses so quickly that they didn't tip over.

Now, there's a neat trick.

As soon as she'd finished drying her eyes, he tipped up her chin and searched her face. What he saw there was more than a woman with a wounded ego. He saw a woman who sincerely wanted to be better. What he thought of her mattered. What she thought of herself mattered. His heart softened and he stroked her cheek with his thumb.

"You're beautiful," he said.

"I know." She chuckled, then shrugged. "Well, I'm not going to pretend I don't know that. Contrary to popular myth, I can see myself in a mirror."

He leaned back and laughed. "Ruxandra, I have to tell you, I was worried that you might not be honest with me."

"Really? Why?"

"Well, you have a reputation of trying to manipulate people."

Her face fell and he immediately felt like an idiot. "I'm sorry. I shouldn't have said—"

She placed a finger over his lips. "No. You're absolutely right. And I want you to tell the truth too."

He looked at her askance. "Even if I know you're not going to like what I have to say?"

She bit her lip and hesitated. Then as if coming to a decision, she straightened her spine and said, "Yes. Even then."

He couldn't help admiring her for that. Still, he wished he had a voice recorder handy.

He offered her his arm. "Shall we go? It's a lovely evening for a walk."

She smiled and said, "Yes, it is."

"What do you mean, she's in the ocean?"

Morgaine pointed to the spot where the pendulum met the map. "I'm sorry, but look. There she is."

Anthony wasn't sure how much witches could see, so with trepidation he asked, "Is she all right?"

"I'm still getting the sense that she's alive."

"And in the middle of the Atlantic Ocean."

"Well, not *in* it. More like on it."

"Whew. Is there an island there?"

Morgaine studied the map closely. "It doesn't look like it."

Anthony scratched his head. "So she must be on a ship. What would make her suddenly decide to go for a cruise if she wasn't compelled?"

"Maybe she was."

Anthony swore under his breath. "Who would compel her, if not my ex? My wizard friend assured me he protected her from all Ruxandra's tricks. Hell, he even accidentally protected her from *my* abilities. I tried to mesmerize her and couldn't do it…twice."

"You couldn't mesmerize her? Can you touch her?"

"Yes. Of course."

"But you said Ruxandra *couldn't* touch her, so the spell worked."

"Yes… What are you getting at?"

Morgaine smiled. "Can you communicate with her telepathically?"

"Uh... It happened once when we were intimate. I've been reaching out to her with my mind, but she's not answering me."

"She's probably too far away. Anthony, do you know what that means?"

"I'm not sure. What are you thinking?"

"Claudia is your beloved."

Anthony had hoped but wasn't sure. Vampires only had one beloved in their lifetimes. Many never found theirs. "How do you know? Does it have something to do with my not being able to compel her?"

"Yes. That's another sign. That's when Sly and I first suspected we were connected on a different level. I *wanted* him to compel me, and he couldn't. I had hoped he could ease my agoraphobic symptoms, so I really, really wanted it to happen."

Anthony didn't know how to respond. If Claudia were with him, he'd be overjoyed. On a deep level, he'd suspected they were blessed in that way, but with the horrific news that she was somewhere unreachable and in who knows what shape... He almost hoped she had broken her sobriety and was able to comfort herself with... No. He wanted her health and happiness above all else. That meant not abusing a poison she couldn't control.

He dropped his head in his hands.

A moment later the door opened, and he heard Sly ask, "You called me, darling?"

"Yes. I thought you might be able to commiserate with Anthony. Remember when I was kidnapped by your maker and held as bait?"

Anthony looked up and Sly came over to him. "Boy,

do I ever. I was never so terrified." He placed a hand on Anthony's shoulder. "But my clever wife got away."

Anthony sighed and leaned back. "I'm afraid this is a little different. My ex is the only person I can think of who'd want to harm my beloved, and Ruxandra isn't holding her as bait. She's still in Boston, but Claudia is somewhere in or on the Atlantic Ocean. *And* she has no knowledge of magic to get away."

"Shit," Sly said. Then he looked at Morgaine and she squirmed uncomfortably.

Anthony watched and waited, realizing the couple must be communicating telepathically.

At last, Morgaine sighed. "I can't. I'm sorry, but the ocean is one of those wide-open spaces I'm afraid of. Jeez, it doesn't get any wider and more open than that."

"But with astral projection, you wouldn't really be there," Sly protested.

"I know, but it doesn't work that way, honey. My mind has to be convinced I *am* there for astral projection to work. I'd still see what's there and what's *not* there. No land. Nothing familiar. Nothing safe—"

"Are you saying that a person who knows how to astral-project might be able to find her?"

Morgaine's gaze dropped to the floor. "Yes, but I can't. Maybe my cousin could help. If you have a picture of Claudia..."

"No need. I have Sadie. My niece can astral-project." Anthony rose and strode over to Morgaine. He took out his wallet and handed her all his cash. "Thank you. I have a way to look for her now."

"I'm glad I could help, but this is too much."

"How about another bottle of Vampire Vintage? Is there enough to cover that?"

"More than enough." Morgaine rushed off to the kitchen.

"Please let us know when you find her," Sly said. "And if there's anything else we can do…"

"I won't hesitate."

Morgaine hurried back with a shopping bag and added his two bottles to whatever she'd put in the bag. It had some heft to it, so she must have given him four or five bottles of the stuff.

"Drink a glass of it now and before you go into the sun."

"Don't overdo it, though," Sly added. "It'll still get you tipsy." He smiled at Morgaine as if he had firsthand experience.

Anthony thanked the couple profusely and hurried down the stairs.

Now that he had the precious Vampire Vintage, Anthony didn't have to go back to his lair in the morning. He could stay up for twenty-four hours and concentrate on finding Claudia.

It was incredible to see the sunrise again.

Until Sadie had some news, he could fill in for Claudia at the tea shop. He couldn't wait to see Sadie and tell her what he'd found out. He also couldn't wait to see the expression on her face when he showed up at her door during the day.

He was on his way there when he spotted Kurt.

"There you are. I've been looking for you."

Kurt halted and stared. "Anthony?"

"Why haven't you been returning my calls?" he demanded.

"I lost my phone. It's the damnedest thing. I've looked everywhere for it. I was just on my way to the store to get a new one."

"At least you weren't ignoring me."

"I wouldn't do that. So, what's up? And speaking of that, how are you up? It's daylight!"

"I'll get to that later. Claudia's still missing. I was hoping you knew where Ruxandra's lair is."

"Uh, yeah. I do. But she invited me in last night and Claudia definitely isn't there. Are you sure Ruxandra is behind it?"

"I can't think of anyone else who'd want to harm her."

Kurt tucked his hands in his pockets and gazed at the pavement.

"What?" Anthony asked.

"I think you might want to consider other possibilities. Ruxandra and I have spent a lot of time together recently. I really don't think she has Claudia."

Anthony didn't want to give Kurt too much information in case he accidentally tipped off Ruxandra—or she compelled him. But his buddy defending the mother of all jealous ex-girlfriends gave him pause.

"Are you two getting close?"

Kurt smiled. "As a matter of fact, yes. I'm happier than I've been in a long time. I think she is too."

"That's great, but are you sure she didn't compel you to think that?"

"She can't compel me. She tried it three times last night and it never worked."

"Why was she trying to?"

"I asked her to. She wasn't up to anything sneaky.

We were just curious about why it didn't work and tried a few experiments."

Could Kurt be Ruxandra's beloved? The thought startled Anthony.

"Can you read her mind?"

"Uh…that's not something I can do as far as I know."

"Hmmm… Have you been intimate with her yet?"

Kurt recoiled. "That's kind of personal, isn't it, bro?"

"Yeah. Sorry." *Whatever Kurt and Ruxandra are to each other really isn't important. Stay on task.*

"I was about to see Sadie. Maybe we can all meet at the shop. Nick and Brandee too. Maybe by putting all our heads together, we can come up with something."

"How about Drake and Bliss? Bliss is Claudia's best friend."

"I'd thought about that, but I didn't want to worry her. Maybe I can ask Drake to come by himself."

"I don't know about that. From my experience, husbands and wives as close as those two share everything."

Anthony sighed. "You're right. I'll wait until and unless there are no other options."

"Uh, please don't take this the wrong way, but I'm not sure I can be of much help, and my priority is finding that damn lab. Can you handle the Claudia situation without me?"

Anthony caught himself a moment before he let out a growl. Kurt was thinking of the greater good. It was understandable that his own thinking might be skewed toward finding his beloved, but Kurt had been trying to find missing paranormals, including his best friend.

"Are you getting any closer?" Anthony asked.

"Yeah. Nick and I are pretty sure we've got the right neighborhood."

"Then you should follow up."

"I can let you have Nick for your meeting. He might have some insight as a PI that I wouldn't have. I won't try a bust without him and a vamp or two, though. Ruxandra has already promised to help, and I think Sly and Morgaine would lend a hand."

"Ruxandra is helping?" Anthony asked incredulously.

"Yes. She was happy to volunteer. I don't think she's as selfish as she was in the past. Either that or she never was, but you didn't see it because of her singleness of purpose."

"Good. I wish you luck, my friend."

"You too," Kurt said. "We're going to need it."

Chapter 15

Anthony welcomed each person or para as they arrived for the meeting at the tea shop. Fortunately, it wouldn't open for another two and a half hours, so they had time to talk privately.

Sadie brought two pots of hot tea to the table where Anthony had already set out cups and some cookies he'd found in the kitchen. Nick and Brandee, Sly and Morgaine, Sadie and himself just fit around the two square tables he'd pushed together.

"Thanks for coming, everyone. I hope that by putting all our heads together this morning, we can come up with a way to locate Claudia and bring her safely home."

"Before we begin," Nick said, "I have to ask the obvious. How are you here? The sun has been up for a few hours."

Anthony nodded to Sly and Morgaine. "Through the generosity of friends. Again, I can't thank you two enough for sharing your cure with me."

"It's only temporary," Morgaine reminded him.

"Still, I'm humbled and grateful that you trusted me with it."

Sly smiled. "I can't think of anyone more trustworthy. Look what you've done here." He made a sweeping gesture to include the whole tea room. "You had a dream of creating a safe place for paranormals, and you've done it."

"I love the idea of a tea shop," Morgaine said. "It feels so much safer than a bar. I'm going to make it my goal to come here by myself in the future."

"That would be wonderful," Sadie said. "Good for you and good for us. If you'd like to do some tea-leaf readings, let me know. I can't keep up with the demand some days. Perhaps if you had appointments..." Apparently the other psychic knew about Morgaine's challenge with agoraphobia, but didn't know if others were aware.

Morgaine smiled. "I'd like that."

Anthony cleared his throat. "And now for the matter at hand. Morgaine did her locator spell and discovered that Claudia is somewhere far off the East Coast. Has that changed, Morgaine?"

"No. I double-checked it a few minutes ago. She's still somewhere between forty and fifty degrees longitude, and forty-two to forty-three degrees latitude."

Sadie's brow wrinkled. "I'm afraid I don't know much about nautical terms. Can you show me on a map?"

"Yes." Morgaine dug a map out of her purple satchel and spread it across the table. "Here," she said and pointed to an area, tracing her finger in a circle about an inch in diameter.

"I'll bet it's a lot more territory to cover than it looks like," Nick said.

Brandee piped up. "If you can pinpoint her location, I can bring her back."

Anthony's heart leaped. "You can?"

"Yes. I'm not supposed to tell you how but I will, *if* I can trust all of you to keep this in the strictest confidence..."

"Absolutely," Anthony said, and the others added their resolute affirmations.

"I'm a muse," Brandee said. "The powers-that-be needed a new one to handle some of the modern technologies that have come into existence since ancient times. I can zap myself to an exact location if someone calls out for help."

Anthony scratched his head. "Zap?"

"For lack of a better word." Brandee shrugged.

"Has Claudia called out for help?" Sly asked.

Brandee's brows knit. "Unfortunately, no. I haven't heard any pleas from the middle of the Atlantic."

Sadie sighed. "So, it's up to me to find her with astral projection. But how do I relate the exact location to you?"

Nick rubbed the stubble on his chin. "It sounds like she might be on a ship. Can you interact with the captain if you're in astral form?"

"No. Unless there's a spirit on board, I won't be able to communicate with anyone."

"If you can get to the bridge, you may be able to spot the location with their instruments," Anthony said hopefully.

"I can certainly try," Sadie said.

Anthony didn't want to push her, but he couldn't wait much longer. "When can you go?"

"Well, I need total peace and quiet. May I use your office?"

"Please do," Anthony said.

Claudia had given up on communicating with anyone onboard. No one could ignore a damsel in distress so completely. She had to conclude that they couldn't see or hear her. Well, okay, she wasn't exactly a damsel.

She'd even kicked the captain, and he rubbed the sore spot but blamed the ache on his "old bones."

"Fuck it," she said. She located "the head," which was what they were calling the bathroom, and used it. "Finally. Ah…"

If only the thing flushed like a regular toilet, one of the four guys onboard might investigate the noise. *Fat lot of good that would do. Everything I've tried to get their attention is just spooking them into thinking they have a ghost onboard…and we're still bobbing out in the middle of nowhere. If only I could figure out how to use the radio and send out an SOS or a Mayday or whatever…*

She finally had her "sea legs" and managed to get to the cockpit of the boat—or whatever it was called—without her stomach roiling. Inspecting the instruments, she grew even more frustrated. She saw rectangles labeled GPS, Horn, Anchor Light, DC Outlet, Trim Tabs, Spreader Light, Spotlight, Overhead Light, Navigation Lights, Bilge 1, Bilge 2, Bilge 3, CB, and Radio—which she tried to use without success. Also VHF, Deck Light, Wipers, Depthfinder, Radar, Fishfinder, Windless, Fresh Water, Transom Light, Downriggers, Livewell 1, Livewell 2, Livewell 3, Cockpit Light, Baitwell, Salt Water, Washdown, Accessory, AMP, Spare, Toilet, Underwater Lights, and four dials that were labeled RPM, MPH, Volt, and Fuel, which looked as empty as her hopes.

Maybe an old-fashioned fishing boat would have had low-tech equipment she could figure out, but the instrument panel on this boat looked as confusing as any airplane cockpit she'd seen in movies.

Shit.

From out of nowhere a stray thought surprised her.

She wondered if one of the guys had a bottle of rum stashed somewhere.

Anthony watched as Sadie lay on the thick Oriental rug in his office. Brandee said she'd stay with her but promised not to interfere. The others waited in the tea room. He didn't know where he should be. Here, in case Sadie needed him? Or in the tea room, out of the way? Just then, the phone rang.

Anthony grabbed it and said, "I'll take this in the other room." Closing the door behind him, he answered.

"Anthony, it's Kurt. Are Nick, Sly, and Morgaine there?"

"Yes. Should I put you on speaker?"

"Yeah. I think I found the place."

Anthony halted. "You found the lab?"

Nick shot to his feet and demanded, "Where?"

"Hang on." Anthony pushed the speakerphone button and let everyone in on the conversation.

"It's here in Central Square. We walked right past it a dozen times."

"Jesus." Nick breathed. "Which building? How do you know it's the right one?"

"Well, I'm not positive it's the right place yet, but I'd bet a thousand bucks on it. I've watched a couple geeky types come and go in shifts. They carried some equipment into a white van a few minutes ago. The basement windows of the building are covered in newspapers from the inside and a corner of one came loose. I could see a couple cages but nothing in them."

"I remember that place. I tried shifting and sniffing those windows with my heightened sense of smell. I even waited across the street in my other form, but there was nothing suspicious that I could see or sniff out."

"If that paper hadn't come loose, I'd never have had a clue. The place looked abandoned."

"Yeah, it did. Someone obviously went to a lot of trouble to make it look that way."

"Anthony, I should go," Nick said.

"Of course. Can you two wait until I can join you before you rush in there?"

"The more backup, the better," Nick said. "But tomorrow night is the full moon. If they have wolves, as we suspect they do, we've gotta get to them tonight. Kurt? What do you think?"

"I figured we'd do the bust during the night. There's apt to be less staff on, and we can include Ruxandra. So, tonight it is."

Nick gasped. "Ruxandra? Psycho, unpredictable, homicidal Ruxandra? Uh…no offense, Anthony."

"None taken. Every word is the truth. Kurt, are you sure you want her along?"

There was a long pause on the other end.

Suddenly a loud thump and cheers sounded from Anthony's office. "Excuse me, everyone," he said. "I think I should look into—"

The door burst open and Sadie shouted, "Come quick. Claudia's back!"

Anthony forgot all about Kurt, Nick, and the lab. He charged into his office and saw a damp, confused Claudia, wide eyed and open mouthed, gaping at her surroundings.

"Darling!" he shouted out and rushed over to her. He grasped her and hugged her hard, yet she didn't react as he would have expected. She went stiff and didn't embrace him back.

She must be in shock.

When Claudia could speak again, she said. "I know this is a dream, because a moment ago it was broad daylight and Anthony's here. Also, a moment ago I was on a fishing boat stranded in the middle of the ocean. But I don't remember falling asleep."

Brandee hit the side of her head. "Jeez! The guys on the ship need rescuing too. I'll be right back." And she disappeared before everyone's eyes.

Claudia took a step back and shivered.

Anthony gently rested his hands against her arms and rubbed to warm her. "You're not dreaming."

"Then how..."

Sadie said to Anthony, "Claudia used the radio and sent out a Mayday." Then she faced Claudia. "That's how Brandee located you."

"But I couldn't make the radio work."

Sadie smiled, but a look of concern crossed her face. She turned to Anthony and asked, "Is it all right to tell her about Brandee?"

Anthony nodded. "I think Claudia deserves the truth." He tucked her damp hair behind her ear. "And I want the truth about how you got on that ship in the first place."

"Ruxandra found a way around Kurt's spell, using physics. She surrounded me with her arms and flew. I don't know how she flew, but...well, I figured it must be another vampire thing."

Sadie glanced up at Anthony. "So, she knows?"

"Yes," he said. "She's been incredibly understanding."

Claudia pushed at his chest until he reluctantly let

her go. "I'm not feeling quite as understanding as I did before I was locked up in a windowless room and then transported to a ship whose crew was hypnotized into thinking we should sail to France."

Anthony balled his fists. "That's it. Ruxandra will never bother you again."

He didn't know if the murderous rage he was feeling showed in his eyes or not, but Claudia backed up another step.

"What are you going to do?" she asked.

"What I should have done a long time ago." He grabbed the office phone, hit the speed-dial number for Kurt, and waited a few seconds for him to answer. Then he simply barked, "Where's Ruxandra's lair?"

Kurt hesitated, then asked, "Why? What's going on?"

"She almost killed Claudia—despite your protection. Now she's going to pay."

"I'm sorry, buddy. I can't be part of that."

"Kurt..." he growled. His friend didn't answer. "Kurt? Dammit, talk to me."

When there was still no response, Anthony realized his good friend was switching allegiances and had hung up on him. He slammed the phone back in its cradle. "Fuck!"

Claudia winced. "I—uh...I need to call my sponsor."

Anthony took in a deep breath and nodded. "Of course."

Claudia edged around him until she reached the phone. "Um...alone, please?"

Anthony couldn't help feeling a little hurt. She'd rather talk to someone over the phone than take comfort from him. Yes, he was probably a little frightening when he was angry, and she'd never seen him lose his cool like this, but of all people, she should understand why.

"We'll be right outside the door," he said.

"No. I need complete privacy and you can hear through doors."

He sighed out the breath he'd sucked in earlier.

"You know what?" she said. "I'll just call her from my apartment. I—I want to change into some dry clothes first."

"Of course. You must be chilled to the bone." He removed his suit jacket and draped it around her shoulders. She tried to refuse it, but he insisted. He also insisted on walking her to her door.

"You know you can't tell your sponsor about any of this."

She simply stood on the sidewalk and stared straight ahead.

"I mean it," Anthony said a little more forcefully than he should have.

Claudia tipped up her set jaw and gave him what looked like a defiant glare. "She wouldn't believe me anyway."

Claudia paced across her living room, hoping her sponsor hadn't missed her for a couple days. *Fat chance.*

"Hi, Gaye."

"Where have you been?"

Claudia hoped she could deflect all the obvious questions and avoid lying, but it was going to be difficult. "Um. It's good to hear your voice too. I'm fine, by the way."

"Oh. Yes, I guess I skipped the pleasantries, but I've been worried about you. I tried to call several times, and it went straight to voice mail."

"Sorry. It couldn't be helped." *Truth.*

"Why not?"

"I didn't have my cell phone with me." *Truth.*

"All right. But why didn't you tell me you were going…where did you say you went?"

"I didn't, and I can't."

Gaye muttered something under her breath. "Are you sober?"

Claudia gritted her teeth. It was a *miracle* she was sober right now. Part of her really wished she could escape into the bottle, but all the craziness would still be there when she sobered up—plus she'd have a hangover.

"Yes, I'm sober. I'm just tired, but I wanted to call so you wouldn't worry. And I need to ask you something too."

"Well, it's too late to avoid the worry thing, but what's your question?"

Claudia took a deep breath and hoped she wouldn't set off Gaye's alarm bells. "I need a place to go to think. Just for a night. Someplace where no one will disturb me."

"What you need is a meeting."

"Gaye, I can't. Not tonight. I'm exhausted."

Gaye didn't say anything for several seconds. Finally her voice gentled. "What's going on, Claudia? You don't sound like yourself at all."

"I know." She felt herself choking up and took a deep breath, hoping to keep the tears at bay. "But I can't tell you. At least not yet. I really need to get away and be by myself for a night or two."

"That's the last thing you need. Trust me."

"I do trust you, but—"

"No buts. Either you trust me to know what's best for you or you don't."

Oh God. Now what could she say? She trusted Gaye, but she really couldn't divulge what was bothering her. Ever. She was nearly lying when she said she couldn't tell her "yet."

"Claudia, there's a saying that you're only as sick as your secrets."

Oh, great. Another saying. Another tidbit of wisdom. "I'm sorry. I *swore* I'd never tell another human being." *Truth.*

Another long silence followed. "Is it legal trouble?"

"No. I'm not covering for anyone so they won't get arrested. It's not that kind of thing at all. Can you please stop guessing?"

"Why? Are you afraid I might guess right?"

Claudia almost burst out laughing. Who would ever guess she'd been dropped onto a fishing boat by a vampire and set adrift.

"I'm sorry. I really shouldn't have called. I'll go to a hotel or something."

"Please don't. I'll respect your privacy, but you really shouldn't be alone. My sister is in the program. She has a guest room and her home is alcohol free. Let me give her a call, and I'll see if she can give you a safe place to stay."

"Thank you. I'd really appreciate it."

"I'll call her right now and get back to you in a few minutes. You'll answer when I call back, right?"

Claudia let out a sigh. "Yes. Of course."

"Okay. Talk to you in a few."

Claudia went straight to her bedroom and packed an

overnight bag. She had to get going before the tea room opened and Anthony came looking for her. She'd call him as soon as she was on her way. Worrying people who cared about her never seemed to work out well. On the other hand, she realized, people *did* care about her. A mixed blessing, at best.

No sooner had Anthony entered his office and closed the door, than he found himself on top of a frozen mountain surrounded by many more snowy peaks.

"Oh, fuck."

Mother Nature appeared in front of him with her arms crossed. "Well, you really screwed the goat this time."

"Goddess, please understand—"

She pointed at him and roared, "No. *You* understand. Humans are *not* supposed to know about paranormals. Now, thanks to you and your rogue ex, your current girlfriend knows about vampires and muses. Magic and powers. What's next? Are you going to introduce her to the whole Supernatural Council?"

"Of course not."

"I might."

"What?"

"I might take her to headquarters and explain the whole thing to her…then transport her to a loony bin and watch her tell them how she got there. They'll keep her forever."

Anthony had never felt so powerless and panicked. "Gaia, please. I need your help. I believe you can do anything. You can reset the world to right before I met Ruxandra—"

The goddess reared back and laughed. The eerie echo mocked him.

"Of course I *could* do that, but why would I? Just to accommodate you? How important do you think you are?"

"I..." Anthony sighed. There was nothing he could say to that. He supposed that even one minor change like letting Ruxandra die would affect hundreds or thousands of other incidents, like a ripple in a pond.

Gaia must have taken pity on him, because the next thing he knew, they were sitting in his office.

"I will help you, but not the way you want me to. That would be too easy and you'd never learn. Now, go to your girlfriend and make sure she tells *no one* what she knows. I want your personal guarantee."

"But how can I promise that when it depends on *her* choices and behavior? I can't mesmerize her, or I'd have done it already.

Mother Nature smirked. "I'm sure you'll think of something."

Claudia opened her apartment door and walked straight into a solid wall...named Anthony Cross.

"Going somewhere?" he asked.

"Please, Anthony, let me go. I won't divulge your precious secret."

"I didn't say you would."

They stood toe to toe, staring at each other. Finally, Claudia said, "I was going to call you from the road. I really can't work today. I need a day to get my head on straight."

"I was here to tell you the same thing. Don't worry about the tea shop. Sadie and Morgaine said they'd help Chris and Angie handle it."

"Who's Morgaine?"

"A friend of Nick's. You may have met her husband a while ago. His name is Sly Flores."

Claudia didn't recall either name, but who these people were wasn't important right now. "I need to go, Anthony."

"We need to talk."

Claudia sighed. "What about?"

"About us."

From the severe expression on his face, she wondered if he'd decided this whole relationship was more trouble than it was worth. Having that on her mind for the next two days wouldn't help matters. Maybe it was best to talk to Anthony first and then catch the commuter train to Gaye's sister's house out in the suburbs.

"May I come in?" he asked.

Claudia stepped aside and Anthony entered. He didn't go much beyond the threshold, as if he might need to snatch her arm if she tried to run off. He took the overnight bag from her hand and placed it beside the sofa.

"If you still want to leave after we talk, I won't stop you."

She nodded and closed the door.

He wrapped her in a tight embrace. "I'm so relieved to know you're all right." When she didn't respond, he took a step back and studied her. "You are all right, aren't you?"

"Basically. No harm was done physically, but I don't know how much more I can take psychologically."

"I understand." He took her hand and led her to the sofa. "Sit. Let me get you a cup of tea or coffee."

"Don't. I should just hear you out and get going before I fall asleep on my feet."

Anthony sat and pulled her down onto his lap. "Claudia, I don't know what I would have done if anything happened to you. I was half out of my mind while you were gone."

He stroked her hair, which was now nearly dry, but she probably looked like she'd been in a windstorm. It didn't seem to matter to him. He gazed at her with love in his chocolate eyes. Part of her resolve melted.

She really did love him, and yet things had to change. She couldn't keep looking over her shoulder and wondering what Ruxandra was going to do next.

As if he'd heard her, he said, "I'll make sure Ruxandra never bothers you again."

"How? She seems really determined to get me out of the picture." Suddenly a horrible thought struck her. *He wouldn't, would he?* "Are you going to k-kill her?"

Anthony fell eerily silent. Finally, he said, "I'm responsible for this. All of this. I'll take care of it. I promise."

"You didn't answer my question."

"Because I don't know the answer."

His jaw was set and his expression hardened.

"I can't condone that. I certainly don't want you to go to prison, and I'm against murder in any case…"

Anthony snorted. "My kind don't go to prison."

"But you do murder."

He hung his head. "I won't pretend it doesn't happen.

However, in order to live among humans, we try to be very careful. There are cameras everywhere now."

"So, are you saying it's an option as long as humans don't find out about it?"

He cupped her cheek. "I'm not saying anything right now. You're not the only one who needs to think. I just want us to face this together…as we've always done."

As much as she appreciated being included in determining a more permanent solution to the Ruxandra problem, it implied a conspiracy. Having a hand in another's demise—no matter how minor—would in all likelihood affect her sobriety.

She had to make Anthony understand. "I can't do this."

He grasped her hands and held them tight. "Please don't give up on us. I'll fix this. Just promise you won't do anything rash."

She sighed. It looked as if she didn't have to add "mend a broken heart" to her to-do list, unless it was the only way to save her own life. "I'll give it one more night. If she's not…restrained in some lasting way, I'll have to leave. How stupid would I feel if I just hung around and let her kill me next time?"

"Not as stupid as I'd feel devastated." He flipped her onto her back and kissed her hard. Her head spun. She wanted to open herself and beg him to fill her.

When he lifted his head, he whispered, "I love you. So much. I won't risk losing you again. I don't care what I have to do."

Claudia wished he'd stop insinuating that murder was still on the table. But what other permanent solution could there be?

She held his face in her hands. "I love you too, but the

idea of being an accessory to murder isn't sitting well. I mean, I blamed myself for my sister's death, and I had no advance warning whatsoever. I feel like I have to protest, but even so, it's hard to do." She mimicked how she felt by speaking deadpan. "Oh, stop. Please don't."

A hint of a smile crossed his face. "I'm not talking about murder—yet, but don't worry. I'll think of something. I just want to be with you now. I want to hold you and make love to you."

There was something he wasn't telling her. It sounded as if he'd come to some kind of decision even though he hadn't said anything. She was too tired to let this debate go round and round in her head, so when Anthony said he wanted to make love again, she pushed all other thoughts away and let him carry her to her bedroom.

Chapter 16

Anthony had hoped she'd let him in the front door. He never imagined she'd forgive him so soon and let him into her bedroom. There was more to talk about, but he was grateful for the chance to cement their emotional bond. Words could wait until later.

He gently laid her in the middle of the bed and removed her shoes. She had changed into jeans and sneakers, but he pulled them off like loafers and tossed them aside.

"Hurry," she whispered.

Oh, what the hell. She knows what I can do. He moved so fast that they were naked and lying beside each other in less than three seconds.

She giggled. "I didn't mean *that* fast, but it's good to know I don't have to wait when I'm horny."

He grinned. "I'll never make you wait for anything if I can help it. I want to give you the world, Claudia."

"I don't want the world." She draped her arms around his neck. "Just you."

He dove for her lips and kissed her for all he was worth. Their tongues met and tangled. Before long, she was breathing heavily and stroking his backside. He had never felt so hard, but he needed to ready her first.

He broke the kiss and crawled down until he was eye level with her breasts. "You're beautiful, Claudia."

He suckled one breast and massaged the other.

Increasing the pressure with his mouth, he pinched her other nipple and rubbed it with his thumb.

She moaned and murmured, "…so good."

When he switched to the other breast, giving it the same attention, she arched and moaned louder. His hand traveled downward and rubbed her mons. As soon as he'd finished with the other breast, he scooted down farther.

"So pretty," he said, stroking the trimmed hair as if she were a kitten. Then he parted her folds and let his tongue explore. She writhed and moaned, especially when he came close to her sweet spot and dodged it at the last minute.

"Don't tease, Anthony. I need you."

He wouldn't make her wait, just as he'd promised. He laved her clit and then licked it with the speed of a hummingbird's wings.

Claudia arched and stiffened, then emitted moans and cries that rose to a crescendo. She grasped the sheets in two white-knuckled hands, as if trying not to fly off the bed. When she shook and screamed out his name, he was elated.

"You're so responsive," he said.

She simply dragged in huge lungs full of air and panted. When at last she could speak, she said. "I'm boneless."

"I have enough bone for both of us." Anthony glanced down at his steely rod and hoped she had the energy to finish.

She grinned. "Let's do something about that." Rolling up onto her elbow, she grasped his cock, and the warm squeeze of her hand hardened him even more. She began to bend as if to take him in her mouth, but he stopped her.

"I won't be able to hold back if you do that."

"But I want to give you the joy you just gave me."

"You do, my love. Believe me, you do." He gently pushed her onto her back and said, "I want to make love to you." He almost said "forever" but caught himself just in time. She'd seemed upset when immortality was mentioned before. If anyone should be upset, it should be the one who had to carry on long after losing his true love.

He couldn't think about that. Claudia was here with him now. He'd make love to her as if tomorrow would never be.

She spread her legs wide and welcomed him into her embrace. He positioned himself at her opening and entered slowly.

"Are you all right?" he asked, concerned for her because of his size.

"I'm fantastic," she said.

He chuckled and pushed on until he was fully seated. "Yes, you are."

He began his rhythm, and the glorious push and pull created strong physical sensations. Perhaps because his emotions were involved, he experienced a greater depth of feeling with Claudia than he had with any woman. You'd think in almost four hundred years he'd have found something close, but no. Nothing came close to his love for Claudia. His elation while joining with her was beyond compare.

He sped up and she matched him thrust for thrust. Tingles at the base of his spine signaled he was close. In only a few more seconds his climax seized him. He knew what it was like to fly, and this release was like flying without leaving the room. He rode it to the very last aftershock. Finally, completely sated, he rolled onto his side and stared into her eyes. There was no danger of mesmerizing her. She had already mesmerized him.

Making sure no one saw him, Kurt waited for Ruxandra a few doors down from her lair. Now that things were going so well between them, he didn't want to jeopardize what they had. A little niggling doubt needed to be taken care of, but he knew how to do it—if she'd cooperate. If not, that would tell him what he wanted to know too.

She emerged looking fabulous as always. She relinquished her trademark red clothing in favor of night-blending black. *Smart girl. Er...woman. What do you call someone who turned vampire over two hundred years ago at age nineteen?*

She smiled when she saw him and they ran to each other, embracing when they met. All they needed was a meadow of wildflowers and a slow-motion camera.

His lips captured hers in a long, romantic kiss. She used tongue, but that was no surprise. *She's French, after all.*

"Are you ready for the raid?" he asked.

"You bet. I haven't participated in a good raid since the Civil War."

Kurt couldn't help the little shock wave of surprise that rippled through him. "I keep forgetting you were around during that time. Which side did you fight for?"

"No side. I just had fun running into a good skirmish, knowing I was immortal."

"But you're a female. Didn't the soldiers stop you?"

"Not when I was beating the crap out of the enemy." She chuckled.

Kurt suddenly realized she was teasing. "You're funny. Who knew?"

"I did. I guess I haven't had a chance to express it for a while. Anthony certainly didn't appreciate my jokes."

"Well, I do." He kissed her again, and then tucked her hand into the crook of his arm and began walking toward the subway.

She was smiling.

This is as good a time as any to ask her if she'll let me do a truth spell. He was nervous about her reaction, but if she flipped out and refused to help him in the raid, he still had Sly and Morgaine to mesmerize the lab geeks.

"Honey, can I ask you something personal?"

"Of course. You may not get a pretty answer, but my history is my history and I can't change it."

He admired her attitude, even though he'd already decided not to judge her for things she'd done in the past. What mattered was what she was doing now and what she hoped to do in the future.

"I wasn't going to ask about your history. I'm more interested in the here and now."

"Oh. Well, that's okay too. What do you want to know?"

"Are your feelings for me real? I don't mean to insult you, but it seems that you've been stuck on Anthony for so long, and this sudden willingness to be with me might be a ploy to make him jealous."

She stopped walking and her eyes shadowed for a second. Then she sighed. "I can see why you might think that. I've done it before, but not this time. I really like you, Kurt. And you seem to like me."

"I *do* like you. More and more as I get to know you better."

She smiled.

"You're so pretty when you smile."

She grinned and said, "Oh, pish posh."

He chuckled. "No, really. When it comes from the inside, you can tell. You seem happy."

"I am. No one has said anything nice to me in a long time."

"Seriously?"

"Well, no one I didn't compel to do it. Sometimes I was so desperate for a compliment that I'd make a thrall say something like that. But as you said, when it comes from the heart, you can tell."

He took a deep breath. *Okay, this is it.* "You might be better at recognizing the truth when you hear it than I am. Here's the thing. I really, really want to believe we're both in this equally. Could you…I mean… Would you be willing to let me put a truth spell on you? On us?

She stiffened and her mouth opened as if to fire off an angry retort, but the words never came. After a few quiet moments, her posture and expression relaxed. "I guess I can understand where you're coming from. I haven't been exactly trustworthy in the past."

"I won't ask you to do anything I'm not willing to do myself."

She smiled and cupped his cheek. "That's why you're still standing here. If you'd insinuated I was the only one capable of deceit, you'd be fifty feet down the sidewalk, spread eagle, wherever you landed."

"You say the sweetest things."

She chuckled. "I'm sorry. Threats are sort of a reflex, but I'll work on it."

"Good. And you'll let me try the truth spell?"

"I'll consider it."

"If that's the case, I think we might work as a couple."

Anthony woke up with a start. *Where am I? This isn't my lair.* He glanced over at the empty spot beside him.

It all came flooding back. He had been in Claudia's bed. Actually, he had been in *her* several times. Had she worn him out? Or had the Vampire Vintage wine's effects worn off and he went into his death sleep?

That thought upset him. Had Claudia witnessed it? Had she tried to rouse him, only to realize he was as close to dead as a person can get without decomposing?

He jumped out of bed and dressed quickly. *Maybe she's in the kitchen or living room.* When he rounded the corner, he spotted the note on her door. Without even rushing over to it, he was able to read the comforting and alarming news. She'd gone to a meeting and would be back.

He mulled it over and realized the meeting would be good for her. She probably needed a sobriety pep talk, even if she couldn't tell anyone what she'd been through. At least he *hoped* she wasn't telling anyone. The more he thought about it, the more worried he became.

Mother Nature wouldn't bring him back from that mountaintop again.

It was night time. That much he was sure of, even without looking outside. He didn't need the Vampire

Vintage unless he wanted to stay up during the day, so he didn't need to get a bottle out of the desk drawer in his and Claudia's office.

Suddenly another worry entered his mind. Had he explained to Claudia what was in those bottles? What if she'd found them? Was she out on a bender somewhere?

Oh, gods.

If only he knew where the meetings were. He could check and see if she was there. *Wait. There must be a way to look them up. Otherwise, how would anyone find them?*

He jogged down the stairs to the tea room. The place was closed. He used his key and went straight to his office. First he checked the bottom desk drawer. All bottles were there, and with the exception of the one he had opened himself, they were still full. *Whew!*

He fired up the computer and searched for local AA meetings. The site he tried first seemed like the right one. He called the service office, and to his surprise, someone answered. Apparently they had staff at night as well as during the day. Probably a good idea.

He was told there was a meeting going on nearby and jogged to the church where, in all likelihood, he'd find Claudia. A couple of guys were smoking cigarettes outside the ground-floor entrance.

"Is this where the AA meeting is?" he asked.

"It sure is. Welcome, brother."

"Oh. I'm not here for myself. I was hoping to find my girlfriend inside. Do either of you know Claudia?"

The guys looked at each other, then back to him. "I guess you don't realize what the second A in AA stands for."

The other one said, "It's an anonymous program. Who we see and what we hear stay in these halls."

Anthony slapped his forehead. "Of course. Well, I'll just go inside and check for myself."

The guys frowned but didn't attempt to stop him. One called after him, "If you want help with your drinking, stay after the meeting wraps up and we can talk."

Did he look that disheveled? He finger-combed his hair as he entered. People were just milling around, drinking coffee. He spotted Claudia among the crowd and strode to her.

"I was hoping I'd find you."

"Anthony! What are you doing here?"

A short woman with red hair put her hand on Claudia's arm. "If you need me, I'll be right over there." She pointed to another crowd of people and joined their circle."

"Is this what you do here? Stand around and talk?"

She chuckled. "No. This is the break. The meeting will restart in a few minutes."

"Are you okay? I mean…did you need to talk to me about anything?"

Her forehead creased. "I'm fine. Why did you think I'd need to—Oh…" She leaned in and whispered, "That death-sleep thing?"

"So you *did* witness it."

"Yeah, I guess so. I woke up after a very restful nap," she said and winked. "You were lying there with your hands crossed over your chest, looking paler than usual. I didn't bother trying to wake you."

She woke up next to a dead body and was okay with it?

"You prepared me for it." It was as if she'd read his mind. Maybe she had. "I wasn't scared as soon as I remembered what you'd said. I just got dressed in the bathroom and read my big book until it was time to leave for the meeting."

"I—I'm amazed. I thought you'd be upset."

"The old Claudia would have. The new Claudia is working on her serenity, despite life's challenges."

"Wow."

"Yeah. The program seems to be working."

The short woman returned. "Is everything okay?"

"Yes. Gaye, this is my boyfriend, Anthony."

Ah...I'm meeting the renowned sponsor.

"Yes, you are. So be nice."

Anthony took Gaye's outstretched hand and kissed her knuckles. "Any friend of Claudia's..."

The woman's eyebrows rose. "You didn't tell me he had such old-fashioned, charming manners, Claudia."

At least the woman was smiling and didn't seem to be using sarcasm.

"Yes. Anthony is a real gentleman."

"A rare find these days," Gaye said. "So, what do you do, Anthony?"

"I own the tea shop Claudia manages."

"Oh, that's right. I forgot. You changed it from a bar to a tea room just for her?"

Anthony wrapped his arm around Claudia and gave her a side squeeze. "She's worth making changes for."

"Funny. She says the same thing about you."

A shock wave ripped through Anthony. Had Claudia told her sponsor how many "little changes" she'd had to make to accommodate his "condition"?

"Don't worry. She's just talking... She doesn't know anything."

Whew. Thank goodness for the ability to communicate telepathically.

"So, is there anything else you wanted to tell me?"

"No. I just thought I'd check in." Anthony felt like he was being dismissed. Maybe he was.

Claudia pointed to a guy stepping up to the podium. "The meeting is about to start again."

"Okay. I might be going to Cambridge. If it's too late by the time I get back, I'll just see you tomorrow."

"Okay," she said and tipped up her face to give him a peck.

He didn't mean to act like a demonstrative jealous lover who laid claim to his woman in public, but he couldn't help it. The majority of people here were men. Some appeared to be young professionals. He swept her into his arms and kissed her deeply as he dipped her toward the floor.

"Wow!" Gaye said.

When he righted Claudia, she giggled. "'Wow' is right."

He grinned and tossed a casual, "See you later," over his shoulder and sauntered outside.

Now that his mind was at ease, he could concentrate on the second most important thing in his long life. Getting rid of that damn lab. He took his cell phone out of his pocket and called Kurt.

There was no answer for a few rings, then a panting voice answered. "Where've you been? We had to start the fun without you."

Anthony got directions to the lab and took off as fast as he could fly. He arrived minutes later and found Kurt questioning a researcher while Ruxandra restrained him. Nick and Sly were working on opening the huge glass cage using brute strength.

"Where are the keys," Kurt demanded.

"I seriously don't know, man. It's not up to me to feed 'em or let 'em out. I'm just the night staff."

"They're not dogs," Ruxandra growled. "They're *people.* How dare you—"

Anthony held up one hand to silence her tirade. He leaned in close to the guy and caught his glance. A second later, the guy blinked.

"It's no good, Anthony," Kurt said. "He can't be mesmerized. Ruxandra tried."

Surprised, Anthony straightened. "Why? Is he her beloved too?"

"Huh?"

Kurt must not know.

"I think they discovered some kind of immunity to compulsion."

"Crap." Anthony scratched his head. "Either that, or he's some kind of paranormal too."

"But why would he condone researching his own kind?" Kurt asked.

Anthony got in the researcher's face and raised his voice, hoping to intimidate him the old-fashioned way. "What else have you learned about us?"

"I don't know anything," he said. "I'm just like a… like a night watchman. I'm here in case something goes wrong."

Anthony remembered Sadie mentioning an old-fashioned night watchman's spirit. This guy didn't match the description. He wore a white lab coat.

"You're lying," Anthony said. "Your coat has your name on it. They don't issue lab coats to night watchmen."

"It—it was a joke," the man said. He shook in fear, and a trickle of sweat rendered a path from his temple to his cheek.

Anthony looked closer at the coat's signature. "Dr. Odd. Okay, let's say it's a joke. It still sounds more like you're a researcher than a night watchman."

"I'm not responsible for any of this. I swear."

"I had heard there was some kind of spirit watching over the building. What do you know about that?"

The guy's eyes widened and he glanced up at the ceiling. "I never heard about a spirit. You mean this place is haunted?"

Kurt shook his head. "We can't get anything out of him. We might have better luck with the paras. Can you help Nick and Sly?"

Anthony surveyed the room. The large glass cage appeared to be sound- and shatterproof. Both Nick and Sly were charging it with various heavy objects like chairs, fish tanks, and empty cages. The people inside seemed to be shouting and pounding on the glass, with no luck. One of those people was his friend Tory.

Several cages held the conventional lab animals anyone would expect. Mice, dogs, and rabbits mostly. Then he spotted a large fish tank. Some kind of Lucite cover kept a merman from escaping. It looked as if only a small padlock held the cover in place.

"Maybe I can talk to him," Anthony said.

As he stalked over to the tank, the researcher yelled out, "Not him. He bites."

Anthony took great pleasure in letting his fangs descend. "So do I," he said.

The researcher trembled and scooted farther back in his chair, until Ruxandra showed her fangs too. He turned enough to get a look at her and screamed. He yanked harder, trying to get away, but Ruxandra just laughed.

"We agreed not to terrorize anyone, Ruxandra. We're better than that."

She put away her fangs and looked as if she were about to argue, but to Anthony's surprise, she sighed and said, "You're right. Sorry."

Anthony returned his attention to the giant tank. The guy inside was madly pointing to something. A nearby desk. The vampire didn't know what was important about the desk, but if the guy could talk, perhaps he'd find out.

Anthony ripped off the padlock and opened the top about an inch. The merman swam over to him. When his nose and mouth breached the surface, he inhaled deeply. After a few more deep breaths, he said, "Are you here to rescue us or take credit for the others' findings?"

"Huh? As you can see, we're trying to free the paranormal captives. What's your name?"

"I'm Jules. Jules Vernon. Thank the gods you're here. I tried to escape, and they locked me up so tight I could barely get any air."

"Can you help us? Have you seen where they keep the keys?"

"I'll tell you everything," Jules said.

"I'd like to let you out of here, but I have to admit I don't know anything about your kind. Dr. Odd over there said you bite."

Jules laughed. "Only when stupid researchers try to pull off pieces of me and study them under a microscope."

Anthony took a closer look and Jules pointed to his side. It looked like a few scales were missing where they met his skin, and a chink in his flipper said he'd been cut there as well. Anthony's heart went out to the poor merman. He threw off the lid and watched the merman pull himself up to sit on the edge of the tank. As the water sluiced off his tail, the tail formed into legs. Now completely naked, the man pointed to a shelf a few feet away and said, "Towel, please?"

Anthony spotted the shelf of towels. The man's waist was slender, so one towel would probably do the trick, but he grabbed two just in case. Jules transferred his legs to the outside of the tank and jumped down.

Anthony handed him a towel which the guy wrapped around his private parts. Then he reached for the other towel and dried off his hair and torso, legs and feet. Anthony grabbed a couple more towels so the guy wouldn't have to stand around in damp ones.

"Thanks," he said when he was dry, covered, and comfortable.

"Where are the keys to the big cage?" Anthony asked.

"There aren't any. It's a code. The keypad is on the side next to the door."

"Do you know the code?"

"No, and I'm not sure the guy you're holding knows it, either. He has keys to the padlocks in the desk drawer. That's what I was trying to point to. But I've never seen him open the big glass cage."

"Listen to him," the researcher said. "He's right. I don't know the code."

"He's also the only one who has never hurt me—or anyone else that I know of. He mostly sits and reads all night."

Kurt took a nearby chair and faced the researcher. "So, it seems as if you might have a conscience."

The guy nodded eagerly. "Oh, yes. I wouldn't hurt any test subject. I needed the job to pay my rent, but if they'd asked me to experiment on anyone, I would have refused."

"You're not completely blameless, lab-rat boy." Kurt said. "You could have reported the abuse."

"To whom? They always documented their work carefully, saying they needed to justify their funding, so I assumed it must have come from a grant or something. But I never heard the name of the source."

Nick, who had joined them, growled. "Who would fund research like this?"

Anthony shook his head. "What have we all been afraid of? That the government would discover our powers and want to dissect us. Or maybe they'll try to brainwash us and then use us as ultimate soldiers or secret weapons, right?"

"Shit. You think the government is behind this?"

"I don't know, but it's clear we need to find out. Even if we can get our hands on each staff member and erase the memory of what they've been doing here, somebody somewhere knows about it. We're still at risk until we find out who."

Nick grabbed the guy by the hair and tipped his head back until he could see his face. "Why can't you be mesmerized?"

"I—I don't know."

"He's lying," Nick said.

"And he knows a lot more than he's telling us," Kurt agreed.

Anthony remembered a secret weapon they had on their side. "Is there something you can do with magic, Kurt?"

He chewed his bottom lip. At last he said, "There's a truth spell..."

"Do it!"

"I need certain things."

"I'll keep an eye on the place while you go get whatever you need," Anthony said.

Kurt chewed his lip again. "Okay. But it'll take me an hour to get to my apartment and back."

Anthony cursed under his breath. "One of us will have to go. You know you can trust me, don't you?"

He hesitated slightly. "Yes. I mean, of course, but..."

"What aren't you saying, Kurt?"

"Can we step outside for a moment?"

Anthony glanced around. Nick, Sly, and Ruxandra could handle one little researcher, but what about the merman? He didn't know him at all.

"I'll help keep an eye on him too," Jules said. Then he grinned at the man, showing two rows of jagged teeth.

"No. Don't leave me with him," the researcher said and squirmed.

Anthony was conflicted. He knew he could trust Nick, but he still wasn't convinced Ruxandra had found an altruistic side. Nick wasn't as fast as she was, but Sly was. He didn't know Sly well, but Nick had vouched for him.

At some point, he'd have to trust that all the paras were on the side of their fellow paras. His plan to have them get to know, trust, and work together seemed to have worked well enough. The only loose cannon was Jules. He scrutinized the merman, who was eyeing the researcher like he'd make a good snack.

"Jules. You have to leave this guy alone. We need him to tell us what he knows. Can you do that?"

The merman crossed his arms and didn't take his gaze off Dr. Odd. "Why should I? I know where they keep their keys."

"But do you know their computer passwords? You've already told us you don't know what the combination to the glass cell is."

Jules sighed. "No. And I see your point. There's a chance that he might. He does write up a short shift report on that one." He pointed to a laptop on a desk in the corner.

"So, you won't hurt him?"

"Fine. Better yet, I'd like to get back to my pod."

"I thought you said you were kicked out of your pod," the researcher said.

"Nah. I left. Personality clash with the leader. I thought I could make it on my own, but clearly there's strength in numbers."

"So there are more of you?" the researcher asked.

Jules gave a sharp, toothy grin again. "Still trying to get information out of me, eh? Well, you can suck it."

Anthony glanced at the others in his vicinity. "Any objections to letting this man get back to his kind?"

The others either shrugged or said they had no objections.

"You're free to go," Anthony said. "But you'll need clothing. Otherwise you'll just trade one jail for another."

"Yeah. I don't have any. When they fished me out of the river, I was in fin-form."

Anthony took the coat off his back and handed it to the man. "Here." He walked him to the door. "You might want to avoid the river. Too many people could spot you there. And stay away from the Navy Yard in Charlestown."

"Don't worry. I'll take the subway to the aquarium. I can slip into the sea nearby. No fishing boats there."

"Good luck, my new friend," Anthony shook his hand. "And if you decide to visit land again, you can find me at Boston Uncommon."

"The tea room?"

Anthony's jaw dropped. "How did you know?"

"It's all the day guys could talk about. They said they'd found a hotbed of paranormal activity there. If you don't kill them, they'll know where to find you too."

Anthony's lips thinned. "Yes. They found a couple of us there. I hope to avoid killing them as long as we can mesmerize them. Do you know why Dr. Odd can't be mesmerized?"

"I have a theory, but I'm not sure if I'm right."

"I'd be glad to hear it."

"I've seen them giving him injections. I think he might be the one they're trying to transfer the supes' powers to."

Anthony swore. "That makes sense. Has anyone else on the staff been injected?"

"No. He seems to be their guinea pig. Well, him and the actual guinea pigs."

"Thanks for offering your opinion. That gives us something to go on."

"Sure." The men shook hands, and Jules sprinted

down the stairs and off into the night. Before he disappeared, he called out, “Thanks for the coat.”

Anthony smiled and silently wished him luck. His smooth legs were bare from the calves down. He looked a little goofy, but as long as he was covered, he’d be okay.

Chapter 17

Kurt had given Anthony the list of ingredients needed from his apartment. While he was nearby, he figured he'd see Claudia, thank her for being so cool with everything, and give her a good-night kiss.

Instead of a kiss, he got a virtual slap upside the head in the form of a note tacked to her door. Apparently, she had gone to a friend of a friend's house "to think." He swore.

I knew she was accepting what happened with Ruxandra too easily.

Part of him was hurt. She didn't trust him when he'd said he'd take care of the situation once and for all. Another part didn't blame her. How could she have faith in his plan when he didn't have one? He wouldn't kill Ruxandra, but did Claudia know that? He had been quite angry when they talked about it…but she knew him better than that, didn't she?

Anthony dropped his head in his hands. This was a disaster. He needed to make things right, but how could he if she was incommunicado?

Clutching at his last hope, he tried to reach out to her telepathically.

Claudia… Sweetheart… Can you hear me?

He waited. When no response followed, he tried again. *Nothing.* Was she not answering him because she couldn't hear him, or because she didn't want to? Or maybe she wasn't able to? It wasn't like Claudia to take off without making sure the tea room was covered.

The tea room! Was she hiding out down there? Even if she wasn't, his Vampire Vintage was there, and he might need a flask with him if things at the lab took longer than planned. Charging down to the tea room, he found it locked. That was no big surprise. He used his key to get in and then entered the office.

She wasn't there, either.

He raked his hands through his hair and paced back and forth in front of his desk for a few moments. He couldn't think of anything that would help his cause except to give her the time she needed and have faith that she'd call him when she was ready.

And he had to get back to Ruxandra to make sure her nicey-nice behavior wasn't just an act. Perhaps she'd hired someone to take Claudia away and never called off that person. One thing was for sure… Part of that truth spell would be used on Ruxandra.

He let out the deep breath he'd sucked in when he saw the note.

I'd better get to Kurt's apartment and find those ingredients.

Twenty minutes later, Anthony had everything on Kurt's list and had arrived back at the lab. Everyone seemed to have calmed down. Dr. Odd had stopped struggling, and Ruxandra had relaxed her grip on him. Nick and Sly were trying different combinations on the locking mechanism to the side of the large glassed-in cage.

"Did you find out anything more while I was gone?"

"No. We were waiting for you. What took you so long?" Kurt asked.

Anthony waved him over to the door. Step outside. I want to talk to you privately for a moment.

"In other words," Ruxandra called out, "you don't want me to overhear you."

"Dr. Odd might overhear us too, honey," Kurt said. "We don't know which of our powers he may have now."

Good point, Anthony thought. He was surprised he hadn't thought of it himself. His mind was divided between freeing his friends and finding Claudia, so he wasn't as sharp as he should be.

The two of them stepped outside. As soon as the door was firmly shut, Kurt asked, "What did you want to talk about?"

"Claudia's gone."

Kurt's eyes rounded. "Again? But Ruxandra's been with me all evening."

"I know. She left a note saying she had to go somewhere to think, but anyone could have made her write that. I called Sadie, Chris, and Angie to see if Claudia had mentioned her absence to any of them, and they all said no."

"That's not like her, is it?"

"No. She's always taken her managerial responsibilities seriously. I can't imagine she'd leave us in the lurch."

"So, what are you thinking?"

"I'd like to use some of your truth spell on Ruxandra to see if she hired anyone to harm Claudia and didn't call him off. I know you'd believe her, but—"

Kurt held up his hand. "I understand. It's a distinct possibility. I was hoping to use the truth spell on her anyway. I need to know she's not pretending to be into me, just to make you jealous."

"Another distinct possibility. Although she seems different. It looks like you might be a good influence on her."

"Don't sound so surprised."

"I'm not. I mean…"

Kurt laughed. "I know what you meant. Let's get this spell started. I think we have to begin with the researcher."

"That's fine, but when it's Ruxandra's turn, how will you get her to cooperate?"

"Well, I can start by asking. I brought it up briefly and she said she'd consider it. If she has nothing to hide, she should agree."

Anthony rolled his eyes. "Good luck with that. Is there a plan B?"

"No."

"Okay, then. She'll either cooperate or pitch a fit. I can't wait to find out which."

This time it was Kurt who rolled his eyes. "Let's get back in there. The longer we stay out here, the worse it looks."

"Fine."

Kurt took the censor and copal out of his bag and set them on a nearby desk. He knew the aroma of copal would encourage liars to expose the truth. It had the added benefit of affecting Ruxandra without her knowing it. However, it was subtle.

"Ruxie, honey. Can you continue to hold him for me?"

"Of course," she said.

He'd worded his request so she'd have to say "yes."

Even so, she could have let go of the researcher and bolted if she were afraid of being affected.

The commanding spell Kurt would have to use on the researcher left no choice. The liar would reveal the truth, the whole truth, and nothing but the truth. He always wondered why it wasn't used in courts of law. Oh, yeah, because most people were skeptical of magic, if not downright disbelievers. Once he'd done his thing, though, no one in this room would doubt it worked.

He set the copal on a charcoal disk, placed them in the censor, and lit it with a match. Soon, the coal caught and the copal smoke began to fill the room. Meanwhile, Kurt took the purple candle from the brown paper bag and dressed it with Command and Compel Oil, a concoction he'd made himself.

Kurt faced the researcher. "What's your real name?"

Sweat broke out on the man's forehead and he bit his lower lip, presumably to keep from spilling the information.

Kurt took some of the oil and rubbed it into his own palm. "I *said*, tell me your name."

"George."

"Good. Is George your first or last name?"

The guy hesitated again. Kurt cupped the smoke in his hand and directed it to the man's nostrils.

"It's my first name," he said.

"Now we're getting somewhere. What's your last name, George?"

"Robbins."

"That's appropriate since he's been robbing our kind of their freedom," Ruxandra said.

Good. She isn't afraid to talk.

"Sit tight. I'll just be a minute." Kurt tore a chunk out

of the paper bag and wrote the guy's name on it seven times. Then he wrote his own name over the other ones. He placed the candle over the paper and lit it.

As it burned, he closed his eyes and chanted. "Darksome night and shining moon, harken to the wizard's rune. East, then south. West, then north, Hear! Come! I call thee forth!

"By all the power of land and sea, be obedient to me. By all the might of moon and sun, As I do will, it shall be done."

When he opened his eyes, he focused his gaze on Dr. Odd and demanded, "George Robbins, I command and compel you. Tell me the truth!"

The candle flame grew to five or six inches. The widening eyes around the room said everyone knew magic was afoot.

George trembled. "What do you want to know?" he asked in a small voice.

Nick stepped in front of Kurt and asked, "Mind if I take over?"

Because Nick was a PI and former cop, he probably had some good interrogation techniques.

"Be my guest," Kurt said.

Nick got up into the guy's face and asked, "What's the code to open the big, glass cell?"

"I don't know. Only the day and evening guys know."

"How many guys are there?"

"Five."

"What kind of research is going on here?"

George squirmed but answered, "We're trying to discover as many different types of paranormals as possible, catalog them, and see what their special abilities are, if any. Those who demonstrate superior strength, senses, speed, and the like will be examined more thoroughly."

"How did you discover paranormals exist?" Nick asked.

"A little over six months ago, one of the guys found a merman in the river in front of our university. We captured him in a net and held him in one of the basement rooms. He tried to bargain for his release by telling us about the other paranormals he knew of in the area. When we verified his information, we rented this facility and went after funding to build more sophisticated cages, buy equipment, and hire trained researchers."

"But you didn't let him go? Did he give you misleading information?"

"No. Everything he told us was true."

Nick swore under his breath. "And we let him walk," he said to Anthony. "Never mind. Freeing the captives and damage control are what we need to do now. Justice can wait."

Anthony stepped forward. "Do you mind if I ask him a few questions?"

"You probably should. I'm too angry to think straight."

Nick seemed to know all the big men in the cage. Kurt only knew Tory. The woman and boy huddled together in the corner didn't seem familiar to anyone, but Anthony's heart went out to them. If the woman knew the full moon was tomorrow night, she had good reason to be afraid.

Anthony leaned down and stared the man in the eye. When he blinked, Anthony's mouth thinned. Then he straightened and folded his arms. "Why can't you be mesmerized?"

"I don't know," George said. "Maybe it has to do with the blood they transfused into me."

Anthony's brows shot up. "Whose blood did they give you?"

"I don't know. It's a blind study. The results might be skewed if I knew."

"Fuck," Anthony muttered.

Kurt decided it was his turn. "So, they shot you full of paranormal blood and left you here alone? That doesn't seem right."

"That's not quite true," George said. "See that rabbit over there?"

The three paranormal interrogators glanced at the cage holding a white rabbit. There didn't seem to be anything abnormal about it except the cage was larger than the usual size for a rabbit.

"Yeah," Kurt said. "What about it?"

"That's my coworker, Kim Lee."

Claudia tossed and turned. And not because she was sleeping in an unfamiliar bed at Gaye's sister's house in Brookline. The small family had been more than kind and welcoming to her. More importantly, they didn't pry or ask why she needed a place to stay. It was the best situation she could imagine at a time like this, but everything within her screamed she shouldn't be here.

Am I running away from my problems? Claudia never thought of herself as the type to shirk her responsibilities, but wasn't that what she was doing? She hadn't contacted anyone to say she was okay and when she'd be back to work…because she didn't know the answer to that.

Could she leave Anthony in the lurch? Damn it all, she still loved him. If she didn't show up tomorrow, she'd cause Angie, Sadie, and Chris unnecessary stress too. But she couldn't very well explain that their boss was a vampire and might be contemplating murder.

She couldn't just lie there. She sat up and turned on the bedside lamp. The clock beside her said it was 3:00 a.m. If she were home, she'd putter out to the kitchen, pour herself a glass of milk, and watch an infomercial or read until she couldn't keep her eyes open. But this wasn't her place and she didn't feel comfortable helping herself to their food and TV.

She let out a big sigh and was about to get up and slip on her robe when a woman appeared at the foot of her bed.

Shit. She rubbed her eyes. The woman didn't go away. She looked familiar, but Claudia couldn't place her. She wore a long, white robe belted with vines, and her white hair hung down to her waist.

At last Claudia found her voice and asked, "Are—are you my fairy godmother?"

The woman reared back and laughed loudly.

"Shhh… You'll wake the family."

"No I won't."

Claudia was confused. She must be dreaming. There was no better explanation for a woman just appearing at the end of her bed at three in the morning, *but it feels so real.*

"Look. I don't usually do this, but you're a loose cannon. I can't find your boyfriend, or I'd tell him to make sure you keep your trap shut."

"My boyfriend? You mean Anthony?"

"Yeah. For lack of a better term. I know to you he's ancient, but to me he's just a boy. And you...you're a mere infant in the scheme of things."

"What are you talking about?"

"Look. I'm not Anthony's silent partner or whatever gibberish he told you about me. I'm Mother Nature. Gaia. Goddess to you."

Claudia's jaw dropped and she couldn't breathe for a few moments. "That's where I'd seen you. On the stairwell outside my apartment."

"Yes. You interrupted a very important conversation, so instead of disappearing, I just changed into contemporary clothing and made up a convenient lie about my identity. I tried to warn him away from you."

"Why?"

"When a paranormal becomes involved with a human, it puts all of them at risk."

"But...I wouldn't tell anyone. I wouldn't know how. Nobody would believe me."

"That's not technically true. Most folks are grounded enough to think you're nuts, but some are getting a little too close to the truth. All they need is verification. And if you give that to them, it'll make me very angry." She stared at Claudia intensely. "You don't want to make Mother Nature angry."

Claudia imagined earthquakes, hurricanes, and volcanic eruptions, and wondered if the goddess was angry when those things occurred.

"Oh, yes," Mother Nature said. "I can do that and more."

Claudia sucked in a quick breath. "You can read my mind?"

"Just the vivid images. I'm not so much for words. I prefer to read the pictures."

Claudia visualized her favorite magazine with beautiful photography of nature and foreign cultures.

The goddess smiled. "Yeah, I have a good side, too, although you'd never know it to listen to the ingrates that live on this planet. All they ever do is complain. Most of the time, they don't even look at or appreciate the beauty I've put right in front of their faces."

Claudia nodded slowly. "I think I know what you mean. People in the city can get so caught up in the hectic pace that they miss a lot of subtle beauty."

Mother Nature narrowed her eyes. "You're not just patronizing me, are you?"

"No. I wouldn't do that. I believe what you just said. I've experienced it myself."

"From now on, make a conscious effort to appreciate the pleasant gifts I give you…not that you ingrates deserve any of them."

Claudia worried her lip. "Um. If I'm dreaming, will I remember your advice when I wake up?"

The goddess rolled her eyes. "Oh, for crap's sake. You're not dreaming. I'm right here." She reached out and grabbed Claudia's arm. Giving it a shake, she said, "Could I do that if you were dreaming?"

"I—I guess not. Dreams can feel pretty real, though."

"Fine. I'll leave you a reminder of my visit. But before I go, I need you to promise you won't divulge anything you know. You met my muse, Brandee. You won't tell anyone what she did for you. You've met vampires…"

"A few," Claudia said.

"Look, I don't care if you meet three or a hundred. Shut up about them, okay?"

Claudia's eyes rounded. "There are a hundred of them?"

Mother Nature pinched the bridge of her nose and muttered something about stupid humans.

"But didn't you create humans?"

She snorted. "Yeah. As food. But then you got better and better at survival and decided you were the top of the food chain. What can I say? When you guys evolve, you evolve!"

"Eek. You created us as food?"

"Well, duh. A tiger's gotta eat. Now man has wiped out almost all of my beautiful tigers."

Claudia didn't know what to say, except that the woman scared her.

"You'd do well to keep that healthy fear alive, but call it respect. I hate intimidating people if I don't have to."

"S-so, is that all? You just want me to keep my knowledge of paranormals to myself, appreciate the beauty of nature, and maintain a healthy respect for you?"

"Ding, ding, ding. We have a winner. Do you think you can do all that?"

Claudia nodded.

Mother Nature extended her fist with her little finger extended. "Pinkie swear."

Incredulous, Claudia looped her own pinkie finger around the goddess's. "Pinkie swear," she said. "Can I at least tell Anthony about our meeting?"

Mother Nature smiled. "I'll make that one exception. Everybody needs one confidant. More than one and the blabbermouth will be sent to a lonely, lonely place, like Death Valley. Understand?"

"Ummm…I guess so."

"Your boyfriend knows what I can do. I told him to dump your ass. Apparently he'd rather freeze atop the Matterhorn than live without you."

Claudia melted inside.

"*Now* do you understand?"

"Yes. I understand."

"Good. Now lie down and I'll help you get to sleep."

Claudia didn't remember anything after that until she awoke with the sunrise. "Boy, that was some dream," she muttered.

She jumped out of bed feeling rested and refreshed. When she turned around, a vine lay on her pillow.

It was almost time for a shift change among the researchers. George had been kept away from any communication with the outside world, but was treated better than the captives. He continued to answer questions honestly, to the best of his ability. It was clear to Anthony that the people they needed to talk to were coming in on the day shift.

Sly knew a couple of shifters that could help them keep an eye on the entrance without creating suspicion. They both shifted into birds. One was a raven and the other, a falcon. They both lived in his building, so he called Morgaine. She said she'd wake them and send them over.

Nick had alerted his werecop contacts to patrol the area and not to interfere unless they were needed. One good howl would call them into action.

The paras in the glass cage had settled down,

realizing their friends were devoting all their resources to freeing them.

While it was a "hurry up and wait" situation, Kurt escorted Ruxandra to the far end of the building to talk. Anthony's hearing was so sharp that he'd be able to overhear—but they didn't necessarily know that. All he had to do was tune out the background conversations between Nick, Sly, and George, and he was privy to all Kurt and Ruxandra were discussing.

He knew he should give them their privacy, but his curiosity won out. He grabbed a book off one of the shelves and found a stool in a quiet corner. The other guys would leave him alone, figuring he was reading—not eavesdropping.

"Ruxie, I want to ask you to do something for me."

Ruxie?

"Sure, honey. Anything."

And honey? She'd better not be leading Kurt on.

"I hope you won't see this as mistrust, but my heart is on the line here. I know how strong your feelings for Anthony have been in the past—"

"Yes. I told you, it's in the past. Not now."

"Regardless… Would you allow me to try the truth spell on that? It's important. I won't ask you anything else if you don't want me to."

There was a long pause and Anthony expected Ruxandra to erupt any second. This is just the sort of thing she'd throw a hissy fit over.

"I—I guess so. I can understand how you might be worried about that."

Anthony's brows shot up. He quickly schooled his expression so the other guys wouldn't ask what he'd read that was so shocking.

"So, you'll let me?"

"Yes. Ask me anything. When do you want to do this?"

"There's no time like the present."

"Don't you need your candles and everything?"

"I have a few extra supplies in my bag," he said.

Anthony had wondered why Kurt only used half the items he'd sent him to his apartment for. Now he knew. Apparently Kurt had been hoping to do this all along. *Smart man.*

There was an elongated silence in which Anthony imagined Kurt setting up his altar and preparing the brown paper with Ruxandra's name on it. Then he heard the smack of a kiss.

Anthony smiled. Surprisingly, he wanted his ex-girlfriend to be happy, and not just so she'd stop being such a pain in *his* ass.

"Okay. Are you ready?"

"Go ahead," she said.

Kurt uttered the same words he'd said before, but in a much quieter tone of voice. After a brief silence he asked, "What are your full name, birthplace, and birth date?"

Ah, good. All things he can check.

"My name is Ruxandra Marie Fournier, and I was born in Provence on November fourth in seventeen forty-nine."

"That makes you 265 years old. Is that correct?"

"Yes."

Anthony was intrigued. Ruxandra was as vain as any woman about her age. To admit it so easily and dispassionately *must* mean she was under the influence of magic.

"What was your father's profession?"

"He was a farmer."

"Was he kind to you?"

"Not always."

"All right. Let's move on. How do you know Anthony Cross?"

"He's my maker. He saved me. I had been beaten, starved, choked, and left in a ditch to die."

"Who did that to you?"

"The Marquis de Sade."

There was a pause. He imagined Kurt taking in the information Anthony already knew. It wasn't a pretty picture. A beautiful nineteen-year-old girl, too young and *supposedly* innocent to suffer such cruelty and be left for dead.

But unless Kurt asked the right question, she'd never admit to going there voluntarily.

"How did you meet the marquis?"

"I was hired by one of his servants—as a prostitute."

Wow. That truth spell really works. No sugarcoating at all.

"Do you hate me for it?" she asked.

Kurt chuckled. *He actually chuckled!*

"No. I never had a servant to do it for me, but I hired the occasional lady when I was lonely. Nobody's perfect."

"Anthony hated it when he found out."

"But he didn't hate *you*."

"He was angry, and I don't think he understood. Unmarried daughters who scare off potential suitors eventually end up on their own."

"But you were only nineteen."

"Yes. An old maid, in my father's opinion."

"Where was your mother?"

"Dead. She died when I was eleven."

"Just when you needed her most, I imagine."

"Maybe. I wouldn't know."

"Did you have any brothers or sisters?"

"Yes. Three of each."

"Wow. Seven kids. Where did you fall in the birth order?"

"Youngest. The boys helped my father with the farm. My three older sisters took care of the house. I felt fairly useless. My siblings considered me spoiled."

Even Anthony hadn't known that. He'd never met her family, and she didn't like to talk about them. He figured she must have been the black sheep. If she scared off potential suitors with her acerbic tongue, she may have been asked to leave.

"Okay. Let's get back to Anthony. Are you still in love with him?"

"No."

"Why not?"

"He doesn't love me. He doesn't even like me."

"Are you sure about that?"

"Yes. He's in love with Claudia."

"I think so too. Are you able to let go of him and let him be happy with her?"

"Yes. I didn't used to think so, but now I do."

"Can you envision a future with me?"

"Yes. I was using you at first. I thought I could make Anthony jealous. But I don't want to do that anymore."

"So, your affection for me is real?"

"Yes."

"And what about Claudia? Can you let go of her too?"

"Yes."

"Will you try to harm her?"

"No."

"Did you try to harm her in the past?"

"Yes. I wanted to, but I couldn't."

"I know. I cast a powerful protection spell around her."

"That's not what I meant."

"Oh. What did you mean?"

"I knew someone who would kill her for a price. I had the money but stopped myself from going through with it. I knew it was wrong."

There was another long pause. Anthony was hanging on every word. He hoped this wasn't too good to be true.

"Do you regret wanting to harm Claudia?"

"Yes."

"I'm glad to hear that. Can you promise it will never happen again?"

"Yes."

"I'm proud of you, Ruxandra. You've overcome a lot."

"I love you, Kurt."

There was another long pause. At last Kurt whispered, "I love you too."

Chapter 18

"It's seven a.m. Go time," Nick said.

The birds outside squawked three times, signaling the approach of visitors.

Anthony and Sly had fortified themselves with a few swigs of Vampire Vintage from their flasks and then plastered themselves against the wall on either side of the front door. Nick kept his weapon trained on George but remained out of sight. George had strict instructions to behave normally—or else. And just to reinforce the "or else" part, Ruxandra was hiding beneath his desk. Kurt stood next to the control panel, ready to program in the code as soon as the others forced it out of the day-shift guys.

They didn't know if the two researchers would arrive together or separately. But with only three squawks from outside, it sounded as if just one had arrived. No matter. They'd hang on to the first until the other showed up.

The inner door swung open, and both Sly and Anthony waited a few beats for the door to swing shut behind the guy. He spotted Sly first. Just as the door was about to close, he yelled out a warning and tried to bolt back outside.

Anthony caught him by the scruff of his neck and pulled him back inside. Sly ran outside, presumably to grab the one who was right behind him.

Only a moment later, the room was full. Two scared

researchers were held immobile by two angry vampires. Two shapeshifters stood guard at the door. Nick stepped out from behind his partition and Ruxandra rose, grasping George's arm.

"What's the code?" Kurt yelled out. Tory was right on the other side of the door, ready to lead the charge out of the cell. The naked men lined up behind him, but the woman and her son remained a respectful distance away.

The researchers glanced at Kurt and then stared at each other. The older researcher was the one Anthony had seen with Maynard at the tea room. To Anthony's disappointment, the other researcher was a scrawny Asian kid with glasses, not Maynard.

"It's no good," George said with a sigh. "One of them is a wizard with a truth spell. If I'd had the code, they'd be gone by now. Since I'm the only one who can't be compelled, the vamps can get it out of you too."

The young kid said, "Way to go, George. I guess that truth spell worked real well on you."

"Yeah, it did the job," he said nonchalantly.

"That's why we didn't trust you with the details," the other researcher bit out.

Anthony shook the older guy, and when he caught the researcher's gaze, he ensnared him. "What is the code? Tell me, now."

The researcher was trying not to answer. When he opened his mouth to speak, he slapped his own hand over his mouth and mumbled.

Sly shook the younger kid, who purposely diverted his eyes.

"Mmm…this one smells good, and I'm kind of hungry. Are you hungry, Anthony?"

"Famished. Do you mind sharing? He might be tasty, but you'll probably be hungry an hour from now."

The guy shivered.

Sly and Nick chuckled. At last, Nick approached the researcher who was still mesmerized and pulled the man's hand away from his mouth. He clasped both of the researcher's hands behind his back and cuffed him with a zip tie. He did the same with the kid, despite his attempt to resist.

"Okay. Let's try this again. What's the code to the large glass cell?" Nick asked.

"It changes every day," said the mesmerized researcher. "The computer randomly selects a new number and gives it to us each day."

Nick poked the man with his gun. "Then go ask the computer what the damn code is."

"I can't type with my hands tied."

"Fine. Tell George how to do it. And by the way, what's your name?"

"Dr. Grant."

"Interesting. Which brings us to another question. Where did you get the grant money to do this research?"

"A pharmaceutical company."

The paranormals all glanced at each other, confused.

"Not the government?" Kurt asked.

"No. It was a private company."

Nick crossed his arms. "What did they intend to do with us?"

"They wanted to know if paranormal fluids, organs, or brain tissue could be made into drugs to give people better lives."

Anthony wanted to drop the guy on the floor. Sure. It

sounded like a noble cause, but at what expense? Killing some to give others their abilities? Would these researchers feel the same way if the study involved human beings who just happened to be extra strong and healthy?

Nick growled.

"You'd better get that code soon, George," Kurt called out. "Or I think someone might eat your coworker."

"Should I do it, Dr. Grant?"

"No!" the Asian kid shouted. "If you let them open the cage, we'll have even more pissed-off shifters out here."

Anthony caught Dr. Grant's gaze again. "You don't have a choice. I'm going to free your hands, and you're going to go to your computer. You will not only retrieve the code, but also print out every bit of information you have. That includes contracts, bank accounts, personnel files, and shift notes. I want to know every single thing that has gone on here—right from the day you decided to open this hellhole. After that, you'll delete it all."

Claudia arrived at the tea room a few minutes late. She'd had to get home and take a shower before going to work, and the subway from Brookline to Arlington Street seemed to take forever. She'd call and thank Gaye's sister later, or maybe send flowers or a fruit basket. Or a thank-you card. Yeah, no one was ever allergic to cards—as long as her friend Bliss, the creator of Hall-Snark cards, didn't make them.

When she walked in, a few customers were already enjoying breakfast.

Angie looked up. "Hey, Claudia. How are you feeling?"

"Uh…feeling? Fine. Why?"

Angie met her by the cash register. "Anthony said you weren't feeling well yesterday. Isn't that why he worked during the day for you?"

"Oh, yeah. I'm fine now. Just a twenty-four-hour bug."

Angie lowered her voice and whispered behind her hand. "Are you sure it wasn't honeymoon cystitis?"

Claudia rolled her eyes. "Positive. I need to do something in the office. I'll be out in a minute."

Try as she might, Claudia couldn't get Anthony out of her head. Apparently she was hopelessly in love with a vampire, and there was nothing to be done about it.

She placed her purse in one of the desk's locked drawers and pocketed the keys. She thought about how Anthony trusted her so completely with his business. Not just the tea room, but the bar before that. She'd paid back his trust with loyalty, hadn't she? Yesterday was the first time in over five years that she'd left him in the lurch.

And I'm supposedly recovering from irresponsible behavior, she chided herself.

Well, the only thing she could do was get back to handling her responsibilities as quickly as possible. She'd do a fast inventory of the shelved items and see if Chris needed anything.

She no sooner stepped out of the office than the bells above the door jingled.

Maynard. Just who I don't want to see. It was too late to duck behind the register. He'd spotted her and was pointing at her.

"You and I need to have a talk," he said.

She let out a long sigh. "I don't suppose I can defer, can I?"

"No. You really can't. There's something important I have to tell you."

She thought about refusing again, but the tea room had customers. A public argument was never a good idea.

"Angie, I'll be in the office. Knock if you need any help. Seriously. Anything at all."

Angie glanced at Maynard, probably recognizing the troublemaker from the other night. "Same goes, boss. If you need me, I'm right here."

Claudia smiled. How lucky was she to have Angie? The girl was not only a terrific employee, but one who genuinely cared about Claudia as a person.

She escorted Maynard into the office and shut the door. Instead of sitting in the chair beside him, which would put them on equal footing, she purposely sat behind the desk. This was *her* territory, and he'd better remember it.

"Claudia, I want to warn you about something…as an old friend. I realize you're taken, and this has nothing to do with trying to get you back."

She nodded. "Go on."

"This place…" He gestured with an open palm, indicating in the whole room. "Where you work…"

"Yeah. What about it?"

"It's paranormal central. You *do* know what paranormal means, don't you?"

Patronizing as usual. "Yes. I'm aware of the term and its meaning."

"But did you know paranormal beings exist? Vampires and shapeshifters of all varieties live in and around the city."

Should she act surprised? Mother Nature didn't

want her talking about this with anyone but Anthony. Somehow, she couldn't give Maynard the satisfaction of being the first to bring this shocking news to her attention. So, she folded her arms. "What of it?"

He paused, obviously examining her reaction. When she didn't give him one, he cleared his throat. "I don't think you understand. I work in a research lab studying such creatures. They're extremely dangerous."

She sighed.

"Claudia! Are you listening to me?"

"Unfortunately, yes."

Maynard leaned forward and pounded his fist on her desk. "You need to leave. Get out of here. Right"*—pound—*"fucking"*—pound—*"now!"

"And just leave my staff and customers with these supposedly dangerous creatures?"

"Ever heard of self-preservation?"

"Yes. I'm familiar with that term too, but sometimes the world isn't as black and white as you seem to believe it is."

"Look." He dug a piece of equipment out of his pocket. "This registers paranormal activity, and the other night when I was here with my friends, it went nuts."

"I'm sorry your equipment was defective. Maybe it's the number of electronic devices in the area. Beacon Hill is a tiny area with a large population."

"No. That's not it. My meter wasn't defective. It was registering some disturbing facts. For instance, your boyfriend is a paranormal. I've been trying to warn you away from him ever since that night." He leaned back in his chair again. "But you haven't been around."

"Maynard, I have a business to run. Thank you for

stopping by and delivering your message. I'll take it under advisement."

"Take it under advisement? Claud, this isn't a decision to ponder. I told you. You need to get out of here."

The ugly nickname made her wince. "And I have the right to decide what I need. Right now, I need you to leave." She rose, ready to walk out and resume her work, leaving him exactly where he was, if she had to.

He leaped to his feet. "For God's sake. What's the matter with you? Haven't you ever heard any of the vampire legends? How about werewolves? Guess what, dear. They're true. And tonight's the full moon."

"Guess what, Maynard. I'm not your dear. And I've lived through many full moons right in this very spot. Now run along." She waved her hand in a sweeping, dismissive gesture. She was being patronizing, yes, but she wanted him to know what it felt like.

His mouth hung open and he didn't look like he was planning to leave, so she did. She even closed the door behind her.

Anthony came breezing into the tea room, saw Claudia and rushed to her, sweeping her off her feet. His lips captured hers in the mother of all passionate kisses. She twined her fingers in his hair and breathed in the scent that was *her* Anthony. He tasted a little bit like wine, but at the moment, she didn't care. He tasted more like love.

Maynard stepped out of the office just as Anthony was setting her on her feet. He glanced up and his eyes narrowed.

"Excuse me, Claudia," Anthony said. "I need a word with your friend."

"He's not my friend anymore."

Maynard tried to skirt around them, but Anthony placed himself between the researcher and the door. He stared at the weasel and said, "You're going to come into the office with me and listen to what I have to say."

Claudia was surprised to see Maynard follow Anthony into the office like an obedient dog.

Anthony told Maynard to sit, and the mesmerized researcher did immediately.

"I have a few things to tell you. First of all, the research facility in which you worked has taken on a whole new direction. You no longer study paranormal abilities. In fact, you and your colleagues scoff at the idea of paranormals. You've disproved their existence altogether.

"Your grant is now funding a whole new area of research. You and everyone you work with are planning to build ultra-realistic sex dolls.

"You use robotics, as well as your expertise in computer technology and biophysics. All of you will learn a great deal about plastics and manufacturing in the coming months. You're working with a model named Ruxandra to make sure you get it right.

"The pharmaceutical company is no longer funding your group. I am. You will report your progress to me via email. Do you understand all of this?"

Maynard nodded.

"Any questions?"

Maynard shook his head woodenly.

"Good. You'd better get back to work. Your coworkers are drawing up plans and making lists of what they need as we speak. You enjoyed your short visit with your old girlfriend, but you've achieved closure. You don't need to bother her again."

"Yes. I should get to work," Maynard said.

"That's right." Anthony rose and buttoned his suit jacket. "You enjoy your job and can't wait to get there."

Maynard walked out of the office without a backward glance. Smiling, he practically skipped out the front door and down the stairs to the sidewalk.

Anthony found Claudia behind the register, writing down the names of the prepackaged teas they needed to order.

"Wow. He looked like he couldn't wait to get out of here. What did you say to him?"

"I'll tell you all about it later. We'll have to wait until we're alone tonight. After closing, we're having a celebration for Tory."

Angie rushed over. "Did I hear you say something about Tory?"

Anthony smiled. "Yes. We found him. He's alive and well."

"Oh, thank God!" Angie laid her order pad over her heart. "When can I see him?"

"Right now he's calling his family to put their minds at ease. He said he'll stop by to see you as soon as he's had a shower and changed his clothes."

Tears welled up in Angie's eyes. "I can't believe how long I took him for granted. He was always so good to us. Especially me. I felt safe whenever he was around. I've missed him so much."

"Be sure to tell him that when you see him."

"Don't worry," she said, grinning. "I will."

As Angie returned to the table she'd been waiting on, Claudia sidled up to Anthony and whispered in his ear. "I have a few things to tell you too."

He turned and kissed her again. This time, it was just a peck since they were in the workplace, but it felt wonderful to touch his lips to hers anyway. "I hope it's good news."

"It is."

"Do you have to keep me in suspense? Maybe you can give me the Cliffs Notes version."

"I love you, Anthony. I've changed my mind about a lot of things over the past two days, but that's one thing that's been unshakable."

"You don't know how happy I am to hear that."

Later, Claudia flipped the *Closed* sign over and turned the lights down low. She and Angie were preparing the tea room for Tory's welcome-home party. Meanwhile, Anthony was in the office tallying up the day's receipts.

Claudia knew there would be some paranormals among the guests, but she didn't know who or what they were. She was determined not to let her nerves get the better of her. Maynard had told her enough to worry her, but Anthony had again promised she'd be safe.

He had also warned her not to let Angie know—about anything. Claudia couldn't help wondering why.

All the tables were pushed together and Chris had baked a cake. Angie was setting the last place when the door opened. They weren't expecting guests for another hour, and Claudia thought she'd have to shoo out a customer who was ignoring the sign.

Tory stepped in and Angie dashed over to him, jumping into his arms. He caught her easily, and they hugged each other like neither one would ever let go.

Claudia couldn't help smiling as she witnessed the happy homecoming. "Um. I'll just step into the office for a few minutes," she said.

Neither one of them looked her way.

She closed the office door behind her and pulled a chair around the desk so she could whisper to Anthony. She knew enough about paranormals to realize they had superior hearing.

"Why can't Angie know about Tory? What does she think happened to him?"

Anthony laid down his pen and took Claudia's hands in his.

"Promise you won't get mad?"

"Mad? Why would I—Oh. You think I'll react badly if you insult Angie."

"No." He took a deep breath. "You already reacted badly."

"Huh?"

"The incident I'm going to tell you about happened a year ago. You don't remember it because…well, Kurt and Sly took care of that."

Her eyes widened. "You mean my memory was erased? The same way you said you could erase memories if you had to?"

"Yes. Are you sure you want me to tell you more?"

"Are you kidding? You'd better tell me all of it now."

He looked like he was trying to stifle a smile. "When Brandee and Angie lived together, Angie overheard a conversation between Brandee and Nick. He was trusting his girlfriend at the time with sensitive information but didn't realize her best friend and roommate was hearing every word. Well, Angie went a little nuts. She disappeared for a night, and when she returned, she'd made a decision to break her promise to Brandee and tell you all about it."

"Me?"

"Yes. She felt that as the manager, you needed to know the bar had paranormal patrons. She even outed *me*."

"Oh!"

"Yeah. Well, you called an emergency staff meeting and asked who else knew about this. Apparently you weren't convinced Angie was in her right mind, but you were willing to hear her out and see if there was anything to it."

"That sounds like me."

"Yes. And it's one of the things that makes you a great manager. However, one of the waitresses freaked out and went screaming out of the office, telling everyone in the bar that vampires and werewolves were invading Boston."

"Let me guess. Robin?"

"Yes." He chuckled.

"And that's funny, because..."

"Well, because the damage control was successful. Believe me, if it hadn't been contained, I wouldn't be laughing about it. I might not even be here. Remember my so-called business partner?"

Claudia tossed her hair over one shoulder and couldn't wait to show Anthony how well she was able to handle the paranormal. Telepathically, she said, *Oh. You mean Mother Nature?*

Anthony's jaw dropped. *"You know about Gaia?"*

Yes. She visited me last night. We had a very interesting conversation. That's one of the things I was going to tell you about later.

He took a moment to recover and she couldn't help gloating a little bit inside. *See darling? I may be handling the paranormal end of things better than you think.*

"I should say so. What did Gaia tell you?"

Just that I shouldn't talk about the paranormal with anyone but you. She made me pinkie swear.

Anthony laughed out loud. "Pinkie swear? Really?"

Claudia sat up straight. "Yeah. She understood I'd have to confide in someone, and she said I could talk to you…but never to let anyone else overhear us. Now I know why."

"Wow. I guess she must really like you. She threatened to leave me stranded high in the Alps if I told anyone."

Claudia shrugged. "Maybe I proved myself trustworthy."

"I'd say there's no maybe about it." He smiled and raised her hand to his lips.

"So…paranormals," she continued. "Are you going to fill me in on our guests?"

He hesitated but only for a moment. *"We'd better do it telepathically so no one can hear us."*

Perfect. Okay. So who's who?

"Before I tell you anything, I want you to remember you've counted most of them as friends for a long time. I don't want that to change."

Neither do I.

"All right." Anthony rubbed her palms with his thumbs. *"If you think you can handle it, I'll start small.*

Tory is a shapeshifting coyote. Angie may never know that. He doesn't have to shift during a full moon as a werewolf does, and he doesn't need to drink blood or stay away from sunlight. In essence, he can live his entire life as a normal man if he chooses to."

For Angie's sake, I hope that's what he decides to do.

"For everyone's sake, I think he will."

Okay. One down. Who's next? Claudia asked.

"You know Brandee is special, but she didn't used to be. She was as human as you and Angie until she and Nick were engaged."

So what happened?

"Gaia needed a new muse and offered her a position as muse of photography. Wait, it was more than that. Muse of still and moving images, I think."

Considering Brandee's career in photography, that makes sense. But did that happen after she and Nick got together, because she proved herself trustworthy with a secret of his?

"Bingo."

So, Nick's a...

"Nick's a werewolf."

Claudia tried to let that sink in. *Okay. Yeah. That makes sense. He's a big man and he'd have to let Brandee know why he couldn't be with her during full moons. Right?*

"I'm sure that was part of it. I was with him when he told her everything, just in case."

In case her memory needed a "do-over"?

Anthony chuckled. *"Yes. He even shifted in front of her and let her see his other form. She was naturally nervous but accepted him fully."*

Wow. That took guts on both their parts.

"Yes. But she had to know the truth. And he wanted her to see that she was perfectly safe with him in either form. I hope you know his guarantee of safety includes you and everyone here."

I don't doubt it.

"You should also know he helped me get Boston Uncommon off the ground. He, like me, had a vision of paranormals meeting in a safe space and getting to know each other as friends."

It seems to have worked.

"Yes, but there are still some age-old rivalries out there. We don't run around recruiting hostile factions and try to play diplomat. We're just available for those who want to get along."

That sounds like the best way to handle it.

Anthony gave her a smile that spoke of genuine admiration. "You really are amazing, you know that?" he said out loud.

"Hmmm…I guess I am." Claudia giggled. *So, what about the rest? Kurt?*

"Wizard but human. Not paranormal at all."

Sadie?

"Sadie is human too. A human psychic. Both of them are aware of the paranormals in our midst. If they're comfortable here, that should say something, right?"

Claudia nodded. *What about Morgaine and Sly? You said they might be coming tonight.*

"Sly is the vampire who mesmerized you and Angie, Malcolm, Robin, and Wendy way back when all hell broke loose after that emergency staff meeting. Kurt froze time long enough for him to do it."

But Sly can walk in daylight.

"And thanks to him, I can too."

She squeezed his hands. *Remind me to thank him later. So, what about his wife, Morgaine?*

"Witch first, then she became a vampire when she married Sly."

She became a... Was it by choice?

"Yes. It was definitely her choice. Apparently he'd already lost a wife and grieved for years. Because she's his beloved, she figured it would be even worse if she died."

Claudia had to remember to breathe. She had never considered the possibility of becoming a vampire. *I'm betting it's not like converting to Judaism, is it? Once it's done, it probably can't be undone.*

"That's correct. In case you're wondering, I don't want you to do that for me."

As selfish as it sounded, Claudia was relieved. Rather than dwell on it, she continued their conversation.

Can Morgaine do spells like Kurt can?

"Yes. I guess there are subtle differences between wizards and witches—mostly moral, and they don't always get along."

Chalk up another unusual friendship because of Boston Uncommon.

Anthony grinned. *"By Jove, you've got it."*

Claudia took in a deep breath and let it out on a sigh. "I guess that's enough for now. Any more information and my head might explode."

Anthony cupped her cheeks and said, "We can't let that happen. It's such a pretty, pretty head."

Chapter 19

THE PARTY HAD GONE WELL. ANGIE SPENT MOST OF the evening on Tory's lap, and everyone had fun teasing her about her "get it yourself" attitude. Anthony and Claudia had just said good night to the last of the partygoers when the bell over the door tinkled again.

In walked Ruxandra.

Anthony's back stiffened.

"What's she doing here?" Claudia asked telepathically.

Kurt followed her in and said, "Hi, Claudia. I'm glad you're still here. Ruxandra has something she wants to tell you."

Anthony stepped in front of Claudia, almost as if it were reflex.

"It's okay, Anthony. I'm not going to hurt her. *Ever.*"

Was that too much to hope for? Anthony caught Kurt's eye and he nodded.

Moving to Claudia's side, Anthony wrapped his arm around her shoulder protectively and noted a tremor. Apparently Claudia needed to be convinced as much as he did.

"Well, Ruxandra. Go ahead. Say what you came to say."

Ruxandra reached for Kurt's hand, as if she needed confidence. A definite change was taking place in her, and Anthony just prayed it would continue.

"I'm sorry, Claudia," she said. "I know I did some

terrible things to you, and I don't expect you to forgive me, but that doesn't change how sorry I am."

After a long pause, Claudia finally said, "I can understand how hard it is to realize you've hurt someone and apologize, *especially* when you don't think you'll be forgiven. I've been in that position too."

Ruxandra's eyes rounded. "You have?"

"Yes. I may not have meant to hurt anyone, but I did. Apologizing is the right thing to do. You may or may not help the other person forgive you, but the important thing is that you do it. It's the first step in eventually forgiving yourself."

Ruxandra hung her head. "I don't know if I'll ever forgive myself for some of the things I've done…especially to you."

Claudia stepped away from Anthony. The spot where she had been curled into him cooled, or perhaps the chill that invaded him was dread. She stepped forward and extended her arms. If Anthony hadn't just taken a breath a few moments ago, he'd have gasped.

Ruxandra looked up, surprised. As soon as she realized she was getting a hug instead of the slap she deserved, she relaxed and opened her arms.

The two women held each other and Anthony thought he heard sniffling, but he couldn't be sure. Kurt pulled a handkerchief out of his pocket and handed it to Ruxandra.

Oh, my gods. I never thought I'd see the day.

Ruxandra was crying.

Anthony and Claudia had finally locked up and made their way upstairs to Claudia's apartment. He placed his hands on her shoulders and smiled like he had some kind of pleasant surprise in store.

"Would you like me to spend the night? Or longer?"

Surprise didn't quite cover the emotion that Claudia felt. Shock was more like it. "Seriously? You want to sleep here?"

"I've always wanted to stay the night with you, honey. I couldn't before Sly gave me his temporary cure for the death sleep and photosensitivity. Now I can—if you want me to."

She grinned. "Of course I want you to." She'd often thought about how wonderful it would be to fall asleep all curled up in his arms. "I'd love that. But what did you mean when you said, 'or longer'?"

He glanced at the floor and scuffed his shoe as if he were nervous. "I was wondering if you'd like us to live together."

She threw her arms around his neck. Instead of answering him verbally, she just planted her lips on his and kissed him for all she was worth.

"I take it that's a yes?"

"Yes. That's most definitely a yes."

Anthony swept her up in his arms and carried her to *their* bedroom. He set her on the end of the bed and unbuttoned her blouse as she unzipped his trousers. She had always wanted to pleasantly surprise him in the bedroom. Tonight would be the night.

He was just reaching for her bra when she grasped his erection and sucked it into her mouth. He leaned back and groaned. Claudia went to work giving him the best blow job she knew how. It must have been pretty good because he was moaning and gently cupping the back of her head, allowing her to do whatever she wanted to him.

She'd never much cared for the act, but with Anthony it was different. She *wanted* to do this. And it wasn't just that she wanted to give him the kind of intense pleasure he always gave her. She loved the intimacy it created between them. She loved *him.*

"Oh, baby…that's so good," he whispered.

She had always wondered if she could possibly measure up to his former lovers. They'd never discussed it, but she had the feeling there had been more than Ruxandra. A lot more. Considering his long life, that wasn't much of a stretch.

She hadn't realized she was projecting her thought until he answered her telepathically.

"You don't have any competition, sweetheart. Not in the present or the past. And there won't be any in the future, either."

Claudia felt a momentary urge to cry. She held it back in favor of the warm feelings flooding her. She wasn't the emotional mess she had once been, but she could still be swamped by strong feelings…this time, feelings of unmitigated love.

She broke the suction just long enough to tell him she loved him out loud and to swirl her tongue around his girth a few times.

"I love you too, darling. So much," he murmured.

Whether he called her "baby" or "honey" or "darling," she felt the sincerity of his words. It was almost too much. She sucked him harder, longing to bring him the same joy she felt.

He pushed gently against her shoulders until he

popped out of her mouth. "I'll have nothing left if you finish me now."

"That's not true," she said.

He laughed. "You know me well. But I want to give you what you need too."

"Right now, all I need is you," she said and reached for him again.

He stepped aside, scooped her up, and tossed her onto the middle of the bed. She gasped, then giggled as she bounced. He leaped onto the bed and braced himself on either side of her. Gently lowering his weight, he captured her lips and kissed her thoroughly.

Claudia wrapped her arms around his waist and stroked his back. He was still wearing his shirt and shoes, and his pants were around his ankles, but she could stroke his buttocks and give them a good squeeze.

He sat up just long enough to pull his shirt off over his head and kick off his shoes and slacks. Then he assisted her with her skirt and bra. She was still wearing her red lace panties, but they proved no barrier at all.

He stroked her mons over the panties, then slipped his finger beneath them. He found the little bud of sensitive flesh and rubbed. She arched her back and moaned. The intense sensations at her epicenter grew white hot. Before she knew it, she exploded in an earth-shattering orgasm. Her moans turned to screams of ecstasy, and her thighs vibrated wildly.

When he had taken her to her last aftershock, she felt completely boneless. She was glad she'd given him his blow job first, because she doubted herself capable of it now.

Anthony easily slipped off her panties and positioned

himself between her legs. She was about to raise her knees so she could lift her buttocks and meet his thrusts, but instead, he hoisted her legs over his shoulders.

"Is this the proverbial legs-behind-the-ears position?" she joked.

"Oh, gods. I didn't think of that." He began to slip her legs off, but she clasped her ankles around his neck. "No. I want to try this," she said.

"Are you sure?"

"God's, yeah," she said, teasing.

He grinned. "I think you'll like it."

He cradled her bottom and then entered her inch by delicious inch. They gazed into each other's eyes the whole time. Claudia felt so complete. She always did when she and Anthony made love, but this…

He began his rhythm and she cooed her pleasure. Her eyes closed of their own volition and she used the darkness to simply feel. His thrusts and parries were slow and sensuous. She let him pick the pace and was glad of that. She'd never have guessed he liked it slow.

"I love you so much, Claudia," he whispered.

Her name rolled off his lips, sounding like a caress. She didn't want to do anything to break the spell, so she answered him telepathically.

I love you too.

She continued to concentrate on the glorious sensations of his intimate strokes. She felt a flutter from deep within. She'd never had an orgasm without direct contact to that little exposed bundle of nerves, but she'd heard that the clitoris was much larger on the inside of the body. That must have been what he was stroking.

Before she knew it, she climaxed in a way she never

had before. Subtler, deeper, more… She abandoned thought and let the new sensation wash over her. As her inner muscles fluttered, Anthony stiffened and jerked a few times. She opened her eyes and watched his face as he climaxed. Eyes closed, he let his head fall back and his mouth opened. He let out a long breath and stilled.

Then he looked down at her and his smile warmed her heart. She felt tears brimming in her eyes. Would he know she was crying from happiness?

He must have. He slid out slowly and gently lowered her bottom to the bed. Then he lay beside her and gathered her in his arms. He wrapped himself around her as if sheltering her from the world and all its storms.

She let out a long sigh and enveloped him with her free arm. "Thank you."

"For what?"

"The gift of yourself."

Anthony woke to the sound of female voices. One was definitely Claudia's, but he couldn't quite place the other one. It sounded familiar.

He knew he could lie there and eavesdrop, but that wouldn't be right.

What time is it? He rolled toward the bedside table on which Claudia kept her old-fashioned alarm clock. She said she didn't trust digital clocks because when the power went out, the alarm wouldn't get her up. More reason to love her. She wouldn't let him down by being late to work.

The battery-operated analog clock said 10:30, but was that a.m. or p.m.? Either he'd slept a few minutes or several hours. When had he last had any Vampire Vintage? Its effects were temporary, and judging by his total lack of bloodlust, he was still enjoying its neutralizing effect. It must be the same evening. Besides, Claudia would be at work if it were morning.

Anthony got out of bed and dressed quickly.

When he rounded the corner, he was surprised to see one of his former waitresses from when the place was a bar. Bliss. Of course, he knew Claudia and Bliss were friends, but he hadn't seen her since the fire.

He cleared his throat to let the women know he was there. They glanced his way at the same time.

"Anthony. So nice to see you." Bliss rose.

"You too," he said. "You look well, Bliss."

She grinned. "I couldn't be any better if I tried."

He didn't hug his waitstaff while they worked for him, but this was Claudia's friend and no longer his employee. He strode to her and extended his arms. She looked surprised but took the cue and hugged him.

"Wow. Claudia, you've really loosened him up."

Anthony's browns rose. *What did she mean by that?*

Claudia answered him telepathically. *"She remembers you as reserved and serious."*

Ah, yes. Back when he was worried about Ruxandra's jealousy, he'd kept all his female employees at arm's length…if not farther. He hardly smiled then.

He suddenly realized what a difference Claudia had made in his life. And now that Ruxandra was truly remorseful for her former behavior, he might be able to relax even more. "How's Drake?"

"Good. Although he's being more careful on the job now that he chose to give up his immortality for me."

"He did that?" Anthony didn't mean to sound so shocked. He'd certainly do it, if it meant not having to survive without Claudia. "How?"

Bliss worried her lip, then whispered, "I'm not allowed to tell. I shouldn't have said anything." Then in her normal voice she said, "Damn it. I'm such a blurter."

Anthony realized who had to be behind it. There was no other explanation. "Gaia did that for him?"

"Shhh..." Bliss glanced around the room furtively as if expecting the goddess to show up.

"Sorry," Anthony said. "I know we're not supposed to tell anyone who doesn't know, but we already do."

Bliss's brows rose. "*Both* of you know?"

Claudia chuckled. "Yes. At first I was told she was Anthony's business partner, which was weird because he'd never mentioned having one. Later on, she told me the truth."

Bliss's mouth hung open.

"Tell me more about what she did for Drake," Anthony said. *Perhaps there's a way I can convince her to do the same for me.*

"I wouldn't want you to. Not without a lot of thought."

I don't have to think about it. I don't want to live without you.

"And what if you go first? I don't want to live without you, either."

Bliss looked from one to the other. "Are you two having a telepathic conversation?"

Both Claudia and Anthony must have looked shocked, because Bliss laughed. "Yes, I know some paranormal couples can do that."

"Can you and Drake?" Claudia asked.

"No. It's not part of dragon DNA. I know werewolves and vampires can talk to their true mates that way. Congratulations, by the way!"

"So you know about me?" Anthony asked.

"Yes. Drake told me everything. Not right away. I think he was worried that I might go running to Claudia and tell her she was working in Paranormal Central."

"Why didn't you?"

Bliss chuckled. "The lady we spoke of a moment ago can be pretty darn persuasive."

"Ah, yes. That's very true." Anthony would have smiled, had the trip to the Alps not been so threateningly cold. Without warm blood in his veins, he'd have frozen like a Popsicle in minutes.

Suddenly, Gaia appeared. "You didn't think that just by talking in code, I wouldn't know you were referring to me, did you?"

Bliss jumped. "I'm sorry, Goddess. It's just that they…well, they already knew—"

"Oh, relax." Gaia plopped down onto the sofa next to Claudia. "I have to talk to them anyway."

Uh-oh. "About what?" Anthony asked.

"A job offer."

Claudia's brows knit. "But we already have jobs."

Mother Nature waved away the thought. "It's not for both of you—just you, dear." She patted Claudia's hand. "Besides, it won't take you away from your work all that much."

Bliss fidgeted as if she knew what was coming. "Uh, maybe I should go."

Claudia glanced back and forth at her friend and Mother Nature. "Are you sure? I mean, maybe you could—"

Before Claudia could finish her sentence, Bliss disappeared.

"What just happened?"

"Relax. She's fine. I just sent her back to her beautiful home. She's busy fixing up a nursery, so she has plenty to do to keep her occupied for a while."

"Oh. Okaaaay."

"I know what you're thinking."

"You do?" Claudia asked, wide eyed.

"You were wondering if she's pregnant."

"No. She told me she was the minute she walked in the door."

"Oh. Of course, she would." Mother Nature rolled her eyes.

"So, this job offer..." Anthony reminded her.

Mother Nature nodded. "Yes. Let's get back on track. Anthony, sit. This doesn't involve you, so be quiet."

He didn't like being commanded like a dog, but the all-powerful one was not someone to argue with. He lowered himself onto the adjacent armchair.

Mother Nature focused on Claudia. "I need a few new muses."

"Muses? Like Brandee?" Claudia asked.

Mother Nature crossed her arms. "You know about her too?"

"She rescued me. Please don't be mad. I might not be here if not for her."

Gaia let out a sigh. "Actually, that makes my job easier, so I'll let it slide. Yes. Just like Brandee. Technology has created the need for a whole new set of muses. Brandee is familiar with photography, so I made her the muse of still and moving images. Whatever she did to rescue you must not have had anything to do with her area of expertise, because it wasn't in her report."

"No. There were no cameras involved."

"Okay. I'll ask her about it later. Back to the job offer…"

"First…" Claudia raised a finger. "Did I just get Brandee in trouble by telling you that she rescued me?"

"No. Not at all. I trust my muses to do what's best for the greater good. She must have rescued you for a reason. Perhaps my offer has something to do with that."

"Yes," Anthony interjected. "The offer. What is it, and does Claudia have the right to refuse, if it's not something she wants to do?"

"I'm getting to that, Mr. Antsy-Pants."

Anthony thought he'd better not get on her nerves any more than he already had and leaned back in his chair.

"As I said, I need a few new muses. And yes, you have the right to refuse. Bliss did. I tried to talk her into it, offering all kinds of incentives, but what can I say? The woman can be ridiculously stubborn. I even grew a money tree in the middle of her living room."

"Wow. What job did you offer her?" Claudia asked.

"Muse of electronic written communication. Email and such."

"Jeez! I can understand not wanting *that* responsibility. I hope that's not the job you're offering me. I'm not very tech savvy."

"No. I'm aware it's not your area of expertise." Mother Nature shrugged. "I'll find someone for that eventually."

Claudia was chewing her lip, and it was all Anthony could do to wait for Gaia to get to the point.

"I need a muse of middle management. I thought you'd be good at that."

Claudia's eyes widened. "Seriously? That's almost as bad as muse of the Internet. Do you know how many frustrated, angry managers have dumbass bosses who have no idea what's going on, and..."

Anthony cleared his throat.

"Oh!" She looked at him sheepishly. "Sorry, hon. I didn't mean you."

He smirked. "I didn't think you did."

"You'd be able to alleviate some of that frustration," Mother Nature said.

Claudia's brow wrinkled. "How?"

"Just whisper in their ears whatever will help. Like, 'Hey, it's a paycheck' or 'It's almost Friday...' You know. Whatever you told yourself to get through another boring day."

Claudia winced. "I didn't cope that well. Actually, I stayed because I was secretly in love with Anthony. I drank the frustration away after I got home each night."

"Oh. Well, in that case, forget it. You'd suck at that," Mother Nature said.

Claudia laughed. "I'm afraid so. The last thing I want to do is create more alcoholics."

Gaia turned her gaze on Anthony. "You knew all this?"

"I only found out after the bar burned. I had no idea prior to that. I was busy trying to keep my own feelings under wraps."

"But now you know. And you don't have a problem with an alcoholic girlfriend?"

"I don't think of her that way. She's Claudia. Not a disease. Besides, she's working hard to change. All I can do is admire and support her."

Mother Nature nodded. "You're a good man, Anthony. I'm glad I didn't leave you on that mountaintop."

"Gee, thanks."

Gaia sat up straighter and glanced from one to the other. "So, what should I do with the two of you? You've been a huge pain in the ass."

Claudia's jaw dropped. "We have?"

"Well, your boyfriend has. He was the one who created a paranormal meeting place with humans in and all around it and gave me more gray hairs than I already had. I'm amazed it didn't blow up in your faces...much."

"I had a dream of creating a safe environment for those of us who wanted to put aside the old prejudices," Anthony said. "I knew I couldn't be the only one who wanted to achieve that, and you have to admit, it was successful."

"There's one success I'm aware of that your little band of misfits were responsible for."

He was about to take exception to the word "misfits" when Mother Nature held up one palm.

"Save it."

Claudia looked from one to the other. "I'm confused."

Anthony sat on the arm of the sofa and laid a hand on her shoulder. "The lab in Cambridge. I didn't want to worry you by telling you we raided the place."

Claudia's eyes rounded. "You what? When?"

"Last night and this morning. That's when we rescued Tory. We also freed the other paranormals they had in their cages."

"Is everyone all right?"

He smiled. "Everyone's fine." He regarded Mother

Nature and said, "I should probably fill you in on the details."

"That won't be necessary. I had a chat with the wizard."

"Kurt knows about you?"

"He does now. I arrived shortly after you left. He and his girlfriend were helping the researchers to refocus their energies and intellect on a whole new project."

"The sex dolls."

"Yes. Apparently Kurt and Ruxandra are helping in the lab until the plans are firmly cemented in place."

"Sex dolls?" Claudia asked.

Gaia snickered. "You don't mind your boyfriend financing their new venture, do you?"

"They had to discontinue their funding from the pharmaceutical company, but *somebody* has to pay them," Anthony volunteered.

"No. That's not a problem as long as I don't have to be involved in it."

"Neither of us do, honey," he said. "I'm just providing the financing and getting progress reports. Kurt and Ruxandra will keep an eye on the lab and staff."

"And eventually you'll make millions," Gaia said.

Claudia scratched her head. "But how did you explain the change to the pharmaceutical company?"

"Kurt took care of that," Anthony said.

"With my help," Mother Nature added. "He's great when it comes to magic, but not so hot on getting from point A to point B and back in a snap. He had to alter paperwork in more than one place. That's where I came in."

"So he was busy. That's why he didn't make it to the party until after it was over."

"Correct."

"How about the memories?" Claudia asked. "Won't the people at the company who provided the grant know something funny is going on?"

"Nope. I took care of that too," Gaia said, proudly.

"You can do that?"

The goddess rolled her eyes. "Just who do you think you're talking to?"

"Oh."

Mother Nature rose and paced. "But I do owe you and your friends a debt of gratitude. And perhaps a reward." Gaia stopped pacing and faced Claudia. "You're not a mother, but I gave you a maternal instinct. Maybe you'll understand this. When you have a child that's 'special' in any way, you tend to be more aware of that child."

"Okay. I guess so."

"Well, I know so. My paranormals are my special children. Most of them began as regular human beings, but through no fault of their own wound up coping with some pretty extraordinary circumstances. Like a child who's been in an accident."

Anthony crossed his arms. "If we're so special, why do you threaten to send us to places we couldn't survive, like icy mountaintops or active volcanoes?"

"I gather you've talked to Nick Wolfensen." When he didn't respond, she sighed. "Oh, come on… All parents make threats they don't keep."

"Hmmm. It sure felt like you meant it."

She planted her hands on her hips. "I probably did at the time. But you're still here, aren't you?"

"Yes."

"Okay. Quit complaining. So, now I have a dilemma."

"What's that?" Claudia asked.

"I'd like to reward your boyfriend for saving some of my special children, but he disobeyed me in the first place."

Anthony's brows shot up. "I did? I don't recall that."

Mother Nature snorted. "No. You wouldn't. I sent Balog to tell you not to open your bar. He was incompetent and didn't accomplish his task. Needless to say, he won't be rewarded any time soon."

Anthony rubbed his chin. "Oh, yes. I remember now. He said he was afraid it would be a bad influence on Adolf Junior."

"Yes, then he arranged a couple of thugs to start a bar fight. None of that deterred you."

"Had you come to me yourself and explained your objections, I'd have been disappointed, but I'd have listened," Anthony said.

"And that's why I don't run around telling everybody what to do."

"Huh?"

"I like to see how my children handle circumstances on their own. None of you will learn anything if I keep saving you from yourselves."

Anthony followed her logic but was still a bit confused.

"I underestimated your determination. When you set your mind to something, you make it happen," Gaia said.

"I think that's a compliment."

"Don't get all puffed up. Want to see what I thought of your idea when I first heard of it?"

"See?" Anthony asked.

Gaia sighed. She drew a circle in the air and a picture—more like a 3-D movie—came into focus.

~

The goddess paced with her hands behind her back. She whirled on Mr. Balog and narrowed her eyes.

"You're sure he's a vampire and he's opened a bar for all paranormals?"

"That's the intel I've gathered."

"Hmph. I cannot think of a stupider idea. Can you, Balog?"

"No, ma'am."

She balled her fists. "What have I told you about calling me 'ma'am'?"

He bowed and stepped back. "My apologies, Gaia, er, Goddess."

"That's right. Gaia or Goddess. I may be older than dirt, but you don't have to rub it in my face by calling me 'ma'am.'"

"I'm sorry."

Gaia folded her arms. "Apology accepted. Now what are we going to do about this bar? Before the werewolves and vampires have a pissing contest in front of the humans."

"Pissing contest? Do you really think they'd—"

"Gaaah! It's an expression, you Romanian dimwit. Get with the lingo of your adopted land. Do you think I brought you over here for nothing?"

"Yes, Goddess. I mean, no, Goddess. I mean…"

She waved away his confusion. "The paranormal beings must never reveal their supernatural status to humans. That's the only thing I demand of them." She threw her hands in the air. "Are you sure you've made that abundantly clear down there?"

"Yes, Goddess."

She sighed. "Fine. Try to talk that vampire out of his ridiculous plan."

"Yes, ma—I mean, Goddess."

She narrowed her eyes at him again and he stood stiffly, trying not to do anything to anger the powerful Gaia.

At last she seemed satisfied. "All right. You have your orders. Now get out of my office building."

Turning from the now-dark and disappearing screen to Claudia and Anthony, Mother Nature said, "Think it over and tell me what—other than your freakin' paranormal meeting place—is your fondest wish."

Anthony vacated the arm of the chair and sat next to Claudia. Taking her hand and gazing into her eyes, he said, "I'd like to be human again. To live a normal human life with my beloved."

Mother Nature smiled. "I thought you might say that. There are some important details you should be aware of first."

"Like?"

"You'll lose all your heightened senses."

"A mixed blessing at best."

"You'll have faults. Just like any other human."

"I have faults now."

"You won't be allowed to know the paranormal world exists—just like any other human. That means you might lose some friends."

"Why? Can't they just keep their paranormal identities a secret?"

Gaia laughed. "Yeah. Like they've been doing that perfectly. Look. If you become human and accidentally discover some of your friends are paranormal, you'd freak out just like you were learning of it for the first time."

A stab of sadness overwhelmed him. He thought about losing dear friends without whom his dream would never have been realized. Friends like Nick and Tory and Kurt.

"I trust them to keep their identities a secret. All you need to do is ask them to treat us like any other humans."

"Riiiiight. That might interfere with your closeness. Trusting friends with your secrets is part of friendship. Who would you say is your closest friend?"

"Other than Claudia? Kurt, probably."

She laughed. "Do you remember the first day you met?"

"Of course."

"Let me show your girlfriend what I mean."

"Why?"

Mother Nature raised one eyebrow. "Why not?"

Anthony didn't know what Gaia was up to, but there was nothing about that day that would upset Claudia. Eventually, he shrugged and said, "Go ahead."

Gaia smiled. She drew a large circle in the air and a scene appeared in it, again kind of like a movie. Claudia sat up and paid attention.

All three of them watched and listened.

A knock on the front door of the brand-new bar surprised Anthony, and he whirled toward the sound. Instead of opening the door, he strolled to the bow window that looked out onto Charles Street. He could make out a casually dressed male, but it was no one he had met before.

"At least it's not Ruxandra," he muttered. He'd gone to a lot of trouble to give her the slip when he'd snuck out of New Orleans, masking his scent and leaving everything behind. He hoped she'd think he had met his true death.

He strode to the heavy oak door and opened it wide. "Can I help you?"

"Funny," the five-year-younger Kurt said. "I was about to ask you the same thing."

"Come again?"

"Thanks. I hope to come here often." The stranger-at-the-time gave Anthony a bright grin, making him wonder if he had found another friend, perhaps of the paranormal variety.

"Come in." Anthony stepped aside and let the man enter. "Are you looking for a job?"

He shrugged. "Maybe."

"What position are you interested in applying for?"

"I was thinking of something a little outside the box."

Anthony scratched his head. "Have a seat and tell me about it. By the way, my name is Anthony Cross, and you are..."

"Kurt."

Anthony wondered why Kurt didn't give his last name, but it didn't really matter. Until he heard the man's idea, this would be nothing more than an exploratory meeting.

"So, what is this out-of-the-box idea you have in mind, Kurt?"

"Well, it's like this. You're going to need someone

like me to handle unusual situations if things get dicey." He leaned back in his chair and draped an arm around the finial, looking like he owned the place.

"What do you mean by someone like you?"

"I'm an ex-marine...and a wizard."

Anthony couldn't help his surprise. His reaction showed on his face, and the guy laughed.

"Seriously. I figured you could use an undercover bouncer. I'll just hang out and drink, like a regular. That way it won't spook the clientele, but you can rest assured that if any disagreements get out of hand, I can fix whatever happens pretty quickly."

"How?"

"I can freeze time. Well, not exactly time. It has to do with quantum physics, but instead of explaining how it works, why don't I just show you?"

Anthony's curiosity demanded he explore it... whatever it was. "Okay. As they say in Missouri, 'Show me.'"

"Look at your watch."

Anthony's Rolex indicated it was eight thirty. A moment later, it was eight forty-five and he hadn't seen the hand move.

"Shit."

"No shit." Kurt grinned. "I can't erase minds, but that's where you come in. I *think* you can do that with hypnosis. Right?"

Anthony gave him a sidelong look.

"So, how about it?" Kurt persisted. "Do we make a great team, or what?"

"How much do you want per hour and when can you start?"

Mother Nature folded her arms. "They're *real* good about not revealing themselves *or* each other *or* any of their unusual abilities, aren't they?"

Anthony shook his head hard as if to erase the nostalgic image. "How did Kurt know what I was? I never asked him."

"And you never will if I do this for you."

Anthony paced and muttered out loud. "I'd just assumed as often happens when one opens oneself to the universe, serendipity or 'coincidence' stepped in. But now that I think about it, Nick must have told him."

Mother Nature tipped her head. "Like I said… So, are you changing your mind?"

When he considered being able to live a normal life with his normal wife, who he'd propose to as soon as he had a believable birth certificate… "I really want my humanity back. All of it. Good and bad. But do I *have* to lose my friends? Can't you just strongly warn them not to say anything? Make it really clear to them what will happen?"

She let out a huge sigh. "Give me a day or two, and I'll see what I can come up with."

Anthony's gaze snapped to the goddess's face. "You can…" He rolled his eyes. "Never mind. I forgot who I was talking to."

Gaia laughed. "Now you're getting it."

"But there's one thing you should know."

"Oh? What's that?"

"One of your *special* children has been a thorn in my side for centuries. I know it was my fault for turning her, but is there any way you can turn her back or keep her away from us? She only recently lost her goal of making our lives a living hell, and I'm not ready to trust it yet."

"Ruxandra."

"You're aware?"

Mother Nature sighed. "Yes. I've seen you struggle to handle her, and I have to give you props for patience. She can be a handful."

"You got that right," Claudia said.

Holding up one palm, Mother Nature continued. "I've witnessed the new relationship, and her bond with the wizard is real."

"I'm glad to hear that," Anthony said. "But I'm still apprehensive."

"What about turning her human…" Claudia asked. "I know she doesn't deserve it as a reward, but it might be a really good idea for everyone concerned. I can't imagine—"

Gaia held up her palm to interrupt Claudia. "Do you have any idea how hard this is to do? We're talking about rearranging DNA."

Claudia's shoulders slumped. "I guess it's out of the question. I just can't help worrying that we'll be even more vulnerable if we don't know what she's capable of."

"She's not interested in bothering you anymore."

Anthony looked at her skeptically. "How can you be sure?"

Gaia snickered. "That's one of my strokes of genius—not just for her, but for many jilted lovers."

"What is?" Anthony asked.

"Ever heard this little ditty? *The fastest way for a*

woman to get over a man is to get under another one." Who do you think invented that?

Claudia's hand covered her mouth. Anthony didn't know if she was trying to stifle a gasp or a chuckle.

Gaia composed herself after her own hearty laugh. "I think they'll be bitten by the travel bug at some point. A little wanderlust will keep them out of your hair."

"But we'll still be friends?" Anthony asked.

"You'll get postcards from all over the world."

Claudia smiled. "That sounds good to me. Does it work for you?"

He returned her smile. "Yes, it does."

Brandee placed the *Back in five minutes* sign in the glass front door of her photography gallery and lifted her adorable baby girl from her playpen. "Ready."

Gaia folded her arms. "I know you don't like to close in the middle of the day, but this is going to take more than five minutes."

"Like how much longer?"

"At least fifteen."

Brandee chuckled. "It's a ballpark figure. No one will hold me to it."

Smug minor goddess. "You like being your own boss, don't you?"

Brandee grinned. "You know it."

"As my muse, you are technically in my employ, and you know how I don't like to micromanage."

"Yes. I'm grateful for that."

The powerful goddess waved her hand at the sign and

suddenly it read, *Back in fifteen minutes.* "On the other hand, sometimes I do."

Brandee grimaced. "Message received."

"Good. Now gather up all the regulars and meet me at Boston Uncommon."

"But it's Tuesday. It's closed today."

"Exactly. We need to meet without the human staff. Is that a problem?"

Brandee shrugged. "No. I guess not. As long as they don't suddenly decide to show up."

"I've taken care of that. The bosses are sleeping in today, and there's no way the employees will come in on their day off."

"That's for sure. Well, I guess you've thought of everything. I'll get the group together and we'll be there in a few minutes."

"Good."

The goddess disappeared and reappeared in the tea room. Her muse did as she was told and gathered the owner and manager's wide circle of paranormal friends and sympathizers. In a matter of seconds the room began filling up.

First to arrive was Nick who lovingly took their baby girl in his arms. Then Brandee disappeared again and returned with her brother-in-law, Konrad, and his wife, Roz. Next, Sadie the psychic. After that, Tory, Kurt, and Ruxandra. Drake and Bliss. Eventually, Sly and Morgaine.

"Is that it?" Gaia asked.

"Other than friends of friends, I believe so. If we think of anyone else, we can fill them in," Brandee said.

"Fine. Now here's the deal, folks." Mother Nature paced in front of the group with her hands clasped behind her back. "I'm rewarding Anthony and distracting him at the same time."

The guests glanced at each other.

"He needs to give up the crazy idea that paranormals can meet in a public place like this and all get along. Eventually this foolish plan will backfire."

"You don't want us meeting in a safe place?" Nick asked. "We never would have been able to take down that lab if not for our ability to work together."

"It's too risky," she said. "There are humans working here. You know damn well how I feel about humans learning that paranormals exist. It's the biggest mistake you can make." She eyed the whole group. "As you all know."

Most of the members nodded their heads.

"Do you want another lab popping up, doing experiments on you?"

They all shook their heads.

"Right. I understand a merman outed you. He's been dealt with. I don't think he'll find much water in the Sahara Desert. Am I making myself clear, people?"

Everyone nodded.

"Exposing your kind makes me very angry, and you *don't* want to make me angry." She glared at each and every one of them in turn.

Kurt raised his hand. "We get it. But why isn't Anthony here?"

Mother Nature folded her arms. "I'm getting to that. Anthony's fondest wish is to become human again. That means he'll be mortal. He'll eat regular food, he'll poop, and he won't go into a death sleep at sunrise. As a result, he and Claudia will have to have every memory of paranormals erased."

Bliss gasped. "Are you saying Drake and I can't be friends with Claudia and Anthony anymore? She's my best friend."

"Of course not, but you'd better not slip up." Gaia pointed a long, unmanicured fingernail at each one of them. "That goes for *all of you* who befriend them or any other human."

"We won't. Don't worry," Nick said.

"You'd better not. There are still active volcanoes, and I can drop any of you into one if you really piss me off. Any more questions?"

"Um…I read tea leaves here. Can I still work?" Sadie asked. "I've never revealed a peep about the paranormal element to humans."

"That's true," Kurt said, "In fact, the one time we had a breach, it was Sadie who convinced everyone they were being ridiculous."

Mother Nature tapped her lips. "All right, but be extra careful."

"I will. I promise," Sadie said, and crossed her heart.

It was the first time Gaia had met the human psychic, and she couldn't help being impressed by how relaxed she was in such exceptional company.

"How did you wind up in this peculiar band, human?"

"Anthony's my seventh great-uncle and was best friends with my beloved until he met his true death."

Mother Nature smirked. "Well, you've got the lingo down. You've never divulged the existence of paranormals to anyone?"

"No, Goddess."

"Not even a priest?"

"No, Goddess. Never. Anthony calls me Aunt Sadie,

so people know we're related, but we shifted our relationship to make it look natural."

Satisfied, Gaia said, "Good."

"What if we want to meet here just to have tea and talk about the weather? Is that okay?" Ruxandra asked.

"I'd rather you stay away from this place. You're skating on thin ice as it is. But if for some inexplicable reason—one that I can't even imagine right now—you absolutely have to be here, remember…no hints, no whispers, not even a conspiratorial wink to each other. That goes for everybody. You're just friends. Got it?"

"Yes, Goddess," she said. The others nodded or murmured in agreement.

"Excuse me, Goddess. I have a question," Tory said. "There may be occasions when we *should* talk to each other paranormal to paranormal. If we meet somewhere else, is that all right?"

"Did you have a particular place in mind?"

"I have a large home on the hill."

Gaia narrowed her eyes. "Your girlfriend is human."

"Yes."

"And you're going to keep all paranormal discussion from her?"

"Absolutely."

"The answer is still no."

"What? But if she's not there…"

"She will be."

A slow smile crept across Tory's face. "Are you saying what I think you're saying?"

"Yes. Find another place, because soon it'll be her home too."

"Hallelujah!"

Kurt slapped Tory on the back. "Congrats, man."

Mother Nature purposely used her bored voice so they wouldn't get carried away. "Yeah, yeah. Many happy returns. So does anyone else have a place?"

Sly and Morgaine glanced at each other. A moment later they said in unison, "We do."

"Ah, yes." Gaia chuckled. "The brownstone on Beacon Street. That place was a hotbed of upheaval a few years ago. Are there any unknowing humans living there now?"

"No. I'm the building's super, and my daughter owns the place," Sly said. "Her husband is one of us, and every tenant has some paranormal secret to keep. We even have an empty apartment we could use."

"Is it on the ground floor?"

"Uh, no. Second floor."

"Perfect. No pesky reporters peeking in windows. Use that."

An audible sigh of relief filled the room.

Mother Nature regarded their expressions. "You genuinely like each other, don't you?"

They all answered in the affirmative.

"You even trust this one?" She pointed to Ruxandra.

Some of them squirmed.

Ruxandra place a hand over her heart. "I know I've been a horrible person—even for a vampire, but I'm doing everything I can to change that now. Right, honey?" She turned to Kurt.

"I believe her," he said. "And she's under a truth spell so everyone can."

The rest of the group smiled and the closest ones patted Ruxandra on the back, murmuring encouragement.

"Well, I'll be darned. His stupid experiment worked. That doesn't mean I want it to continue. At least, not here."

"But you said we could still be friends with Anthony and Claudia," Bliss reminded her.

"Go out to dinner as a foursome. Stop by one at a time and talk about mundane things. I don't expect you'll stop caring about them."

"Good, because we won't," Drake said. It was the first time he'd spoken up, but he was probably just worried about his wife being best friends with Claudia. Gaia didn't like the way he said it, but she understood why.

"Would you like to rephrase that, Dragon?"

"Uh…okay. I doubt we'll stop caring about our dearest friends."

Mother Nature considered his wording and decided he was demonstrating the proper respect for her. The absolute minimum, but she'd let it go. "Yes… Well, I'm satisfied, for now. But if I have to put out any fires…"

"You won't," Drake promised.

She turned to her trusted muse. "Brandee, be sure everyone gets the address of the new meeting place and then return everyone to their homes or businesses."

"Yes, Goddess."

Morgaine pulled several business cards out of her pocket and handed them to the others. Gaia snagged one.

"Psychic readings. You do these out of your home?"

"Yes, Goddess. Many psychics do."

"That means humans frequent the place," Gaia said.

"Sometimes. I also do readings over the phone."

"Are you willing to do all your readings over the phone from now on?"

"Yes, and I will. I promise. No more unsuspecting humans in the building."

"Hmmm." Gaia shrugged. "Okay. I guess we've covered all the bases. Have nice lives."

"Troops, we've gotta fly," Brandee said, and they all disappeared.

Anthony and Claudia woke up on a blanket in a shady spot of Boston Common.

Anthony sat up and looked around to get his bearings. *Oh, yeah. We were having a picnic on the Common.*

Claudia sat up next to him. "Wow. I can't believe we fell asleep in the middle of a bright sunny day…on Boston Common, no less!"

"Yeah. We must be working too hard."

She sighed. "I really want to make the tea room a success."

"I know, but apparently closing one day a week isn't enough. Wednesday isn't a busy day. Why don't we take both Tuesdays and Wednesdays off? Or better yet, why don't we hire an assistant manager? We could actually get away once in a while."

"Like where?"

Anthony had been waiting for the right time to propose. This might be it. He rose, took the ring box out of his jacket pocket, and then dropped onto one knee. "Like on a honeymoon. A brief one, but we can take a longer one later."

Claudia's mouth formed an almost perfect O, reminding him of a certain sex act she performed so well.

"Are you asking me to marry you?"

He chuckled. "I suppose I should actually say the words, huh?" He took her left hand in his right. "Claudia Fletcher, my love, my life, my only... Will you marry me?"

She grinned. "Absolutely, yes."

He slipped the solitaire diamond ring onto her third finger. She rolled up onto her knees and threw her arms around his neck. They shared a long kiss until someone walking nearby yelled out, "Get a room."

They chuckled. At last Anthony said, "Let's have lunch. I'm *starving*. I feel like I haven't eaten in *years*."

Claudia opened the picnic basket. "Let's see...what do we have here? Ah, a steak sandwich—that must be yours. And for me, a chef salad. Perfect."

She handed the sandwich to Anthony as well as a cloth napkin and soft drink. Then she took out her salad, and as she was removing the plastic wrap, he took a big bite of his sandwich.

"Mmm...I don't think I've ever tasted anything so good."

Claudia chuckled. "If you do say so yourself."

He swallowed and cocked his head. "What do you mean?"

"Well, you were the one who put together the lunch..."

Huh? He wracked his brain, and for the life of him, he couldn't remember doing it. He stared at her. "I thought *you* made the lunch."

They paused for a few moments, gaping at each other. Then, as if they were too happy to care, they just shrugged and chowed down.

Acknowledgments

Many thanks to the members of New Hampshire and Massachusetts twelve-step groups, who taught me what I needed to know to write Claudia's journey to recovery.

As always, I want to thank the following people for their unwavering dedication and help.

The women of Leah Mae's Tea Room in Haverhill, MA. They answered all the questions I had while serving me high tea.

Mia Marlowe, my fabulous, almost famous critique partner. If you like my sense of humor, go check out her historical romances. Oftentimes, her "quips" wind up in my books! Ha! She'll be the first one to tell you, "Be careful what you say around a writer." (Heh heh.)

Nicole Resciniti, my fabulous agent, for her feedback, encouragement, and belief in me. When she says things like, "You did it again!" and I know she means it in a good way, it's priceless.

Also my editor for this series, Leah Hultenschmidt. I could always count on her to be kind when she twisted my arm.

How to Date a Dragon

by Ashlyn Chase

Let the sparks fly

Bliss Russo thought nothing exciting ever happened in her life. Until her building caught on fire and she had to be carried out of the flames in the arms of a gorgeous fireman. Sure, her apartment is now in shambles and she'll have to start her huge work project completely from scratch. But at least her love life is finally looking up…if only she can find her red-hot rescuer again.

Dragon shapeshifter Drake Cameron is the last in his clan, and the loneliness is starting to claw at him. He's met only one woman who might be able to stand the shock of his true nature. After all, she barely batted an eyelash when her home burned down. And feeling her curves against him was just as hot as any inferno. Just when he thinks he'll never track her down, she walks into his firehouse—with no idea what she's about to get herself into…

"[Ashlyn Chase] entertains with a voice that makes reading her stories pure pleasure. It's like spending time with your favorite friends."—*Night Owl Romance* Reviewer Top Pick

"Zany characters, sarcasm, sizzling sensuality, humor, originality, arson, dragons, passion, romance, and true love abound in this delightfully entertaining story."—*Romance Junkies*

Flirting Under a Full Moon

by Ashlyn Chase

Never Cry Werewolf

Brandee has been dumped in every way possible, but by text is the last straw. That's it—she's officially done with men. Unfortunately, she's just been told her "soul mate" is the drool-worthy hottie all her friends call One-Night Nick.

Nick has been searching for true love for one hundred years. After all, werewolves mate for life, and he does not want to mess this up. As soon as he kisses Brandee, he knows she's the one. But how will he convince a woman who knows nothing of paranormals that she's about to be bound to a werewolf forever?

"Hot sex scenes and a breezy tone with a nice, happily-ever-after ending makes Chase's story a fun read." —*Booklist*

"It made me laugh, crafted a mystery that had me guessing, and the romance was sweet, steamy, and paranormal." —*The Romance Reviews*

For more Ashlyn Chase, visit:

www.sourcebooks.com

The Vampire Next Door

by Ashlyn Chase

Room for Rent: Normal need not apply

This old Boston brownstone is not known for quiet living... first the shapeshifter meets his nurse, then the werewolf falls for his sassy lawyer, but now the vampire is looking for love with a witch who's afraid of the dark...and you thought your neighbors had issues!

Undead Sly is content playing vigilante vampire, keeping the neighborhood safe from human criminals, until Morgaine moves in upstairs. Suddenly he finds himself weak with desire, which isn't a good place for a vampire to be. And Morgaine isn't exactly without her own issues—will the two of them be able to get past their deepest fears before their chance at "normal" slips away...

Praise for *The Werewolf Upstairs:*

"Witty and wonderful...the entertaining plot, humor, sizzling sensual scenes, and romance make this story unforgettable." —*Romance Junkies*

Strange Neighbors

by Ashlyn Chase

He's looking for peace, quiet, and a little romance...

There's never a dull moment when hunky all-star pitcher and shapeshifter Jason Falco invests in an old Boston brownstone apartment building full of supernatural creatures. But when Merry MacKenzie moves into the ground floor apartment, the playboy pitcher decides he might just be done playing the field...

A girl just wants to have fun...

Sexy Jason seems like the perfect fling, but newly independent nurse Merry's not sure she's ready to trust him with her heart...especially when the tabloids start trumpeting his playboy lifestyle.

Then pandemonium breaks loose and Merry and Jason will never get it together without a little help from the vampire who lives in the basement and the werewolf from upstairs...

"The good-natured fun never stops. Chase brings on plenty of laughs along with steamy sex scenes." —*Publishers Weekly*

Unclaimed

The Amoveo Legend

by Sara Humphreys

She brings out the beast in him...

She works hard to be normal...

Tatiana Winters loves the freedom of her life as a veterinarian in Oregon. It's only reluctantly that she agrees to help cure a mysterious illness among the horses on a Montana ranch—the ranch of the Amoveo Prince. Tatiana is no ordinary vet—she's a hybrid from the Timber Wolf Clan, but she wants nothing to do with the world of the Amoveo shifters.

But there's no escaping destiny

Dominic Trejada serves as a Guardian, one of the elite protectors of the Prince's Montana ranch. As a dedicated Amoveo warrior, he is desperate to find his mate, and time is running out. He knows Tatiana is the one—but if he can't convince her, he may not be able to protect her from the evil that's rapidly closing in...

Praise for *Undone*:

Spellbinding...This fast-paced, jam-packed thrill ride will delight paranormal romance fans." —*Publishers Weekly*

For more Sara Humphreys, visit:

www.sourcebooks.com

About the Author

Ashlyn Chase describes herself as an Almond Joy bar. A little nutty, a little flaky, but basically sweet, wanting only to give her readers a scrumptious, satisfying reading experience.

She holds a degree in behavioral sciences, worked as a psychiatric RN for several years and spent a few more years working for the American Red Cross. She credits her sense of humor to her former careers since comedy helped preserve whatever was left of her sanity. She is a multipublished, award-winning author of humorous erotic and mainstream romances.

She lives in beautiful New Hampshire with her true-life hero husband, who looks like Hugh Jackman with a salt-and-pepper dye job, and they're owned by a spoiled brat cat.

Want more smart, steamy, and laugh-out-loud-funny paranormal romance?

Read on for excerpts from the previous books in the Flirting with Fangs series by Ashlyn Chase:

Flirting Under a Full Moon

How to Date a Dragon

Flirting Under a Full Moon

Over the din of clinking ice and lively conversation, the entire bar heard waitress Brandee Hanson wail, "Dumped in a text message? *Really?*"

Suddenly the place quieted. Heat crept up her neck, and she dropped her BlackBerry into her apron pocket. She was about to slink off to the ladies' room when Sadie Maven, the owner's eccentric aunt, waved her over to the booth she regularly occupied.

"Have a seat, dear. Let me do a quick reading for you—on the house." Sadie was already shuffling her tarot cards.

Brandee slumped onto the opposite bench and set down her tray.

"I had a premonition about you just now." Sadie winked. "It might make you feel better."

Brandee sighed. "I'm all for feeling better. Just don't talk about my love life. I've sworn off men."

"Since when?"

"Since just now."

Sadie spread the cards across the table. "Pick one."

Brandee pulled one card from the middle and turned it over. On it was a picture of a couple entwined in a passionate embrace, and the text beneath proclaimed: *The Lovers*.

"Ah. I was right. You'll meet your true love soon. In fact, he could be the next man to walk through that door."

Psychic Sadie nodded toward Boston Uncommon's Charles Street entrance.

Brandee gazed at the door expectantly. It swung open and a tall, blond, broad-shouldered hunk of a man breezed in.

Oh no. It couldn't be. "One-Night Nick? Are you kidding me?" She burst out laughing.

Sadie shrugged one shoulder. "You never know…"

Brandee picked up her tray and returned to work, still chuckling and shaking her head.

"What put that smile on your face, beautiful? Besides seeing me, of course." Nick Wolfensen grabbed a stool and sat on it backward. Even with the stool's height, his big feet hit the floor. His powerful thighs bulged under his blue jeans. That wasn't the only bulge she thought she saw.

Brandee knew her regulars and Nick was a good tipper. She'd play nice, even though Sadie's omen sat uncomfortably in the back of her mind. "Just something Sadie said. I think I've served her one too many White Russians."

"Well, you haven't served me at all, girl. I'm parched."

"What can I get you?"

"Whatever Sam Adams you have on tap."

"Coming right up."

Usually Angie would get Nick's beer, but the bartender looked engrossed in a conversation. Brandee lifted the part of the bar that flipped up and strode in. "It must be your evening off. You're not in uniform, and you're ordering a brew."

Nick frowned. "Yeah, kind of."

His set jaw and the twitch in his cheek told her she shouldn't pursue the subject. She simply grabbed a frosted mug and held it at an angle under the tap like

Angie had shown her. It created less froth and made room for more beer.

When she set it in front of him, his cocky smile returned. "Ah, you're a good girl. I'd sing 'Brandy' but you've probably heard it a few thousand times."

"Yeah, thanks for not doing that." Brandee played the song in her head, and when the words pointed out what a good wife she would be, she scurried away, mumbling, "Well, I gotta get back to work."

She grabbed a clean rag and wiped down a table that didn't need it. Over her shoulder she caught Nick unabashedly admiring her rear end. She quickly moved on to another empty table and made sure she was facing him. As soon as she bent over to reach the surface, her V-neck dipped. Now he was gazing at her cleavage like he might drool. She bolted upright.

Oh, my Fruity Pebbles. Why can't he turn around?

Nick rose, left his beer on the bar, and strolled over to her. He leaned down so he could whisper in her ear. "When, Brandee?"

She tried to look casual. "When what?"

"When are you going to let me show you the time of your life?"

She smiled, thinking what that might entail, but quickly schooled her expression. "I'm not that kind of girl."

He tried to look innocent, but she knew it was an act. Players like Nick scared her. Not that it stopped her from fantasizing about him. Handsome, charming, intelligent, and dangerous. Whether she had just been dumped or not, he wasn't the kind of guy she needed right now—or maybe ever.

Nick backed up a step. "What are you talking about?"

Brandee rested a hand on her hip and tried to look uncompromising. "I know your reputation. They don't call you 'One-Night Nick' for nothing."

"At least I'm honest about it. I never lead girls on by saying, 'I'll call you,' then leave them to wonder why I didn't. A lot of guys do. I treat a woman to an awesome night she'll never forget. I'm just not interested in getting tied down right now."

She lowered her voice. "Look, I'm not saying I want to get married either. But casual sex isn't my style."

He feigned shock, then boomed in his baritone, "Who said anything about sex? Of course if that's what *you* want, I'd be happy to oblige."

"Oh, my Playboy penthouse… Lower your voice, dammit." She glanced around, but people seemed to have lost interest in her. They continued their own conversations or preoccupation with the football game. *Thank you, Tom Brady*.

"What's your penthouse got to do with anything?"

She chuckled. "I don't live in a penthouse. I live over the bar. That's just something I do when I'm shocked. Instead of saying, "Oh my God—I substitute some other word or words for God."

"Are you religious? Don't want to take the Lord's name in vain or something?"

"Heck no. It's just way overused. I don't want to wear it out." She faced Sadie, who she knew took an interest in all the waitresses' love lives. Sadie shuffled her tarot cards with a knowing smile on her face.

He chuckled. "I'm not going to lie to you, Brandee. I think you're sexy as hell, and redheads are my weakness, but if you can't allow yourself a night of fun without some damn commitment…"

She sighed. “It’s not like that.”

“Then what is it?”

She couldn’t put her feelings into words. Sure she’d like to have a good time, but was one night worth the trouble and expense of getting a full body wax and a mani-pedi and buying a new outfit? She needed her tips to pay for her photography supplies. A night with the handsome cop would probably steal her breath away, but she didn’t want to risk losing her heart too.

He waved and walked away. “Forget it.”

By the time he had retaken his stool and started watching the game, Brandee regretted her hesitancy. Damn it all, Nick was hot. His blond hair was growing out just enough to curl around his ears, and his sapphire blue eyes were impossible to ignore. A suspect wouldn’t stand a chance against that intense stare. Hell. *She* didn’t stand a chance when he looked at her with those gorgeous eyes.

Still, “No casual sex, no matter how tempting the guy might be” was a good policy. She *did* want to fall in love and get married some day. Even a protected one-night stand could result in a life-altering “accident.” And if that happened, it would *not* be with a playboy like Nick Wolfensen.

A man who only dated to have a night of fun with a different woman each time must be extremely superficial. How satisfying could that be? What would make someone do that? Had he been hurt so badly he didn’t want to risk it again? She couldn’t think of any other reason.

Sadie caught her attention and held up her empty glass, calling for another.

Oh my pickled herring…that woman can put them away. But her nephew owned the bar and he’d told the staff to keep her happy. Not only did Anthony seem genuinely fond of his aunt, but she was good for business. To sit at her booth and have a tarot card reading, the patron had to meet the one-drink minimum.

When Brandee delivered Sadie's fourth White Russian, the fortune-teller said, "You know, my Dmitri was like that once."

"Like what?"

She smirked. "You should know better than to feign innocence with a psychic."

Brandee rolled her eyes. "Fine. So, you had a commitment-phobic boyfriend."

Sadie shuffled the cards again. "It wasn't that as much as he wanted to be free when the right woman came along. He really didn't like the idea of hurting anyone." She flipped over a card. "I think your Nick is doing the same thing."

"First of all, he's not *my* Nick."

Sadie pushed the card across the table toward her. "If you say so."

Brandee glanced at the card, then stared more closely. It was the same one. A man and a woman entwined in a passionate embrace. The Lovers.

Oh, my heartbreak…I'm toast.

"What's got your jockstrap in a twist?" Konrad asked.

Nick sat across from his twin brother, with a big mahogany desk between them. "It's nothing." He reached out and ran his hand over the polished surface, glancing at the gleaming brass plate that read Dean Konrad Wolfensen. "Jeez, I can't visit you without feeling like I've been sent to the principal's office."

Konrad laughed. "Maybe you were there too many times when we were kids. What's going on?"

"I quit."

Konrad's jaw dropped. "The force?"

"Yeah, what else do I have to quit?"

"Why?"

Nick fidgeted in his seat. He couldn't very well say his brother's high-profile court case had damaged his credibility, could he? Just because they looked exactly alike and Konrad had incurred public wrath and humiliation, Nick couldn't be absolutely sure that was the only reason his honor had been questioned—more than once—even though he had done nothing to deserve it. He hated the idea that it might be his brother's fault.

"I was butting heads with some of the guys."

"What about?"

Nick shrugged. "Nothing in particular. John Q. Public has been pissing me off too."

"Are you sleeping?"

"Not well."

"You look like you've lost weight."

Nick glanced down at his baggy Dockers. "Yeah, maybe a little."

"Sorry, Bro. I hate to say it, but it sounds like symptoms of depression."

Nick laughed. "Me? What do I have to be depressed about?"

Konrad gave him a sympathetic smile. "You just stood up for me as my best man. Maybe without realizing it…"

"You think I'm jealous? Of you?" Nick was about to

let out another bellowing laugh, but he thought better of it. He didn't want to insult his brother—or his new sister-in-law. Roz was a great girl and Konrad had found his true mate. Marriage was right for him. Nick didn't want to settle for less than that, and he didn't have to. He just had to be patient—correction—*more* patient, but it better not take much longer. At one hundred and one years old, Nick's secret wish was to find the *right* one without being attached to the wrong one.

"So tell me about quitting the force after nine years. It can't be over a few personality clashes."

Nick shifted uncomfortably. "What are you, my shrink now?"

"No, of course not, but you called and said you wanted to see me."

"I was bored."

Konrad leaned back in his big, oak armchair. "You were bored? You interrupted my workday because you were bored?"

"Hey, sorry I bothered you." Nick rose, ready to walk out.

"Stop. I didn't mean to run you off. You're here now, and I'm sure you weren't in the neighborhood. Newton isn't exactly around the corner."

"Nah, you're right. I should let you get back to work."

"Not if you need me. Look, I know you're not telling me everything. What's going on?"

Nick let out a long sigh. Konrad was right. There was more to it than just quitting his job. His lifestyle didn't hold the same glamour it once had, but he didn't dare voice that thought. Everyone was quick to tell him he needed to find a nice girl and settle down. Better to blame his boredom on job dissatisfaction. "I need to work for myself. I'm tired of taking orders, but I don't want to give them either."

"Then you're kind of fucked."

"Not necessarily. I thought of a way to work for myself without taking on a bunch of pesky employees. I'm getting my PI license."

"Private investigator?"

"No, public idiot. Of course private investigator. I'd be perfect for it. With my experience as a cop, I know the law—and how to get around it. As a paranormal PI, I can corner a niche market. There aren't any others in Boston."

"I don't know," Konrad said. "Public idiot sounds a lot more fun."

Nick snorted. "Well, I've made up my mind. I'm going to be a paranormal PI. There's only one thing left to do. I need three upstanding citizens to vouch for me."

"So that's why you're here?"

"That and to see my brother and his lovely wife."

"Stay for dinner. I'll give Roz a call." Konrad picked up the phone.

"If it's no trouble. Since she's an attorney, I was hoping to ask her to be one of my three upstanding citizens."

"I'm sure she'd be honored."

"I'll get out of your hair and see who might be hanging around the teachers' lounge. Is it okay if I stop back later to see what she says about dinner?"

"Why don't you wait a minute? Then you won't have to interrupt me twice."

After a brief conversation, Konrad ended the call with a whispered endearment. He grinned and hung up.

A pang of envy took Nick by surprise. *Damn it,*

maybe he and everyone else is right. All I need is the right girl...wherever she is. So why is it taking so long?

"Roz said she'll thaw another steak. Not to worry. You're always welcome."

"Thanks. Well, I'll let you get back to work. What time should I show up at your apartment?"

"Six would be good."

"I'll be there. Meanwhile, I'll see if I can find two more upstanding citizens who will vouch for me."

Konrad rose. "What about me?"

Good God. How can I turn down my brother's generous offer without offending the hell out of him? My identical twin brother, who got busted for the biggest art heist in history, won't go a long way toward credibility. Even though he was proven innocent, people will believe what they want to believe.

"I think you're too close. I mean, really...it's like getting your mom to say what a good boy you are."

"Yeah. I can see that. Well, good luck finding any of the fifty pack members who love you to attest to your character."

Nick smiled. *Yeah, there are advantages to being in good stead with one's werewolf pack—at last. I'm glad I wasn't the only one who believed in my brother's innocence.*

"One-Night Nick? Was Sadie sober?" Brandee's bartender-roommate stretched the kinks out of her shoulders after a long shift.

"I think so. I can usually tell when Sadie's had enough." Brandee dropped onto the soft sectional in their living room, removed her shoes, and massaged her aching feet.

"Do you think she was dealing from the bottom of the deck?"

"Nope. She was shuffling the cards as she always does."

It was nice of Angie to attempt to discredit the psychic to make Brandee feel better, but Sadie was never wrong. *Never*.

"Did she come right out and say it was a prediction?"

"Kinda, sorta, not really."

"What exactly did she say?"

"Something about having a premonition that I'd be meeting Mr. Right soon. Then she said the next man through the door could be the love of my life…and Nick walked in."

"She said 'could.' That means she *could be* wrong."

"Have you ever known Sadie to be wrong? I think she just says 'could' because she doesn't want to imply a person has no free will. Maybe she's afraid of being wrong if a person is determined to prove her wrong."

Angie gave her a sympathetic look. "Maybe. Or maybe there really aren't any guarantees. I know she's constantly been right before, but there's always a first time to mess up, right?"

"Let's hope so. I need my heart broken like a nunnery needs a condom dispenser." Brandee rested her elbows on her knees and dropped her head in her hands. "I thought maybe the jerk-face who dumped me was my ticket out of Boringsville."

Angie scrutinized her. "What do you mean?"

"You know. Living above the place I work. Struggling to make ends meet and hopefully save a little money for a rainy day. Hell, I thought I might even be able to afford my dream of owning a gallery if he and I…" She let out a long sigh. "Forget it."

"You're kidding. You really expect some guy to swoop in and rescue you from a life you don't like?"

"No! Oh, my female gigolo…no." Brandee shook her head emphatically. "It's just damn hard to make it as an artist and support myself at the same time."

"Did you think he was Mr. Right?"

She shrugged. "Mr. Possible, maybe." *Time to change the subject*. "By the way, as soon as you're ready for bed, can I commandeer the bathroom for the rest of the night?"

"Oh, crap. Did you forget you're lactose intolerant again?"

Brandee snorted. "No. Do you hear me burping up a lung? And for your information, I don't *forget* my condition. I just forget to take my medication with me sometimes and then can't resist a special treat.

"I want to set up a temporary darkroom in the bathroom. I *have* to begin selling my work, not just to get a few dollars ahead, but also to build a name for myself."

"I get that. So what do you have to do to sell your photographs?"

"Create a look or product no one else has. Make my name synonymous with that product. Capitalize on opportunities for publicity, and make everyone who can afford my work want to collect it."

"That's all, huh?" Angie gave her a sympathetic look. "I'll get you a glass of wine."

"I'll get it. You do that all day."

Angie was already walking toward the kitchen. "It's how I show I care."

Brandee chuckled. "It's how you support yourself. Besides, I know you care. Otherwise I wouldn't have told you what I'm going through."

"Yes you would," Angie called from the next room. The refrigerator door opened and clunked shut. A few moments later she strolled back into the living room, holding two glasses of white wine. "You tell me everything."

"Do you ever get tired of it?"

"Tired of what? Your train wreck of a life?"

"Not just mine. Lots of people tell you more than you want to hear. It looked as if someone was talking your ear off when I was getting Nick his beer."

"Nah. That was just a tourist wanting recommendations for cheap hotels. Like fifty bucks a night."

Angie handed her a glass of Chardonnay, and Brandee took a welcome sip. "Fifty dollars? In this city?"

"Yeah, that's a hoot, huh? I tried to recommend the hostel I'd heard about, but they weren't interested."

Brandee leaned back against the loose pillows. "So, getting back to me…if you were in my knockoff shoes, would you accept a date with Nick Wolfensen?"

"Not unless he changed his policy."

"That's what I was thinking. But how do you tell a guy to completely change his lifestyle?"

"Just come right out and say it. Someone needs to." Angie sipped her wine.

"I guess so. I've got nothing to lose if there's nothing to gain."

Angie scratched her head. "I think that made sense."

Brandee thumped her feet onto the coffee table and crossed them at the ankles. "Okay, I'll confront him."

"Good. Do it where I can watch."

"Pervert."

"Nick, I know this is your first case, but we're desperate. The mayor's stepdaughter has been kidnapped."

"Desperate?" *That's hardly a vote of confidence*. "If you're so desperate, why use a brand-new PI? There are plenty of options for a kidnapping case." *Nick wanted the job, but his cop instincts told him something didn't sound right*. Captain Hunter had arranged this meeting fifteen minutes ago. They met at Boston Uncommon but left the bar immediately so they could talk in private.

"There are paranormal circumstances, and we don't have time for lengthy explanations."

"I see. What are these 'circumstances'?"

"She's a fire mage."

Nick's eyebrows shot up. "Shit." He stopped at a bench and glanced around. No one was within earshot, so he and Hunter sat down. "Do you think the kidnappers know this?"

"Don't know. No ransom demands have been made. There's been no contact at all."

"Any witnesses?"

"A neighbor thought she heard something like a muffled yelp of surprise, but when she looked out her window she didn't see anything."

"Where were her parents?"

"The mayor was at City Hall and her mother was in the house. She didn't think she needed to supervise a twelve-year-old in her own backyard. Now she's sick with guilt."

Nick felt for the poor woman. The best way to help her was to find her daughter. "So they may have kidnapped her for her power." Nick rubbed his chin. "The criminal who's not looking for money is usually looking for some kind of power."

"It gets worse. The girl doesn't know what she can do yet. A female fire mage won't realize her power until the first solar eclipse after she hits puberty. Her mother kept putting off telling her."

"Shit. She's untrained and unprepared. Her parents must be frantic."

"To put it mildly." The captain rested his hand on Nick's shoulder. "This case could make or break your career. I wouldn't blame you if you decline, but I hope you won't. I think you're our only hope."

How could he refuse? Not only would he feel responsible if anything happened to the girl, but she could burn the city to the ground if the kidnappers couldn't teach her how to control the power she didn't even know she had—the power to set fires with no more than a thought.

"I'll do my best."

The captain let out a long breath, as if he'd been holding it for a while. "You'd better do better than your best. The next solar eclipse is in nine days."

How to Date a Dragon

"I'M NEVER ATTENDING A DESTINATION WEDDING AGAIN."

Bliss Russo dragged her garment bag and carry-on up the ramp to her Boston apartment building. Her purse had fallen off her shoulder ten minutes ago and dangled from her wrist. She needed the other hand to hold her cell phone to her ear so she could bitch to her friend Claudia.

"Oh, poor you. Someone made you go to Hawaii." Claudia chuckled. "The bastards."

"Seriously… do you know how long the flight is? Or I should say flights. First there's the leg from Boston to L.A., then L.A. to Honolulu, and finally Honolulu to Maui. Two days later, I go from Maui to Honolulu. Then Honolulu to L.A. Then L.A. to Boston. Plus I had to follow Hawaiian wedding tradition—at least what the bride's parents assured us was the tradition—and party all night. I haven't slept for days."

"You're exaggerating."

"No, I'm not. Unless you count the five-minute nap I took at LAX. I was so exhausted, I woke up on the chair next to me when the guy I had apparently fallen asleep on got up and left."

"Sorry. Okay, you're right. It was a lousy, miserable thing to make you do. So where are you now?"

"Almost home. In fact, I'll probably lose you in the elevator. Give me a few days to sleep and I'll call you back."

"Call by Thursday if you can, and let me know if you want to go out Saturday night."

Bliss jostled the door open, and one of the residents held it while she maneuvered her luggage through. "I shouldn't. I worked a little harder and got a few days ahead so I could go to this damn wedding in the first place, but I really can't afford to take any more time off. The competition will crush me."

"That's what you get for landing in the finals of your dream reality show. What is it? America's Next Great Greeting Card Designer?"

"It's not called America's Next… oh, forget it. I'm at the elevator now and I'm too tired to care. I'll call you."

"Okay, sugar. Sweet dreams."

"Thanks." Bliss hung up and dropped her phone into the bowels of her purse. She yanked and stuffed her luggage into the tiny elevator, which she rode to the second floor. Eventually, she dragged everything to her door, rattled the key in her lock, and brought it all into her bedroom. Passing out on top of her bed fully dressed seemed like the only good idea she was capable of having, so she donned a sleep mask, did a face-plant, and stayed that way.

Hours later—or maybe days—Bliss awoke to a deafening blare. Still disoriented, she had no idea what the hell the noise was or, for that matter, if it was night or day. She tore off the sleep mask and still couldn't tell what was going on. But what was that smell?

Oh. My. God. Smoke! That ear-piercing screech is the friggin' fire alarm.

Bliss tried to remember what to do. *Oh yeah, crouch down low and get the fuck out of Dodge*. Thank the good Lord she lived on the second floor, because she couldn't use the stupid elevator.

Bliss remembered just in time to put her hand to the door before opening it. It didn't feel as though there were an inferno on the other side. Staying low, she opened the door. The smoke was so thick she could barely see. She held her breath and charged toward the end of the hall.

Suddenly, her head hit something firm and she fell backward. "Oomph." The sharp intake of breath resulted in a coughing fit.

Looking up to see what she had hit, she realized she had just head-butted a firefighter's ass.

He swiveled and mumbled through his mask. "Really? I'm here to save you, and you spank me?"

Despite her earlier panic, Bliss felt a whole lot safer and started to giggle. *Oh no. My computer!* "Wait, I have to go back…"

"No. You need to get out of here, now." The firefighter lifted her like she weighed nothing—an amazing feat in itself—then carried her the wrong way down the rest of the hallway, through the fire door, and down the stairs.

"Wait!" She grasped him around the neck and tried to see his face through watering eyes.

His mask, helmet, and shield covered almost his whole head, but she caught a glimpse of gold eyes and a shock of hair, wheat-colored with yellow streaks, angled across his forehead. She thought it odd that the city would let firefighters dye their hair like rock musicians.

As soon as they'd made it to the street, she could see better and noticed his eyes were actually green and almond shaped. She must have imagined the gold color. He set her down near the waiting ambulance and pulled off his mask.

What a hottie! But I don't have time for that now. She staggered slightly as she tried to head back toward the door.

He grabbed her arm to steady her. "Hey," he shouted to one of the paramedics. "Give her some oxygen."

"No, I'm fine. I don't need any medical attention." *Thanks to the gorgeous hunk with the weird hair.*

"Please… let them check you out."

"I'd rather let *you* check me out." She covered her mouth and grinned. "Sorry. It must be the smoke inhalation.

He laughed. "Seriously? First you grab my ass, and now you're hitting on me?"

"I didn't 'grab your ass.' For your information, I ran face-first into your… behind."

"Oh. Well, pardon me for being in the way."

His smile almost stopped her heart—or was it the lack of oxygen? Regardless, she *had to* rip herself away from him and get her computer out of the building before it melted. No matter how hard she pulled, he didn't budge.

"You need to go back in there for my computer. Apartment twenty-five, halfway down the hall."

He took off his gloves. "Look, I'm sorry, miss, but if I went back in there now, my chief would have my hide."

"But my whole life is on that computer. I'm in the finale of a huge TV competition."

He didn't seem impressed, so she tried again.

"It's my greeting card business and all my newest designs are there. This show would pay for a whole ad campaign and give me fifty grand if I win." Realizing she sounded like a babbling idiot, she pressed on. "I've worked so hard to make it this far. If I lose my work, I'll never catch up. I'll wind up presenting a half-assed portfolio, and not only can I forget about winning, but it could ruin me!"

Drake couldn't believe what he was hearing. His weakness might be beautiful brunettes, but did she honestly expect him to risk his life for an object that could be replaced? Could she not see smoke pouring out of the building? Sure, he could probably manage it, being fireproof and all, but after the chewing out he got the last time…

"Don't you keep a backup file online?"

"No. I don't trust the Internet," she said with the saddest expression in her beautiful brown eyes. "There are too many hackers out there, and this greeting card competition is outrageously competitive. Pleeeease!"

All this hoopla for a piece of paper that reads, "Roses are red. Violets are blue?" The brunette didn't appear to be insane, no matter how stupid this reality show sounded. There were crazier things on TV.

His chief had already warned Drake about risking his neck and told him to knock off taking stupid chances. He'd lucked out the last time. The mayor, a big dog lover, heard that Drake had gone back into a two-alarm blaze to rescue a greyhound. Then Mr. Mayor made the chief disregard any thought of suspending Drake by giving him a medal. But that sort of luck wouldn't hold, especially if this insubordination was about an inanimate object.

Drake reached out and physically turned the woman

around so she could see the inferno behind her. The feel of her soft, warm skin sent an unexpected jolt of awareness through him.

Her hands flew to cover her mouth, and the same sad, desperate sound all fire victims made as they witnessed the destruction and loss of something precious eked out. The tears forming in her eyes did him in.

If he weren't fireproof, running back into that building would toast him like a marshmallow, but being a dragon, he knew he could do it.

"Ah, hell." Before anyone could stop him, he dashed in the side entrance. He could always say he thought he heard a call for help.

"Stop. Oh, crap," was what he really heard. Apparently the brunette had changed her mind, but he was committed now.

Second floor, halfway down the hall, he repeated to himself until he found it. She had left her door open. Fortunate for him, not so much for her apartment. Smoke and flames were everywhere. He felt the familiar tingle just under his skin that signaled an impending shift. *Fan-fucking-tastic*. Skin became scales. Fingers became claws. His neck elongated, and out popped his tail, creating an unsightly bulge in the back of his loose coveralls. His wings were cramped and folded up under his jacket, but it couldn't be helped.

His sight was greatly improved in his alternate form, and he spotted the Mac on her glass tabletop. The flames hadn't reached it yet, so he did his best to grab it with his eagle-like talons and carry it against his chest.

Lumbering down the hall, he wondered where, and if, he'd be able to shift back before anyone saw him.

Maybe it's cooler in the basement—but what if I get trapped down there?

Instead of heading down another level, he opened the emergency door just enough to toss the laptop onto the grass outside. The outside air was so much cooler that he thought he might be able to shift back right there.

Concentrating on his human form, he inhaled the fresh air and sensed his head and body shrinking and compacting. He glanced down and saw his human hands again. His back felt enormously better without squished wings digging into it.

Ah... I made it undetected.

Or had he? The brunette was standing a few feet away, wide-eyed and open mouthed—hugging her computer.

"What the..."

The handsome firefighter, who had appeared like some kind of dinosaur in the smoke only a moment earlier, stepped out of the building and stretched as if trying to work a kink out of his spine. He whipped off his mask and stared at her.

Bliss scrubbed her eye socket with the heel of her hand. *My eyes must have been playing tricks on me*. There was no other possible explanation. Between her jet-lagged brain and smoke-filled vision, her mind's eye had concocted a reptilian form that was really her hero firefighter.

Oh, fuck it. "Thank you!" *He deserves a reward*. She rushed up to him and cupped the back of his head, dragging him down until she mashed her lips to his in the mother of all adoring kisses. He wrapped his arms around her back and pulled her against him, returning her kiss. She fit his body as if they'd been made for each other. The fire he'd just rescued her from had nothing on the heat in his kiss.

Unfortunately for both of them, the chief came striding around the corner along with the paramedics. The paramedics led her away while her hottie fireman received the dressing-down of a lifetime, complete with explicit and crude language.

"Please don't be mad at him," Bliss called over her shoulder. "It's my fault. I asked him to go back in." But it was too late. A paramedic slapped an oxygen mask over her face as she heard the chief sputter the words "suspended" and "get the hell out of my sight" to her hot hero. She tried to wrestle off the damn mask, but by the time she did, he was gone.

Upon their return to the fire station, the guys whistled at a curvaceous blond waiting for them with a camera. Drake vaguely remembered the chief saying something about their posing for a calendar.

"Terrific," he muttered.

The chief spotted her and groaned. Then he pointed at Drake. "He goes first."

As they hung up their jackets, the chief strode to his office.

"Drake, buddy," Benjamin said, "I'd hang around and watch, but I gotta shower." He slapped Drake on the back and jogged up the stairs with the rest of them.

Drake glanced down at his filthy hands as the blond sashayed over to him.

"Hey there, handsome," she said.

"Look, I hate to make you wait, but I should shower before you take any pictures. We just..."

She finger-walked her way up his chest. "Oh, I know. You were out fighting fires and saving people. I think that's sexy as hell. Don't change a thing. Except, take your shirt off."

Drake stifled a groan. He was tired and about to be suspended. This was the last thing he wanted to do right now.

Figuring he was in enough trouble for defying the chief's orders, he whipped off his white undershirt, faced the blond female photographer as if she were a firing squad, and asked, "How do you want me?"

She chuckled and raised one eyebrow.

"Uh... What should I be doing?" he asked.

From the look in her eyes and the way she licked her lips, the answer was X-rated. Maybe they shouldn't have sent a woman to shoot the annual firefighters' calendar. At this rate it would be December before she finished taking the pictures.

"I don't want to be rude, but I really don't feel like doing this right now." When she didn't respond, he waved a hand in front of her eyes. "Hello," he said to break through the woman's vacant stare.

"Your hair... I've never seen yellow streaks like that. They're like primary colors."

"Yeah, it's unusual, and before you ask, it's natural. My whole family has them." *It would be so much easier if I could just come out and say it's how dragons know each other by clan*. But, of course, he could not. Dragons were governed by the same rule every paranormal faction had to live by—namely not to reveal their existence to humans. To do so would cause widespread panic, witch hunts, and they'd probably wind up as government lab rats.

"Oh, um…" At last she seemed to remember her professionalism. "Pick up that hose and stand a quarter-turn to the right."

Drake did as he was asked and she clicked her shutter release.

"Um, you might want to hold it higher."

Drake realized he was holding the nozzle right in front of his junk as if it were a limp phallus. He dropped it and grabbed an ax instead, resting it on his shoulder.

"Oh, yeah. That pose really shows off your muscles." She moved and clicked. Moved and clicked some more.

"Act like you're having fun. Smile," she said.

Drake rolled his eyes. "Fighting fires isn't exactly a laugh a second."

"Maybe if you think about something pleasant, it'll produce the look I'm going for."

Let's see… something pleasant. Unfortunately, he couldn't come up with much of anything at the moment. He had just lost the last friendly dragon he knew—his mother—a few weeks ago and still didn't feel like his old jovial self. Plus he was in trouble with the chief. He'd never work his way up the ladder at this rate, and the job was his life. Maybe his buddies were right. He needed a hobby.

"You're still looking awfully serious. Here, let me try something."

"Christ," he muttered.

She set down the camera and strolled up to him. Unbuttoning her blouse enough to expose lush cleavage, she said in a low, sultry voice, "Think of the fun we can have after I finish the shoot."

He raised his eyebrows. *Think of the horror when you find out I'm a dragon.*

"No, that's still not the expression I want. What's the matter? Are you having a bad day?"

"You could say that."

"Anything I can do?"

"Nope." He'd have to take his punishment just like any other firefighter who did what he'd done, regardless of his inability to burn. He should be grateful for the chance to delay facing the chief, but to be honest, he just wanted to get it over with.

As Drake was thinking about what to tell him, Chief Tate strolled out where they were shooting.

"Are you almost done here?" the chief asked.

The photographer backed away and quickly buttoned her blouse. "Ah, yes. I'd like one more pose..."

"I'll wait." Chief Tate stuffed his hands in his pockets and rocked back and forth on his heels.

Shit, I'm in bigger trouble than I thought. Drake decided to have some fun with the shoot after all. He set down the ax, moved beside the chief, and threw his arm around Tate's shoulder. "Here. Take one of me and the chief. I'll pay you for it."

"Huh?" Chief Tate leaned away and frowned at Drake. "What the hell for?"

"A memento. If I'm about to be fired, I'd like a picture of my old boss for my scrapbook."

Chief Tate reared back and laughed. "I'm not going to fire your ass, Cameron. I probably should for taking such a dumb chance. This isn't like the time the mayor heard about you saving a damn dog and was impressed. You won't be getting a commendation for this one."

The photographer grinned. "Wow. A commendation from the mayor! Now there's something to smile about."

The chief snorted. "Yeah, I told him to take off the word 'bravery' and make it a citation for stupidity."

Shrugging one shoulder, Drake said, "It figures." At least it didn't sound like he was getting canned. That was a relief.

Chief Tate addressed the woman without looking at her. "Don't encourage him. He risked his life for a damn pet. Cameron, you're just lucky the mayor's a big dog lover."

The photographer got even more excited, if that were possible. "Oh, he is. I've photographed him, and he has pictures of his greyhounds right on his desk."

"Is that right?" The chief didn't sound impressed, despite his words. "Look, as soon as you finish up here, Cameron, come to my office."

"Sure thing, chief."

The photographer cozied up to Drake. She held out a card. "If you had a shirt on, I'd tuck this in your pocket."

He took the card and glanced at it.

Suzanne Bloom
Blooming Great Photography
617-555-8349

He smiled and she said, "Freeze." Backing up a couple feet, she snapped a few more pictures. "There. Now I have what I want."

Yeah, your phone number in my hand.

~

"I've got to do something to make this right, Claudia." Bliss sat at her friend's breakfast bar, running her fingers over the smooth granite.

Claudia took a sip of her coffee. "Look, he saved your business and possibly your place in the competition. Why don't you make him a card?"

"A Hall-Snark card? What would it say? *I'm sorry I got you suspended, but you looked great in suspenders?*"

Claudia grimaced. "Ah, no. I'm sure you can do better than that."

Bliss slumped over and rested her cheek on the cool stone. "My computer didn't survive, by the way. Well, I mean, the hardware did, but I think the rest is fubar."

"Fubar? What's that?"

She leaned back and sighed. "Sorry. It's something my brother Ricky, the ex-marine, says. It means fucked up beyond all recognition."

Claudia chuckled and opened the laptop in question. She hit the power button and a light came on. "Are you sure? It looks okay."

"I tried to boot it up several times, and all I can get out of it is, 'Operating system not found.'"

"Don't give up yet. There's something called forensic data recovery. You'd be surprised what the FBI can get off computers that were supposedly destroyed."

"I doubt the FBI would consider a reality TV show about a greeting card competition worthy of their time or equipment." Bliss cupped her chin and rested her elbow on the counter. "I don't know what I was thinking. He could have died. I don't even know his name..." She lifted her head and sat up straight. "Wait. The back of his jacket said Cameron."

Claudia set a tall glass of ice water in front of Bliss. "There you go. Is that his first name or last?"

Bliss sighed. "I don't know."

"What did the other guys' jackets look like? First names or last?"

Bliss rested her chin on both palms and her elbows on the counter. "I don't know. I only had eyes for him—as they say."

Claudia chuckled. "Oh, yeah. You've got it bad."

Bliss took a long swallow of her ice water. Her parched throat welcomed the cool liquid. "You want to know the worst thing about all this?"

"What?"

"Forget that my home and all my belongings except my precious laptop are toast. I have to go back to Winthrop and live with my annoying parents for who knows how long. If I don't win the contest, it could be forever." She groaned.

Claudia rubbed her friend's back. "I wish I could let you move in here, but my place is just too damn small. We'd get on each other's nerves, and our friendship is more important than anything to me."

"I know. I feel the same way. But I do have to go home. I lost my glasses in the fire. I think I have a spare pair in my old bedroom. Some of my old clothes might still be there, and I'll need them, if they fit. Stupidly, I didn't get renter's insurance, and now I have zero money and no time for shopping."

"So, have you told your parents yet?"

Bliss took a deep breath and let it out slowly. "No, but I have to soon, before they see it on the news. They'll have a fit."

"Not because you need a place to stay, I hope."

"No, that's not it." She snorted. "They're always hoping us kids will come home for dinner… or a month. No, they'll be upset because one of their precious spawn had a brush with death. And they're going to try to get me married off and living in the suburbs."

"Oh, boy. I don't envy you, but at least your parents aren't stuck on the idea of your marrying a rich guy."

"Seriously? Yours are like that? Do they know what you do?"

Claudia laughed. "They know I work on Beacon Hill, but they don't know I manage a bar. If they did, they'd have a fit. I'm supposed to be rubbing elbows with Boston's elite."

"What do they think you do?"

"All they know is that I got my MBA and I manage a small independent company on Charles Street. Technically, that's true, so if you ever see them, don't mention the bar. Actually, the less said about my job, the better."

"You completed your business degree? I thought you still had another semester to go."

"I finished it in December."

"Congrats. So, are you looking for a better job?"

"Nope."

Her friend confused her sometimes, but Bliss had other things to think about right now. "Unfortunately, if I go back home, I can look forward to a lot of arranged, so-called accidental meetings with eligible young men.

My parents will want him to be Italian so they can have a whole passel of *paisano* grandkids."

"With a name like Cameron, it sounds like your hero might be Irish," Claudia said.

"Or Scottish. I think I remember seeing a Cameron clan wearing their tartan kilts at that Highland Games thing we went to."

"Oh, yeah. Who could forget those sexy kilts?" Claudia waggled her eyebrows. "So... what does your guy look like?"

"Tall, about six feet. Rugged, great firm ass, green eyes, and hair that's hard to describe. It's not blond or red. It's kind of sandy or light brown with actual yellow streaks. Not highlights like you see on other people. I'm talking about a primary color in half- or quarter-inch stripes."

"Interesting... What else?"

"He has a side part and it's long in the front—right to his eyebrows. It kind of angles across his forehead. All shaggy and sexy." She sighed.

"He sounds like a hunk."

"Yeah, and if you ever see him, keep your mitts off. He's mine."